SAFEGUARDING THE SURROGATE

DELORES FOSSEN

THE TRAP

CAROL ERICSON

MILLS & BOON

First Published in Great Britain 2021
by Mills & Boon, an imprint of HarperCollins*Publishers* Ltd
1 London Bridge Street, London, SE1 9GF

www.harpercollins.co.uk

HarperCollins*Publishers*
1st Floor, Watermarque Building,
Ringsend Road, Dublin 4, Ireland

Safeguarding the Surrogate © 2021 Delores Fossen
The Trap © 2021 Carol Ericson

ISBN: 978-0-263-28340-2

0621

SAFEGUARDING THE SURROGATE

DELORES FOSSEN

Chapter One

Kara Holland stood in the darkness and waited for the
killer.

With her heartbeat throbbing in her ears and her back
pressed to the barn wall, she tried to listen for any sound
to alert her that he was coming. Nothing. Not yet. But
she'd done everything she could to lure him out and
make him come after her.

And she was ready.

She had the Glock gripped in her hand, and thanks
to the hours of firearms training, she knew how to use
it. If that failed, if he somehow got the jump on her,
she'd fall back on the hand-to-hand moves she'd also
learned. Of course, those things didn't guarantee that
she would stop him, but she had to try. She was tired
of living with this smothering weight of fear.

Finally, she heard something. The sound of a car engine. Then a door closing. He had finally come for her.

The next thing she heard were the footsteps, slow and
cautious. They were coming straight toward her barn.

She'd purposely turned off all but the single light
in the tack room, and Kara had left the door cracked
just enough for a thin beam to pierce the darkness. She

stayed in the shadows by a stack of hay bales, but when the killer came in the barn, she'd be able to see him.

Kara could certainly hear him.

Along with the footsteps, the hinges creaked on the barn door, and she pinpointed every bit of her focus while she lifted the Glock. And she took aim.

"Kara?" the man called out.

She groaned, mixing it with some muttered profanity, because she instantly recognized that voice. Not a killer. But Deputy Daniel Logan.

"What are you doing here?" she snapped once she could manage to speak.

"Checking on you," Daniel snapped right back.

When he stepped into that beam of light from the tack room, she had no trouble seeing the riled expression on his face. Or the rest of him for that matter. He was wearing his usual jeans and work shirt on his tall rangy body. His Mercy Ridge deputy's badge was clipped to his belt.

"I'm fine," Kara assured him. Of course, that wasn't true, and he could clearly see that. After all, she was waiting in her dark barn while holding a gun. "You can go."

"No, I won't." Daniel sounded "all cop" with that one-word response. And he didn't budge, either. In fact, he came closer, meeting her eye to eye.

"You shouldn't have come," Kara insisted.

"I wanted to have a look around and see for myself if the rumors were true. They are," he added in a snarl. "What the hell are you thinking?"

"You know what I'm thinking," she fired back.

That only caused him to release a long hard breath.

No doubt one of frustration. Well, she was frustrated, too. And scared. Especially scared. Something that she'd hoped to end tonight.

"Two surrogates are dead," Kara reminded him. Not that a reminder was necessary. Daniel knew because she'd already told him. She'd taken the news articles to him right away when she had learned about the dead women. "Both used the Willingham Fertility Clinic in San Antonio."

Just as Kara had done. Again, no reminder was necessary for Daniel since the reason she had used the clinic and become a surrogate was to carry a baby for Daniel and his wife, Maryanne. Maryanne had also been Kara's sister.

As it always did, just remembering Maryanne made her feel as if someone had clamped a vise around her heart. It was almost certainly even worse for Daniel. It'd been nearly two years since Maryanne had lost her battle with breast cancer, but sometimes it felt as fresh as if it'd just happened.

When the grief came in these thick waves, Kara just reminded herself that she'd kept her promise to her sister. Kara had gone to the fertility clinic and used in vitro to get pregnant with Daniel and Maryanne's baby. The pregnancy and delivery had gone like clockwork, and Kara had given birth to a healthy baby girl, Sadie. But Maryanne had died four months before Sadie was born. Maryanne never got to hold the precious baby she'd so desperately wanted.

Now, the murders had happened. Murders that added another layer of emotion to the grief. And that emotion was fear.

"First of all, there's no proof that the murders are connected to the Willingham Fertility Clinic," Daniel explained. He was definitely repeating himself since he'd tried to convince her of this before. "One of the women was likely killed by an abusive ex-boyfriend. The other is still listed as missing."

"There were signs of a struggle in the second woman's house," Kara quickly pointed out.

He nodded. "Even if she was attacked, that doesn't mean there's a link to the clinic." Daniel certainly sounded convinced of that, but...

"Yet you're here to check on me," she said. "You must think there's a credible threat or you wouldn't have come."

This time he scrubbed his hand over his face after he nodded again. "I'm a cop." He paused, his jaw muscles at war. "I'm your friend. And I'm worried about you. You said you thought someone was following you and watching you when you were shopping in San Antonio."

"Someone was." Kara was sure of that, but it hadn't been more than a gut feeling. "And I think someone got into my truck when I was there. The doors were unlocked, and I'm sure I locked them. I could also tell someone had riffled through the glove compartment."

Daniel only sighed because they both knew that could have been a would-be thief. It wasn't that hard to break into a vehicle. "If you truly believe someone wants to kill you, then why the hell would you offer yourself up like this and try to draw him out?"

"Because I'm tired of being scared," she blurted out. Much to her disgust, her voice trembled. She hated that. "I've always been the strong one. No choice about that."

He nodded. "Because you had to take care of your sister after...well, after."

Daniel obviously hadn't wanted to blurt out what followed that "after," but he was talking about her parents being murdered. That'd happened when Kara had barely been eighteen, but she'd done a decent enough job raising Maryanne, who'd been three years younger. Heck, she had even continued to run the family ranch and had made it even more profitable than when her folks had been in charge.

The fear made her feel weak.

It made her feel like a coward.

"The second anniversary of Maryanne's death is coming up," Daniel said several moments later, "and I think it's just stirring up bad memories for you. It's certainly stirring up some for me," he added in a mumble.

Kara had no doubts about that. *None.* Daniel had loved her sister, and even though he hadn't approved of Maryanne opting for egg harvesting at a time when she should have been concentrating on her health and recovery, their marriage had held strong. Daniel had been as devastated by Maryanne's death as Kara had.

Daniel glanced around as if trying to figure out what to do, and his gaze came back to hers. "So, what was your plan? To let word get around that you'd be working in your barn, *alone*, for the next couple of nights. Then wait, hoping that a killer will come in here after you?"

Yes, that had been the plan, and Daniel had made it seem like a stupid one. It hadn't felt stupid, though, when she'd come up with it. However, it had felt desperate. Which it had been. This fear, and the threat, had to end.

"I've been having nightmares," she admitted. "Bad ones. And I couldn't get my mind off Brenda McGill and Marissa Rucker. Brenda's the surrogate who was found dead, and Marissa's the one who's missing."

Daniel made a sound to indicate that he understood that. "Then you started to dwell on the similarities between you and the women."

Again, the answer to that was yes, and there had indeed been similarities. Even Daniel couldn't deny that. Brenda and Marissa had both become surrogates to family members who'd had trouble carrying children. Both of them were brunettes—just like Kara. Both women had also lived in or near small towns. So did she. Kara lived on her horse ranch that was a good five miles from the town of Mercy Ridge where Daniel's own ranch was located.

"I know you don't believe this applies to my situation," she went on, "but there are fanatics out there. People who don't believe that surrogacy should be legal. The clinic admitted to me that they get threatening letters all the time. In one of them, the person said he was responsible for Brenda's death and that there'd be other murders."

None of that was an exaggeration, but as Kara heard her own words, she knew why Daniel was looking at her with what could only be sympathy in his otherwise cool gray eyes. Which, of course, only made her feel worse than she already did. Daniel shouldn't be here. His concern for her shouldn't have pulled him away from what he needed to be doing.

"You've obviously put in your usual shift at the sheriff's office, and you should be home with your daughter," Kara said. "How's Sadie?" she added, not only hoping to remind him that he should be on his way but also because she genuinely wanted to know.

The corner of his mouth lifted into a smile, but then he winced a little. "She repeated a bad word that she heard me say when I dropped my phone."

Sadie definitely was in the "little pitcher, big ears stage," and she was constantly babbling. She was also the spitting image of Daniel with her dark brown hair and smoky gray eyes. Just remembering the image of that precious little face caused Kara to relax some.

Daniel checked his watch. "Why don't you follow me home, and you can see Sadie for yourself? She should still be awake. And if you want, you can even stay the night in the guest room."

It was a nice offer, one that might not please Daniel's nanny, Noreen Ware, who was a stickler for keeping Sadie's routine. Still, Kara thought a glimpse of the baby might soothe the rest of her frayed nerves.

"Thank you," she muttered. "But just seeing Sadie should be enough. I won't stay long, and then I can come back here."

Daniel lifted an eyebrow. "Here as in the barn?"

"No. I'll stay in my house." With the doors locked and the security system armed. Kara tipped her head to the Glock she was holding by the side of her leg. "I'll put this in the house first."

Daniel walked out of the barn with her. "If you stay the night at my place, you could see Sadie in the morning and have breakfast with us."

He was obviously still concerned about her state of mind, and while spending time with Sadie and him was tempting, Kara pulled back a little. Something she always did when it came to Daniel. After all, he was an attractive man. Incredibly hot. Something she had been aware of since she'd been old enough to notice the opposite sex. But after Daniel had started dating Maryanne in high school, Kara had made sure to keep any tugs from the attraction in check. That was much harder to do when she was under the same roof with him.

"Thanks, but I'll just say good-night to Sadie and then come home," Kara answered, though she would still have to deal with the worry and fear that a killer had her in his sights. That's why she glanced around the backyard as they walked from the barn to her house.

Daniel looked around, too. The kind of glances a cop made. It eased some of the tightness in her chest to know that he hadn't outright dismissed her concerns, but there was still a good fifty feet between the house and the barn. That was plenty of space for a killer to come after her.

He made it up the back porch steps ahead of her, and when he reached for the doorknob, she realized he was going in with her. "You should lock your door," he commented when he opened it.

Kara froze. "I did." She took the keys from her jeans pocket to show him. "In fact, I've been making a point of locking up since I heard about the surrogates. I also use my security system when I'm sleeping." She hadn't turned it on, though, for her "stakeout" in the barn.

Daniel's forehead bunched up, but he certainly didn't freeze. He hooked his left arm around Kara, positioning her behind him, and in the same motion, he drew his gun. That sent her heartbeat into overdrive.

"You're sure you locked it?" he whispered.

"Positive."

He gave a quick nod. "Stay close and keep watch behind us."

That nearly robbed her of her breath, but Kara managed a nod, too. She was right behind Daniel when he stepped into her kitchen. As he'd done in the yard, his gaze fired all around, but he didn't go far. Only enough to get her inside, and then he eased the door shut behind them. That would prevent them from being ambushed. Well, hopefully it would.

But the killer could be anywhere in the house.

They waited there for what seemed to be an eternity, and Daniel lifted his head, obviously listening. Kara did the same, but the only thing she could hear was her too fast breaths. She tightened her grip on the Glock, hoping that would steady her suddenly raw nerves.

Her house was old and didn't have a modern open floorplan. That meant they couldn't see any of the other rooms from their position so that was probably why Daniel took several quiet steps to the side and peered into the kitchen.

"I don't see anyone," he whispered.

That didn't put her at ease because there were three bedrooms, a living and dining room, her office and two bathrooms. Plenty of places for someone to lie in wait for an attack.

Maybe the killer had gotten in and was now waiting to go after her. If so, he might not come out if he knew Daniel was there. Kara didn't want the guy to be able to stay in hiding. She wanted him out in the open so this showdown could take place. Then and only then would the danger finally be over.

Daniel motioned for her to follow him as he stepped into the kitchen. No one was there, and when she peered into the living room, she could see that the front door was shut, the chain lock still in place. Nothing in the room had been disturbed. It was just as she'd left it over an hour ago when she'd gone out to the barn. It was the same for the dining room when they went in there to look around.

Since the house only had one floor, Daniel headed to the hall next, and Kara was able to take in everything in a sweeping glance. All the bedroom doors and the one to her office and the hall bathroom were open. Just as they normally were. That meant Daniel and she would have to go into each room to make sure no one was there.

Daniel didn't waste any time doing just that. He went into the first guest room, his gaze shifting from one side of the room to the other. When they went inside, he checked the closet as Kara looked under the bed.

No one.

They repeated the process on the next bedroom and got the same results. However, the moment Daniel went through her office door, Kara knew something was wrong. The curtain was fluttering in the night breeze. And she soon saw why. The window was open.

Daniel didn't ask if she'd left it that way. Probably because like her, he saw the bits of glass on the floor. Someone had broken the window, slipped a hand through and unlocked it to get inside.

"Keep watch," Daniel reminded her, and he took

out his phone to text for backup. Kara hadn't thought anything could rev up her heartbeat even more, but that did it.

While he waited for a response to his text, he glanced in every corner. The intruder wasn't here, and that left just one more place in the house. Her bedroom suite. Lots of places to hide in there, too.

His phone dinged, and Daniel checked the screen. "Barrett's on the way," Daniel told her in a whisper. "He'll be here in a few minutes."

Barrett was not only Daniel's brother, he was also the town sheriff, and his ranch was only a couple of miles from Kara's place.

As she'd done in the other rooms, she looked around to see if anything was missing. And there was. Her laptop was gone, and the bottom drawer of her desk was open. The small metal box she kept there was also open, and the money that would have normally been inside was missing.

"A burglar," Daniel added, his voice still barely audible. "Someone who knew you wouldn't be in the house. He could have come in through the window and gone out through the back door."

Daniel was right. Why else would the back door be unlocked? Plus, she had put out word that she'd be in the barn tonight. And that made Kara want to kick herself. She'd practically invited someone to break in.

With Kara right behind him, Daniel went out of the office, back into the hall and headed for her bedroom. Her first thought was her jewelry box that would be sitting right on the dresser. She didn't have a lot, but there were several rings and a necklace that had once belonged to her mother and grandmother. That made Kara want to rush inside the room when Daniel walked through the door.

But instead she froze in her tracks.

The lamp on the nightstand was on, the milky light practically spotlighting her bed. In the center of it was a woman with long brown hair. A stranger.

And her dead eyes stared up at the ceiling.

Chapter Two

Daniel felt the quick punch of shock and dread before his instincts kicked in, and he pushed Kara behind him. He definitely didn't want her touching the body and contaminating the scene, but there was a bigger concern here.

The killer could still be in the room.

No way could he leave Kara alone, so he nudged her with his elbow and tipped his head to the closet and adjoining bathroom to let her know he had to check them out. She gave a shaky nod, and she started walking when he did, but she didn't take her eyes off the dead woman.

Kara was as tough as nails. He knew that. And she'd even been with Maryanne when she drew her last breath. They both were. But murder was different, and even though Daniel hadn't had a chance to examine the body, he figured this was a homicide.

Moving as fast as he could, he went to the closet. No one was lurking in there. Next up was the bathroom, and he held his breath until he threw back the shower curtain. No killer there, either. In fact, the only signs of one were the office and the bedroom.

"Do you know the dead woman?" Daniel asked Kara once he had her back in the bedroom.

Kara shook her head, and the breath she dragged in was shaky, long and hard. He wasn't sure if it was a good thing or not that this was a stranger. If it was someone she knew, it might make it easier to figure out how she'd gotten here and why she'd died. But he knew from personal experience that it could crush you to lose someone you knew.

Maryanne's death had certainly crushed him.

"Why is...*was* she here?" Kara asked. Her voice was ragged and with hardly any sound. Because her arm was right against his, Daniel could feel her muscles trembling.

Daniel wanted to get started on answering that *why* question so he motioned for Kara to stay put, and he went closer to the bed. He didn't recognize the woman, either, but he made a mental description of her. Brown hair, brown eyes, slim build, midtwenties. She was wearing a yellow dress. And jewelry. Gold earrings, a heart necklace and three rings. Apparently, the person who'd put her here hadn't seen fit to rob her.

There were bruises on her wrists and what appeared to be a puncture mark on her right forearm. Maybe from a syringe. If so, it was fresh, and it could mean she'd been drugged.

When Daniel moved to the other side of the bed, he saw something lying next to her. It was a Texas driver's license, and without touching it, he leaned in to see the name on it.

"Mandy Vera," he relayed to Kara. "According to her address, she's from San Antonio."

Kara repeated the name several times, but then she shook her head. "It's not familiar. How did she get here?"

Daniel wasn't sure, but judging from those bruises, she hadn't come willingly. However, before he could consider more than that, he heard a vehicle pull up in front of the house. Seconds later, there was a knock at the door.

"It's me," Barrett called out.

Good. Because Daniel not only needed backup, he also wanted his brother to take charge of the crime scene so that he could get Kara out of there. After all, the killer could still be hanging around. And that made Daniel want to curse. Kara had tried to make herself bait, and it could have worked. She could have been the one to end up dead in that bed.

With Kara still close to him, Daniel went to the door and opened it. He didn't offer any explanation to Barrett. Daniel just motioned for him to follow them back to the bedroom. With a puzzled look on his face, Barrett stepped in. Then he froze for a second before he went to the body.

"What the hell happened?" Barrett demanded.

"Not sure. Kara and I came in from the barn and found her like this. The window's broken in Kara's office so that appears to be the point of entry. It's just up the hall, and there are some items missing."

Daniel immediately saw the questions in his brother's eyes. Eyes that were a genetic copy of his own.

"You didn't see who did this?" Barrett asked, aiming that question at Kara.

She shook her head, pushing the wisps of her dark

brown hair from her face. "No. I was in the barn when Daniel got here."

"She was trying to draw out the killer," Daniel supplied.

No need for him to add more to that because Daniel and Barrett had already discussed Kara's obsession with a possible surrogate killer. And here he hadn't even believed there was a killer.

Well, he sure as heck believed it now.

Of course, he had to stay objective and look into the possibility that this wasn't connected to anything to do with surrogacies. If it wasn't, then it would give them another puzzle as to why this had happened. But one thing was for certain, it was connected to Kara. Someone had gone to a lot of trouble to stage a crime scene like this. There had to be a reason for that, and Daniel would make it his priority to figure that out.

Along with keeping Kara safe.

"So, if the killer came through the office window, how'd he get her in here in the bedroom?" Barrett muttered. "He must have broken in and unlocked the back door to bring in the body."

"I only heard Daniel's truck when he drove up," Kara said. "And yours. I didn't hear another vehicle."

"How long were you in the barn?" Daniel asked her.

She had clamped her teeth over her bottom lip and had to release it before she spoke. "Over an hour."

Plenty of time for someone to do this. "The killer could have parked on a nearby ranch trail, walked to the house with the woman, broken in and then murdered her."

Barrett nodded. "If so, there could be footprints or

tracks. I'll get a CSI team and the medical examiner out here right away."

Daniel took out his phone as well, and he checked the time. The Willingham Fertility Clinic was already closed for the night so he called his contact Loretta Eaton, the office manager. He wasn't sure how much info Loretta could give him without a search warrant, but this was a start.

"Mandy Vera," Daniel said to Loretta after he identified himself. "I'm pretty sure she was just murdered, and her body was left here in Mercy Ridge." Though he'd have to verify that her driver's license wasn't a fake. "I need to know if she had any connection whatsoever to Willingham."

Loretta's sharp sound of shock made Daniel wish he'd sugarcoated that just a little. Of course, it was impossible to sugarcoat murder.

"Her name doesn't ring any bells. I'm home right now and don't have access to the files," she said, "but I'll go into the clinic and check."

"Thanks. Text me as soon as you know one way or another."

"I will. Uh, how was this woman killed?" Loretta asked.

Daniel had no intention of giving her any other details. Not until he figured out who was responsible for this. Probably not Loretta, though. The woman was in her midsixties and petite. Still, she might say something to the wrong person.

"I can't get into that right now," Daniel answered. "But it'd help a lot if you check those records for that name."

Loretta repeated her assurance that she would, and

Daniel ended the call. Barrett, too, had finished his call and was studying the body.

"The ME will have to confirm it, but it looks like strangulation," Barrett said. "There doesn't appear to be any blood or tissue under her nails."

Daniel had noticed that as well, and that likely meant Mandy hadn't struggled while she was being strangled. Maybe because she'd been too drugged to do anything to stop the attack. Or maybe her killer had worn gloves and long sleeves. But Daniel figured if the woman had been conscious, she would have definitely fought back, and the covers on the bed didn't appear to have been disturbed.

"There are marks on her forearm," Daniel explained. "It could have been the way the killer got the drugs into her."

Barrett made a sound of agreement, and when he kept his attention on Kara, it caused Daniel to look back at her. There wasn't much more color in her face than there was the dead woman's, and the pupils of her dark brown eyes were too large. She looked as if she might be in shock. No surprise there. However, it was a reminder that she shouldn't be here.

"I can't have you pack anything to take with you," Daniel told her. "Everything in the house has to be treated as a crime scene."

He followed her gaze as it drifted over his shoulder to the framed photo of Sadie and him that she had on her dresser. Daniel knew that she loved Sadie, but there were plenty of photos of just his little girl and even some with Kara and Sadie. He wasn't sure why her choice of pictures unsettled him, but what was more unsettling was the look in her eyes when their gazes met. She quickly turned from him, as if she hadn't wanted to give away what she was thinking.

Or feeling.

Hell. He wasn't stupid, and he'd felt that tug inside him sometimes when he looked at Kara. A tug he hadn't wanted, but it was just a basic primal urge. After all, she was an attractive woman. However, Daniel hadn't wanted her to feel that same attraction for him.

"You okay?" Barrett asked, and that's when Daniel realized his brother was volleying glances at Kara and him.

"Fine," they answered in unison. Which, of course, only made them sound guilty of something.

"Fine," Daniel repeated, changing his tone so that he sounded like a cop. Thankfully, he didn't have to add more because he heard a familiar voice at the front door.

"It's me," someone called out. Leo, his kid brother and fellow deputy.

"We're back here," Barrett told him.

Several seconds later, Leo appeared in the doorway, and as Daniel and Barrett had done, his gaze swept around the room. Blowing out a slow breath, he put his hands on his hips. "Damn," he grumbled.

That about summed up how Daniel was feeling, but his brother's arrival was good news. Now, he wouldn't have to wait around to get Kara out of there.

"I'm taking Kara to my house," Daniel explained. That would accomplish a couple of things. She wouldn't have to keep staring at the body, and he could check on Sadie. He had a good security system, but he'd feel better once he was sure the nanny and his daughter were okay.

Barrett nodded. "Walk with them to Daniel's truck," he added to Leo.

Kara made a soft groan, one that had come from deep within her chest. No way had she forgotten that a killer had been here, but maybe it had just occurred to her that he could still be lurking around.

She didn't resist when Daniel took hold of her arm to guide her out of the room, but she did look back at the dead woman. "We have to find out who did this. We have to stop him."

The *we* concerned Daniel a lot, and it caused Leo to give him a raised questioning eyebrow. No way did Daniel want Kara involved in this investigation. But she already was. The trick would be to keep her safe and not allow her to set herself up as bait again.

"You're taking her to your place?" Leo asked when they reached the front door.

Daniel nodded, but he felt the split second of hesitation in Kara. He didn't want to read too much into it. After all, before they'd found the body, he'd already talked her into going to his house to say good-night to Sadie. But this would be more than just her popping in. It was going to take a day or two for the CSI team to process the scene. Only then would Kara be free to return.

The question was—would she want to go back? Would she ever be able to walk into her bedroom and not see the woman's dead body? If the answers to those questions were no, then she might be at his place longer than either of them wanted.

When they went out the door and onto the porch, Daniel immediately looked around for any signs of the killer. Nothing. There were no trampled down plants or grass. Leo was doing the same thing, and he used the flashlight function on his phone to examine the gravel and dirt driveway in front of the house where Barrett, Daniel and he were all parked.

Still nothing.

Of course, he could have screwed up any prints when he'd driven in. It hadn't been on Daniel's radar that a killer could have just been there. Just the opposite. He'd come to tell Kara that there was no reason for her to lure out a killer who didn't exist. Now he knew differently and wondered how soon it would be before Kara said *I told you so.*

Or blamed him for this.

If he'd just listened to her, there might not be a dead woman lying on her bed. He might have been staking out her place and could have caught the guy red-handed.

"I'll have to come back in the morning to check on the horses," Kara muttered as Daniel helped her into his truck.

Her comment actually made him feel better because it meant the shock was wearing off. "I'll have one of my ranch hands do it."

Daniel had four who worked for him, managing the herds of Angus cattle that he raised, and he'd send one of them here to her place. No way did he want Kara out in the open like that until they had some answers. He was pretty sure those answers would confirm something he already felt in his gut.

That Kara was in danger.

With that unsettling thought going through his head, Daniel started his truck as Leo headed back to the house. Daniel would have driven away had his phone not buzzed with a call. When he saw the name on the screen, he knew he had to take the call right away.

"It's Loretta Eaton from the fertility clinic," he relayed to Kara, and he hit the answer button while he continued to keep watch around them.

"Oh, God," Loretta immediately said. And Daniel felt that same avalanche of dread that he heard in the woman's voice. "It's true, Deputy Logan. God, it's true. Mandy Vera was one of our surrogates."

Chapter Three

Kara didn't have to hear what Loretta had said to Daniel. She could tell from his softly muttered profanity and the grim look on his face that what the woman from the fertility clinic had told him wasn't good news.

"Thanks for letting me now. I can't talk right now. I'll call you tomorrow," Daniel told Loretta, and he ended the call.

"Mandy was a surrogate," Kara stated.

Daniel hesitated for several moments before he nodded, and he fired off a text. "I'm letting Barrett know. He'll want someone from SAPD to go out to Mandy's place and have a look around."

Yes, and maybe they would find something, especially if that's where the killer had gotten his hands on the woman. But if that's where it'd happened, then why hadn't he just murdered her there?

The answer to that settled like ice in her bones.

"This is personal," Kara managed to say. "He set all of this up to taunt me."

Daniel didn't deny it. Couldn't. Because he knew as well as she did that there was no other logical reason for why Mandy had been brought here and posed liked that in Kara's bed. It had all been set up to shock and terrify her. And it had worked. The fear slid through her, breath to bone.

But so did the anger.

Kara had felt plenty of anger when she'd set her plan of bait into motion. She hadn't wanted to feel helpless, and she'd gone into that barn, waiting for the worst to happen. However, the anger she'd felt then was a drop in the bucket compared to what she felt now. The monster who'd murdered Brenda and now Mandy wasn't going to get away with this.

"I didn't hear anything about the killer posing Brenda's body or moving it to a location away from the place she was killed," Kara said as Daniel drove away from her house. "You read the police reports. Was there any mention of that?"

Even in the dim light from the dashboard panel, she could see the rock-hard set of his jaw muscles. He was still glancing around, no doubt looking for the person who'd murdered Mandy. "None." This time when he cursed, it wasn't muttered. "I didn't believe you. I didn't believe there was a killer."

She heard the guilt in his voice and knew this was something that would eat away at him. But Kara had no intention of holding his feet to the fire on this.

"You had to look at this as a cop," she reminded him. Like Daniel, she also continued to keep watch, but there were lots of woods on the rural roads between their two ranches. "Besides, there wasn't a lot of evidence to convince you that someone was targeting surrogates."

"You knew there was a killer," he snapped.

It wasn't much consolation for her to know that she'd

been right all along about her being in the crosshairs of a killer. "Because I sensed someone following me. Because I was paranoid," she added in frustration. "I've been paranoid for the past thirteen years."

He didn't have to ask what had happened thirteen years ago to make her that way. Daniel knew. That's when her parents had been murdered. But not just murdered. A ranch hand her father had fired, Lamar Darnell, had stalked her parents and taunted them with threats for weeks. Before the cops could find Lamar and arrest him, he'd shot and murdered her mom and dad and then turned the gun on himself.

There was that old saying that what didn't kill you made you stronger. Well, their deaths hadn't killed her, but Kara had known she wouldn't go through something like that again without a fight. For all the good it'd done.

A woman was still dead.

"I should have handled this a different way," Kara whispered, talking to herself. "I should have tried to find out the names of the surrogates so I could contact them and warn them. I should have looked harder to find some kind of evidence to give the San Antonio cops a push to get involved."

Daniel groaned, and he shook his head. "If you need to blame someone, blame me. I didn't listen, but I'm listening now. Whoever's doing this might have a beef against the fertility clinic. Maybe against the idea of surrogacy itself. Either way, I want access to the files. I want to read some of that letter they got from the guy claiming to have killed Brenda."

Kara wanted that, as well. In fact, she'd asked for permission to read that letter and any others of a threatening nature, but her request had been denied. Maybe Daniel could use his badge to get to them, and that in turn could lead them to suspects.

Maybe an insane one.

"Mandy was a brunette, too," Kara murmured, and just that little detail caused her stomach to twist into knots. "Just like Brenda and Marissa. Just like me."

"Yes," Daniel said, and he paused for several moments. "Often a killer like this will stick to the same type of victim and the same method of murder."

Kara thought about that. Brenda had been beaten to death, and from the looks of it, Mandy had been strangled. They still didn't know what had happened to the missing woman, Marissa, but Kara had the sickening feeling that they'd find her dead, too. And everything was pointing to their being surrogates at the same clinic as the reason for their deaths.

"You think there's more than one killer?" she asked, trying to focus on the investigation rather than the images of the dead woman.

Daniel lifted his shoulder. "It's too early to say. Maybe. Or maybe he just got carried away with Brenda. He could have beaten her because she fought back."

True, and that didn't ease the stomach knots any. It only proved to her that whoever was doing this would use any means to reach his goal.

And his goal was to kill.

"All the surrogates who used that clinic will need to be contacted," Kara said. "They should know there's a possible threat."

He made a sound of agreement. "It's tricky when getting access to medical records, but maybe the press can help with that. When the news media picks up on the two murders, possibly three, and all were former patients at Willingham, then—"

When he didn't finish that, Kara turned to him and saw that he was looking in the rearview mirror. At first, she didn't see anything other than the darkness, but then she spotted the vehicle.

A black truck with the headlights off.

"It just pulled out from a side road," Daniel said.

Kara's heart immediately jumped to her throat. There were other ranches and houses out here, and while there wasn't a lot of traffic, there was still some. Still, everything inside her went on alert because this could be the killer, especially considering the driver wasn't using the headlights.

Without looking at her, Daniel passed his phone to her. "Text Barrett and let him know that we're being followed."

Kara tamped down her nerves and did as Daniel asked. She also kept her attention nailed to the side mirror so she could see the truck. The driver still had the headlights off, and they stayed that way even after Daniel flashed his own lights. Even though the truck was behind him, he'd be able to see the lights go on and off.

Despite the fact that Kara had been expecting a reply from Barrett, the dinging sound from Daniel's phone nearly had her shifting her gun to take aim. "Barrett's on the way," she relayed to him.

Kara did a quick estimate and figured Daniel's brother could be there in five minutes or so. Then, maybe they could stop the truck and figure out what was going on. It could turn out to be nothing. Or this could be a huge break. One that would lead them to catching a killer.

"I don't want to go to my place just yet," Daniel muttered.

"I agree." Kara couldn't say that fast enough. If this was a killer, no way did she want him going to Daniel's doorstep. Sadie was in the house, and if there was trouble, she could be hurt.

That reminder gave Kara a new surge of anger that steadied her hands and her mind. She'd already lost too many people she loved, and she would do whatever she needed to do to stop it from happening again.

"He lowered his window," Daniel said, his voice hard and tight. He drew his weapon while he continued to drive. "Get down on the seat."

Kara wanted to argue with him, to remind him that she could help him keep watch. But this wasn't the time to distract Daniel with what would no doubt be a disagreement. The cop in him wouldn't want her to take any unnecessary risks—even if he was taking one just by staying behind the wheel.

The reality of that risk hit her hard when she saw the hand snaking out from the open window of the truck. Oh, mercy. The driver had a gun.

And he aimed it right at them.

She slid lower into the seat but not so low that she wouldn't be able to provide backup. And she did that just as the bullet slammed into Daniel's truck. The sound she heard was of metal ripping into metal. Not once but three times. That sent her heart pounding and her grip tightening on her Glock.

"Hold on," Daniel ground out, and he hit the accelerator.

This wasn't exactly a good road for speeding. There were a lot of curves, even a bridge, and it would be so easy for them to crash. Still, they needed to get out of range of those bullets.

"Text Barrett again," Daniel told her. "Tell him we're under fire."

Before Kara could do that, the sound of another shot blasted through the air. This one didn't hit Daniel's truck, but the shooter immediately sent another shot their way. Then another. Worse, the guy was managing to keep up with them. Both trucks were flying down the country road.

She sent the text, knowing that at the speed they were going, it would take Barrett even longer to reach them. However, he could likely manage to get them some backup that could arrive faster since they were headed in the direction of Mercy Ridge.

Daniel sped past the turn that would have taken them to his ranch, and then he cursed. Kara risked sitting farther up in the seat so she could look in the side mirror again. What she saw sent her heart to her knees. The shooter had slowed down and taken that turn.

He was heading to Daniel's ranch.

Daniel slammed on the brakes, the tires squealing against the asphalt, and he turned his truck around. Not easily and not fast. It was hard to do a U-turn on such a narrow road, and the maneuver ate up precious seconds, but Daniel finally got them turned around.

"Call Noreen," Daniel snapped, but Kara was already doing that.

With the lead the driver of the truck had on them, he would make it to the ranch before they did. Kara tried not to let that terrify her. Terror wouldn't help right now. She just needed to let the nanny know what was going on so she could do whatever possible to keep a killer from getting into the house.

Thankfully, Noreen answered on the first ring, and Kara didn't even bother easing into this. "There's trouble. A gunman is on the way to the ranch," Kara blurted out.

"Kara?" Noreen said. "Why are you calling? What's going on?"

"I don't have time to explain everything. He'll be there within minutes so you need to make sure all the windows and doors are locked. Turn on the security system if it's not already on and then take Sadie into one of the bathrooms. Do it now," Kara snapped when Noreen didn't respond.

"I'm checking the doors." Noreen finally said. "God, what's happening?"

"We're not sure, but this gunman could try to break in. Are the doors and windows locked?"

"Oh, God," Noreen repeated. "We keep the windows locked, and the doors are, too." Kara heard some soft clicks. "And I've just set the security system."

"Stay on the line and get Sadie to the bathroom," Kara instructed.

Daniel muttered something, maybe a prayer, and he continued to speed through the night toward the ranch. She could hear their gusting breaths, but that was the only sound.

Until the next shot.

It seemed to come out of the blue, and it blasted through the window right next to her head. The safety glass tumbled down onto her, and Kara didn't even have time to bring up her gun before the gunman fired another bullet. Then another.

"Get down," Daniel yelled.

She did but not before she saw the black truck. Not on the road ahead of them. The driver had pulled off onto a trail, the front of the truck facing them.

With a hail of bullets coming directly at them, Daniel's truck lurched to the right, and that's when Kara knew their situation had gone from bad to worse. Because the gunman had managed to shoot out at least one of the tires.

Fighting with the steering wheel, Daniel kept going, and the bullets kept coming. The shooter's truck did, too. From the glimpse that Kara got in the side mirror, the driver had bolted out behind them again. And that meant they were now headed for Daniel's ranch.

"Do you have Sadie in the bathroom?" Kara asked Noreen.

"Yes." Noreen's voice sounded even shakier than it had before.

Kara could also hear Sadie fussing, and that was like a fisted hand on her heart. Sadie could be afraid. She was too young to understand what was going on, but the little girl had no doubt picked up on her nanny's fear.

The shots started again, and Daniel's truck did another lurch. Mercy, the gunman was trying to stop them, and if he succeeded, they'd be sitting ducks. He could continue to fire until he killed them both.

"I'm not going closer to the house," Daniel snarled.

Unlike Noreen, there was no fear in his voice. Just some raw anger. Something Kara totally understood.

She wanted to make this gunman pay hard for what he was doing.

"Text Barrett again and give him our location," Daniel added, and he finally brought his truck to a stop.

Kara knew that it was necessary for Barrett to know where they were so that there wouldn't be the possibility of being wounded by friendly fire, but she wanted to help Daniel with this showdown. Still, she sent off the text, tossed the phone onto the glass-strewn seat and levered herself up so that she could return fire. Beside her, Daniel did the same.

There was another sound. Not gunfire this time. But rather the gunman throwing his truck into Reverse. He flew backward, whipping the truck onto a trail so that he could turn around.

Daniel bolted out from cover, taking aim, and he fired two rounds into the cab of the truck. However, it was already too late.

The killer was speeding away.

Chapter Four

While Daniel waited for an update from Barrett, he paced across his living room and watched Kara. He had to hand it to her—she was looking a lot steadier than she must be feeling.

And she was doing that for Sadie's sake.

Kara was pulling off the steady facade, too, because Sadie showed no signs that anything was wrong while Kara read her a story. They were snuggled up on the sofa with Sadie in her lap. Of course, Sadie was only eighteen months old and thankfully too young to realize something bad had happened.

The calm veneer wouldn't last for Kara, though. Daniel was certain of that because he figured it wouldn't last for him, either. Right now, he had plenty to do, what with trying to find out what the hell had happened with that attack, but once Sadie was in bed and Kara and he started talking about it, the emotions would be right there at the surface.

The fear, too.

After all, their attacker was still at large, which meant he could return for another round. Since the shooter was also likely the same person who'd murdered Mandy, it wouldn't be a friendly encounter.

Sadie clapped when Kara finished the book and gave Kara a kiss on the cheek. That was Noreen's cue to get Sadie moving. The nanny was also keeping up appearances, trying not to let it show that she was worried, but Daniel would have to talk to her soon, too, and try to reassure her that he'd do whatever it took to keep them all safe.

"Remember, you get to sleep in the bathtub," Daniel told Sadie.

That caused his daughter to grin. She believed this was some kind of an adventure. Like indoor camping with the bedding that he'd put in the tub for her. However, it was much more than an adventure. It was for her own safety. If a gunman fired shots, Sadie would be safer in the tub than in her crib. Daniel would add a level to that safety by sleeping on the bathroom floor next to her.

As usual, Sadie doled out good-night kisses and hugs first to Kara and then to Daniel. He let the hug linger a couple of moments. Just having his baby with him settled him down a little. However, it also reminded him of how high the stakes were right now. His little girl could be in danger, and he needed to find out why because the why often led to the who.

"What kind of updates have you been getting?" Kara asked the moment Sadie and Noreen were out of earshot.

Obviously, Kara had noticed that during the time she'd been reading to Sadie, he'd been getting texts.

Some had been from Barrett, others from Leo, but neither of them had good news.

"There's still no sign of the killer," he said, giving her the worst of it first. Until they found him, they couldn't make an arrest, and the threat would continue.

Kara nodded, and she stayed quiet a moment, no doubt trying to come to terms with that. "Anything on Mandy?"

"Some, most of it is still preliminary, though. Cause of death is likely strangulation. San Antonio PD is going through her place now, and they've told us there are signs of a struggle."

Another nod from Kara, followed by some deep breaths. She was trying to steady herself. Good. Because even though she had a darn good reason to fall apart right now, Daniel was hoping she wouldn't. He needed both of them to hold things together so they could figure out the safe thing to do about Sadie. About Kara, too, since she was almost certainly the killer's target.

But why hadn't the guy just killed her tonight?

Kara had put out the word that she'd be in the barn, and he could have gone in there after her. It could be this was some kind of cat-and-mouse game, or maybe the killer was a coward. It was one thing to take and drug an unarmed woman like Mandy, but he must have known that Kara would be armed and ready for him.

"The crime scene unit is out at your house," he went on after glancing through his texts. "They've found two sets of footprints outside your office window. There are some drag marks, too. So maybe the guy had drugged Mandy before he got there, revived her enough so she could walk at least part of the way and then gave her a second dose of the drug once he got her inside."

Of course, the killer could have incapacitated the woman other ways, smothering or a blow to the head, but it didn't really matter. He'd gotten Mandy into Kara's house, murdered her and staged the body. Maybe as a threat to Kara to tell her to back off her investigation into the missing and dead surrogates, maybe just to torment her.

The tormenting was definitely working.

She shook her head. "I didn't hear anything to let me know someone was in my house."

At the moment, he considered that a good thing. "If you had, you might have gone inside to check things out and been killed."

Daniel hoped that was a warning she'd take to heart. He didn't want Kara setting up any more traps for this snake. She certainly didn't jump to defend what she'd done. Nope. Her emotions went in the other direction. Her eyes filled with tears.

"Oh, God. Daniel, I'm so sorry."

Hell. He'd hoped she would be able to keep the aftermath of all of this at bay. Apparently not. Those tears didn't spill down her cheeks, but she was blinking hard to keep them from falling.

Daniel figured this was a mistake the size of Texas, but he went to her and pulled her into his arms. Kara practically sagged against him, her head landing on his shoulder. He didn't want to notice how well she fit. Didn't want to notice her scent that he immediately took in. Or the soft breathy sigh she made.

But he noticed.

Having her this close was a reminder that she was an attractive woman. And that he was a man. Something he'd been noticing more and more whenever he was around Kara.

It'd been nearly two years since he'd lost his wife. Since Kara had lost her sister. It was only natural for Kara and him to tap into the grief they shared for the loved one they'd lost. Grief that could still slice to the bone.

Added to that, there was Sadie. Kara had carried his little girl for nine months, and Sadie and she had DNA in common. These were all the things that Daniel had gone over and over. All the reasons he kept giving himself for why he felt this connection with Kara. At the moment, though, those were not the reasons his body was having this reaction to her.

A bad reaction.

He felt the stir of familiar heat and knew if he let it continue that it would put a serious dent in his resolve to keep his hands off his late wife's sister. Sexual heat could do that. It could make excuses and blur lines that shouldn't be blurred.

And that's why Daniel stepped back from her.

He'd hoped that Kara was so caught up in her near meltdown that she wouldn't notice how fast he'd moved away from her. But she did notice. Her eyes came to his, their gazes connecting, and he saw something he wished weren't there.

The same blasted heat that he was battling.

Kara was battling it as well, and in that long look they gave each other, many things passed between them. Things best left unsaid, and that's why Daniel decided to do something to put an end to this nonverbal conversation.

He went into the adjacent kitchen to get himself a bottle of water. What he really wanted was a beer or a shot of something stronger, but until the killer was caught, he was essentially on the job. Plus, he didn't want anything, including this lust for Kara, to cloud his head and therefore his judgment.

"How secure are the grounds around your ranch?" Kara asked, joining him in the kitchen.

She didn't look at him. A smart decision. That meant she'd learned her lesson about making long eye contact with him. Added to that, it was a good question. Too bad his answer was going to suck. He considered softening it some, but that could end up being dangerous. He didn't want Kara to have a false sense of safety that could end up getting her killed.

"I have four hundred acres," he reminded her. "Along with barns and other outbuildings. There are at least a half-dozen old trails that thread through the area. And in the middle of all that sits this house."

She nodded, drew in another of those unsteady breaths. "I've brought danger to your house, to your daughter."

"Wrong. The killer did that by going after us tonight." He paused, added the rest that she needed to hear. "I could have been the target."

Now it was surprise that flashed through her eyes. "You?"

"Me," he verified, and he tapped his badge to let her know that he was referring to his being a cop. "I've arrested people who might want to get back at me."

In fact, just a couple of months ago he'd had a tense run-in with a nearby rancher, Neal Rizzo, who'd threatened him. Mandy's murder pointed to the other surrogates and the fertility clinic, but Daniel had to look at this from all angles. And one big angle was that Mandy's killer hadn't launched another attack until after Kara and he had left for his ranch. It would have been easier for the killer just to go after her when she was alone. But he hadn't. So, maybe Kara and he were both targets.

"I'm going through all my old cases," he went on. He'd have a chat with Rizzo, too. "We'll take as many precautions as we can."

They'd already done that by closing all the curtains and blinds, locking all the doors and arming the security system. He also had several full-time ranch hands and another part-time one who could help keep an eye on the house and grounds. But even all of that might not be enough.

"There are just too many places for someone to lie in wait," Daniel continued a moment later. "Or someone could climb up one of the trees and take shots at the house. That's why Noreen will be sleeping in her bathroom tonight, and you'll be staying in the guest bathtub. It won't be especially comfortable, but it'll add another safety layer."

Kara didn't give him even an argumentative glance about that. "You'll take precautions, too?"

He nodded. "No pj's for me tonight." Though he was more of a "boxers and tee" kind of guy, and in his earlier days, commando. "I'll be wearing Kevlar." And he'd be armed to the hilt. He didn't like carrying a gun with Sadie around, but he couldn't risk having to run for his weapon if the worst happened. "Keep your Glock with you."

She nodded as if that were exactly what she'd expected him to say, but Daniel could still see the tension, and the fear, this had caused her. Tension and fear, though, were better than not being prepared if this killer came after them again.

"Because it's already getting late, we need to stay here for the night," Daniel went on, "but tomorrow, I'll find someplace safer." He'd been mulling that over, while no place was a 100 percent safe, he had an idea. "I'm considering moving the four of us to the Serenity Inn in town."

The inn was on Main Street, only two buildings away from the sheriff's office. Along with having a security system and motion-activated exterior lights, the open yard would make it harder for a gunman to sneak onto the grounds.

Harder but not impossible.

"I'm sure I can talk Ellen into closing the inn to everyone but us," he added. Ellen Deavers owned the place and rarely had visitors anyway since Mercy Ridge wasn't exactly a hotbed for tourism. "We can get the adjoining rooms on the second floor, and one of the other deputies can sleep downstairs."

"That might work," Kara said after releasing her bottom lip that she'd been biting. "We'd still have to keep Sadie away from the windows."

"Noreen and you, too," he emphasized. "I don't want either of you taking any unnecessary risks."

Especially since the necessary ones were plentiful

enough. After all, Daniel would have to take them out in the open to get them from his ranch to the inn.

"You're okay with connecting rooms?" Kara asked.

Daniel couldn't pretend that he didn't know exactly what she meant. This was about the heat that was still in full simmer mode. Being under the same roof with Kara could send it from simmer to boil. But again, it was a risk he had to take. No way did he want her out of his sight as long as she was in the crosshairs of a killer.

"I'm okay with it," he said.

Again, their gazes held, and it seemed as if she were trying to figure out if that were true. However, she didn't get a chance to do that because his phone rang, and when Kara saw Barrett's name on the screen, it got her attention. It got Daniel's, too, because this was almost certainly connected to the investigation. He hit the answer button and put it on speaker so that Kara could hear.

"I've got bad news," Barrett immediately said. His brother didn't wait for them to verbally respond to that, but inside, Daniel felt the punch of dread. A moment later, the dread was confirmed when Barrett added, "There's been another murder."

Chapter Five

Loretta Eaton, the office manager at the fertility clinic, was dead.

That was the thought that had run through Kara's head most of the night, and it was one of the reasons she hadn't gotten much sleep. Of course, it hadn't helped that she'd spent the night in a bathtub and knew that Sadie had done the same. Kara hated that such measures had been needed to keep the girl safe. Hated even more that such measures would have to continue, well, indefinitely.

From what Daniel and she had learned, Loretta had gone into the office to check the files on Mandy and according to the San Antonio cops, the woman hadn't made it out of the building alive. When Kara had finally gone off to "bed," they hadn't yet received a time of death from the medical examiner, but according to the security login, Loretta had been in the fertility clinic about two hours before her lifeless body was discovered by a janitor.

Kara hadn't needed any further proof that all these deaths were connected to Willingham Fertility Clinic, but Loretta's murder added to the weight of the case.

There were now three confirmed deaths: Mandy Vera, Loretta Eaton and Brenda McGill. Marissa Rucker was still missing, and Kara could only pray that she was still alive and would stay that way. If Marissa had figured out what was going on, that her life was in danger, maybe she went into hiding. At the moment, that was the best possible scenario when it came to Kara's fellow surrogate.

Kara finished her shower and dressed in jeans and a top, and she used some makeup that one of Daniel's ranch hands had brought over from her place. Whoever had processed her house for evidence must have cleared the items since they'd been waiting for her when she got up.

She tried her best to hide the dark circles under her eyes. Even though Sadie probably wouldn't notice something like that, Kara didn't want to give the little girl any reason for concern. Ditto for Daniel. He was already worried about a killer and didn't need to spare any of his thoughts to her well-being.

Following the smell of coffee and the sound of Sadie's babblings, Kara made her way to the kitchen. Everyone was already up, making her feel a little like a slacker. Sadie was in her highchair eating bits of scrambled egg and cut-up fruit. Noreen was at the stove, and Daniel was at the table, sipping coffee while he read something on his laptop.

Noreen was wearing one of her usual loose cotton dresses and white sneakers, and she gave Kara a quick smile that didn't quite make it to her weathered blue eyes. Since Noreen was a local, Kara had known the woman her entire life, and she was as steady as they came, having raised her three now grown sons on her own after her husband had been killed when the boys were children. That steadiness would come in handy with what they were facing.

Daniel glanced up at her, studying her face, and her frown. Obviously, her makeup attempt hadn't fooled him one bit. She must have looked as exhausted as she was.

"Nantie," Sadie greeted, which was her attempt at *Auntie*. Thankfully, she was grinning and showed no signs of stress.

"Good morning, sweetheart," Kara murmured, giving Sadie a kiss. Her dark curls were haloing around her pretty face, and her gray eyes practically sparkled.

Sadie added a hug to the kiss, her sticky fingers leaving bits of egg and strawberry in Kara's hair. She didn't mind. Despite the horrible circumstances, it felt good to see her niece first thing in the morning. It was a rare treat that would help her get through this.

"Have some coffee," Noreen offered, and she stopped scrambling more eggs to get Kara a mug.

Kara filled the mug to the brim, certain that she would need lots of caffeine to make it through the day, and she turned back to Daniel to ask if there were any updates. However, before she could say a word, his phone rang.

"Barrett," he mumbled, already standing. "I need to take this." He answered it while walking out of the room. Obviously, he was worried about Sadie overhearing something she shouldn't.

Noreen sighed, shook her head. "Daniel's worried sick," she whispered. "So are you."

Kara didn't deny it. Couldn't. "How about you?" she asked the nanny. "How are you holding up?"

"About as well as can be expected," she said, still whispering. "I'm trying to stay calm for Sadie's sake."

Kara was trying to do the same. "Did Daniel talk to you about all of us staying at the inn?"

She nodded, dished up the scrambled eggs that she then handed to Kara. "I've already gotten Sadie's things together. Eat," she added, stepping away from her to load the dishwasher.

Kara wasn't hungry. In fact, her stomach was in knots, but she had to eat. She wouldn't be any good to Daniel and this investigation if she walked around with a light head.

She ate standing, her back against the counter and her gaze on the living room where Daniel was talking on the phone and pacing. Whatever Barrett was telling him had caused Daniel's forehead to bunch up.

"You're worried about him," Noreen said, startling Kara and causing her to practically snap toward the woman.

There'd been something in Noreen's tone. Something that went beyond concern for their safety. That same something was in the woman's eyes, and it made Kara believe that maybe Noreen had picked up on the attraction between Daniel and her.

Noreen managed a slight smile. "I always figured Daniel and you would get together."

It was a good thing that Kara had already swallowed the coffee and eggs, or she would have choked. "It's not like that between Daniel and me," she assured the woman.

Noreen shrugged in a "suit yourself" gesture. "I think it's what your sister would have wanted, too."

Kara didn't even want to consider that. She didn't want that idea in her head. But it was too late. It was already there. It had been for months now. Before Maryanne died, Daniel had been her sister's husband. Period. Of course, Kara had noticed he was hot. She would have been blind not to see that, but he'd been hands-off. Now, her body was nudging her to test that hands-off rule.

And that could be a huge mistake.

If Daniel and she did try for a relationship, and it failed, Sadie could end up being hurt. Kara didn't want any awkwardness between Daniel and her. It just wasn't worth the risk.

She mentally repeated that to herself. Twice.

But, oh, her body could spin some images. Unfortunately, those images were fueled by actual memories of the time she'd seen him and his brothers skinny-dipping in the creek. Even then, he'd been Maryanne's, but that hadn't stopped the memory of him, naked, lean and amazing, from being branded in her mind.

"Let me get Sadie cleaned up while Daniel and you talk," Noreen said.

It took Kara a moment to pull herself out of her heated daydream and realize that Daniel had ended his call with Barrett and was making his way back into the kitchen. One look at his somber face and Kara knew this was a conversation that Sadie definitely shouldn't overhear.

Sadie insisted on giving her daddy a sticky kiss and hug before Noreen whisked her away. It didn't take long, but during that handful of seconds, Kara could feel the anxiety build inside her.

"Has there been another murder?" she came out and asked.

"No." He dragged in a long breath. "Barrett got an update from the ME about Loretta. She died from blunt force trauma. Multiple blows to the head," Daniel added in a mumble. "Barrett saw the crime scene photos, and he said there was a lot of rage in the attack. Plenty of overkill."

That turned her anxiety to an ice-cold chill. Kara could almost see Loretta's beaten body, could feel the terror the woman had gone through before some monster ended her life.

"Are we dealing with two attackers?" Kara asked, forcing her mind back on the investigation. The only way she could help Loretta now was to find her killer and get justice.

"Maybe, but there was over an hour between the attack on us and Loretta's estimated time of death. That's plenty enough time for our attacker to make it to the clinic." Daniel paused. "San Antonio PD found several tiny cameras planted throughout the clinic. Ones that didn't belong to the clinic's security system."

Kara took a moment to process that. "The cops believe whoever planted the cameras knew that Loretta was there and went after her?"

He nodded. "The question is why. Loretta had already confirmed that Mandy Vera was a surrogate, but she'd also searched some other files. We don't have the details on that yet, but we should soon." Daniel checked the time. "Someone from the clinic should be calling me any minute now."

Good. Maybe that person would be able to tell them what Loretta had been searching. It had to be more than simply providing them info about Mandy since Daniel would have gotten that intel shortly after he verified who she was. Of course, maybe the killer just wanted Loretta dead so that she couldn't give them anything that would help the cops catch him.

Overkill and caution.

Take out a potential threat before it became a real threat.

Of course, when the cops continued to dig, they might discover that Loretta had some kind of connection to the killer. Maybe even be an accomplice. But if that were true, it didn't seem as if the woman would have been so quick to cooperate with them by confirming the info she'd given them on Mandy.

"San Antonio PD is giving me access to the files of the murdered surrogates and the missing one," Daniel continued. "They're not dismissing the theory that Brenda was killed by her abusive boyfriend, but in light of everything else, they're going to treat her murder as connected to the others."

"Good," Kara murmured, and she felt the knotted tension inside her ease up a little. "Maybe there's something from the crime scene that can help ID the person."

Daniel nodded and stared at her as if he wanted to say more. More that might not be connected to the murders. He finally huffed and groaned softly. "I don't want this thing between us to get out of hand."

Kara definitely didn't ask him to clarify what *thing*.

She knew. And she just happened to agree with him. Unfortunately, she wasn't sure their feelings for each other were in their control. It was hard to turn off the heat when you didn't know how or when your body kept urging you to do something about it. Still, she made a sound of agreement and hoped that being under the same roof with Daniel wouldn't break down the defenses she was trying to build to contain this heat.

As if relieved over the interruption, Daniel immediately took out his phone when it rang. "It's the fertility clinic," he relayed to her, and he hit the speaker function as he answered, "Deputy Logan from Mercy Ridge."

"Hello," the woman said, and that one-word greeting seemed very shaky. Of course, with a murder inside the clinic, Kara suspected that tensions and fear were running high. "I'm Betty Hyde. I was Loretta's assistant, and I'll be taking over her duties until they can hire someone else."

The woman's voice not only cracked but Kara could hear her breath break into a sob.

"You were close to Loretta?" Daniel asked.

"No. Not really. But... God, she's dead. Someone killed her."

"I know. I'm sorry." In contrast, Daniel kept his voice level and calm. "I know this is a hard time for you and everyone else there, but I'm hoping you can help."

"Yes," Betty muttered. "The other cops told me that you needed copies of any threatening letters and emails we've received in the last year. I've got those for you. Well, I have the letters, including the one from the person who claimed to have killed Brenda McGill, but someone hacked into our computer files about two months ago and deleted a lot of stuff. Including the email threats."

Daniel and she exchanged a knowing glance. Kara seriously doubted that was a coincidence. One of those deleted threats would have likely pointed to the killer.

"There are two letters in particular that caught my attention," Betty went on a moment later. "The first is the one that mentioned Brenda. There's no name, no signature and the crime lab wasn't able to find any DNA on it. The police still have the original, but there's a copy here in our files."

Kara hadn't known the letter had been tested, but she was glad the San Antonio cops were taking those kinds of measures. Too bad the person who'd written it hadn't left behind any kind of trace evidence.

"And the other letter that caught your attention?" Daniel prompted.

"There's no signature or return address on it, either," Betty explained. "I can send you a copy of it."

"Do that," Daniel insisted, giving the woman his email address. "In the meantime, give me the gist of the letter."

"The person threatened the clinic," Betty said without hesitation. "Other clinics in the city were threatened as well, and the same language was used in each one. Using a lot of profanity, he said he was going to make everyone pay, that we'd all be sorry for turning innocent young girls into surrogates."

"He?" Daniel questioned. "You're sure the person who wrote it was a man?"

"Yes. Well, I'm sure if he's telling the truth. He

claims to have had a daughter who was talked into becoming a surrogate, and she died."

Kara immediately got a flash of a memory. When Maryanne and she had been researching the clinic, Kara had read something about a surrogate dying shortly after giving birth.

"Do you know the name of the surrogate who died?" Kara asked. Then she remembered that she hadn't introduced herself so Betty wouldn't have any idea who she was. "I'm Kara Holland. I was a surrogate at Willingham, and last night someone tried to kill me."

Kara heard the woman's sharp intake of breath. "So, you think this is connected to what happened to Loretta?"

"I do. Do you keep records on the surrogates after they deliver?" Kara pressed.

"No, I'm sorry. The surrogates or the biological parents choose the facility and hospital where they want to receive medical care."

That had been true in Kara's case. She'd chosen to give birth in Mercy Ridge, and she'd had no follow-up with Willingham Clinic after Sadie's birth. Still, she pushed.

"I remember hearing about a surrogate who died," Kara said. "This would have been well over two years ago. I seem to recall she died from a blood clot a few days after she delivered."

"I'm sorry," Betty repeated. "I don't know anything…" Then she paused. "Wait. I do recall something like that." Kara heard the click of keys on a computer keyboard. "I wasn't working here then, but I heard someone mention it."

Obviously, Betty was searching for a name. Something that Kara was also doing. She remembered coming across the woman's name during her research. It had been an awful tragedy, but Kara hadn't put the blame for her death on the clinic.

"Clarice Stroud," Betty blurted out. "She was a surrogate here, but she died at a hospital in Austin."

Bingo. That was the same name Kara had seen, and she looked up at Daniel to see if he thought it might be an important connection. He did.

"I'll want a copy of that second letter," Daniel reminded the woman, "and I'll contact SAPD to have them pick up the original. I want them to have another look at it and send it to the lab."

"Of course," Betty agreed. "I'll get that copy to you right away."

"One more thing," Daniel said. "Could you give me the next-of-kin contact for Clarice Stroud? It's important," he added when she made a sound to indicate that might be a problem. "This could end up saving another woman's life."

"Oh, God," Betty muttered, and after a few seconds, Kara heard more clicks on the keyboard. "Clarice only had one next of kin listed. Her father, Eldon Stroud. He lives on a ranch about thirty miles from where you are. Mercy Ridge."

Daniel jotted down the address Betty gave him, and the moment he ended the call, he made another one. To Barrett.

"We've got a possible person of interest in the murders," Daniel immediately told his brother. "I need you to get Eldon Stroud in ASAP for questioning."

Chapter Six

Daniel read through the copy of the letter that Betty had just emailed him. The woman had been right about the profanity and the threats. The venom was practically coming off the words in dangerous, heated waves, but Daniel zoomed right in on one particular sentence.

Somebody will pay for what happened to my girl.

Daniel didn't know the background of why Clarice Stroud had become a surrogate, not yet anyway, but if this letter was truly her father's rantings, then he obviously believed his daughter had been pressured into going through with a pregnancy. A pregnancy that had perhaps contributed to her death.

That caused Daniel to stop, and he cursed while he pressed in Barrett's number again.

"What's wrong?" Kara asked. She was shoulder to shoulder with him as they sat at the kitchen table reading the letter on his laptop.

"Whoever hired Clarice could be in danger," he managed to explain right before Barrett answered. He ignored Kara's gasp and told his brother what was going on. "Eldon's daughter, Clarice, was a surrogate who died shortly after giving birth. We need a court order to find out whose baby she carried."

"I'll get on that," Barrett assured him. "I'm still trying to get in touch with Eldon. He's not answering his phone so I'm going to send a deputy out to his place."

Good. Daniel wished he could be the one to go out and face down this man, but he couldn't leave just yet. Not until he had Noreen, Sadie and Kara moved into the inn where they'd hopefully be safer than they were here at his ranch.

"Go ahead and send Leo out here with a cruiser," Daniel added to his brother.

He didn't want to drive them to the inn in his SUV in case of another attack. The cruiser was bullet resistant, something that he prayed they wouldn't need. Still, he wanted to take the precaution.

When he got Barrett's assurance that he'd take care of sending the cruiser, Daniel stood to check on Noreen and see if she was about ready to go, but the sound of an approaching vehicle stopped him. It was barely eight in the morning, and he wasn't expecting any visitors.

"Stay back," he warned Kara.

With the attack from the night before still way too fresh in his mind, he drew his gun and went to the front of the house to look out the window. The person he saw caused him to mutter some profanity.

"Who is it?" Kara asked. He could hear the real question in her fear-laced voice. *Is it the killer?*

"It's Neal Rizzo," he spat out.

There was no need for him to explain to her who that was. Mercy Ridge was a small town where everybody knew everyone else's business. That meant there wasn't anybody over the age of five who hadn't heard about Daniel's run-ins with Neal Rizzo, his neighbor who liked to stir up trouble. If there was a beef to find, Rizzo would locate it and try to make it worse.

That was especially true after their last run-in.

A couple of months ago, Daniel had gotten an anonymous tip that Rizzo was a member of a militia group that might be stockpiling weapons, and Daniel had gone over to Rizzo's ranch to have a chat with him. He hadn't arrested Rizzo. Hadn't gotten in his face. *Too much.* But he had made it clear to Rizzo that if he was involved in any illegal activity, he'd uncover it and arrest him.

Rizzo hadn't taken that well.

Judging from the tight muscles in his face when he stepped from his truck, the man still wasn't taking it well.

"Stay back," Daniel repeated to Kara.

He disengaged the security system so he could open the door. Daniel stepped onto the porch, and as expected, that stopped Rizzo from coming closer. He doubted that Rizzo would do something stupid like open fire—especially considering that two of Daniel's ranch hands were watching—but after the attack from the night before, he wasn't taking any chances. He didn't want Rizzo any closer to his house than he already was.

Rizzo had brought his own ranch hands, and while they stayed in the truck, Daniel thought they looked more like hired thugs than cowboys. Maybe they were part of the militia group. If so, it was stupid for Rizzo to bring them here and try to rub it in Daniel's face.

"Some of your livestock broke fence and got onto my property," Rizzo snarled.

Daniel looked at his ranch hand Tanner Parnell to see if he knew anything about it. Tanner nodded. "It happened about an hour ago, and I was coming to tell you." Tanner shot Rizzo a narrow-eyed glance. "But it doesn't look as if the livestock tore down the fence. My guess is that someone did it."

Tanner gave Rizzo another of those glances, probably to emphasize that he believed Rizzo or one of his men were responsible. Daniel wouldn't put it past Rizzo to give an order like that.

"I'll send you a bill because your livestock tore up some of my pasture," Rizzo went on. "The next time it happens, something bad could happen to them. Maybe my men will mistake them for deer and shoot them."

"Then your men are dumber than dirt if they can't tell the difference between an Angus and a deer. But just in case they are that stupid, you should probably know that the laws have tightened up on that sort of thing. The legal thing to do is inform me that my livestock are on your property and give me a chance to remove them."

That sure didn't help the tight muscles in Rizzo's jaw. Every inch of him vibrated with insult and anger.

"And FYI, if you did shoot my cattle," Daniel went on, "I'd have to examine the fence that you say they broke. Outside authorities would be called in to help with the investigation. It'd be interesting to find out if there's any trace evidence or DNA that would ID the person responsible. That could result in all sorts of charges like destruction of property and cattle rustling."

Daniel hadn't known for sure that Rizzo or his men had indeed cut that fence, but he knew it now. Rizzo confirmed it with the stone-cold glower he aimed at

Daniel. The man certainly didn't jump to deny that he'd done such a thing or that he'd ordered it to be done.

"This isn't over," Rizzo spat out. "You're not just going to stick your nose in my business and get away with it."

Daniel tapped his badge. "Your business is mine when you're suspected of doing something illegal. The investigation into your involvement in the militia is open and ongoing. Cutting my fence isn't going to make me step back on that."

That kicked the man's anger up even higher. "You deserve to go down," Rizzo threatened. "You deserve to burn in hell."

With that, Rizzo turned and stalked back to his truck. With his hand on the butt of his weapon, Daniel stood there and watched as he sped away. Even though Rizzo was gone, his rage still hung in the air like a dark and dangerous cloud.

"You think we should set up cameras out in the pastures?" Tanner asked.

It was something Daniel had already considered. Not because of Rizzo. But in case the threats from the killer continued. After all, he couldn't stay at the inn indefinitely, and he'd have to beef up security in order to be able to live here with Sadie.

"Arrange for the cameras," Daniel instructed Tanner, and the hand took out his phone, no doubt to get that started.

But Daniel continued to stand there. Thinking. Remembering that look on Rizzo's face. The anger in his threat.

And he had to consider something.

The timing of this fence incident was maybe not a coincidence. News of the attack had to be all over Mercy Ridge, so maybe Rizzo wanted to add to the troubles. Or worse.

Maybe Rizzo was the cause of them.

Even though it was probably a long stretch, Daniel went back to something that Betty had said. The fertility clinic's records had been hacked into two months ago. That was around the same time that Daniel had confronted Rizzo about his ties to the militia. Rizzo knew full well that Kara, Maryanne and he had used that clinic to have Sadie, so maybe...

Hell.

Was that possible?

Had Rizzo set some kind of sick plan in motion? One with an ultimate goal to stop him from digging further into the militia investigation?

"What's wrong?" he heard Kara ask.

He glanced over his shoulder to see her in the foyer. A new wave of worry was in her eyes.

"You heard what Rizzo said?" Daniel asked, going back in. He moved her away from the door so he could shut it and reset the security system.

Kara nodded and studied his face as if trying to figure out what was going on in his head. He doubted she would believe his theory, but he laid it out for her, anyway.

"Rizzo's bad news," he said. "I haven't been able to prove it, but he's connected to a militia that's involved in illegal arms sales."

Daniel paused only so he could figure out the best

way to word the rest of what he was about to tell her, but Kara spoke before he could say anything else.

"You believe he's involved with the surrogate murders and last night's attack on us?" she asked.

Believe was a strong word. Right now, it was just something that had started to take root, and it could end up causing him to take a wrong turn with the investigation. "Rizzo's got motive to want to get back at me, but he's not stupid. He has to know if something happens to me now that he'd be a prime suspect."

Kara nodded. "But if Rizzo used the fertility clinic as a cover, then your death could be pinned on the surrogate killer."

He was glad she'd reached the same conclusion he had. Yes, it was possible that Rizzo was behind this.

Possible.

But a stronger suspect was Eldon Stroud. Daniel needed to question the man ASAP, but he'd also do some checking to see if there was anything to connect Rizzo to the murders. Unfortunately, with those militia ties, Rizzo wouldn't have necessarily had to hire a killer because he could have had one of his fellow militia cohorts do the deed. If that'd happened, there wouldn't be a money trail. Still, people talked, and it wasn't easy to keep multiple murders and attempted murders a secret.

When Kara grew quiet, Daniel looked at her. Yeah, the fear was back, and he doubted it was all for her. The baby she'd carried and loved was caught up in the middle of this. And he might be the reason for the danger.

Daniel silently cursed.

"This isn't your fault," Kara murmured as if she'd

known exactly what he was thinking. She touched his arm, gave it a gentle rub with just two of her fingers. "Even if it's Rizzo who's behind all of this, this isn't your fault," she emphasized.

He wasn't sure he could believe that, and it didn't matter that he'd been doing his job when he'd questioned Rizzo. None of that mattered if the SOB went after anyone else.

Once again, he found himself staring into Kara's eyes. The fear was easing some. Not the worry, though. He figured that was here to stay until they solved this case and got on with their lives. He only hoped that was possible. But it seemed each time he looked at Kara this way, it was sending him further down a very tricky path. One that he knew wasn't smart to go down. Even after the danger ended, maybe there was no turning back from that. Maybe things had already changed and they'd never be able to go back to the way things were.

Daniel welcomed the distraction of his phone ringing. Best not to stand around staring into Kara's eyes. Especially when it was Leo's name on the screen.

"I'm nearly at your place," Leo said when Daniel answered.

"Tell Noreen we're ready to go," Daniel instructed Kara, and he waited for her to leave before he continued with his brother. "By any chance, did you see Rizzo on the road leading here?"

"No." Leo paused. "Why? Is he giving you trouble again?"

"Trying to. I want to see if I can connect him to anything at the fertility clinic or the murders."

"All right," his brother said without missing a beat. "I can help with that. Maybe SAPD can give us something, too. By the way, a couple of the homicide detectives there agreed to contact anyone who's been a surrogate at the clinic for the past two years. They'll warn them of the possible danger and offer protection to any one of them who wants it."

Good. That'd perhaps take a lot of manpower, but it might prevent someone else from being killed.

"I'm pulling up in front of your house now," Leo added.

Daniel did indeed hear the cruiser's engine, and he checked out the window to make sure it was his brother. It was. "We'll be out in a few," he told Leo and ended the call.

He turned to get Noreen, Sadie and Kara, but they were already heading his way. With a diaper bag looped over her shoulder, Noreen was carrying Sadie, and Kara had their suitcases, one in each hand. Daniel wouldn't be able to help her with that because he wanted to be able to draw his weapon if necessary. He hoped like the devil that it wouldn't be necessary, though.

"We move fast," Daniel told them and was thankful that Sadie was smiling as if this was some sort of fun game. "The three of you will go in the back seat. I'll ride shotgun."

Noreen gave a shaky nod. She was afraid but as determined as he was to make this trip fast and safe. Kara's sound of agreement wasn't shaky at all. He could see a steely resolve in her expression. Good. Because he needed everyone to be ready to protect Sadie.

At the knock on the door, Daniel disengaged the security system so he could open the door to let Leo in. His brother kept things light, too, giving Sadie a quick kiss before they hurried out together.

Daniel and Leo stayed on the sides of Noreen and Kara. Using their bodies to shield them. It wouldn't stop a sniper, but if someone had been in place to shoot, Daniel figured those shots would have happened when he'd been talking to Rizzo. Of course, that only applied if he was the target. If it was Kara the killer wanted, then this could turn deadly fast.

He fired his gaze all around the yard and ranch, and the second they all reached the cruiser, Daniel practically shoved Kara and Noreen inside it. His brother had thought to put in a car seat, which looked out of place in the center back of a cruiser, but Daniel was thankful for it. Thankful, too, when he had everyone inside the bullet-resistant vehicle.

Daniel could finally release the breath he'd been holding. No way, though, would his heartrate ease up until he had them safely at the inn. That would be another breath-holding situation, but at least Leo would be able to pull right up to the back porch of the inn. It would still mean they'd be out in the open, but there'd be fewer places for a gunman to hide there. Added to that, Barrett had already sent out reserve deputies to patrol the grounds of the inn.

As soon as Noreen had Sadie in the car seat, Leo took off.

Kara had to adjust the suitcases, which thankfully weren't full-sized, and she stacked them on her lap. It wouldn't make it easy for her to get down on the seat if it came to that, but he hadn't wanted to risk taking the time to put them in the trunk.

"Ites," Sadie blurted out, clapping her hands.

"Lights," Daniel translated for Leo.

About a month earlier, Barrett had dropped by the ranch in the cruiser, and he'd shown Sadie the blue emergency lights. Obviously, they'd made an impression on his little girl.

Leo turned on the lights, including the one on the dash. It was actually the only one that Sadie could see from inside the car, but again, it made an impression. She squealed with delight, and despite their circumstances, it made everyone else in the cruiser smile.

Leo kept the lights on as he drove away from the ranch, and even though a cruiser with whirling lights wouldn't be a deterrent to a killer, it probably wouldn't hurt, either. After all, if the killer had the ranch under surveillance, then he had almost certainly seen Leo arrive.

Not exactly a comforting thought.

Daniel continued to keep watch as they made their way to the road that would lead them to town. Leo was doing the same. He saw that Kara was, too, after he glanced in the mirror. He only looked at her for a split second because something else grabbed his attention.

Leo must have seen it, too, because he hit the brakes, stopping only about twenty-five feet from the turn to the road that led into town.

"What the heck?" Leo muttered, and both Daniel and he drew their guns.

There was a person, a woman, lying on the ground just ahead of them. She wasn't moving but was instead stretched out on her back, her arms and legs forming an *x*. And Daniel had no trouble seeing what was on her light-colored clothes.

Blood.

Chapter Seven

Kara's heart went to her knees. She got just a glimpse of the bloody woman lying on the road before she threw her hand in front of Sadie to shelter her eyes.

Thankfully, the little girl wasn't paying any attention to what was beyond the whirling blue emergency lights, but just in case, Kara directed Sadie's attention to her phone that she pulled from her pocket. Kara loaded a cute kitten video and handed it to Sadie for her to watch.

"Is she alive?" Kara asked, trying to choose her words carefully. She hadn't wanted to say *dead*, though that certainly seemed to be the case.

Oh, God.

Had another woman been murdered?

"It could be a trap," Daniel muttered just loud enough for her to hear.

That gave Kara a jolt of adrenaline. Her gaze flew around, looking for any signs of danger. From the front seat, Leo and Daniel were doing the same. Leo called in the incident to Dispatch, reporting the location of the body. Or maybe not a body at all but rather a person who was pretending to be dead. Either way, Leo requested an ambulance and backup.

"Drive around the woman," Daniel instructed his brother. "Don't stop. The EMTs will take care of her when they get here."

Kara knew that had to be hard for Daniel, especially if the woman truly did need help, but getting out to check on her could result in the killer launching a full-scale attack on them. Sadie could be hurt. Or worse.

Leo inched the cruiser forward, maneuvering around the road so that the woman was on the passenger's side of the cruiser. There wasn't room for him to get around her any other way. That gave both Daniel and Kara the chance to get a good look at her.

Even though her voice and hands were shaking, Noreen managed to keep Sadie's attention on the kitten video. Kara, however, looked down at the ground as they drove past the woman. She definitely looked dead, and it was either an excellent makeup job or else there truly was a gaping hole in her chest.

Seeing all the blood turned her stomach, but Kara forced herself to look at the woman's face.

And she bit back the profanity that came with the shock.

"I know her," Kara blurted out, and she would have bolted from the cruiser to try to help if Daniel hadn't reached over the seat and taken hold of her.

"Stay put," he warned her. And much to her horror, he opened his cruiser door while barking out to Leo, "Cover me."

Leo probably would have cursed had Sadie not been there, but he did cover his brother as Daniel opened his door and leaned out enough so he could reach the woman. It took some doing, and he was obviously trying to stay behind the cover of the door, but he touched his fingers to her neck. He didn't say anything, but the look he gave Kara confirmed it.

The woman was dead.

This wasn't some ruse. Well, not on her part. That didn't mean her killer wasn't nearby, waiting for a chance to kill them. That was no doubt why Daniel didn't waste any time closing his door, and the second he did that, Leo sped away.

"Who is she?" Daniel asked.

Kara's heart was beating so loud, the sound pounding in her ears, that it took her a moment to realize what he'd said. "She's Georgia," Kara managed to tell him. "I can't remember her last name, but…" She had to stop and swallow hard before she could continue. "I met her at the fertility clinic when we were both waiting for appointments. She was a surrogate."

And just saying that filled her with a new wave of dread. Another connection to Willingham Fertility Clinic. Another dead surrogate.

Her breath broke, and she couldn't stop the hoarse groan that tore from her mouth. Sadie clearly thought this was a game because she giggled and tried to imitate it before Noreen got the child's attention back on the video.

"Obviously, the body wasn't there when I drove by less than ten minutes ago," Leo murmured. The moment he was on the highway, he hit the accelerator to get them out of there.

Ten minutes. That wasn't much time, but Kara had no idea how much time it would take to drag a body from a vehicle or the ditch and pose it that way. It was possible Georgia had been dead for hours. Days even. Of course, it was just as possible the woman had been murdered in the short time that Leo was at Daniel's ranch.

Kara tried to tamp down the swell of emotions. Definitely tried to make sure she kept the stark expression off her face so that Sadie wouldn't see it and get upset.

She fired glances all around, keeping watch. Staying alert. There were no signs of the killer, but Kara's thoughts immediately went to Rizzo. This could still be connected to him. After all, the man had just been at the ranch, and while he wouldn't be able to see Daniel's ranch from his place, he could have been watching the road.

Daniel took out his phone, and Kara saw him press Barrett's number. "I need to give Barrett an update about this," he said. However, he didn't put the call on speaker. Again, probably because of Sadie.

"The DB is a female, midtwenties. About five-six, medium build. Brown hair and eyes," Daniel told his brother when he answered. "COD appears to be gunshot wound to the chest." He whispered that last part. "Kara believes the woman is Georgia, surname unknown, and that she was a surrogate at the fertility clinic around the same time Kara was a patient there."

Daniel had managed to deliver all of that info in his cop voice. It was void of emotion, but Kara knew there was no such void inside him. He was almost certainly feeling plenty of anger and disgust, coupled with the need to put a stop to this now. Too many people had already died, and they weren't even close to being able to find the killer and put an end to the danger.

"Georgia Marshall," Daniel said a moment later, obviously repeating what Barrett had told him. Barrett must have already had access to the files from the clinic to be able to pull it up that fast.

Daniel looked back at her to see if she could confirm that, but Kara had to shake her head. "I only met her once, and I'm not sure we even exchanged surnames."

The only reason Kara remembered Georgia was because the woman had made a comment along the lines of her name being the same as the state where her mother had been born.

Daniel gave her a nod, relayed that to his brother and then said, "Eldon Stroud. Did you get in touch with him?"

Kara couldn't hear Barrett's response, but a moment later, Daniel added, "Good. I'll be interested in hearing if he has an alibi for last night and this morning."

Hearing that helped the tightening in Kara's chest to ease up some. Maybe Eldon could give them some answers. Heck, maybe he'd just confess to everything so that Barrett could lock him up.

"Stroud is coming in for an interview this afternoon," Daniel relayed to Kara in a whisper.

"Rizzo showed up at my place this morning," Daniel went on, talking to his brother now. "He's like a pressure cooker about to go off." It seemed as if he was about to say more, but his gaze drifted back to Sadie. She was no longer watching the video, and Noreen couldn't seem to get her attention off Daniel. "Bring in Rizzo for an interview," he finally said to Barrett. "See if you can convince him to be tested for gunshot residue."

That was a good call if Rizzo would agree to something like that. Kara doubted that he would even if he was innocent. Rizzo didn't seem the sort to cooperate with the law, especially when the sheriff was Daniel's brother.

Daniel ended the call just as Leo pulled to a stop at the rear entrance to the Serenity Inn. Other than the owner's car, there were no other vehicles in the tiny parking lot. No one in the yard, either, but Daniel, Leo and Kara still glanced around, making sure it was safe to move Sadie.

Even though Kara often drove by the inn, she tried to look at it with a fresh eye. The two-story white Victorian was one of the oldest houses in Mercy Ridge, and the owner, Ellen Deavers, kept it in pristine condition. Flower beds burst with color, and while there was no fence, low-growing manicured hedges marked the property lines.

Kara glanced at the motion-activated lights that would no doubt flare on if someone came into the yard. There'd be a decent security system inside, too. Ellen was friendly. Welcoming, even. But she was also a woman in her sixties who was often alone. She hadn't wanted her beautiful home to be easy pickings for someone out to steal something, so she'd added far more security than most folks had.

Daniel and Leo got out together, each of them opening one of the back doors of the cruiser. Leo helped get Sadie out of her car seat, immediately rushing her up the porch steps and into the inn. Noreen was right behind them. Daniel took one of the suitcases from Kara's lap, but he kept his shooting hand free as they hurried inside.

Ellen was there in the large kitchen waiting for them,

and she turned on the security system once they'd shut the door. She also handed Daniel a piece of paper with the code and instructions to control the system.

Despite the tense situation, Ellen had a smile for Sadie. By now, though, Sadie wasn't so cheery. Maybe she was picking up on the dour mood because she started to fuss. Adjusting the diaper bag on her shoulder, Noreen took Sadie from Leo.

"Let me read her a story and try to get her to settle down," Noreen suggested.

Ellen nodded. "You can use any room in the place, but there are two large connecting rooms on the second floor. Daniel said something about a deputy staying, too—"

"Cybil Cassidy," Leo provided. "She'll be here before I leave to go back to work."

Kara knew Cybil. She was a deputy who was working on a criminal justice degree. She was young, probably only twenty-four, but from what she'd heard, Cybil was a good cop. She'd certainly come from good stock since her grandfather had once been the sheriff of Mercy Ridge.

"Cybil can stay in a room on the first floor if that works for you," Ellen said. "Maybe the one near the front door?"

Daniel made a sound of agreement, and when Sadie fussed again, he motioned for Noreen to go ahead and take her upstairs. Both Ellen and Leo went with her, each of them taking a suitcase, and Kara had no doubts that Leo would check every inch of the second floor to make sure it was safe. On the bottom floor, Daniel began to do the same.

Kara followed him as they made their way through the large front parlor, where there was a reception desk. Together, they checked the door and every window to make sure they were locked and armed with the security alarm. They also closed the curtains and blinds. It helped settle her nerves a little, but Kara could see much too clearly the images of Georgia lying dead on the road. Images that would no doubt stay with her for a lifetime.

Oh, mercy.

Why was this happening? Why were so many women being murdered? Maybe the interviews Barrett was going to do would give them some answers, but it still wouldn't undo what had already been done. The killer had already taken and ruined so many lives, and there were no guarantees that this wouldn't just continue.

Daniel whirled around to face her, and that's when Kara realized she hadn't quite tamped down the sound that'd torn from her mouth.

"I'm sorry," she said, waving him off when he went to her. "You've got enough to worry about without having to deal with me."

"I want to deal with you," he assured her. Daniel's voice was barely a whisper, and when he pulled her into his arms, he brushed a kiss on the top of her head. "Trust me when I say that I'll do everything I can to keep you safe."

"Ditto." She pulled back, looked up at him and saw his slight smile. "I've always trusted you." But she wanted to wince when she heard her own words. They sounded, well, intimate. As if she meant more than just his keeping her safe.

And she did.

Kara had indeed always trusted him. That had never been a problem between them. The only problem was how to justify the other things she was feeling for him. The heat. The pull of her heart to him. He'd been her sister's husband. Her brother-in-law. And while Mary-anne was alive, Kara would have never let her feelings for Daniel cross any lines.

Never.

However, she certainly felt capable of crossing some lines right now.

It was probably a combination of the danger and the spent adrenaline. And the fact that she'd ended up in his arms again. She wasn't at her strongest right now, and she needed to be. Not to resist Daniel. She was no longer sure that was possible. But she needed to be strong to face whatever the killer had in store for them.

"I should check on Sadie," he murmured, but he didn't move. Neither did Kara. Daniel continued to hold her, and she could feel the conflict going on inside him. The moment ended, though, when his phone rang. "Barrett," he said glancing at the screen.

Daniel stepped back and put the call on speaker. "Are you settled in at the inn?" Barrett asked.

"We're here. How long are you going to be able to spare Cybil?"

"As long as necessary," Barrett assured him.

Because she was still close to Daniel, she could see that relaxed him a little. Kara figured there was also a good chance that Leo would be spending some nights here at the inn. Barrett, though, had his own concerns since his fiancée was pregnant.

"I just got off the phone with SAPD," Barrett continued. "Georgia's roommate reported her missing last night when she didn't come home after working her shift at the hospital. She was a nursing assistant."

"Was?" Daniel said. "You're sure the dead woman's Georgia?"

"Yeah. I'm at the scene now, and I found her driver's license. It was tucked underneath her body, so obviously the killer wanted us to know who she was."

Kara got another flash image of the dead woman. She hadn't seen the license, but she agreed with Barrett. The killer wanted them to know Georgia's identity. Wanted them to know that she'd been a surrogate. That way, the mental torture could start right away. Kara was thinking exactly what he no doubt wanted her to think.

Will I be next?

The killer wanted her scared. Wanted to put her through hell and back. But it fired up the simmering anger inside her. She wanted this SOB caught and punished.

"SAPD's still working on contacting all the surrogates," Barrett added a moment later. "But at least now we have a task force. Since the murders have happened in more than one jurisdiction, the Texas Rangers are coming in to help."

"Good," Daniel answered just as there was a knock at the front door. He motioned for Kara to move to the side of the living room, and once she had, he went to the window and peered out the edge of the curtain.

"Is something wrong?" Barrett asked when Daniel ground out some profanity.

Daniel's reaction didn't send Kara into a panic. To

her, he seemed more riled than worried about a threat. "No," Daniel finally said. "It's just Sean Maynard."

Kara pulled back her shoulders in surprise. Sean was a local rancher, and while he wasn't the absolute last person she'd expected to hear from today, she certainly hadn't been expecting him. Especially not here at the inn.

"Kara?" Sean called out.

Once, Sean and she had been lovers, and for a while she'd thought she was in love with him. However, things had gone downhill fast when she'd agreed to become her sister's surrogate. He'd been totally opposed to it and basically given her an ultimatum. Either him or the surrogacy.

Kara hadn't chosen him.

That'd been well over two years ago, and while things weren't exactly friendly between them, she'd thought that she was no longer on his radar. He certainly hadn't been on hers.

"Kara?" Sean said again, and he followed it with a louder knock.

"I'll call you back," Daniel told his brother right before he ended the call.

He disarmed the security system for the front door and he opened it just a crack. Judging from his defensive stance and the way Daniel slid his hand over his gun, he wasn't taking any chances.

"Is Kara here?" Sean asked. "I need to see her. I need to make sure she's okay."

Kara was certain that her own stance was defensive when she went closer to stand by Daniel's side. Sean's attention immediately shifted to her, but Daniel was firing glances all around the small front yard and the street. He was no doubt looking to make sure this wasn't the start of another attack.

"Are you all right?" Sean blurted out, his words running together. His breathing was way too fast, as if he'd just sprinted there. "I heard someone tried to kill you."

She nodded but was puzzled by his reaction. The reaction of someone who'd expected to find her injured or in immediate danger. Of course, everyone in Mercy Ridge had heard about the attack so maybe the gossips had gotten it wrong and were gabbing that she'd been physically hurt.

"How'd you know we were here?" Daniel snapped.

"I saw her in the cruiser when you pulled into the parking lot of the inn," Sean readily answered.

"I didn't see your truck," Kara pointed out.

Sean tipped his head to Main Street. "I was in the hardware store. I was parked at the back."

Daniel made a show of checking his watch. "We've been at the inn for more than five minutes. It wouldn't have taken you that long to walk here."

The steely tone of Daniel's question caused Sean's shoulders to snap back. "I debated if I should come over or try to call you instead, but I figured a visit would be better. I just had to know if Kara was all right."

She couldn't figure out a reason why he would lie about something like that, but then she wasn't exactly in a trusting mood.

Daniel clearly wasn't about to trust Sean, either, but Kara didn't want this conversation to continue. With the door open, Daniel could become a sniper's target. Best to give Sean the answer he wanted so he'd be on his way.

"I'm okay," she said to Sean, knowing it wasn't any-where near the truth. However, she didn't want to get into a discussion about her well-being with her ex. Es-pecially when her ex was tossing a few glares at Daniel.

"She's fine," Daniel snapped, and he moved as if to shut the door in Sean's face. But Sean's foot stopped him.

"I'm also here to talk to you," Sean insisted. "Both of you," he amended. "I have some information about the murdered surrogates."

Chapter Eight

Until Sean had said that last part—*I have some information about the murdered surrogates*—Daniel had been about to slam the door in the man's face. But hearing that sure stopped him.

"Information?" Daniel repeated, and he didn't bother to take the skepticism out of his tone or the glare he was aiming at Kara's ex.

Being her ex didn't have anything to do with his extreme dislike of the man, Daniel assured himself. No. This had nothing to do with the attraction simmering between Kara and him, and it wasn't the reason Daniel's glare intensified. He had other reasons for despising Sean. The man had treated Kara like dirt after she'd told him about the surrogacy.

"Information," Sean verified, keeping his gaze focused on Kara. "This morning when I checked the mail, there was a letter. Whoever wrote it said you were in danger and that Daniel's responsible."

Well, that got Daniel's attention. Kara's, too, because she moved even closer to Daniel, maybe so he could meet Sean's gaze head-on. However, in doing that, she also put herself in a possible line of fire. That's why

Daniel stepped back, and he motioned for Sean to follow them into the foyer. Daniel also kept his gun ready in case this turned out to be some kind of dangerous ruse.

He'd never thought of Sean as a potential killer, but there was a whole lot of anger simmering beneath the surface. People with that kind of anger could snap.

Had that happened to Sean?

Daniel had to look at it from that angle. Sean was bitter over his breakup with Kara so maybe he could have orchestrated a way to murder both of them to get his revenge. That was a long shot, but Daniel intended to be cautious enough not to overlook anything. Including that Sean might try to attack them now. And that's why he moved Kara behind him.

Sean noticed the maneuver, and it caused him to turn a scowl on Daniel. Daniel scowled right back at him, and he was certain he could pull off that particular expression better than Sean. The stakes weren't nearly as high for Sean as they were for Kara and him.

"Leo, stay upstairs with the others," Daniel called out to his brother. He definitely didn't want Noreen bringing Sadie down right now.

"Is there trouble?" Leo immediately asked.

"To be determined." He kept his glare on Sean. "Tell me about this letter you say you got."

Sean definitely didn't blurt out any info. Instead, he shifted his gaze back to Kara, and Daniel didn't think it was his imagination that Sean was waiting to see if she'd jump to his defense.

She didn't.

That didn't improve Sean's mood, but it should have been what he expected. Kara and he weren't exactly on friendly terms, and women were dying. Anyone who'd had a past grudge with Daniel or her was suspect.

"The letter is in my pocket," Sean finally snarled to Daniel. "Don't shoot me when I take it out."

"Then make sure you don't take out a gun with it," Daniel fired back.

"I didn't have to come here, you know," Sean grumbled, pulling the bent envelope from his back jeans pocket.

Daniel watched the man's every move. "You did if you actually have relevant information about an ongoing murder investigation. That's the law."

The man's glare stayed locked with his, but Sean gave the envelope to Kara. Daniel didn't mind that because he wanted his own hands free in case he had to do something to restrain, or stop, Sean.

Sean's name was typed on the envelope, but there was no return address. The postmark was from San Antonio and had been sent two days ago. It normally only took a day to get mail from San Antonio, but it was possible that it'd been delivered yesterday and that Sean had just now found it.

Possible.

"Should I read it?" she asked Daniel. "Will I contaminate it?"

Yeah, she could indeed contaminate it. If it was actual evidence, that is. That fell into the "to be determined" category, too. Still, the envelope had clearly been handled and opened so any trace or prints that might be there had already been compromised. Added to that, he couldn't send it to the crime lab until he believed this might actually pertain to the case.

"Read it," Daniel instructed.

Making glances from the corner of his eye, Daniel saw Kara slide the letter from the envelope. It was a single page with a few lines of typewritten words.

"'Sean,'" Kara said, reading it aloud. "'If you still care for Kara Holland, you'll get her away from Daniel Logan before he gets her killed. You can save her if you convince her that leaving with you is the only way to keep Daniel and his kid alive.'"

At the bottom of the page was, "From a concerned friend."

Daniel tried not to react to the punch of raw emotion he got from hearing those words. But the emotion barreled through him, anyway. The SOB who'd written that letter had just threatened his daughter. It didn't matter if the threat weren't real because it still sank into him like a viper's fangs. He had to wrestle with the rage that came with that and then force himself to think like a cop.

"Sadie," Kara said on a rise of breath. Obviously, she was also having to deal with the firestorm cause by that letter.

"She's fine," Daniel reminded her. He reminded himself, too. His little girl was safe, and he had to deal with what this letter meant. Or figure out fast if it meant anything at all.

Kara reread the letter, muttering the words this time, while Daniel watched Sean for a reaction. If the man was acting, then he was doing a good job of it because his anger had morphed into what appeared to be worry. Some of Daniel's had morphed, too, and he'd mentally zoomed in on one line.

If you still care for Kara Holland, you'll get her away from Daniel Logan before he gets her killed.

That seemed to put this threat right in his lap. But was it?

Hell.

Maybe.

It was that possibility that had him rethinking this plan to be here at the inn. It had him rethinking everything.

"A concerned friend," Kara said, her voice mocking. "The killer. He didn't have my best interest at heart when he tried to murder us."

No. But this might not be from the killer. It could be some kind of sick game that Sean was playing. But why? To get back at Kara and him?

Possibly. If so, that could point at Sean. At Eldon Stroud, too, if he wanted revenge for his daughter's death. Hell, Rizzo wasn't off that possible suspect list, either, since this could be just another way to torment them. Along with putting some suspicion on Sean.

Rizzo wasn't an idiot, and he would have known about the bad blood between Kara and Sean. Which meant there'd also be bad blood between Daniel and Sean. Rizzo could be trying to tap into that in some way by getting Sean involved in his already messy mix.

"Someone obviously wants you dead," Sean said, stating what was already way too obvious. He pointed to the letter. "It says if you leave Daniel that it'll keep you, him and his baby alive."

Daniel was certain that Kara hadn't missed that part. Certain, too, that she wasn't buying it. He got confirmation of that a moment later.

"This could be a ploy to separate Daniel and me so that it'll be easier to kill us," she said. She looked up from the letter and nailed her gaze to Sean. "Someone's murdering former surrogates, and why would my being with you stop something like that?"

"I could protect you," Sean blurted out.

Daniel's eyebrow rose, and he tapped his badge.

Sean huffed. "You don't have to be a cop to protect her. I could hire bodyguards." He turned to plead his case to Kara. "I wouldn't let a killer get to you. We were close once. Remember that, and maybe then you'll realize that I'd do anything to keep you safe."

"Daniel's doing everything possible to keep me safe," Kara argued.

Daniel hated that he felt any bit of pleasure about her saying that. But he did. Too bad he didn't have as much faith in himself as Kara did.

Sean huffed, propped his hands on his hips. "Does that mean you won't even consider going with me?"

"That's exactly what it means," Kara said without hesitation. "Do I have to remind you that you wanted nothing to do with me when I told you I was becoming a surrogate? Because I certainly don't have to be reminded of it. There's no way I can trust you after you did that."

Sean's next huff was a lot louder, and his eyes narrowed. "Fine, suit yourself, but remember this. If you stay, you're putting his daughter in danger. Is that what your sister would have wanted?" He slid them both a nasty glare. "Of course, I doubt Maryanne would have wanted you sleeping with Daniel, either."

Thankfully, Kara didn't bite on that last part and

try to convince Sean that they weren't lovers. Neither did Daniel, and their combined silence and hard stares must have made the man realize this was one argument he wouldn't win. Cursing them both, Sean turned and stormed out. Unfortunately, Sean nearly smacked right into Cybil, who was making her way up the steps.

"Kara's going to get them all killed," Sean grumbled, maybe to Cybil, maybe just to himself.

"A problem?" Cybil asked Daniel when she stepped in and closed the door behind her.

"Maybe." Daniel tipped his head to the letter that Kara was still holding. "Could you put that in an evidence bag and send it to the lab? Sean said someone sent it to him, and it might be connected to the murders."

"Of course," Cybil answered, heading right back out. "I've got a field bag in my SUV. I can bag it, and Leo can carry it back to the office for a courier to pick up."

Daniel thanked her, and Cybil headed out.

"Do you think Sean's right?" Kara muttered the moment his fellow deputy was out of earshot. "Do you really think I could get us all killed?"

"No." Daniel didn't even have to think before he answered. "Remember, both of us were attacked last night. I believe you were right when you said it'd be easier for someone to come after us if we weren't together. Especially if you were with bodyguards that Sean hired."

Meeting his gaze, Kara made a sound of agreement. "I don't trust Sean."

"Neither do I," Daniel immediately assured her.

He was glad they were on the same wavelength, but that didn't address the problem of keeping Kara safe while in his protective custody. And making sure that

Sadie didn't get caught up in the crosshairs of a killer gunning for them. Moving his baby away from the ranch was a start, but he had to do more.

Daniel's phone rang just as Cybil was coming back into the house, and he answered it while he shut the door and reset the security alarm. It was Barrett, and Daniel put the call on speaker.

"I just got a call that Sean Maynard was at the inn," Barrett greeted.

That shouldn't have surprised Daniel. Mercy Ridge was filled with gossips, but in this case, the talk had happened darn fast since Sean had only been gone a couple of minutes.

"Sean brought Kara a letter that he claims he received this morning," Daniel explained. He watched as Cybil put on a pair of thin latex gloves to take both the letter and the envelope from Kara and slip them in an evidence bag. "Cybil's taking it now. I'll call the lab and see if they can put a rush on it."

"I can do that," Barrett offered.

Even better. As the sheriff, his brother had more pull than he did in that sort of thing.

"Rizzo's coming in," Barrett added a moment later. "This shouldn't come as a shock to you, but he's pissed. Really pissed. It makes me wonder if he's taking some kind of drug that's hyping him up."

"Maybe. Then again, Rizzo's usually riled about something." And being ordered in for a formal interview wouldn't sit well with him.

"True, but I might try to find a way to have him tested."

Daniel definitely didn't like the sound of that.

"You're not going to bait Rizzo and have him throw a punch at you so you can arrest him, are you?"

"No, but that'd be easy enough to do. The man's on a short fuse. But he's bringing his lawyers. Yes, that's plural. *Lawyers*. So, I might be able to appeal to them to help clear their client's name with tests for gunshot residue and drugs. Maybe even a lie detector."

"Good luck with that," Daniel mumbled. He wasn't convinced, but if anyone could do that, it was Barrett. Maybe Barrett could press a few of Rizzo's hot buttons and get him to agree to the tests. Then again, if Rizzo was truly guilty, then there was no way that was happening.

Cybil finished bagging the letter, and she stepped into the living room with it to label the bag and start the record of the chain of custody. By labeling it and then logging it into the database, that would assure the courts and the legal system that the evidence had been handled properly.

"I just got a report back on Eldon Stroud," Barrett went on. "He's got a record. He threatened some of the staff at the hospital where his daughter died and then tried to assault one of the doctors."

Daniel thought about that for a moment. Such behavior could be an "excuse" for someone experiencing grief. "I'm surprised he didn't go after someone at the fertility clinic. I mean, other than sending a threatening letter."

"Oh, he did. Eldon threatened the former clinic director, Dr. Millie Hilburn. She retired about eight months ago, but she reported the threat to SAPD. The gist is that Eldon said he believed she should be punished for luring young women into surrogacy."

Punished could equal murder, and Daniel saw Kara shudder. He was right there with her. "Please tell me that SAPD has offered Dr. Hilburn protection?"

"They have, and she's taking it. She said she believes she saw Eldon following her a couple of times. SAPD hauled him in for questioning, but he insisted he had a right to watch the doctor. That's when she filed a restraining order. That's not his first one. The doctor he assaulted filed one, too."

"Has he served any time in jail?" Daniel asked.

"Two months, that's all, but he's on probation. That's why he doesn't have a choice about coming in for an interview."

Good. Maybe Barrett could use the man's parole to get some answers. Even if Eldon wasn't the person committing the murders, he might know something.

"I'll do a video feed of the interviews to your laptop," Barrett added a moment later. "Text me any questions you want me to ask them."

Daniel assured him that he would, and he ended the call just as Cybil was heading upstairs. She had the evidence bag that she would give to Leo, and then Leo could finally get back to work. Daniel would do the same. He obviously had some calls, and decisions, to make. First, though, he needed to start with Kara while they had a moment alone.

"I'm sorry you're caught up in this," he said, placing his hand on her arm.

He would have said more, but she stopped him by shaking her head. "No, you're not going to apologize to me. I wanted to be a surrogate. I wanted to carry a child for Maryanne and you."

"But remember, this situation might be because of me," Daniel pointed out. "Because of Rizzo."

"Even if it is, you're not apologizing because someone has gone off half-cocked and might want you dead." She touched his hand that was still on her arm. "We'll work together and stop this person. We'll get justice for all the women he's killed."

She sounded resolved enough, but Daniel suspected she didn't want him to see just how shaken up she truly was.

The sound of the hurried footsteps on the stairs had both Kara and him whirling in that direction. It was Leo, and he wasn't carrying the bagged envelope but rather his gun.

"Sadie's all right," Leo immediately said as he raced down the stairs. "She's in the bathtub, and Noreen, Ellen and Cybil are all with her."

His brother's reassurance didn't help. Daniel's heart went into a gallop. "What's wrong? What happened?"

Leo ran past him, heading to take up position by the window. "Someone just spotted a gunman on the roof of the diner across the street."

Chapter Nine

Kara had been on an emotional roller coaster since learning the latest details about the missing and dead surrogates. But this was a threat that cut to the bone.

Because Sadie could be hurt.

Kara wanted to run upstairs to her, but Daniel motioned for her to get down on the floor. She did, but Daniel and Leo didn't. They each went to a window, and with their guns drawn and ready, they peered outside. She braced herself for the sounds of shots. For an attack. And she prayed that Leo or Daniel could take the guy out before he did any harm.

"Who reported the gunman?" Daniel asked.

"Gayla Howard," Leo answered from the other side of the room.

Kara knew her. She was a nurse who worked at the small hospital just up the street. She also lived in an apartment over the hardware store so it was possible Gayla had seen the man from there, and she'd called Leo because they were friends. Thank God she'd spotted him before shots had been fired. Main Street wasn't exactly a bustling place, but at this time of the day, there'd be people going to and from work and the shops.

"Gayla's safe?" Daniel pressed.

"Yeah," Leo answered. "I told her to stay put, and then I called Barrett. He's on the way to the back of the diner now. Jake's with him."

Jake Mendoza was the nighttime deputy, but obviously he'd stayed around after his shift. No doubt because Barrett had been busy with the murder investigation, and Leo and Daniel had been tied up keeping Sadie and Kara safe.

"Do you see the man?" Kara asked them.

"No," Leo and Daniel answered in unison, but the moment they spoke, the sound of Daniel's phone ringing shot through the room. Because every nerve in her body was on edge, Kara felt the surge of adrenaline and better positioned herself in case she needed to help protect Sadie.

"It's Barrett," Daniel said after giving her a glance. No doubt to make sure she was okay. She wasn't. But she didn't want him focused on her right now.

"The guy with the gun's gone," Barrett said the moment Daniel had him on speaker. "No sign of him."

"You're sure he was actually there?" Daniel pressed. He no doubt believed Gayla, but the nurse had to be on edge, too. Heck, everyone in town probably was. It was easy to blow things out of proportion and see threats that weren't there.

At least that's what Kara hoped had happened.

"Three people spotted a man wearing a dark hat and sunglasses on the roof," Barrett verified, dashing Kara's hopes. "Two of them saw the guy climbing down a rope ladder, but no one saw what direction he went. I'm putting out an alert for everyone to stay inside while Jake and I look for him."

"I'll help," Leo volunteered. "Cybil's upstairs with Sadie. Daniel's downstairs with Kara."

"Good," Barrett said. "Go out the back of the inn in case this guy still has the place in his sights. I've called in the reserve deputies, and there's a Texas Ranger on the way."

Kara was sure Barrett and his brothers would welcome the help, but those interviews with Eldon and Rizzo were important, too. Because maybe one of them had hired this gunman.

Or maybe *one was* the gunman.

That seemed a huge risk for Rizzo to take since everyone in town knew him, but with the hat and sunglasses, he perhaps thought it was a chance worth taking. Especially if he'd managed to get off a shot that would have taken out Daniel or her. Of course, the hardest way to hit at Daniel and her would be to go after Sadie.

"I'll reset the security after you leave," Daniel said, following Leo into the back. "Stay down," he told Kara. "I won't be long."

She lifted her head to make eye contact with Daniel before he hurried after his brother. He'd been right about not being long. It took him less than a minute. But that was plenty of time for her worries to skyrocket about Sadie and him.

"What are we going to do about Sadie?" she asked when Daniel ran back through to get to the front window.

This time he didn't look at her, and even in profile

she could see that this was tearing him to pieces. His jaw was set. His body tight and braced for a fight. He was going to have to make some hard decisions to keep Sadie safe. So would she. Except it wouldn't be hard at all to put Sadie first.

"I could be bait," Kara insisted. "I could try to draw out the killer."

"That didn't go so well last time you tried it," he reminded her in a snap.

"No, but it's obvious the killer's getting more…daring," she said because she couldn't think of another word that didn't involve profanity. "He might not be able to resist coming after me if I make it easy for him."

"No," Barrett said before she even finished. "I'm not going to let you get close enough to this snake for him to try to finish you off."

"Then what?" She didn't want to die, but she also didn't want anyone hurt if she could do something to stop it. "I can do this. I can shoot and I know self-defense—"

"No," he repeated, and this time there was eye contact. Daniel shot her a glare for a split second before he turned back to the window. "But we are going to make some changes."

Before he could say what those changes would be, his phone rang. "It's Dispatch," he relayed to her, and she watched as he listened to whatever the person on the other end of the line was telling him. "Eldon Stroud wants to talk to me?" Daniel asked after a couple of seconds. "Put his call through."

Kara shook her head, not understanding why Eldon had phoned Daniel when it was Barrett who'd called him in for an interview. Daniel was clearly puzzled, too, but he took the call on speaker.

"Deputy Daniel Logan," he said when Dispatch switched over the call.

"You already know who I am," Eldon said. Considering his police record and the tone of his threats, Kara had expected the man to shout or spew some venom. But his voice was soft and maybe a little hoarse, the way someone might sound if they'd been sick.

"I do. Why are you calling?"

"I'm here in Mercy Ridge, and I thought you'd have things to say to me. When I found out you wouldn't be in the interview, I decided to get in touch."

"You're here in Mercy Ridge?" Daniel repeated. He checked the time, and Kara knew why. The man wasn't due in to interview until the afternoon, which was still several hours away. "By any chance, were you on the roof of the diner a few minutes ago?"

"No," Eldon answered without pausing or snarling at the question. "But I heard somebody was up there. I'm at the gas station now, and there's talk about it. We're all supposed to stay inside. Was the guy on the roof gunning for you?" he added after a short pause.

"You tell me. What do you know about that?"

"Nothing. I know what you think of me." Eldon's voice was still as calm as a lake. "I've been arrested, and I've spent some time in jail. I lost my daughter, and I've had some trouble dealing with that."

Now there was emotion. Eldon's voice cracked on the word *daughter* and the grief practically poured through. Kara understood that kind of grief. So did

Daniel. They'd both lost Maryanne. But sometimes grief could make you do things you wouldn't normally do.

"I'll do the interview with your brother," Eldon went on. "From everything I'm hearing about him, he's a good man. Is he planning to arrest me for these murders y'all are investigating?"

Kara saw the quick debate on Daniel's face before he countered Eldon's question with one of his own. "What have you heard about the murders?" That was as cop-like as it could get.

"I've been reading about them in the newspapers. The girls were surrogates just like my daughter, and I have to wonder if they were messed over like my girl was."

"Messed over?" Daniel repeated. "How?"

"She was talked into doing that by a so-called friend," he answered without hesitation. "She carried another woman's baby for money, and the people at that clinic talked her into doing it."

Despite his personal grudge against surrogacy and the clinic, Eldon still never raised his voice. But the emotion was coming off him in thick waves.

"You blame the clinic for your daughter's death," Daniel said, and this time it wasn't a question.

"Yes." Eldon said that as gospel. "If she hadn't been talked into carrying a child, then she wouldn't have gotten the blood clot. She'd still be alive." Now, he paused. "Her mother died years ago. My daughter was all I had."

"I'm sorry," Daniel said. No cop voice that time. There was plenty of sympathy in his tone.

"I heard you lost your wife, too," Eldon went on

after he muttered a thank-you. "It twists you up. It breaks you."

"It can. But I have a daughter, and I want to keep her safe. Do you know who's trying to hurt her?"

"Somebody wants to hurt her?" Eldon blurted out.

"It looks that way. If the man on the roof of the diner had fired shots at us, he could have hit my little girl."

Eldon stayed quiet for several long moments. "The little girl you had with a surrogate. Your wife's sister, Kara Holland." And just like that, his tone changed. His voice was still low, but it was now laced with a fire and brimstone kind of judgment.

"My wife and I wanted a child, and her sister carried it for us," Daniel calmly pointed out. "Now, I have a child I love."

"You have her because of surrogacy." Again, that seemed to be some kind of judgment. "But the child shouldn't have to suffer because of the decisions the parents made."

Daniel waited, no doubt hoping Eldon would add more to that. When the man didn't, Daniel prompted him with a very direct question, "Do you know who's trying to hurt Kara, my daughter and me?"

"No," Eldon answered, and Kara so wished she was face-to-face with him so she could perhaps tell if he was lying. Or better yet, she wished Daniel could see him. He'd be a better judge if Eldon knew more than he was saying.

A muscle flickered in Daniel's already tight jaw. "How long have you been at the gas station?" he demanded.

Eldon made an audible sigh. "You're wanting to

know if I have an alibi for the time that man was on the roof. Well, I don't. By the time I got to the gas station, the place was already buzzing of talk about it."

"And where were you this morning?" Daniel pressed, clearly checking to see if Eldon had an alibi for the time the dead woman had been left on the road.

"On the way here. No one I know saw me, and there's no one who'll vouch for what I'm saying. That's a problem for both of us. I can't prove my innocence, and you can't gather enough evidence to charge me with a crime."

"Not yet." That was clearly a warning, and Kara hoped it would shake Eldon enough that the man would spill something important during his interview with Barrett.

"I didn't make the bed you're lying in right now, Deputy Logan. You did. Sometimes, people have to deal with the consequences of their actions."

That sent a chill through her because it sounded very much like a threat.

"If you murdered those surrogates and came after Kara and me, then you'll have to deal with the consequences of your actions, too," Daniel warned him right back. "Not just prison time but a needle in the arm because you'll get the death penalty. Do you think that's the way to honor your daughter's memory?"

Kara held her breath, waiting to see if any of that had gotten through to Eldon, but she couldn't tell because he ended the call. While it was still fresh in her mind, she went back through the conversation, trying to pick out any details that would give away his guilt. Or his innocence. Nothing. She had no idea if Eldon was the killer who'd made Daniel and her his next target.

Before Daniel could even put his phone away, it rang again, and for a moment she thought it was Eldon calling them back. But it was Barrett's voice she heard when Daniel answered the call on speaker.

"There's no sign of the gunman," Barrett immediately said. "Every business owner on Main Street has checked in with Dispatch, and no one has seen him."

What Kara felt went well beyond disappointment. This sickened her and made her terrified for Daniel and Sadie.

"Jake's just searched the grounds around the inn," Barrett went on, "and it's clear. I suspect the guy left the area as soon as he came down off the roof of the diner."

Daniel made a sound of agreement, and she could see his shoulders drop. Again, not just disappointment but a weariness that the danger was far from being over.

"I'll keep Sadie upstairs a while longer," Daniel said. "By the way, Eldon just called me. He claims he's not behind the murders."

"Guilty men usually say that," Barrett grumbled with all the cynicism of a veteran cop.

"Yeah. He might have thought he was clearing his name by calling me, but I just moved him to the top of my suspect list. I'm thinking he called to taunt me because he missed out on firing shots into the inn."

"Where is he?" Barrett immediately asked.

"The gas station. Maybe you can get someone up there to see if he has a weapon in his vehicle. Maybe a dark cap and sunglasses, too, that match the description of what the gunman was wearing."

"I will. I'll get right back to you on that," Barrett assured him.

After another of those heavy sighs, Daniel moved away from the window and came back into the foyer with her. "Don't get your hopes up," he said. "If Eldon had those things, he probably ditched them before he ever went in the gas station. He'd know that he would be a suspect just by being in the area."

Kara had already thought of that, but until she heard Daniel say it aloud, she hadn't realized that she had indeed been hanging on to a glimmer of hope. It felt like another blow to have that taken away.

She tried not to show the disappointment and the barrage of other feelings that were coursing through her. It wouldn't help anyone if she didn't stay strong, but she knew she wasn't fooling Daniel. He was well aware of what she was going through, and that was probably why he pulled her into his arms.

Or so she thought that was why.

But then his mouth came to hers. Not for some chaste peck to comfort her. No. This was the real deal. A hot, hungry kiss. He parted her lips, tasting her. And she tasted him.

Oh, mercy. Daniel tasted as good as he looked.

Her body didn't forget the danger or the murders. Didn't forget that they had so much at stake. However, what he was doing to her kicked up the heat, turning it to a full blaze, and Kara let that fire slide through her. She wasn't sure how Daniel could manage to get her to flash point with just a kiss, but he did it. For a few moments, he made her body burn and her mind cloud.

He also made her want him more than her next breath.

And then he stopped.

He pulled back, looked down at her, and she could see the battle he was having with his own body. Could see something else, too.

The disgust.

Not for her but for himself. He hadn't wanted to kiss her, and he sure as heck hadn't wanted to feel this way. *Welcome to the club.* That kiss had just opened a box that probably should have stayed shut.

Daniel continued to stare down at her, and she saw the regret building. And she also saw something else that she couldn't quite decipher. Not until he spoke.

"I'm going to have to move Sadie to a safe house." Daniel said it fast as if ripping off a bandage from a still healing wound. "And you and I can't go with her."

Everything inside her went still, and she took a moment to let that sink in. No, they couldn't go with her. Because they would just carry the threat with them. Carry the threat to Sadie.

Kara cleared her throat to make sure her voice would sound steady. "When will you take her?"

"It needs to be now," Daniel said, and he started for the stairs.

Chapter Ten

Daniel figured that kissing Kara was about the stupidest thing he could have done. He should have been keeping an emotional barrier between them and not skyrocketing the attraction. But he would have to kick himself for it later.

For now, he had only one priority and that was to keep his daughter safe.

While he made his way up the stairs to check on Sadie and the others, he called Leo, and was grateful that his brother answered on the first ring. "I want to move Sadie to a safe house right away."

Leo didn't question that, and the demand probably wasn't a surprise. The night before, Leo and he had had a phone conversation about this very possibility. Daniel had wanted to try the inn first, but that was for purely selfish reasons. He wanted to be with his little girl and have her close to his family. However, he couldn't take that kind of risk, not with a gunman obviously knowing their location.

"I'll get everything ready," Leo assured him. "I can be ready to leave in fifteen minutes."

He felt some of the tightness ease up in his chest. "Thanks."

Daniel took a moment to gather his breath and stopped in the hall to finish the conversation with Leo before going in to see Sadie. "Since Barrett and the other deputies are tied up right now, Kara and I will follow Noreen, Cybil, Sadie and you to the safe house. Maybe even Ellen, too, if I can talk her into going. That way, I can make sure the killer isn't following you. Once we're sure everything is okay at the safe house, then Kara and I will come back here."

Leo cursed. "You're not trying to draw out the killer and make him come after you?"

Kara had offered herself up to do just that, but if anyone was drawing out a killer, he would be the one to do it. Still, Daniel kept that to himself. "I just need to put some distance between Sadie and me."

"I get that, but it means Kara and you will be doing the return trip without backup."

Daniel hated to use Kara's argument, but he would. He didn't want to pull Cybil or Leo off protection detail for Sadie. "Kara's an expert marksman." At least she was if the gossips had gotten it right. "We'll come straight back here from the safe house."

Which would only take about thirty minutes.

However, it'd take them much longer to get to the safe house since they would essentially have to drive around to make sure no one was on their tails. That would mean Daniel missing the video interviews with their three suspects, but it couldn't be helped.

"I'll be at the inn as soon as I can," Leo finally said. His brother's quick goodbye likely didn't mean Leo was giving up his argument about Kara and him not having backup, but at least he wasn't wasting any more time.

Daniel found Cybil and Noreen sitting on the bathroom floor, and they'd put Sadie in the bathtub along with a stash of toys. She was playing and was thankfully unaware of the scare they'd just had.

"Ellen's in the room across the hall getting some books for Sadie," Cybil explained. "I got a text from Barrett saying the gunman wasn't around so I thought it was okay for her to leave the bathroom."

Daniel silently cursed himself for the reminder that Ellen was also in danger. "It's okay," he assured her as both Ellen and Kara stepped into the doorway. He was glad he had them all there because he wouldn't have to repeat himself.

"We'll be leaving for a safe house in a few minutes," Daniel explained. He looked at Sadie when she grinned at him, and it nearly broke his heart. Since she'd been born, he hadn't gone a full day without seeing her, but that could change.

And all because of a killer.

"I'd like for you to go with them to the safe house," he added to Ellen.

The woman didn't hesitate. Maybe because she'd just gotten the scare of her life with that gunman. "I'll pack a bag," Ellen said, hurrying off after she handed the children's book she'd been holding to Kara.

Kara took the book to Sadie, sat down on the edge of the tub and began thumbing through the pages with her.

"Kara and I will follow the cruiser, but we'll be coming back here to the inn. There'll be some toiletries and some clothes at the safe house," he went on, talking to

Cybil now, "but if you need anything from your place, make a list."

"I have a bag in my SUV," she said. "I wasn't sure how long I'd be staying here at the inn so I packed one."

"Good thinking." He was about to go with her to get it, but he thought of something. "Maybe I can drive your SUV to the safe house and then bring it back here?"

"Of course," she said, fishing out the keys from her pocket and handing them to him. She eyed him, though, with the same concern that Daniel suspected he'd get from Leo. "Kara and you will be careful," she added as a reminder.

Yeah, they would be, but it didn't mean he could keep Kara out of harm's way. She wouldn't want that, though, if it came at Sadie's expense.

Now that everyone knew what was going on, Daniel took Noreen's suitcase that hadn't yet been unpacked, and he headed downstairs to wait for Leo. He didn't have to wait long. Leo was pulling up in the cruiser at the back of the inn as Daniel made it into the kitchen. He disarmed the security just long enough to get Leo inside and made a sweeping glance around the yard.

"You didn't make a mistake bringing Sadie here," Leo said right off. His brother had obviously picked up a lot from his tone over the phone. "We had to know how fast the killer would respond. Now, we know."

Yeah, now they knew. Or maybe they did. If the person on the roof had been the actual killer, then why hadn't he taken a shot? Even getting off one shot could have done some damage. Or worse. It could have killed someone inside.

Daniel doubted the shooter had simply changed his

mind. No. It was more likely that he'd realized he had been spotted and hadn't wanted to take the risk of being gunned down himself. After all, many people in Mercy Ridge carried some kind of weapon.

At the sound of footsteps behind them, Leo and Daniel turned in that direction to see Kara coming in. She exchanged a quick glance with Daniel, but apparently it wasn't quick enough for Leo not to notice that something was, well, different between them. Leo lifted his eyebrow in a way that made Daniel realize that his brother was also picking up on his expressions.

"Don't ask," Daniel warned him when Leo opened his mouth.

Leo just shrugged and winked at Kara. His brother's attempt to lighten things up, though, didn't last. He got very serious when Noreen came into the room with Sadie. Cybil and Ellen were right behind them.

"I can turn on the security system with my phone once we're in the cruiser," Ellen offered.

Daniel nodded and was thankful for the feature. That way, someone wouldn't be able to just sneak in and lie in wait while Kara and he were gone.

"Get in the cruiser as fast as you can," Daniel instructed them. "Kara and I will go out front and get in Cybil's SUV." He gave Sadie a kiss on the cheek, but he tried not to linger too long. He'd be able to say goodbye to her once they were at the safe house.

Leo didn't waste any time, either. He got Noreen, Ellen, Sadie and Cybil out the back door. Daniel waited until they were all inside the cruiser before he locked the back door and hurried to the front with Kara. He drew his gun and wasn't surprised when Kara did the same. He set the lock on the door, and they ran.

Daniel held his breath every step of the way from the inn's front door to the cruiser, and he prayed Barrett was right about there not being any signs of the gunman having stuck around. Cybil's SUV was in the front spot in the parking lot. Not far in distance but plenty far enough.

Kara and he jumped into the SUV and had a couple of seconds to steady themselves before Leo drove out ahead of them. Daniel followed, knowing that he'd stay on edge every second of this trip. As they drove by the shops, both Kara and he glanced at each one. If there were going to be attack, Daniel hoped the person would come after Kara and him and leave the cruiser alone.

"You told Leo that you kissed me?" Kara asked.

Daniel did a mental double take at her question, and it took him a moment to realize that she was trying to ease the thick tension in the air. Of course, talk of kissing her wasn't exactly a tension-breaking subject.

"No, but I believe Leo guessed that's what happened," Daniel answered. Heck, maybe Leo thought it was more than just a kiss and that Kara and he were now lovers. Or soon would be.

He wasn't sure what to think of the small sound she made, and he couldn't see her face to try to gauge her expression. Kara continued to look around, studying their surroundings.

It didn't take long for them to get out of town and onto the road that led to Daniel's ranch, but he knew they wouldn't be going there. Leo would drive past it and keep going for at least ten miles before he started a series of turns that would let them see if anyone was following them. It would be much easier to do that on a country road where the houses were few and far between.

"The safe house can't be linked to any of us," Daniel explained, hoping to relieve her mind a little. Hoping, too, that the reminder would also give him some relief. "It's a place the Marshals set up when they had someone going into witness protection. The witness moved out months ago, but the Marshals kept it in case they or we had to use it."

"So, the safe house is close?" she asked.

"It's in the county about twenty miles from here." So, not nearly close enough, considering that's where Sadie would be.

When they drove by the road to his ranch, Daniel took another look around. He didn't see anyone, but then his house wasn't visible from here. However, he did see one of his ranch hands out in the pasture. He was on horseback and had a rifle sheathed in a saddle case. Obviously, the hand was on alert just as Kara and he were.

They'd only gone about another mile when Daniel saw Leo tap his breaks. His attention immediately slashed to the road ahead. Nothing. But then he caught the blur of motion out of the corner of his eye.

A woman.

She was wearing jeans and a white top, and she was running through a pasture. She was throwing glances over her shoulder as if someone were in pursuit.

"Who is that?" Kara asked, automatically moving closer to the window.

"I don't know," he said.

Just as the sound rang out. Daniel didn't have to guess what the sound was.

A gunshot.

KARA THOUGHT MAYBE her heart had stopped for a few seconds. It seemed as if everything stopped except for that horrible sound that had blasted through the air. Her breath stalled in the throat. Her muscles froze. Still, her first thought was that Sadie could be hurt.

She forced herself to remain calm and checked their surroundings. The shot hadn't gone into the cruiser. Not into the SUV, either. But it had hit something else. Kara watched as the bright red blood spread across the running woman's back. She stumbled, nearly fell, but she regained her balance and kept on running. Kara could see the sheer terror on the woman's face.

And the woman saw them, too.

Despite her obvious injury, she started running toward the cruiser and the SUV.

Another shot came, and Kara fought her way through the shock to try to pinpoint the location of the shooter. She thought maybe he was in the thick woods on the other side of the road. But she couldn't see him. And he'd almost certainly be out of range of their handguns. She was pretty sure whoever was firing those shots was using a rifle.

With his gun ready, Daniel took out his phone and pressed in Leo's number. "Keep going," he told Leo the moment he was on the line. He slowed to a stop on the narrow gravel shoulder of the road and used the phone to motion for Kara to move lower onto the seat. "Get Sadie out of here now."

"What are you going to do?" Leo demanded.

"I'm going to try to save that woman," Daniel answered without pausing a beat. "Call Barrett and get me some backup out here. Call my ranch hands, too, since they can get here faster. But hit the accelerator and keep going."

Kara doubted that Leo wanted to leave his brother and her behind, but he was in charge of precious cargo so he did just as Daniel asked. Kara did drop lower in the seat, but only a couple of inches so she could still keep watch. From over the dashboard, she saw the cruiser speed away.

"You stay down," Daniel warned her, and he hit the latch to put her seat in a near reclining position.

"I can't give you backup like this," she reminded him.

"You're not leaving this SUV," he insisted.

With Daniel's gaze firing into the woods where the shooter no doubt was, he practically climbed over Kara to get to the door on her side. Once he had it open, he got out, his boots thudding when they hit the gravel. The SUV itself would give him some cover, but he could still be shot. Especially if he did what Kara believed he would do.

He was going out into that pasture to rescue the woman.

"Help me," the woman called out.

Kara risked looking at her, and the thin brunette was still coming toward them. Not fast, though, and she was stumbling now and weaving around. Maybe because of the blood loss or the shock of the gunshot wound. She still couldn't clearly see the woman's face, but Kara had to consider the worst-case scenario.

That this attack was connected to the surrogates.

Another shot blasted through the air, causing the woman to scream. The sound turned Kara's blood to ice, and she wasn't sure she could just sit there and let the woman be killed.

"Stay put," Daniel warned her one last time.

Even though there was another blast, he crouched down some and started making his way to the woman. Kara eased up in the seat just enough to watch them. She also lifted her gun, and her gaze snapped toward the woods when there was another shot. So far, none of the bullets had gone into the SUV, but that could change once he hit his target.

The woman.

This brunette was clearly the one he wanted because Kara could see the bullets kicking up the dirt around her. Unfortunately, Daniel was headed right into the path of those shots. At the moment, he might not be the shooter's primary target, but that could change.

The next shot landed even closer than the others. So close that Daniel had to shield his eyes because of the debris from it that flew into his face. He still hadn't reached the woman, and worse, she'd stopped. She was obviously struggling just to stay on her feet.

God, she could be dying. Bleeding to death.

And the shots just kept coming.

Kara had had enough. This time it wasn't fear that sliced through her but rage. No way would Daniel approve of what she was doing, but she needed to create a diversion if he had any chance of rescuing the woman.

She leaned over, rolled down the window of the SUV took aim at the area where she thought the shooter was. Even though she seriously doubted she could actually hit the gunman from this distance, she fired, anyway.

Then she fired again. And again.

The sound from her own shots was deafening in the small space of the SUV, and it caused a sharp pain to pierce through her ears. It was hard to hear, but she didn't miss that the gunman hadn't fired any shots. That's why she sent another two bullets in his direction.

Kara prayed that it had caused him to go on the run even though she would have preferred to stop this monster. She wanted to confront him. But that would have to wait. For now, Daniel and this injured woman had to come first.

"Get down!" Daniel shouted, and Kara was certain he meant that for her.

She did get down but not before she shifted her attention to check on Daniel. The woman was still on her feet. Not for long, though. Kara watched as she crumpled and fell to the ground.

"Call an ambulance," Daniel yelled.

Kara had to fumble through her purse, but she came up with her phone and called nine-one-one. "We need an ambulance," she said, rattling off their location.

Her throat froze, though, when she saw the vehicle in the rearview mirror. For a few terrifying moments, she thought the gunman was returning to try to finish them off.

But it was Tanner Parnell, Daniel's ranch hand.

He was definitely a welcome sight, and she was thankful they'd been so close to Daniel's ranch so that

Tanner could get here this fast. And he was obviously ready to help. He barreled out of his truck, a rifle in hand.

"The shooter was over there," Kara said, pointing to the woods. "But I think he's gone now. Please be gone," she added in a whisper. She didn't want them all gunned down.

Tanner nodded, shifted his attention to Daniel, who was leaning over the injured woman. He headed toward them. So did Kara, and she saw Daniel strip off his shirt and use it to try to staunch the wound. By the time Kara made it to them, though, his shirt was already soaked with blood.

The woman was bleeding out.

Kara got a better look at her face now. She still didn't recognize her, but she appeared to be in her early twenties and had a slim build. There wasn't an ounce of color left in her. A stark contrast to the bright red of the blood on her clothes and Daniel's shirt.

Kara dropped down to her knees and helped Daniel apply some pressure to the wound. Tanner stood over them, keeping watch of the woods and the rest of the pasture.

"Who are you?" Daniel demanded. "Who did this to you?"

"Daisy," she answered, her voice barely audible. "Daisy Burkhart."

Daniel glanced up at Kara to see if she recognized the name, but she had to shake her head. "You were a surrogate?" Kara asked, and she braced herself for the gut punch she knew she was going to get.

Daisy gave a weak nod. "He killed me, didn't he?" she murmured. "I'm dying, aren't I?"

"He?" Daniel repeated. "Who did this to you, Daisy?"

The woman's eyelids fluttered down, and with the last breath she'd ever take, she whispered something.

The name of her killer.

Chapter Eleven

Sean Maynard.

Daniel wasn't sure who'd been more surprised—Kara or him—when Daisy had muttered that name. Of course, Sean had been a suspect since he'd shown up at the inn that morning, but Daniel had put Rizzo and Eldon way ahead of him. Judging from her shock, so had Kara.

He was sure the shock was still there as he sat in the bathroom of the inn and listened to the water in her shower. Daniel hadn't wanted to leave her alone once they'd made it back, but he'd understood when she'd said she had to wash off the blood.

Daisy Burkhart's blood.

Seeing it was a reminder that there was yet another dead surrogate. A murder that he hadn't been able to stop. And it sickened him to the core.

At least Sadie was safe, and that was a huge weight off him. Leo had done as Daniel asked, and he'd gotten Sadie and the others to the safe house. He'd done that, though, with backup from the Rangers since Daniel had stayed with Daisy's body until the CSIs and another team of Rangers had arrived.

While Daniel had still been at the scene, he'd also started the ball rolling on some new security measures. He'd had one of his hands make a quick trip to San Antonio to buy a dozen motion-activated cameras that were now placed on the tops of the buildings around the inn. If anyone tried to get on the roofs, the cameras would trigger an alert that would be sent to his phone.

Once Daniel had finally been able to get Kara back to Mercy Ridge, he'd brought her to the inn and locked down the place. That didn't mean a gunman couldn't still fire shots into the inn, but at least now Sadie wouldn't here.

And there was something else. Something that could work in their favor.

Maybe it'd been a fluke, but the person who'd killed Daisy hadn't been that good of a shot. He'd missed far more often than he'd hit, and he hadn't even tried to shoot Kara and him. This was despite Kara firing at him and Daniel being out in the open where he'd been an easy target.

So, the question was—had Sean been the person pulling the trigger?

Was Kara's ex the killer responsible for all those deaths?

If so, that would make him a serial killer, but it left Daniel with a lot of questions. If Sean was behind this, then his motive had to be getting back at Kara for ditching him. Then why hadn't he simply tried to kill her in the pasture today? Why had he allowed Daisy to find out who he was?

Of course, it was possible all this was a ruse, that the real killer had told Daisy that he was Sean. It was also possible that the shooter was just a hired gun and not the same person responsible for murdering the other surrogates. But if the surrogate killer had been the one pulling the trigger today, then he didn't seem to have any decent sniper skills. That was a good thing for Kara and him. Still, they couldn't take any risks since the shooter didn't necessarily have to be good, just lucky.

Using his phone, he read through an email from Barrett and was trying to force his mind off the dead woman's face and her plea for help when Kara stepped from the shower. He automatically glanced up but just as quickly looked away. Kara wasn't naked but it was close. She had only a towel wrapped around her so he got a glimpse of plenty of bare arms and legs before she put on a robe.

"Your turn," she said. Her voice was strained. With reason. She'd just witnessed a woman being murdered, but Daniel thought some of her nerves were because they were sharing the very small bathroom.

She stepped around him, which was no easy feat, and of course, she ended up brushing against him. Daniel caught a whiff of the shampoo and soap, but her own scent was mixed in there, as well. He tried his best to ignore that. Tried his best to ignore the tug in his body that made him want to reach out and touch her.

"Has Barrett brought Sean in for questioning yet?" she asked.

"A Texas Ranger picked him up and is on the way to the sheriff's office now. Barrett will text me right before the interview starts."

Kara took up the position he'd just left. On the floor with her back against the door. She looked at everything but him, which was a good thing because he started to strip, starting with the loaner T-shirt that he'd gotten from one of the EMTs. His own shirt had been soaked with blood, and the Rangers had bagged it in case it'd picked up any fibers or trace from Daisy's body.

"I got some updates while you were in the shower," he started, shucking off the rest of his clothes. "Sadie's doing great. Leo said she's having a ball since she's got so many people willing to read to her and play with her."

"Good." She sounded relieved. But still tense. He figured that if there were any kind of unusual sound right now, she'd probably jump out of her skin. Or out of that bathrobe.

He didn't want to think about that.

However, imagining Kara's naked body was a whole lot better than some of the other images going through his head.

"The security cameras are all in place on the buildings," he went on.

"You'll be able to see if anyone goes up on one of the roofs?" she asked.

"Yeah. And two of the cameras are angled to pick up anyone coming to the front or back doors here at the inn. If anyone gets on a roof or comes to the doors, my phone will beep with an alert. That should give us time to take cover."

Well, take cover in her case. If he got an alert and pinpointed the killer, then Daniel would try to put an end to this.

"Barrett's phone will beep, too, if any of the cameras are triggered. And he's shifted the times of the interviews," Daniel continued a moment later. "So we'll be able to watch them on my computer. He wants to talk to Sean first, before interviewing the others."

That made sense because if Sean confessed, then there'd be no need to interrogate Eldon and Rizzo. But Daniel didn't see Sean just owning up to murdering at least four women along with attempted murder and attacks on a cop and on his ex-girlfriend.

"If Sean's guilty, why wouldn't he have just run?" he heard Kara ask.

It was the million-dollar question. Daniel had an answer, but he wasn't sure it was the right one. "He would have looked guilty had he run. This way, he can claim his innocence and say that someone's trying to frame him."

And someone could be trying to do just that.

Daniel kept going through those *why* questions that were plaguing him. Why would Sean have let Daisy know who he was? Maybe it'd been for sport, to up the stakes of this cat-and-mouse game. Or maybe it'd just been a mistake. Daisy could have recognized him when he kidnapped her and then managed to get away from him. But that just led him to another why.

Why had Sean and Daisy been so close to his ranch?

He lathered up and quickly rinsed off. "Maybe Sean took Daisy to my place to kill her," he muttered, not figuring Kara would hear him.

But she did.

"It would be a way to hit at both you and me," Kara said. "Sean could have been planning on putting Daisy's body in your house or on your land."

Yeah, but if so, it was stupid when he had ranch hands working today. Then again, maybe Sean hadn't known that. Neither would Eldon. But Rizzo certainly would have.

He turned off the shower, wrapping a towel around his waist before he got out. No robe for him. There'd only been one in the bathroom, and Kara had used it. Maybe being nearly naked wouldn't give his body any bad ideas about Kara before he managed to get dressed.

"Barrett confirmed that Daisy Burkhart was a surrogate at Willingham Fertility Clinic," Daniel went on. No surprise there, but it was something that had to be checked off the list. "She lived alone but was engaged. SAPD is questioning her fiancé, but they don't believe he was involved in this. He has a solid alibi since he was in a meeting with four other people at the time of Daisy's death."

Still keeping her eyes off him, Kara stood so they could go back into the bedroom. They were sharing it, as well. For now. That's because he didn't want her to be too far away from him if there was an attack. But in a couple hours when it was time for them to sleep, he'd have to figure out how to handle that. Daniel was 100 percent sure that he wouldn't be able to keep his hands, and his mouth, off her if they ended up in the same bed.

Kara took some fresh clothes from her suitcase and went into the walk-in closet to dress. Daniel stayed in the bedroom itself and did the same, using some clothes that Barrett had sent over for him. However, he hurried.

The moment he'd finished dressing, he put back on his holster and weapon and then went to the window to look out. This room had a good vantage point where he could see the entire backyard and parking lot. No one was lurking around, but Daniel figured if there was an attack, it'd come from the side or the front. The shooter might get up on another nearby roof and start firing.

His truck was no longer in the parking lot. Thanks to Barrett, there was now a cruiser, a safer option if Kara and he had to make a run for it. Maybe, though, it wouldn't come down to that.

He turned when Kara finally came out of the closet. She was wearing jeans and a loose cotton top, and her hair was still wet from her shower.

And she was crying.

Judging from the way she quickly wiped the tears away, she probably hadn't wanted him to see that. He started toward her, but she waved him away.

"I'll stop," she insisted. "You don't need this."

"Neither do you. Sometimes, though, we can't control things." Which, of course, described him to a tee. He wasn't controlling much of anything right now. Including these thoughts he kept having about Kara.

It was stupid for him to pull her into his arms. Even more stupid to kiss her. But that's exactly what he did. He caught her sound of surprise with his mouth and deepened the kiss. Her stiff shocked response didn't last long.

Nope.

With his thoughts of her whirling and the air charged with sparks of lightning, Kara practically melted into him. Mouth to mouth. Body to body. And the sparks just kept on flying.

It'd been years since he'd kissed a woman like this. With a need that was already so hungry that it felt as if he could take her where she stood. He ached for Kara. Needed her. But worse, he wanted her now.

Daniel expected to feel a flood of guilt over kissing his late wife's sister. In fact, he thought he would have welcomed it because it would have forced him to take a huge step back and rethink this. But no guilt came. Only the heat that kept building and building.

Kara didn't help with getting him to step back. Just the opposite. Her arms went around him, and she pulled him closer, fitting him against her in a way that let him know she'd lost the willpower battle, too.

He could blame that lost battle on the spent adrenaline, the danger. The overwhelming fear that neither of them might live to see another day, but it kept going back to that want. His body had been simmering for her for days now. Maybe longer. And she was right here for the taking.

She slid her hand down his back, her fingers digging into his skin, and she made a silky moan of pleasure. A sound that went straight to his groin. Hell, he was already harder than stone, and Kara had obviously noticed that, too, because she pressed her center against his.

Because his heartbeat was crashing in his ears, it took Daniel a moment to realize the next sound he heard was his phone ringing. He had to pull himself out of the lust trance he was in, and he cursed himself for the lapse. There were too many things going on for him to be kissing Kara.

"It's Barrett," he relayed to Kara, and he put the call on speaker. Also to put some distance between them, he went to the window again and glanced outside.

"Sean's in the interview room," Barrett said the moment he was on the line. "You can log into the feed to watch it. FYI, the Rangers have found nothing in Dai-

sy's phone records to indicate she knew Sean. Her fiancé says he never heard her mention the man's name."

That didn't mean Sean hadn't been the one to kill
her, but Daisy had certainly learned his name from
somewhere. Or rather she'd learned the name the killer
wanted her to.

Daniel went to the small desk where he'd put his laptop, and he booted it up. "Have the CSIs gone into the
woods where the shooter was?" he asked.

"They're there now, and we should have a preliminary report soon," Barrett answered. "Remember to text
me any questions you want me to ask Sean. I'm going
into the interview now."

Daniel hit the end-call button and logged into the
video feed. Sean was seated at the metal table. Brandon Mauer, one of the town's two attorneys, was next
to him, and he was making notes on a legal pad. Sean's
attention, however, was nailed to the camera. He didn't
appear angry—that was a surprise—but he was looking into the lens as if he wanted to send some kind of
message.

Maybe to Kara.

Barrett came into the room, and he set up the interview by identifying everyone for the recording and
reading Sean his rights. Sean spoke the moment Barrett had finished.

"I didn't kill anyone," Sean insisted. "And I have
an alibi."

His lawyer laid his hand on Sean's arm, probably to
tell his client to wait for the questions before he said
anything, but Sean only continued.

"I was on the phone with a rancher who's selling

me some cattle when the attack was taking place," Sean added.

"What time was that?" Barrett countered. "And how do you know what time the attack happened?"

"It happened four hours ago," Sean provided without hesitating. "Something like that gets around so that's how I know. I was on the phone with Mason Ryland over in Silver Creek."

Barrett slid a notepad toward Sean. "Write down his name and contact info. I'll check with him." He gave Sean a moment to do that. "But a phone call doesn't prove your innocence. You could have had that conversation on your cell and still been in the area of the attack. Or you could have finished your business with Ryland and then gone to those woods where you gunned down a woman."

"No." Sean didn't shout his denial. He repeated it and buried his face in his hands for a couple of seconds. "I didn't gun anyone down."

Barrett gave him a flat cop's stare. "The dead woman said differently. In fact, her dying words were your name."

"My client didn't know the deceased." Brandon spoke up. "And there's no physical evidence to link him to this crime."

"Not yet. The scene's still being processed so something might turn up." Barrett combed his gaze over Sean. "The Ranger who brought you in said you'd just gotten out of the shower when he arrived at your place."

Sean shrugged. "So?"

"So, you might have done that to remove any gunshot residue," Barrett reminded him.

"No." This time Sean's voice was a little louder, and the huff he made sounded to be of pure frustration. "I told the Ranger that after my conversation with Ryland, I went for a ride on a new horse. I got sweaty and showered."

"I can't tell if he's lying," Kara muttered. "I should be able to tell."

There was plenty of frustration in her voice, too, and Daniel wanted to assure her that she shouldn't have been able to tell something like that. Some people were just good liars, and Sean might be one of them.

"My client has agreed to submit to a GSR test," Brandon stated. "He also agreed to come here and answer your questions, but as you well know, it's not necessary for him to prove his innocence."

"Yeah, yeah," Barrett grumbled. "I know the burden of proving his guilt is on me, but I've got a good start. I've got a murdered woman who told a cop that your client had killed her."

"A woman who could have been mistaken," Brandon was quick to point out. "After all, she was dying. She could have been confused. Or maybe her real killer wanted her to believe he was my client."

Sean's gaze fired back to the camera. "Is Kara listening to this?" he asked, ignoring everything his lawyer had just said.

"Yes, Kara Holland is watching," Barrett confirmed, giving her full name for the record. "So is my brother Deputy Daniel Logan."

Sean stood, his eyes staring right into the camera lens. "Kara, I didn't kill that woman. I swear, I didn't.

I love you, and I want to make sure you're safe. Please let me see you. I need to talk to you."

Daniel looked at her, and after one glance he could tell that Kara was considering it. "He could be a killer," Daniel pointed out. "He could want to see you to finish whatever sick plan he's set in motion."

She nodded. "I don't intend to see him, but I would like to talk to him." Kara shifted her attention to Daniel. "I might be able to make him angry enough that he'll spill something."

"Does that mean you think he could have committed these murders and attacked us?"

Kara shook her head, sighed. "I just don't know. That's another reason for me to talk to him. I might be able to tell if we're talking."

Daniel cursed the pang of jealousy he got—but hell, it was there. Yeah, Kara and Sean had been lovers, and he shouldn't resent that. She was a grown woman and had a right to a life. But because of those kisses, Kara felt like, well, *his*. Which made him an idiot. A couple of kisses didn't equal a commitment or a relationship. Neither did the feelings he now had for her. But Daniel could see that's where they were heading.

And he had to stop it.

At least temporarily nix it, anyway. Once the murders were solved and he had Sadie safely back home, then he could figure out if things were going anywhere with Kara. He very much wanted things to go somewhere with her. Of course, his body was pushing for sex, and Daniel figured his body was going to get its way on that. It'd be different if Kara had been sending him "hands off" signals, but she wasn't. Just the opposite. There was plenty of need in her eyes.

Daniel texted Barrett, explaining that Kara wanted to speak with Sean. He saw the same hesitation on his brother's face that he was sure had been on his own. A few snail-crawling moments went by before Barrett nodded and fired off a reply.

"Tap into the audio function on the camera feed," Barrett instructed.

Daniel did, and when he was done, Barrett turned back to Sean. He pointed to the small speaker below the camera. "Kara wants to talk to you."

Sean actually sat up straighter in his chair. He had what Daniel could only call a hopeful expression. "Kara? Did you hear what I said?"

"I did," she assured him. "Did you kill that woman? Did you kill any of the surrogates?"

Daniel could see the hope drain away from Sean's face. "No. You shouldn't have to ask me that. We were together for a long time. Years," he emphasized. "You know the kind of man I am."

Yeah, Kara knew he could be stubborn and mean. Maybe even obsessed. But that didn't make him a killer.

"Do you know anything about the surrogate murders or the attack on Daniel and me?" she pressed, obviously skipping over what he'd just told her.

"No." Now the anger flared through his eyes. "I love you. I wouldn't hurt you."

Daniel couldn't help but notice that Sean hadn't included him in that *I wouldn't hurt you*.

"I want us to get back together," Sean went on, standing now. "I can protect you." He muttered some profanity. "I believe someone is committing these murders to get back at Daniel. That's why you should get as far away from him as you can. You sure as hell shouldn't be staying with him."

"I'm not getting back together with you," she said without a shred of doubt in her voice. There wasn't any in her eyes, either, but Sean couldn't see that. The video feed was only one-way. "And why exactly do you think the murders are to get back at Daniel?"

"He's a cop," Sean answered so fast that he must have given it some thought. "I think someone he pissed off or arrested is doing this, and you're caught up in the middle of it. I'm caught up, too, because someone obviously tried to frame me."

Since Sean seemed to be getting more agitated with each word, Brandon took hold of his arm to pull him back in his seat. Sean just threw off his grip and kept his attention glued to the camera.

"I'm not leaving Daniel," Kara said. Then she paused and gave Daniel a look that he couldn't quite make out. She had something up her sleeve, and before he could ask what, she continued, "I have feelings for him."

As a declaration of love, it was pretty tame, but Sean clearly got the gist of it. Or rather the gist of what she wanted him to believe, that is. She'd basically just laid down the law and told her ex that she had a new man in her life.

A man Sean hated to the bone.

"Feelings for him," Sean spat out like the words were distasteful. His stare turned to a glare, and once again he shook off Brandon's attempt to have him sit. "Feel-

ings for a man who could get you killed. I thought you were smarter than that, Kara."

"Oh, I'm smart," she countered. "That's why we're no longer together. That's why we'll never be together again," she amended. "Killing women and attacking me won't cause me to come running back to you."

Sean made a feral sound that came deep from within his throat. "If I were you, I'd be very careful." And it sounded very much like a threat.

Obviously, Brandon heard the threat, too, because he stood and angled himself so that he got in Sean's face. Daniel couldn't hear what Brandon whispered to his client, but it caused Sean to give an angry shake of his head.

"My client and I need a couple of minutes," Brandon said, and this time he took a firmer grip on Sean's arm. "Is it okay if we use the break room?"

"Sure," Barrett answered, his voice far from friendly. "Just don't leave the building." His brother waited until Sean and Brandon were out of the room before he looked up at the camera. "I'm going to my office to call this Mason Ryland and see if he can confirm Sean's alibi. I'll text you when the interview starts back up."

"Thanks," Daniel muttered, and he was about to pause the video feed when he heard a sound. A series of three sharp beeps.

And he drew his gun.

Because someone had just triggered a security camera.

Chapter Twelve

Kara drew her gun, and beside her, Daniel did the same. He also whipped out his phone and pulled up the small split screens for the security cams. It didn't take them long to see who'd triggered the alarm.

Rizzo.

Daniel and she cursed at the same moment, and she wasn't surprised when Rizzo knocked on the door again. It was louder this time and followed by the man's equally loud voice.

"I need to talk to you, Daniel. I think you'll want to hear what I have to say."

That brought on more cursing from Daniel, and he headed down the stairs. "Stay back," he warned her.

At least he hadn't told her to stay put upstairs. Something Kara wouldn't have done. If Rizzo was there to attack them, Daniel would need backup.

"Lift your hands so I can see them," Daniel ordered their visitor, and he didn't go to the door to verify that Rizzo had done it and that he wasn't armed. Instead, Daniel watched the man on the camera feed on his phone.

No gun in sight. Of course, that didn't mean Rizzo

wasn't carrying. Still, it'd be stupid to come to the inn door in plain sight of the cameras and the people on Main Street.

Daniel's phone rang, and he hit the answer button while he eyed Rizzo from the window.

"Is everything okay?" she heard Barrett ask. "The alarm went off for one of the cameras."

"Rizzo's here. I'll see what he wants and send him over to you."

"Be careful," Barrett warned him before Daniel ended the call.

Daniel glanced behind him, no doubt to make sure that she wouldn't be in Rizzo's line of sight, and he paused the security system so he could open the door. Only a fraction, though.

"What do you want?" Daniel snarled.

"A truce," Rizzo said.

She couldn't see either of their faces to gauge their reactions, but Kara was betting that Daniel looked both skeptical and riled. "A truce?" Daniel questioning.

Rizzo huffed. "I'm tired of getting hauled into the sheriff's office for questioning. Tired of you and your brothers hounding me."

Daniel stayed quiet a moment, but Kara figured he was glaring. "You're getting hauled in for questioning because you're a person of interest in an investigation."

She believed Daniel meant the militia case, but Rizzo might not know that Barrett wanted to question him about Daisy's murder and the deaths of the other surrogates and Loretta.

"Yeah, I got that," Rizzo said. "That's why I want a truce. If you really believe I shot somebody, then you'll want to test me for GSR. I'll agree to it. You can test me today."

"Why the change of heart?" The skepticism was still there.

"I just want to have some peace. And FYI, I didn't tamper with the fence your livestock broke through."

Daniel made a sound that could have meant anything. It definitely didn't confirm that he believed Rizzo, and he checked his watch with what no one could mistake as anything but impatience.

"We aren't going to settle our differences here on the porch of the inn," Daniel finally said. "The investigation has to play out. You'll have to be interviewed. After the killer is caught and the Rangers have finished looking into the militia, we'll talk about that truce."

"Killer?" Rizzo questioned. "You mean the woman who was gunned down today?"

"The woman who was gunned down very close to your ranch," Daniel supplied.

Now Rizzo cursed. "You're looking at me for that?" He didn't wait for Daniel to confirm it. "If I was guilty, I would have come up with at least a half-assed alibi and wouldn't have killed her around my own stomping grounds."

"Maybe. But perhaps by setting yourself up like this, you thought it would make you look innocent."

There was more silence before Rizzo grumbled something she didn't catch, and he walked away. Or rather he stormed away, his boots thudding on the porch steps as he left.

Daniel relocked the door, reengaged the security system and went to the window to watch Rizzo leave. He didn't have to say that he didn't trust the man. Neither did she. But Kara thought that Daniel was considering some stronger measures to make sure Rizzo or any of their other suspects didn't come back here.

"The security cameras worked," she said when she thought Daniel was about to launch into an argument of why they should move. "We're less than a minute away from the sheriff's office. Short of sleeping in the break room there, this is about as safe as it can get for us."

"I considered the break room," Daniel admitted after he huffed. "I'm still considering it."

She wanted to go to him and pull him into her arms. Maybe to try to give him some comfort as he'd done for her. Unfortunately, holding him wouldn't just give comfort, though. It would almost certainly stir the heat along with causing him to worry that she was too close to a window. Instead, she was about to tell him that she would go to the sheriff's office break room if that would make him breathe easier, but his phone rang before she could say anything.

"Barrett," he relayed before putting the call on speaker.

"Rizzo just walked in so I'm guessing everything is okay. What'd he want?"

"A truce. Or so he said," Daniel added with a slathering of skepticism. "He could have been scoping out the place to see what kind of security we have."

Barrett made a sound of agreement. "I'll bring that up during the interview. He's going to have to wait, though. Eldon's here, and I'm taking him in next."

"You're finished with Sean?" Daniel asked.

"For now. Sean's still with his lawyer in the break

room, but I'm going to have to cut him loose. Mason Ryland confirmed his alibi. They were on the phone about the time Daisy was dying. That doesn't mean Sean didn't hire someone to kill her, though."

No, it didn't. And it sickened Kara just to consider that possibility. The possibility that Sean hated her so much that he would murder innocent women in an attempt to cover up the real murders he wanted—Daniel's and hers.

"By the way, Eldon asked to see both of you," Barrett went on. "I told him you'd be watching the interview but that you wouldn't be in the building."

"Do you think it'd help if we were there?" Kara asked.

"No. Because it'd mean you going outside. I know it's not far, but I'd rather you stay indoors with Daniel until we get a better handle on all of this."

A handle on this wouldn't happen until they had the killer behind bars. Right now, Barrett had all three of their suspects in the sheriff's office, but it didn't feel as if they were any closer to putting an end to the danger.

"I'm in my office right now finishing up some paperwork, but I'll be starting Eldon's interview in about ten minutes," Barrett added a moment later. "Text me any questions you want me to ask him."

When Daniel ended the call, he rechecked the locks and security system before he led her back upstairs. No doubt so they could watch the interview with Eldon. They did indeed go straight to the laptop, but Daniel took out his phone to text Leo.

"How's Sadie?" Daniel texted.

Kara certainly hadn't put her worries about the little

girl on the back burner, but when Leo didn't immediately respond, it sent the fear skyrocketing. Her frantic mind was already coming up with worst-case scenarios when Daniel's phone dinged. Not with a message but rather a photo.

Of a smiling Sadie.

She was snuggled in Noreen lap while the nanny read her a book. Obviously, Sadie wasn't the least bit worried about being in danger, and Kara was beyond thankful for it. Seeing her, though, was a reminder of just how much Kara missed her. Of course, Daniel felt the same, and she saw the emotions shade his eyes as he ran his finger over the image of his daughter's face.

"She has to stay safe," Daniel muttered, and he sent a thank-you text back to his brother.

"She will." Kara had to believe that because it was the only way she could stay sane.

To get his mind off Sadie, Kara took him by the hand and led him across the room to the laptop. The camera was still on in the interview room, but Daniel had turned off their audio. Probably so that someone in the sheriff's office wouldn't be able to overhear them. However, the audio to the room was still on so they'd be able to listen to Eldon's interview.

As Daniel and she were watching, Esther Ridley, one of the other deputies, escorted Eldon in. Unlike Sean, he didn't have a lawyer with him, but he did immediately look up at the camera.

"Deputy Daniel Logan," the man said, knowing they were watching. "Kara Holland. I needed to talk to you, but the sheriff said you wouldn't be coming in. There are some things you need to know."

Kara glanced at Daniel to get his take on that, but he only shrugged and pinned his attention to the screen. She did the same as Eldon took out an envelope from his pocket.

"Somebody sent me some pictures," Eldon said, speaking directly into the camera. His eyes were narrowed when he pulled out a photo and held it up for them to see.

Kara cursed when she saw the image of the first murdered surrogate, Brenda McGill. It didn't appear to be a crime-scene photo, either. No. In this one, Brenda was sprawled on the floor, face up, her limbs outstretched. The camera had focused on her blank dead eyes.

Oh, God.

Kara's stomach tightened when she realized this could have been taken by the killer.

Daniel hit the button to allow them audio into the room. "Where'd you get that picture?" he demanded while he texted Barrett. He was letting his brother know what was going on.

"Like I said, somebody sent it to me," Eldon insisted. "It came in the mail yesterday. Then, today I got another two."

He took out a second picture, and Kara instantly recognized it, too. It was Mandy Vera, the surrogate who'd been left at Kara's house. This was a shot of Mandy on the bed, right where Daniel and she had found the body.

There was the sound of hurried footsteps, and Barrett came rushing into the room. He glanced at the picture Eldon was still holding up and then at the camera.

"I was just telling your brother and the surrogate he used that somebody's been sending me pictures," Eldon explained, already reaching for the third one. He said the word *surrogate* like it was vulgar.

Barrett had the same reaction that Daniel and she had. He cursed when he saw Mandy's lifeless body. "I'm taking those into evidence," Barrett insisted.

Eldon nodded as if that'd been exactly what he had expected the sheriff to say. "I just wanted your brother to see this last one." He didn't wait for permission. Eldon just held up the third picture.

It was a darker shot than the other two, but Kara could still see the bed. The same bed where they'd found Mandy. But it wasn't Mandy this time.

Kara gasped before she could stop herself.

Because the person lying on the bed was her.

DANIEL FELT THE punch of fear and dread and figured it was a drop in the bucket compared to what Kara was feeling right now. She had gone pale, and her bottom lip quivered as she stared at the image of herself.

Kara shuddered. "Someone broke into my house and took that picture of me when I was sleeping," she said in a hoarse whisper. "God, when I was in bed and sleeping."

"Maybe. Or it could be Photoshopped." But Daniel didn't really believe that.

Judging from the way she frantically shook her head, neither did Kara. For a good reason. The killer had gotten into her house to leave Mandy's body so it wasn't much of a stretch for him to have broken in another time.

Hell.

He thought of all the times Sadie had been there

with Kara. The killer could have gone after them then. He could have taken them both. Hurt them. Or worse.

"This note was clipped to Kara's picture," Eldon went on. He held that up, too, for them, and Daniel had no trouble reading the two words that someone had scrawled on the paper.

She's next.

"The next to die," Kara muttered, dragging in a long breath.

"I'm turning off our audio," Daniel told his brother, and he hit the button to mute the sound from their side. He definitely didn't want Eldon listening in case Kara fell apart. And he thought she might do just that.

Daniel pulled her into his arms and would have kissed her if he thought it would help. It wouldn't. Even the scalding heat between them wasn't going to fix this. The killer—and Eldon—had just shaken her to the core.

"I can't go back to that house," she said, her voice as shaky as the rest of her. "I can't go back home."

That wasn't a surprise. The creep factor was high on this. Especially high, considering that the killer could have murdered her in her sleep.

So, why hadn't he?

If Kara was the target, why hadn't he ended her life then and there?

It was definitely something that Daniel needed to give more thought to, and he could talk that through with Kara. Not now, though. Not while she was trembling in his arms. But soon, the same question would come to her, too. So would the full impact that she'd essentially lost her home. She loved that placed, loved raising and training her horses. It wasn't going to be an easy gap to fill, and while she might change her mind about returning, that would take some time.

"I'm okay," she said several moments later.

It was a Texas-sized lie, but Daniel didn't call her on it. He just kept holding her while he kept watch on the screen as his brother bagged the photos that he took from Eldon.

Eldon looked straight into the camera again. "I figure this sort of thing can mess with a person's head. Of course, I'm figuring her head was already messed up for her to do what she did. Being a surrogate, I mean. People pay in all kinds of ways for the mistakes they make."

That sounded like a veiled threat, but Daniel had to concede that almost anything the man said could be taken that way. After all, Eldon was a suspect, and his showing Kara the pictures could be just part of his cat-and-mouse game.

"I'm having Mr. Shroud wait in my office so I can bag and tag these pictures," Barrett said for Daniel and Kara's benefit. His brother probably didn't want Eldon to have any other chances to take a poke at Kara. "I'll have Esther do the interview with him while I talk to Rizzo. Give me a minute and I'll call to explain what's going on."

Daniel knew it was going to take more than a minute to soothe Kara's jangled nerves. If Eldon had set out to torment her with what he'd shown them, then he'd done a damn good job of it.

"I didn't see any signs of a break-in at my house," she went on, her words and breath hitting against his shoulder and neck. "But it must have happened." He felt her muscles go stiff. "Why?"

He didn't have the answer to that, and Daniel was worried that he might not have it soon enough. As long as the killer was out there, Kara and he wouldn't have any peace. And the child they both loved wouldn't be safe.

Daniel had to put that thought aside when his phone rang. He shifted a little, just enough to answer it, but he kept his arm around Kara. As expected, it was Barrett, and since she was close enough to hear, he didn't put the call on speaker.

"I'll have the photos that I got from Eldon sent to the crime lab," Barrett explained. "He claims he has no idea who sent them."

Daniel jumped right on that. "You believe him?"

His brother sighed. "I just don't know. He's angry all the way to the marrow about his daughter's death so some of that comes through with everything he says. Maybe that's coloring the way I see him."

Daniel was worried the same thing was happening to him. He needed to stay objective because that was the only way to get to the truth.

"The envelopes with the pictures have a San Antonio postmark," Barrett went on. "Eldon admits he's had them in his pocket since they arrived so I suspect any trace will be compromised."

Yeah, so did Daniel, and he was betting that if Eldon wasn't the killer, then the real killer's prints wouldn't be on the envelopes. But that led to an interesting thought.

"Both Sean and Eldon got some kind of correspondence from the killer," Daniel pointed out. "Rizzo didn't."

Of course, that didn't mean Rizzo was guilty. It was

just puzzling why he was the only one of their suspects who hadn't gotten that. Then again, the killer might not be either of the three. All three men could be innocent, and if so, that meant Daniel had no idea who was behind these murders and attacks.

"Is Sean still there?" Daniel asked his brother. He might not be able to pin anything on Sean, but he still wanted to keep tabs on him.

"No. He left with his lawyer about ten minutes ago. I got a court order on the financials for all three men, and the files just came through. I'll be looking through those and will go over the interview statements once they're done. I'll send those to you so you can do the same."

Daniel would indeed look over them. Heck, he'd dig through them, looking for any inconsistencies. Since Barrett would be tied up with the interviews and the aftermath of paperwork that would follow those, Daniel appreciated the tasks. It might help him keep his mind off Sadie. Off Kara, too.

Though that'd be harder to do since she was right next to him.

"How'd you manage to get financials on Rizzo?" Daniel asked.

"Leo. He's been working on that from the safe house, and he cited the latest murder and the attack on Kara and you to expedite us getting the files. He'll also deal with putting some pressure on the crime lab and the ME reports. We need to find out if the killer left any piece of himself at Kara's or the clinic when he killed Loretta."

That would be a break if they did find something, but Daniel figured this killer was too smart for that. Still, mistakes happened, and all it took was one hair or one print to blow this investigation wide open.

Barrett didn't waste any time. Within seconds after he ended the call, the financial files on all three suspects came through. Daniel considered going downstairs to the office to print out copies for Kara to read through, but there was a huge window in there, and it was on the ground floor. He preferred to keep her upstairs. Not that a gunman couldn't fire into this room, too, but Daniel had purposely kept her angled away from the single window so as to not give an attacker a direct shot.

He opened the files on his phone, motioning for Kara to take the laptop so she could start reading. "You take Sean's," he said. "I'll start with Rizzo's. Look for any lump sum withdrawals or checks that could have been used to hire a gunman."

She nodded in agreement and got started. Daniel pulled up a chair across from her, and he dug in. He immediately noticed that this was not just Rizzo's financials, but the file also included the notes from the investigation that the Texas Rangers were conducting. The Rangers had highlighted several large online deposits that had been followed with equal withdrawals less than twenty-four hours later.

None in the past couple of days, though.

These were from at least three months ago, shortly before Daniel had gotten that anonymous tip about Rizzo being part of the militia. There wasn't a large withdrawal or deposit after that.

Did that mean Rizzo had just gotten more careful?

Maybe, but he sure as heck hadn't been before then, and Daniel zoomed in on the pattern that the Rangers were obviously trying to establish. Rizzo was getting deposits from a dummy company. Or rather dummy *companies*. Ones that existed only long enough to make the deposits to Rizzo. Then Rizzo was withdrawing the funds, which would have given him cash.

What Daniel was seeing was a way for Rizzo to launder money or to feed that cash from suspicious sources into the militia—maybe for purchasing those weapons they were stockpiling. It wasn't absolute proof that Rizzo was involved in the militia, but it was grounds to hold the man until Daniel and Barrett could take a harder look.

Daniel took out his phone to call his brother, but it rang before he even had a chance to press the number. And it was Barrett.

"You need to hold Rizzo," Daniel immediately told him. "There are red flags in his financials."

Barrett paused as if he were rethinking what he'd been about to say. "I will, but for now I have a problem. I need someone to get to the hospital."

"The hospital?" Kara and Daniel said in unison. Obviously, she'd heard what his brother had said. "What's wrong?"

"Sean's in the ER," Barrett answered. Then he paused and cursed. "Sean claims that you just tried to kill him."

Chapter Thirteen

Kara wasn't sure who looked more stunned about what Barrett had just told them. Daniel or her. Judging from his tone, Barrett was experiencing the same thing.

"Someone tried to kill Sean," Daniel repeated. "How? When? How bad is he hurt?"

"Not sure of any of that yet," Barrett answered. "But he must not be hurt too bad because he just phoned from the ER and wanted me to get there ASAP."

Daniel grumbled some profanity. "Well, it sure as hell wasn't me who tried to kill him. I've been here in the inn with Kara."

"I know that, but I don't know why he said you did. That's why he wanted me up there right now. But I can't go. I have both Rizzo and Eldon in the building, and I don't want to leave Esther here without backup. At the moment, there's no one else I can call in so I'll reschedule the interviews—"

"No." Daniel drew in a long breath and looked at her as if apologizing.

But it wasn't necessary. Kara knew what had to be done. "The hospital is two blocks from here," she reminded Daniel and Barrett. "We can drive there in the cruiser and talk to Sean. We'll try to get to the bottom of what happened."

"I hate to ask," Barrett said a moment later. "But if someone really did try to kill him, we need to know."

"Agreed," Daniel said. "Kara and I will be at the hospital in a couple of minutes."

However, Daniel didn't budge when he ended the call and put away his phone. He did curse some more. And she saw the apology in his eyes as he looked down at her.

"Don't." She pressed a quick kiss on his mouth and holstered her weapon in the back of her jeans. "We'll be careful."

Of course, being careful was no guarantee that they'd be safe since the killer could have set all of this up as a way of luring them out. But the alternative was leaving a deputy alone with two suspects, and Kara didn't want Esther being put at undue risk or having the investigation stall because Barrett couldn't finish the interviews.

"Besides," she added, "both Eldon and Rizzo are in the sheriff's office. Neither of them will be able to fire shots at us."

After several long moments, Daniel finally nodded, and he got them started out of the room and down the stairs. He had to temporarily disengage the security system to get them out the back door, but once they were on the porch, they hurried.

And held their breaths.

Because they both knew that while their suspects wouldn't be able to shoot them at this exact moment, it didn't mean that one of them hadn't hired a henchman or two to do that job.

Kara's heart was pounding by the time they made it into the cruiser. She still held her breath until the doors were shut and Daniel was driving away from the inn. They both fired glances around them, but Kara didn't see anything out of the ordinary. She hoped it stayed that way.

It took less than a minute for them to pull into the hospital parking lot, and Daniel stopped the cruiser as close to the ER doors as he could get. With their hands on their weapons, they hurried inside. A nurse, Gayla Hayward, was right there waiting for them, and she motioned for them to follow her.

"Barrett called me and said you were on your way," Gayla explained. "We have Sean back here in the examining room."

So he wasn't in surgery or intensive care. That was good because he might be able to answer some questions. Especially one question—why he'd accused Daniel of trying to kill him.

"What's Sean's condition?" Daniel asked.

"He has a gunshot wound to the shoulder. Dr. Tipton is with him now."

Kara knew Dr. Norris Tipton since he'd lived in Mercy Ridge his entire life. It was the same for Gayla.

Gayla threaded them through the ER waiting area and down the hall. The moment they stepped into the examination room, Kara spotted Sean. He was lying on the table, and the right side of his shirt was soaked with blood. He immediately sat up, practically snapping to attention, and he aimed fiery narrowed eyes at Daniel.

"You stay the hell away from me," Sean snarled,

practically pushing the doctor away so he could try to stand. "I won't let you shoot me again."

"I didn't shoot you," Daniel snarled right back, and he went closer. Like Kara, he examined the wound that Dr. Tipton was cleaning. "How bad is it?"

Dr. Tipton gave Daniel a somewhat annoyed glance, probably because he didn't appreciate being interrupted during an exam. "He'll live," the doctor said. "But he'll need stitches, and I want an X-ray just to be sure."

"Could he have done this to himself?" Daniel pressed, causing a howl of outrage from Sean.

"You tried to kill me," Sean insisted.

Daniel shifted his hard gaze to Sean. "No, I didn't. Tell me what makes you think I did."

"Because I saw your badge. The sun glinted off it just as you shot me."

"You claim you actually saw me pull the trigger?" Daniel snarled. "Or did you just see someone with a badge?"

Sean opened his mouth, closed it, and he cursed before he lay back on the examining table. "I saw the badge. But the shooter was about your size and was wearing a black Stetson like you always do."

She heard Daniel release his breath. "So it could have been someone hired to make you believe it was me."

It seemed to be the last thing Sean wanted to do, but he finally gave a conceding nod that it could have happened that way. "Someone shot me," he growled. "Someone tried to kill me."

Daniel shifted back to the doctor. "Could this wound have been self-inflicted?" he repeated, causing Sean to snarl out another protest.

"Not likely," the doctor commented. "The angle's wrong, and there's no stippling. Have a look for yourself." He moved back so that Daniel could see Sean's injured shoulder.

Stippling was gunshot residue that showed on the skin when the bullet was fired at close range. Which a self-inflicted wound would have been. Kara had a look for herself, and she didn't see any gunshot residue on Sean.

"Satisfied?" Dr. Tipton asked, but he didn't wait for Daniel to answer before he added, "Because I need to finish cleaning this wound, and it's best if Kara and you aren't in here for that."

Daniel volleyed glances between the doctor and Sean, but he didn't budge.

Dr. Tipton sighed. "You can wait in my office. We can chat after I'm finished here."

Daniel finally nodded and tipped his head to Sean. "He doesn't leave this area until after we've spoken, understand?"

Both the nurse and doctor made sounds of agreement, and Daniel took Kara out of the room and down the hall to Dr. Tipton's office. It wasn't big, just a cluttered desk with two visitors' chairs. And a large window. Daniel immediately went to it and lowered the blinds after he checked to make sure no one was lurking around outside. He took up guard duty at the door that he partially closed but motioned for her to stay back.

"You think Sean had something to do with his own attack?" Kara asked. "That maybe he set this up to make himself look innocent?"

"Maybe." But there was plenty of room for doubt in his tone.

It did seem extreme since Sean had indeed been shot. A shoulder wound could have been serious had the gunman missed just a little, and the bullet could have gone into Sean's neck. So if Sean had hired this guy, he must have had plenty of faith in his abilities.

Since there was no way Kara could sit, she started to pace. Not easy to do in the small space, and of course, she ended up near Daniel. She placed a hand on his arm, causing him to look at her. Their gazes locked. And held. Until Daniel cursed under his breath.

"I'd hoped this would be over," he said.

She thought he was talking about the danger and not the sizzle of attraction that she felt slide between them. Despite their situation, she smiled. "As long as we keep kissing, I don't think it'll be over."

He sure didn't smile. Daniel looked as if he wanted to glare or curse some more. However, he let out a long sigh, and as if resigned to whatever he was feeling for her, he brushed a kiss on her cheek.

Then her mouth.

It might have been barely a touch, but she felt it all right. Mercy, did she. The heat went all the way to her toes, and her body started to rev up for something it wasn't going to get. At least not right now. She couldn't have Daniel, but Kara had no doubts that soon they'd be lovers. They'd no longer be able to resist this hard pull between them, and they'd land in bed. Maybe whatever happened wouldn't destroy the fragile friendship they'd built for Sadie's sake. Maybe they wouldn't ruin everything.

"I just have to focus on keeping you safe," Daniel said as if talking to himself.

She nodded. "I have to focus on keeping you safe, too."

Now he did smile, and Kara wanted to hold on to that moment. She needed it as much as she needed him. But it didn't last because the sound of Daniel's phone shot through the room, and she saw Barrett's name on the screen.

Daniel answered it on speaker, but he put the phone in his shirt pocket. Probably so he could keep his shooting hand free.

"How's Sean?" Barrett immediately asked.

"Alive. But he's injured," Daniel added. "A gunshot wound to the shoulder. I'm waiting on a report from the doctor."

"Good." But Barrett's tone didn't indicate anything good. It was said almost absently as if it was something to check off an important to-do list. "I'm going to have to let Rizzo go."

Daniel groaned. "No. Take a look at the financials. I think he's laundering money for the militia group."

"I did glance over that, and I'll study it more, but lawyers pressed for his release. There's an emergency at his ranch. Someone set several of his barns and outbuildings on fire. The fire department is on the way there now, but the early reports aren't good. There's damage, and the fire's spreading. It could reach some of his livestock, even his house."

"Damage that Rizzo could have caused so that he wouldn't be arrested," Daniel quickly pointed out.

"Maybe." But Barrett didn't sound at all convinced of

that. "Sean's been shot, and now this happens on Rizzo's ranch. The only one who hasn't taken any hits is Eldon."

True, but that didn't make the man guilty. Or innocent.

"Anyway, I've let Rizzo go," Barrett went on. "And no, I don't like it any more than you do, but if he tries to run, then it'll only add more weight to his involvement in the militia. That weight, though, doesn't link him to the murders or the attacks, and you know it."

Yes, Daniel did know it, and that's why his next round of profanity was from pure frustration. They probably had enough to get an arrest warrant for Rizzo, but if they wanted to prove he was a killer, they had a long way to go.

Kara didn't especially want to put a positive spin on this, but she had to latch onto some hope. Hope that Rizzo would say or do something to incriminate himself. If not Rizzo, then perhaps Eldon or Sean would do that.

"I just let Eldon go, too," Barrett continued a moment later. "Since both Rizzo and he will be out on the street, I want Kara and you to go back to the inn ASAP. I can send Esther to the hospital to get the report about Sean from the doctor."

Again, Daniel stayed quiet a moment as if deciding if that was what he should do. He probably wanted to stay put and see if he could get any proof that Sean had orchestrated his own attack. However, her safety must have trumped that option.

"Okay," Daniel finally said. "I'll text you when we get back to the inn."

He ended the call and laid his hand back over his

weapon. Kara did the same when he gave her the nod to get them moving. Daniel stepped out into the hall first, glancing around as if he expected someone to jump out and attack them. Kara did the same, but the only person she saw was a nurse.

The hospital wasn't huge by anyone's standards, and this section didn't have actual hospital rooms. It was mainly offices for the doctors, examining rooms for ER patients and the waiting area. That's where they headed, passing by the room where they'd last seen Sean and Dr. Tipton. Kara had hoped the door would be open just so she could get a peek at what was going on, but it was closed.

There was a woman holding a crying baby in the waiting room and another woman at the reception desk. Kara knew both of them. The woman with the baby was Shelby Monroe, and the receptionist was Heidi Coltrane, and she gave them nods of greeting as Daniel and she made their way to the cruiser. However, when they were still about ten feet from the ER doors, she saw something she didn't like.

Smoke.

It was billowing right at the door, seeping in, and it only took her a moment to realize that it was some kind of tear gas or pepper spray. Kara's eyes immediately started to sting, and she began coughing. So did Daniel and the others in the waiting area.

Oh, mercy.

Were they under attack?

Had someone done this so they could try to kill them?

"Run," Daniel snapped to the other women.

Shelby was already doing that. Coughing, she clutched the infant to her chest and began running away from the smoke and into the hall where Daniel and Kara had just been. The receptionist did the same, and Daniel and Kara were right on their heels.

Daniel drew his gun on the run, and he glanced behind them. Just as Kara heard another sound. A hissing sound as if someone had struck a very large match. She looked, but it was impossible to see through the thick smoke. Or at least it was until the flames shot up.

Her heart went to her knees.

Someone had started a fire.

Because she could hardly see and couldn't smell anything other than the tear gas, she couldn't tell if there was some kind of accelerant. It was possible the fire would spread fast, and if that happened, people could be hurt.

Dr. Tipton must have heard the running because he opened the examining room door. His eyes widened when he saw what was going on, but like Kara and the others, he began coughing.

"Get Sean and your nurse out of here," Daniel ordered.

The nurse already had Sean in a wheelchair, and both she and the doctor took hold of it to start hurrying down the hall. But the smoke and the tear gas just kept coming at them. It kept choking them. Making it hard to escape.

Which was no doubt what the killer had planned.

He could be making his way through that smoke and gas right now while he wore a mask. He could be coming to kill them.

"Who the hell did this?" Sean snarled.

No one answered him. Probably because no one knew. Well, unless Sean was the person responsible. He could have hired someone to do this, but if so, he'd put himself right in the mix. If a gunman started shooting now, he could hit Sean or any of the rest of them. Including that baby.

That sent a spike of raw anger through Kara. How dare this snake do something to put an innocent child in danger.

Ahead of them, Shelby, who still had her arms wrapped around her baby, stumbled, and Kara didn't know how Daniel managed it, but he sprang toward her, catching them before they could fall.

"Kara, keep watch behind us," Daniel told her, and she tried, but it was impossible to see anything.

Overhead, the sprinklers made a hissing sound a split second before the cold water began spewing down on them. That would help put out the fire. At least Kara prayed it would. But at the moment it was making it even harder for her to see.

"Don't go in there," Daniel said when Dr. Tipton reached for one of the office doors.

Kara knew why Daniel had said that. He didn't want the doctor to go into a room where he could be trapped by the fire. The fire department was almost certainly on the way, but it only took seconds to be overcome by the smoke and flames.

They all kept running, with others joining them, but Daniel stopped when they reached the back exit. He opened the door but motioned for them to stay back.

Because a killer could be out there.

Waiting.

Ready to strike.

And suddenly the stakes were so much higher now that there were so many people who could be gunned down. Kara remembered the wild, almost random shots that'd been fired at Daisy when she'd been running in the pasture. If that happened now, the baby could be hurt.

Even though the water from the sprinkler was getting into Kara's eyes, it helped some with washing away the burning that the gas and smoke had caused. It must have done the same thing for Daniel because he seemed to focus when he looked outside. Then he turned his gaze to her.

"You'll have to cover me while I get them out," he said.

She didn't have to ask who he meant by *them*— Shelby and her child. Kara nodded and stepped into the doorway to watch for a gunman while Daniel hooked his left arm around the woman. He whisked them out of the hospital and hurried them to a car several yards away. He had them get down on the ground and then under the vehicle before he motioned for the doctor to bring out Sean. However, before Dr. Tipton could do that, there was the sound of a blast.

Someone had fired a shot.

Kara couldn't tell what the bullet had hit. She prayed it wasn't Daniel, Shelby or the baby. But she caught onto the doctor to hold him back. It wasn't easy. Because they were all still fighting for their breaths, the instinct was to run. To get out in the fresh air, but that could be a fatal mistake.

She moved ahead of the doctor and Sean, and despite the clogged air, Sean still managed to growl out some profanity. Kara pushed the sound of his voice aside and kept watch. She listened. She heard the howl of sirens, probably both the fire department and Barrett.

There were other voices coming from other parts of the hospital. Shouts for people to evacuate. Which they would almost certainly do. And they might run straight into gunfire.

Kara lifted her head, listening for any sign of the shooter. From the front end of the car, she spotted Daniel doing the same thing. Their eyes met, and it seemed for a second that time froze.

Then a second shot came.

This one smacked into the door just inches from where Kara was standing. She automatically ducked back in, shoving the doctor and Sean farther into the hall and against the wall. She waited, holding her breath and listening for the next shot.

She didn't have to wait long.

This one tore through the front of the car, close to where Daniel had crouched, and Kara risked looking out to see if she could spot the gunman. Thanks to the smoke, she couldn't, and she didn't think this particular smoke was coming from the fire at the front of the building. She thought that maybe their attacker had set off some kind of device to give him cover.

And it was working.

Kara couldn't see him, and she couldn't just fire in his general direction because she might hit an innocent bystander. But she had to do something. As long as there was gunfire, the fire department wouldn't be able to come onto the scene. The hospital could be severely damaged, and there were likely plenty of people still inside.

Instead of aiming at the gunman, Kara lifted her weapon and fired into the sky. It was still a risk since she could hit a power line, but at the moment anything they did carried huge risks. She fired a second shot. Then waited.

It didn't take her long to pick through the other sounds and hear something. Footsteps.

Someone was running. And she didn't have to guess who.

The shooter was getting away.

Chapter Fourteen

Using the binoculars that he'd taken from the cruiser, Daniel stood at the second-floor window of the inn and watched the chaos still going on around the hospital.

Since the sun had already set, it was dark, but the lights on the tall poles in the parking lot still gave him enough illumination to see the scene well enough. The fire department had managed to put out the flames, and everyone had been evacuated from the building itself.

That was the good news.

But the parking lot was a sea of emergency vehicles, first responders and even some patients who were being treated for smoke inhalation and other injuries. They'd gotten damn lucky with the assortment of injuries. None of them had been serious, and that was nothing less than a miracle. It could have been so much worse.

Daniel hated that he couldn't be there to help, but there was no way he could keep Kara on the scene once other law enforcement had come in. Especially since Kara and he were almost certainly the targets of the attack. If they'd stuck around, it would have continued to put others in danger.

That definitely wasn't a comforting thought.

Neither was the fact that despite the latest incident, they still weren't close to making an arrest and putting an end to this exile. Not just for Kara and him but also for Sadie.

He heard the shower turn off and knew that Kara would soon be coming out of the bathroom. Daniel tried to steel himself up and get some of the worry off his face. No need for her to see that on him since she was no doubt feeling plenty of it herself.

This attack had shaken her even more than the other ones. He had felt that when he was finally able to lead her away from the scene. They'd walked out, literally having to step around those getting medical treatment, and Kara was almost certainly blaming herself for what'd happened. It wasn't her fault. Hell, it wasn't his, either.

But it sure felt like it was.

Wearing the bathrobe that she had tightly cinched around her, Kara stepped from the bathroom, her gaze immediately going to his. "Anything new on the gunman?" she asked.

Though she probably already knew the answer to that, Daniel shook his head. "But I did get a call from Barrett just a couple of minutes ago. He said it looks as if both the tear gas and the incendiary device that caused the fire were on timers. They were tucked behind concrete plant holders just inside the ER doors."

She stayed quiet a moment, her forehead bunched up while she obviously gave that some thought. "I'm guessing the security camera didn't catch who put the device and tear gas there?"

Daniel had to shake his head again. "The only cameras are in the areas where meds are stored."

That wasn't out of the ordinary for a small town
hospital in an area with a very low crime rate. Still,
he wished there'd been just one camera to catch whoever had done this. Of course, if there had been, their
attacker might have been able to disarm any security.

"A timer means we can't rule out any of our suspects," she added a moment later. She sighed, pushed
her damp hair from her face and walked toward him to
join him at the window.

Bingo. That's exactly what it meant. Added to that,
there might not have even been a hired gun if the attacker was Eldon or Rizzo. Both men had time to get to
the hospital after leaving the sheriff's office.

But Sean was a different matter.

He'd been right there with them, and he certainly
hadn't fired any shots. So, maybe he had a henchman
helping him. That would explain why the shooter hadn't
aimed any bullets in Sean's direction. Then again, if
Sean had set the timer, he might not have minded being
in the thick of an "escape." Especially if he knew there
was no real threat to him. It could have given him some
kind of sick thrill to watch them run for their lives.

"We don't have proof yet," he went on, "but it appears that the fires set at Rizzo's ranch were also on
timers. He lost two barns, and his back porch was damaged. No injuries, though."

"That's good," she muttered, taking the binoculars from him so that she could look at the hospital. It
wasn't a long look, though. Kara only eyed the carnage
for a couple of seconds before she sighed again and

handed him back the binoculars. "What about Shelby and her baby?"

Here was where he could give her some peace of mind. "Both are okay. Not a scratch on them. They were treated at the scene for smoke inhalation and then released."

"Good," she repeated, sounding a lot more relieved than she had been about the lack of injuries in the fires at Rizzo's place.

Daniel could add to that peace of mind with something else he had to tell her. "Sadie's all right. I called the safe house while you were in the shower. She was already asleep so I didn't get a chance to talk to her, but Leo said she had a fun day."

He welcomed the ghost of a smile that put on Kara's face. He'd had the same reaction, and he wished they could both hang on to it awhile longer. Especially since all the updates he had to give her weren't good news.

"The Rangers are digging through Rizzo's financials," he went on. "But it's possible those deposits and withdrawals are for cattle purchases and sales. The Rangers might not be able to use them to link him to the militia."

That meant they also couldn't use it to arrest Rizzo, which made him a free man. For the time being, anyway. Barrett was still interviewing people who'd been in or around the hospital at the time of the attack. It was possible one of them had seen the person responsible, and maybe that person was Rizzo.

"What about the pictures that Eldon had?" Kara asked. "Are those already at the lab?"

"They are and they'll be processed ASAP since

they're connected to a multiple-murder investigation."
Now he had to pause and take a deep breath before he
gave Kara another dose of bad news. "The San Antonio police found Marissa Rucker's body."

No need to explain who Marissa Rucker was. Kara
knew that she'd been a surrogate. The very one who'd
also used the Willingham Fertility Clinic. And she'd
been missing for several days now.

"How'd she die?" Kara's voice hardly had any sound
now, and she went way too pale. She suddenly looked
ready to face-plant on the floor, so Daniel took hold of
her arm to help steady her.

"She'd been shot," he told her.

He didn't intend to mention that she'd also been
bashed in the head. There'd been plenty of anger in
her attack, but unfortunately not much evidence since
the body had been exposed to the elements for at least
four days.

Kara nodded as if trying to accept that, but he knew
there was no way she could accept something as senseless as another murder.

"Once SAPD pinpoints Marissa's time of death,
they'll want to question our suspects to see if they have
alibis." Of course, even if they didn't have them, it still
might not lead to an arrest. Everything they had right
now was circumstantial.

"Daniel," she whispered. Kara said his name like a
weary sigh and moved closer, putting her head against
his shoulder.

Even though she'd no doubt done that just for comfort, the closeness set off some alarms inside him. He'd
been telling himself to keep his hands off her. Not to

let what he was feeling for her interfere with the investigation. But his body didn't care much about alarms.

Daniel set the binoculars aside and slid his arms around her.

She made another of those weary sigh sounds, and the moment crawled by while he just held her. He didn't pull her closer. Didn't kiss her. However, it certainly felt as if that was going on.

And more.

He got some very clear images of stripping off that robe and taking her to the bed that was only a few yards away. But that would be a mistake. Kara wasn't in a good state of mind right now and wasn't ready for something like that.

Or so he thought.

But he had to do a mental adjustment when she eased back enough to locate his mouth with hers. He might have planned on resisting a kiss, but he sure didn't. Her lips felt as if she intended to make this count. To make this ease some of that tension bubbling inside her.

Daniel was all for relieving tension, all for the pleasure that being with her would give them, but he didn't deepen the kiss. He just let her take the lead. And she took it all right. Her tongue ran along the seam of his lips, and Kara went in to take this to a whole different level.

That *different level* went straight to his groin. Man, her taste got to him and made him want a whole lot more. But more wasn't necessarily a good thing. It could turn out to be something Kara would regret, and that's why he had to give her an out.

"You should probably get some rest," he managed to say when she finally broke for air.

She pulled back enough to meet him eye to eye. "Do you really want me to rest?" Kara asked.

Hell. That was a hard question with an easy answer. No. He wanted her naked and beneath him in the bed. Or on top of him. It didn't matter. He just wanted her, and when Daniel stared down into her eyes, he knew that want was going to win out.

He lowered his head and took her mouth.

KARA HAD FELT Daniel's hesitation. But then she'd also felt that hesitation snap like a twig when the heat took over.

She was thankful he'd lost that particular battle. They'd have to deal with the consequences of this after. But for now, they could be together, and for a little while they could forget the attacks, the murders. The danger. For now, it could be just the two of them and the pleasure they could give each other.

And Kara was certain there would indeed be pleasure.

His scent swirled around her as she sank into his taste. A taste that fueled a wildfire that already had a life of its own. A fire that she was certain would get a whole lot hotter.

The kiss raged on until her mouth felt slightly bruised, and Daniel's strong arm wrapped around her waist, hauling her to him. Not that he had to do much of that. Kara was already against him.

"Kara," he said, whispering her name as he buried his face into her hair.

There was so much emotion in that one word. Both the pleasure and the doubts all mixed with the heat and need. He was worried about this. About her. But that wouldn't stop them. Not with this urgency pushing at them to finish this.

And Daniel got started on the finishing.

He took those lethal kisses to the sensitive spots on her neck. She wasn't sure how he'd known just where to kiss. Where to touch. But he did, and he was very good at it.

Kara tried to kiss him and touch him as well, but everything started to move too fast, and she had to hold on to him to anchor herself. Without stopping that firestorm of kisses, he walked them to the bed. Not gently. Each step seemed to be a battle to milk out every ounce of pleasure. To make and then take even more. Kara very much wanted that more.

The moment her back landed on the soft bed, he shoved open the robe. She was only wearing a bra and panties beneath, and she nearly lost her breath when he skimmed his hot gaze, then his hand, down her body. She hadn't needed anything else to make her want him, but that did it.

Her mouth was so hungry, and she was starved for him when she kissed him. When she got open the buttons on his shirt and touched his chest, she let her fingers trail through the thick mat of dark hair that he had there. Then she kept trailing until she reached his stomach where the muscles tightened under her touch.

His body was perfect, of course. She'd known it would be. She kept touching, kept her hand sliding lower until she pressed her palm over the front of his jeans.

He was huge, hard and ready. That, in turn, made her ready as well, and she felt her own heat pool in the center of her body.

He made a husky sound of pleasure that nearly caused her to melt. That sound, the look he gave her, was a potent weapon in his sexual arsenal.

"Now," she insisted.

But Daniel didn't listen. Apparently, he wasn't done with the kissing and touching because he lowered the cups of her bra, and with the lightest touch, he flicked his tongue over her nipples. First one, then the other. He might as well have doused her with carnal fire because that *now* became a lot more urgent.

"Now," she repeated.

He must have taken her at her word because he went after her panties. He kissed her along the way as he pushed them down. Down. Down. Kissing her right between her legs.

Kara heard her own sound of pleasure, and for a moment she nearly gave in to the pleasure he was creating with his mouth and tongue. But she didn't want to do this solo. She wanted Daniel with her when she climaxed.

With her hands shaking from the need, Kara unhooked his belt and would have freed him from his boxers, but he eased her hand away. "Condom," he said.

He might as well have asked for the moon because she lay there, burning. Needing. And knowing that she didn't have a condom. Thankfully, though, Daniel did. He fished out his wallet from his back pocket and took out the foil wrapper.

Clamping the edge of the wrapper between his teeth,

he shoved his jeans and boxers past his hips. The moment he had on the condom, he was back on top of her.

And inside her.

This was many steps past mere pleasure with that first thrust. Her breath went wild. Her heart pounded. And she wanted him with every fiber of her being.

He moved. Slowly. So slowly. Which only made the need more frantic. Kara pulled at his hips, thrusting hers up to meet him. She didn't even try to make this last. She couldn't. The fire was way too hot for that, and her body wasn't going to settle for anything less than the fast orgasm that only Daniel could give her.

Finally, the heat must have gotten to him, too, because he started to move faster. Deeper. Thrust after thrust. With her lifting her hips to meet each one.

Until she could take no more.

The climax slammed through her, clamping onto his erection and causing Daniel to slide right over that peak with her. She felt his body give way. Heard the hitch of his breath. As his muscles went slack.

She rode out the pleasure from the aftershocks, keeping her arms wrapped around Daniel. The emotions hit her all at once. The incredible sensations of his weight on her. The way his skin felt against hers. His mouth when he sought out her lips for a lazy, sated kiss.

But what hit her most were the feelings that seemed to pour from her heart.

Feelings that Daniel probably didn't want her to have, but there was no way Kara could stop them. Not now. Not after she'd been with him like this.

She was in love with him.

Chapter Fifteen

Daniel lay in the darkness, staring up at the ceiling while he wondered just how much he'd screwed things up.

The sex with Kara had been great. But then that was no surprise. A scalding heat made for scalding hot sex. However, there could be a huge price to pay for it. Kara knew that, too, and he figured she was having as many doubts as he was.

Well, maybe she was.

Maybe she had such deep feelings for him that this would end up hurting her. Daniel hated that, but he wasn't sure there was a way to avoid it. It didn't feel as if his heart was his to give, that he might not be able to forget Maryanne and move on with his life.

He mentally shook his head, though, rethinking that. The fact that he was here in bed with a naked Kara snuggled against him was perhaps proof that he had moved on. He wasn't sure if that bothered him, but he was certainly having some pangs of guilt over not feeling, well, guilty.

"You can't sleep?" Kara whispered, letting him know that she was well aware he was awake.

"Neither can you?" he countered, looking down at her. And thanks to the night-light coming from the bathroom, he got an eyeful. One that made him want her all over again.

The sheet had dipped down a couple of inches, exposing her left breast, and she had one leg on top of the covers. Her face was as beautiful as it always was. Then there was her mouth. It looked a little swollen from all the kissing they'd done, which only reminded him that kissing her had been darn pleasurable and that he wouldn't mind doing more of it again.

Like now, for instance.

Despite the guilt lecture he'd just given himself, Daniel found himself leaning in to brush a kiss over her lips. She moved closer, sliding right into the kiss, which would have no doubt led to more sex.

If his phone hadn't rung.

Daniel quickly disentangled himself from Kara and snatched up his cell from the nightstand. He saw Barrett's name on the screen and checked the time. Since it was nearly midnight, this couldn't be good news.

Sadie.

That was his first thought, and Daniel blurted out his daughter's name the moment he answered. He added a quick, "Is Sadie okay?"

"She's fine," Barrett assured him, but Daniel could tell from his brother's tone that not all was well.

"What happened?" Daniel snapped. He got up and started to get dressed. Kara did the same.

"One of Rizzo's ranch hands just called," Barrett explained. "Rizzo was supposed to be staying in a guesthouse on the ranch grounds since the main house had some fire damage. The hand heard what he thought might be a gunshot coming from the guesthouse so he went to check it out. Rizzo didn't answer when the hand knocked at the door. When he went in, he said there are signs of a struggle, and that Rizzo's nowhere around."

Daniel released the breath he'd been holding. This didn't sound good for Rizzo, but this didn't have anything to do with Sadie or the rest of his family. At least he hoped it didn't.

"So, Rizzo's missing," Daniel concluded.

"That's what the ranch hand believes. He insists he's checked all around the ranch, and he can't find his boss. He says Rizzo's phone is still in the guesthouse. His wallet, too."

Daniel thought about that for a moment. The phone and wallet weren't good. People didn't normally leave those things behind if they went out.

"Signs of a struggle," Daniel repeated. "Maybe the sound of a gunshot. But no blood?"

"No, but I'm heading out there now to have a look," Barrett answered. "I was at my place so I'm not that far from Rizzo's ranch. I told the hand to get out of the guesthouse in case it's a crime scene. I don't want him mucking up any possible evidence."

Daniel didn't like that at all. This could be some kind of trap to lure Barrett into danger. "Do you have backup?"

"Yeah, Esther's meeting me there. She was off duty, but I called her back in to help with this."

Barrett had had to do that because there weren't many options, not with Leo, Daniel and Cybil all tied up with protection details. The night deputy, Jake Mendoza, would be at the sheriff's office, but he would have to stay in town to be able to respond to any emergencies.

"There's more," Barrett continued several moments later. "The ranch hand said that Rizzo's truck is also missing. If someone kidnapped him, then they might be in the truck."

True. But there was another option. If Rizzo had faked an attack to draw Barrett and other lawmen away from town, then Rizzo could be using his truck to come to the inn. Or escape if he truly believed he was about to be arrested.

"FYI, I just tried to contact Eldon," Barrett said. "I was going to ask him if he knew anything about Rizzo, but mainly I wanted to see if he had an alibi. The call went straight to voice mail."

Since it was late, that wasn't unusual. Some people did turn off their phones at night. But nothing about this felt right. Apparently, his brother felt the same way, and that's why he'd called.

"I just want you to make sure your security system is still activated and that no one set it off," Barrett insisted.

"I'll check that now."

Daniel put on his holster and drew his gun. With Kara doing the same thing and following right behind him, they hurried downstairs. The light on the security monitor was engaged, and there weren't any red lights to indicate an open window or door. Still, they went through the bottom floor to check each one.

"Everything's secure," Daniel relayed. He checked the security app on his phone. "And none of the exterior cameras have been triggered."

Of course, if any of the cameras had been, he would

have gotten a signal. Still, Daniel went to the front window and peered out to verify no one was there. He didn't see anyone.

But he saw *something*.

"There's a dark blue truck parked just up the street. I can't make out the license plate, but I think it could be Rizzo's. It's parked just out of range of the security cameras."

Barrett muttered some profanity. "Sit tight, and I'll call Jake to have him check it out."

Since Deputy Mendoza was less than two blocks away, it wouldn't take him long to do that. However, that didn't ease the tight ball of tension that settled in Daniel's gut.

Something was wrong.

And Daniel got confirmation of that just seconds later.

His phone beeped, the sound piercing right through him. Because someone had just triggered one of the security cameras.

KARA TRIED TO steel herself up for the jolt of fear and adrenaline that came. From the moment she'd heard the concerned tone of Barrett's voice, she had thought there might be trouble. She just hadn't considered that trouble might already be waiting for them outside.

"What's wrong?" Barrett asked.

Daniel didn't answer his brother until he'd gone through each of the various screens of the cameras. "I don't see anything, but something or someone tripped the alarm."

Maybe the same someone who'd left Rizzo's truck

up the street. Of course, it might not actually be Rizzo. If the ranch hand had indeed heard a shot and Rizzo had been taken by force, then his kidnapper could have brought the truck here and come close enough to set off the sensor on the camera.

"I need to go back upstairs and view the camera feed on the laptop," Daniel told his brother. "If I see anyone, I'll call you back." He ended the call and shoved his phone back in his pocket.

There was only a small light on the reception desk, but Daniel turned it off before they rushed back up the stairs. Kara tried to listen for any indications of someone breaking in. Or another camera alarm triggering. But there was nothing like that. She could only hear the sounds of Daniel's and her hurried footsteps and her own gusting breath.

Just minutes ago, Daniel and she had been in bed. And while she couldn't say they hadn't had a care in the world, the sex had soothed her raw nerves. So had Daniel. Well, there was no soothing now, not until they were certain that they weren't about to be attacked.

Once they were back in the bedroom, Daniel raced to the computer, but Kara went straight to the window. Daniel had warned her enough to stay out of anyone's possible line of sight so she peered out the side of the blinds. She looked past the cruiser parked there, past the sliver of a backyard and into the area that the cameras wouldn't cover.

Still nothing.

Mercy Ridge had very little nightlife so there wasn't anyone out strolling around, but she looked to make sure a cat or some other animal hadn't inadvertently set off the sensor.

"According to the security log, the camera in the eastside yard was the one that went off," Daniel relayed to her.

He motioned for her to follow him, and while balancing his laptop on his forearm, they rushed down the hall to what was called the east room. It was a large suite and had not one but two large windows that faced that particular part of the yard. Kara went to one. Daniel, the other. But just like the back, Kara couldn't see anything that would have tripped it.

"Maybe someone's playing games," she murmured.

A sick game.

The person could have thrown a rock or something at the camera so they'd get the alarm and go into a scramble. But why? If this was the killer, certainly he knew that Daniel and she wouldn't just go running outside to see if there was a threat. Plus, anyone who knew Daniel would also know that he would tell his brother the sheriff about this.

Then again, Barrett wasn't nearby.

He was out at Rizzo's.

Maybe that ploy had been part of this. Something that caused Kara's heart to pound even harder. But she forced herself to remember that there was a deputy at the sheriff's office. They would have backup if needed. And it wasn't as if Daniel and she were defenseless. They were both armed and wouldn't just stand by while someone attacked them.

Daniel's phone dinged again, and the soft sound went through her as effectively as a scream. Her body braced.

Her hand tightened on her gun. And with her breath held, she waited while Daniel scanned his laptop screen.

"It's the camera at the back of the inn this time," he snarled.

Unfortunately, they couldn't see that particular spot from these windows so they had to hurry back to the room they'd just left. This time it was Daniel who went to the window, but he kept his attention on the laptop.

And he cursed.

That sent Kara running to him, and she looked around his shoulder, trying to see what had caused that reaction. Nothing. Not at first, anyway. Then she zoomed in on a shadow at the back of the yard. It wasn't out in the open but rather next to a spindly Texas mountain laurel tree.

Maybe a person.

It was hard to tell, so she watched, waiting for some kind of movement. But nothing. Kara was so focused on that one spot that she gasped when the sound of Daniel's phone ringing shot through the room. He passed her the laptop so he could take out his phone and answer it.

"Daniel," Barrett blurted out the moment he was on the line. "Is everything okay there?"

"Someone or something keeps triggering the cameras. It could be a kid who thinks this is a fun prank."

Judging from Daniel's tone, he didn't believe that. Neither did Kara.

Barrett stayed quiet a couple of moments. "There's blood in the guesthouse where Rizzo was staying, and there appears to be signs of a struggle."

Kara tried to look at that from several angles. Maybe Rizzo had indeed been the victim of a crime. Heck, he could be dead. Then again, he could have orchestrated all of this to make himself look innocent, and at this very minute he could be waiting by that mountain laurel.

But there was no way she could just focus on Rizzo as the culprit. Eldon could have done this. Or even Sean. His shoulder injury might be the real deal, but that wouldn't necessarily stop him from breaking into Rizzo's guesthouse and abducting him at gunpoint.

"I'm calling in a crime scene team," Barrett added a moment later, "and then I'm heading back your direction."

Good. Because Kara had the feeling that Daniel and she were going to need all the help they could get.

Daniel ended the call and went back to his search for a possible intruder. He slid his cop's gaze from the laptop screen back to the edge of the window. Kara moved, hoping that a slightly different angle would help her get a better look at that shadowy figure, but before she could do that, there was another sound.

A blast.

And the glass from the window came flying at them.

Tossing his laptop aside, Daniel hooked his arm around her waist, pulling her to the floor, but Kara was already heading in that direction. A little too late, though. She felt the shards of glass slice over her face and arms. She felt the sting of the cuts. Felt her blood on her skin.

Felt the fear slam into her.

She turned to make sure Daniel was okay, but she didn't even manage a glimpse of him before there was another shot. Not a bullet this time. But a small metal canister burst through what was left of the window and landed on the floor next to them.

Smoke spewed from it, filling the room.

DANIEL HAD A flashback of the nightmare of the smoke that'd billowed through the hospital. Of Kara and him having to run to safety. Of the shots that'd followed once they'd made it to the parking lot. Even more memories of the bullets that had come within a breath of killing them and the others they'd been trying to get out.

And he braced himself for that to happen again.

At least now they didn't have a baby in the path of those bullets, but Daniel had no doubts that this was going to go from bad to worse in the blink of an eye. Someone could hear the shots and come to try to help. He seriously doubted a killer would just let that happen. No. He'd gun down whoever got in his way because it was obvious whoever was doing this wanted to make sure this was the last attack.

The one that'd leave Kara and him dead.

But who was doing this? Daniel quickly pushed that question aside. It wouldn't help him now because no matter who it was, he had to make sure the person didn't succeed. He couldn't let this SOB kill Kara and anyone else.

"Stay low and start moving," he snapped to Kara, but the anger roiled inside him when he saw her face.

The blood.

Hell, there was so much of it in her hair and on her face that he couldn't tell how serious her injuries were. He wanted to take out the killer for doing this to her. Wanted him to pay and pay hard. But he had to put that on hold and try to get her out of there. No choice about it. The smoke was already starting to smother them.

Regardless of the blood and what had to be pain from her injuries, she started crawling. And despite the coughing, Kara managed to keep hold of her gun. Daniel wasn't sure, however, that she could see well enough to shoot straight.

Each inch they crawled felt like a mile, and he felt the pieces of broken glass dig into his own hands and knees. That didn't stop him, though, because Daniel knew the person who was doing this could continue to send more of that glass raining down on them.

There was another shot, and it ripped into the wall just as they made it into the hall. Daniel quickly reached up and slammed the door shut. A bullet could still go through the wood, but he was hoping to stop some of the smoke from filling up the rest of the house.

Kara sat up, putting her back against the wall while she gulped in some long breaths. Daniel used his shirtsleeve to wipe away some of the blood from her face, but it was too dark to tell if she had any deep gashes. He thought he might have a deep cut of his own on his knee, but he'd have to deal with that later.

It ate up precious seconds, but Daniel took the time to message Barrett to let him know what was going on. "We're under attack," he texted. "Approach with caution. Active shooter in the area."

Maybe that would keep his brother and the other deputies safe. He definitely didn't want them walking into an ambush.

He took hold of Kara's arm and moved her away from the room. Away from the stream of smoke that was already seeping under and around the door. They definitely couldn't just sit there and let the smoke overtake them, but he wasn't sure where he should take her.

And then he caught a whiff of something else.

That "going from bad to worse" had just happened.

"We need to get down the stairs," Daniel told her.

She shook her head, maybe not understanding why he'd said that, but then Kara lifted her head. She sniffed and cursed when she no doubt caught the scent of the accelerant.

Gasoline.

Daniel didn't think the killer had actually gotten it in the house. Probably the back porch, though. But it would still be enough to burn the place down, especially since the fire department wouldn't be able to respond until they were certain there were no other shots being fired.

He considered going back in the room to get his laptop, but it was too risky. Instead, Daniel had a quick look on his phone to view the feed from the security cameras. The phone screen suddenly seemed way too small, but he saw the fire. Not on the back porch but rather the front one.

There didn't appear to be anyone in the backyard where the cruiser was parked. But, of course, a killer wouldn't just stand out in the open for them to see.

Daniel cursed himself for not having brought any Kevlar vests to the inn. Cursed his plan that had brought Kara here in the first place so all of this could be set in motion.

Now, because of the bad decisions he'd made, he might get her killed.

The realization of that squeezed at his heart, and it

sickened him. But Daniel battled back those feelings and got her moving to the stairs. He had to try to get Kara out of there. Later, he could take the time to berate himself.

If there was a later, that is.

Despite the smoke and the fire, Daniel didn't run with her down the stairs. It was pitch dark, and he couldn't risk them falling. Right now, any other injuries could be just as dangerous as the killer's bullets because it could trap them inside.

He didn't know if it was the killer's actual intention to burn the place to the ground, but Daniel couldn't risk staying inside where the smoke could overtake them and leave them unconscious.

Each step was another effort, and despite the darkness, he kept watch. He didn't see anything other than the dark shadows of the furniture, but he could hear plenty. Somewhere in the house, a clock chimed, and the old stairs creaked. And he could hear the crackle of the flames as the fire battered away at the front porch. There was black smoke seeping beneath this door, too.

"This way," he whispered, taking hold of Kara's arm so they wouldn't get separated in the darkness.

Daniel headed to the kitchen, already dreading the wall of windows that he knew was there. There were side exits, two of them, but both of those would put them much farther away from the cruiser. The back door was much closer.

Something that the killer almost certainly knew.

"We'll have to go out there," he heard Kara mutter. It wasn't a question, but it was laced with as much concern as Daniel felt.

"Yeah," he verified. "But we'll take some precautions."

Such that they were. They wouldn't just go running out into the backyard, but they were going to have to get to the cruiser. So that meant using whatever they could for cover.

By the time they reached the kitchen, the smoke had already made it back to this part of the house, and he doubted the front door would hold up much longer. Once it was gone, the fire would begin to make its way throughout the rest of the inn. Daniel didn't know how much time they had before that happened, but he figured they had mere minutes.

With his hold still on Kara, he made sure she didn't go directly in front of the windows. That meant crouching down and heading to the door. Daniel had to turn off the security system—a huge risk since the gunman could sneak inside and ambush them from behind—but he needed to be able to hear. He couldn't do that with the alarm blaring.

"We crawl out onto the porch," he explained. "Stay behind the railing, and we'll make our way to the steps."

If they managed that without anyone shooting at them, then they could go into the yard.

Kara nodded, and using her forearm, she swiped away the blood that was trickling into her eyes. She clearly needed medical attention. If he managed to get her into the cruiser, he could take her to the sheriff's office and call the EMTs to come and treat her.

For now, though, they had to leave.

Daniel sent another text to Barrett to let his brother know that Kara and he would be outside, and then he took out the keys to the cruiser, and using the remote function on the keypad, he unlocked it. Next, he un-locked the back door, automatically pulling Kara to the floor with him.

"Let's go," he said after taking a deep breath.

Daniel opened the door and got them moving.

Chapter Sixteen

Kara began to crawl, her bloody palms pressed against the cool wood of first the kitchen floor and then the porch.

She tried to force her hands to stop shaking. It was hard to do because of the fresh slam of adrenaline she'd just gotten, but she had to stay in control. Well, as much control as she could manage, considering she was bleeding in too many places to count and was terrified.

The terror wasn't for herself but rather for Daniel. She knew he would go to any lengths to protect her. Any. Lengths. That would include putting himself between her and any gunfire that'd come their way.

He could end up dying for her.

And she didn't want that. Kara didn't want to leave her niece an orphan, so if it came down to Daniel and her under a killer's bullet, she'd make sure that he wasn't the one to die.

They'd gone only a few inches outside the door when there was another shot. This one blasted into one of the windows, causing more glass to shatter down on them. And worse, the glass now littered the porch, making it even more dangerous for them to keep going.

"Try to get to the railing," Daniel whispered, and as she'd predicted he would do, he levered himself up enough to cover her body with his.

The railing wasn't far, only about six feet away, but Kara was sure she left a bloody trail each time her hands and knees scraped over the wood. Her heart was pounding so hard that it was throbbing in her ears, making it hard to hear. Hard to think, too. Still, she got there and pressed herself against the wrought iron railing.

She wished the railing had been a solid metal sheet. Or any kind of solid material for that matter. But there were several inches of gaps between each of the metal stakes, and that meant Daniel and she could still be easy targets.

Especially Daniel.

He was still looming over her while he fired his gaze all around the yard, but Kara did something about that. She took hold of the front of his shirt and yanked him farther down.

"If he kills you, then I'll be a much easier target," she managed to say.

She knew it was playing dirty to remind Daniel of something like that, but it worked. He cursed. And he stayed down.

The moments crawled by while they both tried to pinpoint the shooter. Tried to pinpoint other sounds, too. There were no wails of sirens, but Kara heard a vehicle approaching the front of the inn. Probably the fire department. A moment later, she got confirmation of that when Daniel got a text.

He didn't take his attention off their surroundings,

but instead Daniel passed his phone to her. She saw the text from Barrett.

I'm out front with the firefighters, his brother messaged. We'll hold until I get the green from you.

The green. The go-ahead to let him know it was safe to come to the back of the inn, safe for the firemen to get out of their vehicle and fight the blaze. But neither of those things might happen.

What's your location? Barrett texted.

It took some doing because of the blood on her hands, but Kara answered, On the back porch.

She would have added that they were under fire, but there was no need for her to do that. At that exact moment, two more shots came. These came from the back left side of the yard, and both bullets slammed into the window, bringing down yet more glass. Once again, Daniel covered her, his back taking the falling shards.

The anger came, as hot as the fire that slimy snake had set. Whoever was doing this was trying to rip Daniel and her to shreds, and they couldn't just lay there and let it happen. Plus, if the fire wasn't contained soon, it could spread to other buildings. People could be hurt. Or worse.

"I'll fire over his head," she whispered. That way, she wouldn't hit any bystanders. "He might run again."

Daniel made a sound to let her know he wasn't convinced that would happen, but he shifted, levering himself up again. "I'll do it."

And he did. He lifted his gun and fired. Two thick blasts that were deafening.

They waited. Listening. There were no sounds of hurried footsteps. However, there was another shot from the gunman. This one smacked into the porch railing. Obviously, he knew where they were, and he'd given up on the windows. Now, he was going for the direct kill.

Daniel cursed again and used his forearm to cover her head. "Stay down," he whispered. "I'm going to try to get to the other side of the porch." He tipped his head in that direction. "I think I can drop down off the side and get to the cruiser."

"No." She couldn't say that fast enough. "That'd only make you an easy target." Kara had to pause a moment to gather her breath. "We'll both get to the other side of the porch," she suggested. "That'll put some distance between us and the shooter, and when we both drop down to the ground, we can run to the front where your brother's waiting. We'll have backup."

It was an awful plan, one that was filled with risks that could get them killed, but at the moment it was the only chance they had. If this shootout went on much longer, Barrett would likely storm in, and then he could be gunned down. They had to move fast.

And now.

"Come on," Kara insisted, shifting out from beneath Daniel. "Let's just hurry and do this."

She was counting on the gunman not having stellar marksmanship skills. Plus, Daniel and she would have the meager cover of the railing. She prayed both of those things would work in their favor.

"Let's go," Daniel said as soon as he got into a crouching position.

They did. Daniel and she scrambled across the porch. As expected, the shots came, one of them smacking into the railing and ricocheting off with a loud pinging sound of metal striking metal. Another hit the wood pillar on the corner of the porch. No glass this time, but instead they got hit with a spray of splinters.

The moment they were on the other side, Daniel and she dropped back down so they were flat on the porch. She could see better here, thanks to the illumination coming from the lights on Main Street. What she saw past the railing was a row of thick hedges where they'd need to jump, and the trick would be not to get tangled up in them.

Of course, first they had to get over the railing, which meant there'd be seconds where it'd be easier for the shooter to kill them.

"What the hell?" Daniel grumbled.

Kara's head snapped up, and she followed the direction of his gaze. Not toward the shooter. Or rather not from the area where the shooter had fired those last two shots. Daniel was looking at that Texas mountain laurel where earlier they'd seen the shadow.

But there was no shadow now.

No. This was a man. A man with blood on his shirt.

And staggering forward, he fell to the ground.

DANIEL FOUGHT HIS instinct to run to the man who'd just fallen, but he forced himself to stay back. Plus, he had to get Kara to a safer place, and that meant getting her off the porch.

"I want you to climb over the railing and drop down into the shrubs," Daniel told her, and he made sure it sounded like the order that it was. He didn't want her arguing about this, especially when he added, "I'll cover you."

Kara didn't argue, not verbally anyway, but he could see the hard questioning look she gave him. She might have continued that look, too, but the man lying in the yard moaned, and it was definitely the sound of someone in pain. He'd likely been shot. Could be dying. And Daniel couldn't get him the help he needed until he had Kara off this porch.

"Help me," the man said, his voice also laced with pain.

Well, maybe.

And maybe this was all just a trick to get them to go out into the open to check on him.

"Help me," he repeated, and Daniel could see the man struggling to crawl toward them.

He also saw the man's face.

Rizzo.

Daniel had no idea why Rizzo was there, but that blood probably wasn't part of the ruse—if there indeed was one. No. The blood was real, Daniel could smell it, and he could see it on the right sleeve and shoulder of Rizzo's shirt. The injury could have happened when someone kidnapped him and brought him here.

As bait.

If that was the plan, it wasn't going to work. Daniel couldn't *let* it work. He forced his attention back on the area where the gunman had last fired shots.

"Climb over the railing as fast as you can," he instructed Kara.

She certainly didn't jump to do that, and Daniel felt the hesitation coming off her in waves. "Just be careful," she finally said, and she got into a position to make the climb.

Daniel got in position, too. As best as he could, anyway. When she moved, so did he. He stood, took aim at where he presumed their attacker was, and he sent two shots in that direction. From the corner of his eye, he also kept watch of Rizzo. After all, the man could be armed and ready to strike.

Kara got over the railing fast, and Daniel released the breath he was holding when she dropped into the shrubs. Their attacker didn't fire, and Daniel didn't know if that was because he'd ducked or because he was on the move, looking for a better position so he could kill them.

Daniel scrambled over the railing right after her, landing directly in front of her. The shrubs poked and jabbed at the cuts they already had, but Daniel pushed aside the pain and focused.

"Keep watch behind us," he told Kara. He didn't think the gunman could get past Barrett to come at them from that way, but he couldn't take the risk.

"I need an ambulance," Rizzo muttered, still crawling toward Kara and him.

Yeah, he probably did need fast medical attention, but a wounded man could still be dangerous. He could still be a killer. However, Daniel had to rethink that theory when the gunman started shooting again. He'd moved and was now more in the back center of the yard, but Daniel couldn't see him. He could only see where the SOB was aiming.

At Rizzo.

Or at least he was aiming *near* Rizzo. Another shot blasted through the air. And another. Daniel couldn't be sure if either of the bullets had hit Rizzo, but if not, they were coming damn close. He couldn't just crouch there and let a man be murdered.

"Stay down," he warned Kara.

Daniel had to leave the meager cover of the shrubs so he could return fire. He sent what he hoped was three rounds into the shooter. Even if he didn't hit him, it caused him to stop long enough for Daniel to hurry out into the yard and take hold of Rizzo's uninjured arm. He began dragging the man to the shrubs.

And the gunman began firing again.

Daniel felt the searing pain from a bullet as it sliced across his own forearm. Cursing, he didn't let go of Rizzo, but he ducked down, trying to make himself less of a target.

The sound of the shots behind him caused an icy chill to ripple over Daniel's skin, and that chill only got colder when he realized that Kara was now out of the bushes and was trying to stop the gunman from doing any more damage. She was also putting herself right in the line of fire.

Daniel didn't bother to shout for her to get down. She was focused on giving him precious seconds to get to safety. So that's what Daniel did. Still dragging Rizzo, he hurried to the side of the porch. Once they were by the shrubs, he let go of Rizzo, and in the same motion, he pulled Kara back to the ground.

Not a second too soon.

A bullet whipped through the air, cutting through the exact spot where she'd just been standing.

His life didn't exactly flash before his eyes, but it was close. Too close. And he felt a chill of a different kind. One that cut him all the way to the bone. He could have lost her.

Damn it, he could have lost her.

Later, he'd tell her that he hadn't wanted her to risk her life for his. Later, he'd tell her a lot of things. But for now, he just wanted to get her out of there.

Even with Rizzo's injuries and continued mumblings for help, Daniel frisked the man to make sure he couldn't pull a gun on them. But Rizzo wasn't armed. He also didn't seem to have any injuries other than the one to his shoulder, but there was so much blood that Daniel couldn't actually see the bullet wound.

"You're hurt," Kara said, her words rushing out with her breath.

Daniel glanced down at his arm and shook his head. "I'll be okay." He'd need stitches, but Rizzo's injury would also need some medical attention. "See what you can do to help Rizzo."

Kara kept hold of her gun, but she used her free hand to try to apply pressure to Rizzo's shoulder. Rizzo was writhing now, and his arms were flailing around, so she used her knees to pin his hands to the ground. As soon as she'd done that, however, the man went limp. For one terrifying moment, she thought he was dead, but she felt his pulse and realized he'd just passed out.

Daniel kept watch around them and took out his phone. He needed to text Barrett to see if he could pull a cruiser right into the side yard. That way, he could get both Kara and Rizzo into it so that Rizzo could be taken to the EMTs. But Daniel barely had time to take out his phone when something caught his eye.

A woman.

She came walking out of the shadows and into the yard.

"Don't shoot," she blurted out.

Daniel didn't, but he did take aim.

He didn't recognize the woman, a tall curvy brunette with her loose hair partially covering her face, but he could see that her hands were cuffed in front of her. There were also plastic restraints on the ankles of her bare feet.

And she wasn't alone.

Someone was behind her, using her as a human shield, and that someone had a gun pointed at her head.

"Don't shoot," the woman repeated, her voice shaking. She was shaking, too, and even in the darkness, Daniel could see that she was ghostly pale. "If you shoot, he'll kill me."

"He?" Daniel questioned.

Daniel heard her captor mutter something, but he couldn't make out what he'd said to her. Nor could he make out the voice. Was that Eldon or Sean behind the woman? Or was this someone else, maybe a henchman one of them had brought here to do his dirty work?

"Rizzo," she said. "He's the one who set all of this up."

Daniel glanced at the unconscious Rizzo. "Really?" He made sure her captor heard the skepticism in that one word.

There was more muttering. "Rizzo hired someone to scare Kara and you, to get you to back off the militia investigation. But Rizzo double-crossed him. Rizzo was going to kill the two of you and set up his hired gun to take all the blame."

Daniel tried to pick through the whirl of thoughts in his head to see if that made sense. Maybe. "What's the name of Rizzo's hired gun?" Daniel wanted to address the man and not talk through the hostage.

There were more mutterings, and the woman answered, "Ned."

Daniel seriously doubted that was the guy's real name, but it was a start. Now he needed more info fast. First, though, he handed Kara his phone and whispered for her to text Barrett.

"Who killed the surrogates?" Daniel asked. "Did you do that, *Ned*?"

"Rizzo killed them," she said without hesitating. "I'm Annie Cordova," she added a moment later.

Daniel hadn't recognized her face, but he sure as heck knew the name because he'd seen it on the list he'd gotten from the fertility clinic. She was another surrogate. And every instinct told him that she'd had no part in this attack, that she was just another innocent victim that a killer didn't mind using to get to Kara and him.

But who was using her?

Annie frantically shook her head at something that Ned told her, and the moonlight shimmered on the tears that spilled down her cheeks. "He said he'll have to hurt me if you don't swap places with me. He wants you to be his ticket out of here."

"No," Kara insisted. "It's a trap."

Probably. But maybe in Ned's way of thinking, he'd have more to bargain with by using a cop instead of a surrogate. Of course, holding a cop was risky, too, because Daniel figured he was a much better bet at defending himself than Annie would be.

"You're to toss your gun into the yard," Annie went on. "And then step out. He'll let me go when you do that."

"Don't. He'll gun you down," Kara warned him. Her voice was a raw tangle of fear and nerves, and she levered herself up enough to catch onto his arm as if to hold him back.

Daniel knew he didn't have time to think this through. Ned wasn't going to wait, especially not with other cops nearby, and Daniel couldn't stand by and watch another woman die. However, he could make this harder for Ned, or whoever was behind Annie, to kill him.

"Give me your gun," Daniel whispered to Kara.

"You're not going out there," Kara snapped. "You're not going to sacrifice yourself. Promise me you won't do that," she added as she slipped him her weapon.

Daniel couldn't agree to that promise because he'd do whatever it took. He lowered his own gun to the side of his leg, and using his left hand, he tossed Kara's gun into the yard.

"I'm coming out," Daniel said the moment Kara's gun hit the ground. "Let go of Annie."

Daniel levered himself up just a little, his attention nailed to the surrogate. He made eye contact with her and tipped his head down. He hoped she got the message that he wanted her to drop. Once she was out of the way, then he'd be able to shoot the man holding her.

Annie gave a small nod back, and Daniel could see her steeling herself up to do what he'd silently asked.

But she didn't get the chance.

Her captor tossed Annie over his shoulder and started running. Before Daniel could do anything to stop him, they disappeared into the shadows. Even over the thudding of his own heartbeat, Daniel heard the sound of the man's running footsteps.

He was getting away.

"No!" KARA SHOUTED before she could stop herself.

She knew it wouldn't do any good, that their attacker wasn't just going to turn himself in to be arrested, but the sheer frustration and dread had taken over. The gunman couldn't get away, especially not with a hostage. He just couldn't. Because if that happened, Daniel and she might never be safe.

They might never be able to bring Sadie home.

The killer could just wait until they thought they were in the clear and then come after them again. In the meantime, he would almost certainly kill Annie.

"Barrett?" Daniel called out to his brother. "I need you on the side of the porch with Kara."

Kara didn't have to ask why Daniel wanted that. He was going after the shooter. Part of her knew that had to happen, but the other part of her didn't want to risk losing him. She was in love with him. She would have told him that, too, but Barrett didn't waste any time getting to her. The moment he reached Rizzo and her, he gave Daniel the nod to get going.

Daniel did.

He hurried off into the night after the gunman and the hostage he'd taken.

She could have sworn her heart skipped several

beats, and there was a pain in her chest because her muscles were too tense. Kara whispered a prayer and hoped that their attacker wasn't now lying in wait. Waiting to kill Daniel.

"Once Esther gets here, I'll give Daniel some backup," Barrett whispered to her.

With his gun drawn and his gaze firing all around them, Barrett positioned himself over Rizzo and her, obviously giving them protection in case the shooter circled back. If that happened, she wouldn't have a way to fight back since her gun was in the yard where Daniel had tossed it. She was considering whether or not to rush out and get it when she felt something.

Next to her, Rizzo groaned, and he reached down to rub his hand over his leg. "I think he shot me," he mumbled, his words barely coherent.

Kara couldn't see any blood there, but then it was dark so maybe she'd missed it. However, it wasn't dark enough for her to miss the glint of metal when Rizzo whipped out a gun from an ankle holster. Before Kara could even react, he had hold of her.

And he pointed the gun at her head.

For a few stunned moments, she didn't react. The shock of what was happening had left her frozen. Rizzo was behind this.

Rizzo was the one who wanted Daniel and her dead.

Kara didn't have to ask his motive. This was about revenge. This was his way of getting back at Daniel for his accusations about the militia, and that twisted her stomach into a knot. Daniel had just been doing his job, and now this monster was going to try to punish him for it.

By killing him.

By killing all those innocent surrogates.

If Rizzo had managed to get away with this, it would have looked as if Daniel's murder was tied to the surrogacy. To her. To the decision they'd made for her to carry Sadie.

She pushed aside the shock and fear and tried to ram her elbow into him, but Rizzo held on. Not easily. He was breathing hard, but she didn't think it was from pain. All of this had likely been some kind of ruse, and he could have put the blood on himself to make them believe he'd been shot.

Kara made a strangled sound, and she started to scramble away from them, but Rizzo stopped her by pressing the gun harder against her head.

"Move and you die," he told her before shifting his attention to Barrett. "You need to put down your weapon, Sheriff."

Barrett's eyes narrowed, and Kara knew he was doing the same thing she was—assessing the situation. Trying to figure a way out of this. It wouldn't be easy because Kara was literally between Rizzo and him.

She now knew the position of his body was intentional. So were the fake injury and his cry for help. Even pretending to be unconscious while he waited for the exact moment to strike was part of his plan. He'd set all of this up, including the weapon he'd drawn from the ankle holster. Rizzo had likely known that Daniel would frisk him, and he had, but they hadn't considered that Rizzo would have a concealed gun that he was now going to try to use to kill her.

"You know I can't do that," Barrett answered, his voice as icy as the glare he gave Rizzo. "If I put down my gun, you'll just kill all of us."

"Maybe. Maybe not." He might have tried to sound nonchalant, but he wasn't pulling it off. Kara heard the strain of nerves in his voice. Felt it in the knotted muscles of his arm.

"You don't need to do this," Kara tried.

Rizzo's response was a hollow laugh. "Right. Let's just say I need to cover up the mess I made. I just need to wait a couple more minutes to make sure Ned takes care of Daniel."

Her stomach knotted even more. *Takes care of Daniel.* Ned was no doubt Rizzo's hired gun, and Rizzo had given him orders to kill Daniel.

"You killed all those surrogates," Kara managed to say. Maybe she could distract him. Or come up with some sort of diversion so that Barrett could get off a shot.

Rizzo certainly didn't deny committing the murders, nor was there any logic he could give her that would justify why he'd done that.

"You killed innocent women and attacked Daniel and me to cover up your own crimes," she snapped.

The sound of the gunshot stopped Kara from saying more. She felt the punch of dread, and she prayed that Daniel hadn't been on the receiving end of the bullet.

Oh, God.

Had Rizzo's henchman succeeded?

Was Daniel dead?

The thought of it was unbearable, and it sent a slam of rage into her. How dare this miserable excuse for a human being do such things. He had no right to put them in danger. And Kara used that rage, letting it build and soar until she had it pinpointed on the man behind her.

On a feral growl, she slammed her elbow into Rizzo, and in the same motion, Kara shoved away from him. Just in the nick of time. Rizzo pulled the trigger, and the bullet came so close to her that Kara could have sworn she felt the heat from it as it flew past her.

She punched him, trying to knock away the gun, but he fired again. The sound of it blasted through the night and merged with Barrett's shouts for her to get back.

But Kara couldn't get back from Rizzo. Nor could she run. If she did, Rizzo would be on her, and she seriously doubted he would have any reservations about shooting her in the back. No. He was basically a coward, preying on women who'd never done him a moment of harm.

Kara managed to latch onto Rizzo's right wrist, and she clamped on hard so she could try to keep his gun pointed away from Barrett and her. But Rizzo was a lot bigger and stronger than she was, and he'd obviously gotten his own slam of rage and adrenaline.

Barrett lunged toward them, ready to help, but Kara knew he didn't have a clean shot. Plus, Rizzo was using the positions of their bodies to his advantage. If Barrett tried to punch Rizzo, he could end up hitting her. While that wouldn't kill her, it might cause her to move the wrong way, and that could allow Rizzo to get off a shot.

"Put down the gun," someone shouted.

Daniel.

Kara couldn't see him, but there was no mistaking that voice, and she could also hear his running footsteps as he approached. The relief came, even stronger than her earlier rage. He was alive.

But he might not be for long.

From the corner of her eye, she could see Daniel running toward them, cutting through the smoke that had already made its way to the backyard. At the speed he was going, it wouldn't take him long to reach them, and Rizzo might be able to shoot him. Unlike some of his other shots, she doubted Rizzo would miss at such close range.

And Daniel could die.

Using brute force, Rizzo punched Kara with his left fist, and he hauled her to him so that Daniel wouldn't be able to shoot him. However, it would make Daniel an easy target for Rizzo. She couldn't just sit there and let Rizzo gun him down, especially when he was trying to save her.

Kara went at Rizzo again, and she managed to bash her elbow into his face. He cursed her, his growled tone a vicious threat. He turned and pivoted his hand.

So he could point his gun at her.

Kara had only a split second to decide what to do. Daniel was right there, already taking aim. Kara knew she had to move, too. So that Daniel would have the shot. So instead of trying to latch onto Rizzo again, she went limp and dropped on her side to the ground.

Time seemed to slow to a crawl, and she heard herself scream when Rizzo lifted his gun, pointing it right at Daniel. The blast came. A thick syrupy sound that quickly turned to an explosion in her head.

Rizzo had pulled the trigger.

Chapter Seventeen

Daniel didn't brace himself for Rizzo's shot. No time for that. He simply took aim as best he could and fired. Just as Rizzo did.

Rizzo missed.

Daniel didn't.

The shot slammed straight into Rizzo's chest, and Daniel heard the unmistakable sickening sound of the bullet tearing through him. Daniel hadn't meant for it to be a warning shot. That would have been too risky. So, he'd aimed to kill.

Rizzo's body went slack, his own gun sliding from a hand that was no longer receiving the right signals from his brain. Still, the man managed a dry smile.

"You'll never be able to save Annie," Rizzo said, attempting a grin. It was no doubt meant to taunt Daniel.

And it worked.

Because what Rizzo said could be the truth.

"Where's Annie?" Kara asked, her voice tight with the strain from the fear and the fight.

Daniel had to shake his head, and he glanced at Barrett. "Annie wasn't with the hired gun when I caught up to him. Either she got away or he stashed her somewhere."

Or he could have killed her.

Daniel hadn't heard the hired gun fire a shot, but he could have snapped her neck. However, Daniel didn't want Kara to have to deal with that possibility right now. Not when she looked to be barely hanging on by a thread.

"And the gunman, this *Ned*?" Barrett pressed, already getting to his feet.

Daniel tipped his head toward the area where he'd left him. "I had to shoot him, but he was alive when I cuffed him to the door of the dumpster behind the hardware store. He'll be able to tell you where Annie is."

Barrett volleyed a few glances at Kara, Rizzo and him, and his brother must have decided this situation here was under control because he took off running. Daniel heard him call someone, Esther probably, and he barked off orders for a search to find the now missing surrogate and to have the EMTs and the fire department move in. Daniel wished he could help, but there was no way he could leave Kara alone.

Struggling to get to her feet, she hurried to him, her gaze skimming over him, no doubt to check him for injuries. Daniel had a few, just cuts and bruises, but she had a lot more than he did. The nicks were still bleeding, and the right side of her face was swollen.

It felt like multiple punches to the gut to see her like that. To see the injuries that this SOB had caused, but Daniel didn't want Kara to feel his anger. He wanted to give her what comfort he could, so while keeping his gun aimed at Rizzo, he hooked his arm around her and pulled her to him for a hug. But he was the one who was comforted, and Daniel felt the immediate relief of just being able to hold her like this.

"Now, that's touching," Rizzo rasped out. He coughed, then groaned. "Guess you won this round, huh?"

Daniel thought it was a shame that Rizzo had used what little of his breath he had left for that. There'd been no confession. No remorse. Not even a message he wanted given to someone who might care for him. Just that stupid question that drilled home for Daniel just how senseless all the murders and violence had been.

Senseless enough that Kara had nearly died because of it.

Now, he watched Rizzo die. He heard the death rale, saw the life drain from the man's eyes. And Daniel felt both disgust and relief. Rizzo wouldn't be able to hurt another woman or launch another attack.

"We have to get away from the building," Daniel told Kara when he saw the firemen move in to start putting out the flames at the front of the inn. He also motioned to the two EMTs, and he pointed to Rizzo. "He's dead, but Kara needs help."

Kara was shaking her head before he even finished. "No. We have to look for Annie."

"Barrett will find Annie," he assured her, and Daniel hoped that was the truth.

He led her to the back of the ambulance, away from some of the smoke, away from Rizzo, and he had her sit while one of the EMTs started to examine those wounds on her face. The other EMT stooped down to take a look at Rizzo. Daniel stepped back so he could call Esther to see if she could give him an update on the search, but he spotted the deputy.

Not alone.

She was walking toward them, and she had the injured gunman in tow. The guy was bleeding, but he didn't appear to have any trouble walking. The man was definitely in better shape than Rizzo.

Daniel hurried toward them. So did one of the EMTs who'd been by Rizzo. "Did he say where he'd put Annie?" Daniel immediately asked.

He could tell from the deputy's expression that the answer to that was no. Daniel simply put out his hand to stop the EMT from going to the gunman. He didn't say that the piece of slime wouldn't get medical treatment until he talked, but Daniel was pretty sure he got his point across.

The gunman huffed. "I knocked her out and dumped her on the side of garbage bags in the alley."

Daniel texted that info to Barrett as fast as he could, and he instructed Esther to help Barrett with the search. Esther shoved the man to a sitting position on the ground and hurried off.

At the front of the inn, Daniel could hear the firemen getting to work. Maybe they'd be able to save the place. If not, it would end up being yet something else that Rizzo had ruined.

"I want a deal," the gunman insisted, giving Daniel a snarling look. "I tell you everything you want to know about Rizzo, and I get immunity."

Not bothering to keep his language in check, Daniel told him what he could do with his immunity demand.

"You're not calling the shots here," Daniel reminded

him. "You're going down for multiple murders, attempted murders, murders for hire, conspiracy, kidnapping and any other charge I can tack onto that. You'll be on death row before you know it."

Now it was the gunman who cursed. "I didn't kill anyone."

"Maybe not, but accessory to murder will still land you on death row."

Daniel finally saw something he wanted to see. The panic in the man's eyes. "I'm not going down for this," the gunman snapped. "Rizzo was the one who put all of this together."

Bingo. That was a good start, but Daniel wanted to hear a whole lot more. He glanced behind him to check on Kara—she was still being treated—and he gave the go-ahead nod to the other EMT to check the gunman's wounds.

"Keep talking," Daniel told the man as the EMT stooped beside him. "Start with your name and don't stop until you've convinced me to take the death penalty off the table."

Something that Daniel doubted would happen even if the man told them everything. It didn't matter that he might not have actually killed anyone, accessory to murder carried the same penalty as murder itself.

"I'm Ned Kershaw," he finally said. "Rizzo and I belong...*belonged* to the same group."

"The militia," Daniel provided. "The Rangers have proof to put a stop to that." If they didn't already have that proof, they soon would with what he could get from this idiot.

"Yeah, but I can give the Rangers more. I can give

the names of everyone in the group and the location of our stashes. I'll cooperate, and that should help cut back on my sentence."

Maybe, but that'd be up to the Rangers. It was possible they would indeed want to make a deal with him to take down a militia group. For now, though, Daniel was more interested in what Rizzo had done to the surrogates and what he'd tried to do to Kara and him.

"Tell me about Rizzo," Daniel demanded. "What was his part in all of this?"

Ned winced when the EMT cut away his shirtsleeve and began to clean the wound. "Rizzo set all of this up," Ned repeated. "He killed those women. The surrogates from that clinic. He figured that way when he killed you and your woman, that he wouldn't get the blame, that the crazy guy who lost his daughter would."

Daniel shook his head. "Rizzo was going to set up this man to make him look guilty?"

"Yeah," Ned confirmed. "Rizzo sent him some pictures to stir him up. Said he was already right on the edge since he was all broken up about losing his daughter. Rizzo thought maybe the crazy guy would do the job for him, that he'd kill you because it'd look like you were trying to set him up. But the crazy guy didn't take the bait. That's when Rizzo tried to stir up the other guy, too, by shooting him."

Sean. So that explained who'd shot Sean and why.

"Rizzo didn't want this second man dead?" Daniel pressed.

"No. The idea was for him to go after you and your woman. He was one pissed off guy, I gotta tell you, and Rizzo thought he wouldn't have to push him too much.

Still, I guess he didn't push fast enough 'cause Rizzo set all of this up."

Ned was right about Sean's anger level. He was indeed a hothead. But obviously Rizzo hadn't been able to provoke him into committing murder.

"I didn't know about any of that, though, about shooting that man until after it was a done deal," Ned went on a moment later. "When things didn't go the way Rizzo wanted at the hospital, he hired me to help him tonight. All I was supposed to do was hold the other woman. Annie," he clarified. "And I was to fire shots that didn't hit anybody. Especially Rizzo."

Daniel could see Rizzo setting up something like this, but there was one piece that didn't fit. And it was a huge piece. "Why didn't Rizzo just have you gun me down when you had the chance?" He could have easily done that when Daniel had stood to toss Kara's gun into the yard.

"Because he wanted to do it himself," Ned answered without a moment's hesitation. "He said no one but him was gonna put a bullet in you and that he wanted you to watch while he killed your woman."

None of that was a surprise, but hearing it still packed a wallop. Daniel saw that same reaction in Kara's eyes when she walked toward him and stood by him. She touched his arm, and he was surprised at how much that simple gesture steadied him. Actually, everything about her steadied him, but Daniel knew they had a long road ahead of them. It was going to take a lifetime or two to get past the nightmare that Rizzo had created.

"How'd Rizzo ever expect to get away with this?" Kara asked.

"He faked being shot when he fell in the yard," Ned explained while the EMT worked on him. "He had some of his own blood drawn, and he used that. He said that would have been on all your clothes when your bodies were found. He'd planned on putting it on the crazy man's clothes, too. So, when Rizzo just disappeared, it'd look like the crazy man had also killed him."

Rizzo had obviously planned on running. On making a new life somewhere else. A life that wouldn't have involved any jail time for his involvement with the militia or all the murders he'd committed. A life where Kara, he and anyone else who'd gotten in Rizzo's way would have been dead.

Since Ned was still wearing his cuffs, Daniel risked taking his attention off the man for a couple of seconds so he could pull Kara into his arms. She was trembling, probably dealing with an adrenaline crash, but she still looked better than she had a couple of minutes ago. That was in part because the EMT had wiped most of the blood off her face, but Daniel could see the relief there, too. Rizzo was dead. The threat to Sadie was over.

He looked down at her, their gazes connecting, and Daniel realized there was so much he wanted to say to her. Things that would have to wait, though, he realized, because she spoke first.

"I'm in love with you," she blurted out. "And I know the timing sucks for telling you that, but after everything that just happened, I didn't want to wait another minute without telling you."

Daniel just stared at her. He certainly hadn't seen this coming. But he knew it was true. She was in love with him. He also knew she was right about the timing being bad, and his response was going to have to wait. That's because he caught the motion out of the corner of his eye.

Since his body was still on alert, he pushed Kara behind him and pivoted in that direction. However, there was no need for him to take aim. It was Barrett.

And he had Annie with him.

"She's okay," Barrett quickly assured them, and he handed the woman off to an EMT who came rushing toward them.

"He bashed me on the head with his gun," Annie snapped. She sounded more riled than hurt, and she aimed a nasty glare at Ned. "I hope you put him in jail and throw away the key."

Daniel thought that was a stellar idea. He wanted the man in a cage and was certain that's exactly where he'd be.

"She needs to go to the hospital," one of the EMTs said, referring to Annie. He looked at Kara and Daniel. "You two do, as well. You're both pretty cut up, and you're going to need some stitches."

Stitches weren't a picnic, but Daniel thought they were a small price he was willing to pay, considering their injuries could have been much, much worse.

"Go ahead to the hospital," Barrett told them. "All three of you can go in the ambulance, and Esther and I will take care of things here."

Daniel hated to put all of this on his brother and his fellow deputy, but he doubted Kara would go to the hospital without him. That's why he slipped his arm around her and began to lead her to the ambulance that was parked behind the fire truck.

"After the hospital, we'll go see Sadie," Daniel assured her.

That made her smile, and he wasn't sure how she managed to look so darn good when they'd both been beat to hell and back. But she did. Kara looked amazing. So amazing that he couldn't stop himself from leaning down and brushing a kiss on her mouth.

"I'd like that," Kara whispered. She kissed him, too. It was both casual and intimate, the kind of kiss that couples shared even after they'd been together for years. "I like this."

He knew what she meant. *This* was those kisses. Him, holding on to her. Them being together even if it was only for this moment. For this night.

Or longer.

Kara clearly wanted *this* to last for a while. And that was something they needed to discuss. Maybe when they got to the hospital, he could find a minute to talk to her alone so he could ask her about what she'd said to him.

I'm in love with you.

He'd heard the words clearly enough, but Daniel wasn't sure she'd meant them. No. Her emotions had been sky-high, and coupling the danger with the fact they'd had sex must have made her believe her feelings went beyond...

Daniel stopped. Literally and mentally.

With the EMTs and Annie ahead of them, Daniel looked down at Kara. "It's been a tough night," he said, testing the waters. Or something. Heck, he wasn't sure what he was doing, but he suddenly felt off-kilter.

No.

That wasn't it.

He suddenly felt as if everything was…right.

"You're in love with me?" He hadn't intended for that to be a question or for him to make it sound as if it were some kind of miracle. But it was. It fit the miracle label just fine.

"I am." She didn't smile this time, but there seemed to be a contentment about her when she looked into his eyes. "How much of a problem will that be for you?"

Daniel had heard a lot of tough things tonight, including some tough questions. But that wasn't one of them.

"No problem at all," he assured her—after he kissed her again.

This time, though, it was a lot more than a brush of his lips on hers. He made sure that she felt it. Hopefully all the way to her toes. It must have worked because when he pulled back, she had a dreamy smile on her face.

"Good," she whispered. "Because I plan to love Sadie and you for a long, long time."

Since that was exactly what Daniel had in mind, he smiled, too, and kissed Kara again. Soon, very soon, he wanted to get started on that long, long time.

* * * * *

THE TRA

CAROL ERICSON

Prologue

Rule number one. Leave no witnesses.

Their eyes locked. He dropped the dead woman from his arms and took a tentative step toward the onlooker peering from behind the bush. The eyes glowing at him from the darkness widened and looked like a deer's in the crosshairs. The owner of those eyes took flight.

He glanced at the prey crumpled at his feet, and with rule number one pounding in his head, he took off after the witness, the plastic garbage bag encasing his body crackling with each step. He loped through the trees, gun dangling at his side. He'd needed the gun to force Ashley into his car, but he'd strangled her with gloved hands according to the playbook.

As he ran, twigs snapped back in his face, needling into his flesh. He thrashed about for several minutes, but he couldn't find a trail, or any clues as to which direction the person had run.

Had he…or she…even seen him? The body? Tipping his head back, he surveyed the moonless sky between the treetops. Threatening clouds had been hovering over LA all day, even squeezing out a few drops of rain here and there. He'd been using a flashlight to dispose of Ashley's body and had switched it off when he heard the crack of a branch.

Maybe this person was no witness at all. He tugged the cap lower over his face. And maybe he was leaving evidence by chasing this person through the trees. He bent over, hands on his knees, his sweaty palms sticking to the plastic, his breath heaving in his chest.

At the sound of a car engine, he jerked his head up. Too late. Whoever it was had gotten away and might be calling the police right now.

He swung around and stumbled back to the clearing near the trail where he'd left Ashley. Less time now to complete his mission. He'd totally messed up his first kill, but he was determined to finish the job.

Ashley lay where he'd left her, undisturbed. He rolled her onto her back and swept the dark hair from her face. The previous copycat, Mitchell Reed, had selected his victims based on their appearance—brunettes with long hair who looked like some chick who'd jilted him in college. Pathetic loser.

He didn't care what they looked like. All women were whores, just like his mother. He never got jilted. He was the one who did the jilting. He used them, took their money and left. But he never killed them. That would be breaking rule number four. Don't ever murder someone you know. The first copycat, Jordy Lee Cannon, had broken that rule. Pathetic loser.

As the past deeds of the previous copycats ran through his head, he'd been arranging Ashley's body into a position that would facilitate the rest of his tasks. He swept aside the plastic bag and pulled the playing card from his jacket and placed it between her lips. Eyes open or closed? He couldn't remember, so he left hers staring into the cloudy sky.

He fished the box cutter from the front pocket of his jeans and circled to Ashley's left side. Holding her wrist down with one hand, he used the box cutter to slice off her pinky finger. Blood spurted into the carpet of leaves beneath her hand. He dropped the finger in a baggie and sealed it.

A trophy for The Player.

They'd all done it. Severing the little finger of the victims' left hand had not only sent a message to law enforcement that The Player was back—if only by proxy—but also afforded The Player his trophy of choice. He'd be mailing Ashley's finger to a PO box. The other copycats had probably used a different PO box.

He shrugged. A small price to pay. He already had his souvenir of the kill, so he turned from the body to start his climb back to his car.

As he pivoted, he caught sight of the bush where he'd spotted someone hiding. What had that person been doing here at this time of night and alone?

He crept behind the bush and crouched, poking his head to the side to get a view of Ashley. Couldn't even tell that it was a body of a human. And where were the cops? Where was the outcry? The person had seen nothing of consequence.

He put his hands on the ground to hoist himself up, and his palm dug into something hard. He felt around the damp bed of twigs and leaves, and his fingers curled around a small bottle.

He picked up the clean prescription pill bottle and brought it close to his face. As he read the name on the bottle, his mouth stretched into a smile.

He now knew the identity of the witness—and now he could follow rule number one.

Chapter One

Kyra perched on the edge of Quinn's love seat, the one she'd helped Charlotte pick out when she remodeled the Venice house, her hands clasped, her legs bouncing up and down, her face stiff. If Jake kept rubbing a circle on her back, he'd rub a hole right through to her spine.

When the coroner hitched the gurney onto its wheels, something broke inside her. She flung herself off the cushion and dropped to her knees next to Quinn's lifeless body ready to be transported away forever. "He can't be dead. Are you sure? Are you sure he's dead?"

Even as the words left her lips in a strained, high-pitched tone, she knew the truth. Quinn was gone, the only father she'd ever known.

"Kyra, let me take you away. You've been here long enough. You can't do anything for Quinn now. You gave him everything at the end. He's with Charlotte."

Kyra hadn't shed a tear yet—not when they walked into Quinn's house and found him on the floor, not when she cradled his head in her lap as Jake told her Quinn had no pulse, not when Jake called 911, not when the EMTs pronounced him dead of a suspected coronary. Now her throat closed and her eyes ached, and when Jake pulled her up and crushed her to his chest with one arm, she buried her head against his shoulder and the floodgates opened.

She sagged against Jake as the wheels of the gurney spun out of the house. Quinn would never return to this house he'd shared with Charlotte, the house that had been her refuge when she'd been a mixed-up foster kid.

With the emergency personnel gone, the house creaked and sighed. The seawater lapped against concrete barriers that kept it away from the houses that hugged the banks of the canal. It seemed to whisper, "Charlotte, Charlotte." Is that what Quinn heard when he sat on his porch alone?

Jake stroked her hair. "I'm so sorry. I know Quinn was everything to you, as you were to him. He was so proud of the woman you've become. You couldn't have made him any happier."

She raised her head from the shirt she'd stained with her tears and took in the small house with a watery gaze. "Nothing will ever be the same again."

"Nothing ever is."

She balled her fist against her stomach. "What am I going to do?"

"What are you going to do?" He swept his thumb across her cheek, catching several tears. "You're going to carry on, just like Quinn would expect you to do. You're going to do your job. You're going to enjoy your life. You're going to honor Quinn."

Honor Quinn. Kyra curled her hands around Jake's shirt. "I'm going to find The Player."

Jake's body stiffened. "I don't think Quinn would want you to go down that path."

"Really?" She released her hold on Jake's shirt and paced to the sliding glass door that led from Quinn's kitchen to a deck over the canal. She stared at the moonlight cascading across the water.

"The Player was Quinn's one failure as a homicide detective. The Player murdered my mother, along with four other women, he encouraged and inspired three copycat killers—that we know of—and he's still alive. He's still out there spreading evil, tormenting me, and Quinn learned that truth a few weeks ago." She whipped around, a steely resolve replacing the sorrow that had sapped her strength over an hour ago. "That's *exactly* what Quinn would want me to do."

Jake opened his mouth, snapped it shut, took a step toward her, stopped. "Before we get out of here, do you know if Quinn had an attorney?"

"Terrence Hicks. Why?"

"I know Hicks. He specializes in financial planning for cops. Used to *be* a cop." Jake spread his hands as if to encompass the house. "You should contact him to let him know about Quinn's death, although when a giant in law enforcement like Quinn passes, everyone knows."

"I think I have Hicks's card." Her gaze darted around the room. "I—I can't go through any of Quinn's stuff right now."

"Of course not." Jake crossed to the front door and removed the keys Kyra had left there when they first entered Quinn's house and saw his body. "Let's lock up and get something to eat."

She widened her eyes and crossed her arms over her midsection. "There's no way I can eat anything."

"Do you want me to take you home? Do you want to be alone?"

The old Kyra would've given an emphatic yes to that question, but the new and improved Kyra heard something in Jake's voice. She peered at him through her lashes, still wet with tears.

He bobbled her key chain in one hand while holding

on to the doorjamb with the other, his neck stiff and his jaw tight. He'd lost Quinn, too. The two of them had gotten close, shared a bond as homicide detectives. Jake revered the old detective, but had a soft spot for him, too. He'd miss Quinn almost as much as she would.

Taking a deep breath, she straightened her spine and walked toward Jake. She wrapped her arms around his waist and said, "I want to be with you."

He dropped his head and kissed the top of hers. "I was hoping you'd say that. I don't want to go home alone. I want to talk about Quinn."

They wound up at her apartment in Santa Monica, much closer to Quinn's Venice house than Jake's place high in the Hollywood Hills. Jake ordered a pizza on the way, and by the time they and the food got to her place and Jake had opened a bottle of wine for her, she managed a few bites.

She brushed the crumbs from her fingertips over a paper plate. "The coroner will do an autopsy, right?"

"Yeah, but we know he had heart disease, already had two stents, and the EMTs indicated a coronary was likely." He pinged the side of her wineglass with his fingernail. "More wine?"

"Yes, please." As she watched the ruby-red liquid swirl into her glass, she asked, "Did anyone check for signs of forced entry?"

She felt Jake's eyes on her, probing, so she grabbed the slice of pizza on her plate and forced herself to take another bite.

"I did—everything locked up tight from the inside, not even a window cracked open. He probably closed up against the rain earlier in the day." He toyed with the crust on his plate. "No signs of a struggle. No defensive wounds on his hands. I did my due diligence as a detective before the first responders got there. What are you suggesting?"

The bite of pizza felt like sawdust in her mouth, so she washed it down with another gulp of wine. "I'm suggesting what any good detective might suggest, given Quinn's status at the LAPD. A retired detective with one cold case on his record, a cold case that has gotten hot in the past several months due to the copycats emulating The Player, and an admission by Quinn that The Player was still alive and directing the copycats."

"We think that's the case, or at least some of us do." He held up his hands in defense. "I believe he is, but it can't be verified."

"Quinn told us about information the copycats' puppet master passed along to them, information only The Player could've known. Then we have Mitchell Reed, Copycat Three, who kidnapped your daughter and was willing to exchange her for me—to please The Player."

Jake squeezed his eyes closed for a second, most likely remembering the moment he realized a serial killer had snatched his daughter. "We think that's why he wanted to make the trade, but The Player never showed up to claim you, did he?"

"I don't think you gave him enough time. You tracked Copycat Three down through Fiona's burner phone and rushed in there to save my life." She wiped her fingers on a crumpled napkin, and then took his hand. "I think that's about the third or fourth time you've come to my rescue."

"You saved my daughter. I'm never going to forget that." He brought her hand to his lips and pressed a kiss against the back of it.

"I'd do it all over again, but I couldn't save Quinn, could I?"

"From a heart attack? No, although you tried your

best. You did more than his own doctor did, monitoring his diet—" he lifted his beer "—his alcohol."

"I shouldn't have allowed him to have any." Her bottom lip quivered and she tossed back some more wine.

"Quinn was a grown man. He did what he wanted, lived life on his own terms. Can't ask for more than that." He raised his bottle. "To Quinn."

"To Quinn." Her nose stung, and she glugged down the remainder of the wine.

Jake tipped the neck of his beer bottle at her. "You'd better slow down yourself or you're gonna end up in a world of hurt. You're not fooling me with those little nibbles of pizza. You have nothing in your stomach but red wine sloshing around in there. So eat up, or back away from the booze."

Sniffling, she surveyed him through watery eyes. "Oh, God. Is that how I sounded with Quinn? Because it's really annoying."

He rolled his eyes to the ceiling. "That's exactly how you sounded with Quinn, but it must've sounded more lovable coming from you because he complained, but he didn't mind—he didn't mind anything about you."

A tear rolled down her cheek. "He was my savior. Do you know, he's the one who personally took me to the Department of Children and Family Services when my mother had been murdered? I was covered in blood and…"

"Wait. I thought your mother had been strangled like all the rest."

"She had been, but during the struggle, because my mom fought like hell, she grabbed a vase and it broke on the floor. She cut herself on it, and I cut myself on it when I discovered her body the next morning. When the police showed up after I called 911, I was hiding in my bedroom. Then Quinn showed up, and I just knew everything was going to be okay."

"DCFS should've allowed him and Charlotte to adopt you. For all the issues that may have presented, how is it not better than foster care?"

Kyra lifted her shoulders. She'd been through this with Quinn and Charlotte a million times. It didn't change a thing—didn't change that she'd lived in more foster homes than she cared to remember, culminating in the one where she'd killed a foster father in self-defense and to protect the younger girls in the home.

But Jake knew all about her sordid past, and it hadn't scared him off. When her phone buzzed, she blinked, wondering where the sound was coming from. Jake had been right about the two-plus glasses of wine on an empty stomach, but she was entitled to numb the pain.

Jake handed her the phone. "It's Billy."

"Why is your partner calling me?" After staring dumbly at the display for a few seconds, she answered. "Hi, Billy."

"Hey, Kyra. I heard about Quinn. Just want to let you know how sorry I am. If there's anything I can do for you, let me know."

Fresh tears spilled from her eyes. "Thank you, Billy. Do you want to talk to J-Mac? He's right beside me."

"That's where he should be, baby. No, I don't need to talk to him. Just called to offer my condolences on your loss and make sure you're doing okay, but if J-Mac's with you, I know he'll take care of you."

She thanked Billy again and ended the call. "I guess the word is out about Quinn's death."

"I knew it wouldn't take long." He held up the bottle. "More wine? Warm bath? You should eat more, but I'm not going to force you. Something besides pizza?"

"I'm okay." She stroked the cheek of the man who would stick by her through anything. He'd already proved that, and Quinn had approved of Jake. Quinn had had plans for them and their future, hers and Jake's—marriage, children. Now Quinn wouldn't be there to share in their future. Maybe those plans would all fall apart now.

"I do have one request."

"I will feed Spot if he comes meowing at your door."

She lifted a corner of her mouth, the closest she could come to a smile right now. "That, too, but could you stay the night? Just hold me? I couldn't bear waking up in the middle of the night alone and thinking about Quinn."

"I will absolutely spend the night with you. Like I said earlier, I don't much feel like being alone, either."

Her phone buzzed again, and she glanced at it, still clutched in her hand. "It's Captain Castillo. Hello, Captain."

"Hello, Kyra. We heard about Quinn. I'm—I'm devastated. Such a loss. I'm so sorry."

"Thank you, Captain Castillo. It was a shock finding him on the floor like that."

Castillo paused. "Heart attack? That's the word, and I know he had his difficulties."

"That's what it looks like now, but they're going to do an autopsy."

"They are?" Castillo's voice cracked and Kyra glanced at Jake.

"Jake said they probably would, given who he was."

"He's right. They probably will." Castillo cleared his throat. "Let me know if you need anything. Anything at all, anything the department can do for you."

"I will. Thanks again, Captain." He ended the call, and Kyra set the phone next to her paper plate, the cheese on her pizza hardening into an unappetizing glob. Her stomach gurgled. "That was nice of him."

"Castillo and Quinn always shared that bond of being the first ones at the scene of your mother's murder."

"Were they?" She tilted her head.

"Castillo was working patrol at the time. He's the one who responded to your 911 call. As soon as he walked into your mother's house, he called Quinn because he knew they had another one of The Player's victims on their hands. Quinn was nearby, so the two of them were at the house alone with you…and your mother's body for several minutes before the hordes showed up. I guess you left the bedroom for Quinn, but you wouldn't come out for Castillo."

"That's weird. I'm sure I read that, but I don't even remember. I knew Castillo had worked the case with Quinn, but I just thought he was on the original task force."

"Yeah, he was. After your mother's death, Quinn asked Castillo to join the task force. Castillo's career took off after that. From what I heard, it never hurt to have Detective Roger Quinn in your corner."

"And now he's never going to be in anyone's corner again. Certainly not mine." She dropped her head to her hands.

Jake lightly squeezed the back of her neck. "I'm in your corner now—and I'm not going anywhere."

She wouldn't be able to answer without bursting into tears again, so she just pressed her body close to his.

Spot's meows broke the spell, and Jake pushed off the couch. "I'm going to feed this mangy cat. Why don't you get ready for bed? I'll clean up everything here and join you later."

Kyra dipped her head and rose woozily from the

couch. Her eyelids drooped and she silently thanked that bottle of cabernet. Without it, she never would've been able to sleep tonight.

As Jake bustled through her kitchen, she brushed her teeth and washed her face with cool water. No need to remove her makeup. Her tears had already done that job. She smeared on some night cream, shed her clothing and crawled between the sheets.

Her eyes grew heavy, waiting for Jake to join her. Then the harsh ring of his work phone jolted her awake.

His body shifted beside her as he removed his arm from her waist. She peered over his shoulder at the digital clock and realized with a start that she'd drifted off and had slept through the whole night.

Jake's voice mumbled a hello. The mattress bounced as he shot up against the headboard. "You're kidding. Tell me you're kidding."

Rubbing her eyes, Kyra struggled to sit up, her hand squeezing Jake's bicep. "What? What's going on?"

Had they found out something about Quinn's death? Something suspicious?

Jake growled into the phone. "When will it end? When will this end? I'm on my way."

He said goodbye and tossed his phone onto the nightstand. Then he twisted around and cupped her face with one hand. "We have another copycat killer. Our fourth."

Kyra clutched the covers in her fists. "He's taunting Quinn—even in death."

Chapter Two

Jake navigated the trail on the way to the body's dump site more sure-footed than he usually was, as he hadn't bothered to return home to change into a suit. The soles of his running shoes crunched the pebbles and twigs that littered the path beneath him.

No place to park a car here, so the killer must've carried the victim from the parking area almost a half a mile away. Strong. Bold. Sure of himself.

Kyra functioned as the task force's victims' rights advocate and all-around hand-holder and typically accompanied him to a crime scene, but he'd convinced her to stay behind today. On the heels of Quinn's death, she didn't need to be out here thinking about the one who escaped Quinn's net twenty years ago, the one who killed her mother.

He beat his partner to the scene, even though it had taken him almost an hour to reach the Angeles National Forest from Kyra's apartment in Santa Monica. As he tromped down the trail toward the yellow tape beckoning him through the trees, he caught the scent of pine that wafted down from the higher elevations of the park. The sun still dappled the ground between the leaves swaying above, but a distinct chill in the air had Jake hunching into his jacket.

The patrol officers guarding the body stood at attention when he approached. He didn't recognize them. The Angeles National Forest, the site of several dumped bodies over the years, didn't fall into the jurisdiction of LAPD's Northeast Division, but LA County's entire law enforcement world knew to call in the Copycat Player Task Force.

The name of the task force had morphed with the three different killers it had investigated and brought to a rough justice. They'd dubbed Jordy Lee Cannon, the first copycat, the Copycat Player for mimicking the MO of The Player. Little did they know at the time, they'd have three more killers terrorizing women in LA. The second killer, Cyrus Fisher, had earned the name Copycat 2.0, and they'd taunted the third copycat, Mitchell Reed, by calling him Copycat Three.

However, once they'd learned that the original serial killer, The Player, was responsible for encouraging and leading this new crop of killers, they'd decided to go back to Copycat Player for the task force name. In Jake's mind, he'd call this new guy Copycat Four. He just had no words or snappy nicknames left in his arsenal for this wave of evil.

He shook hands with the officers and then slipped on a pair of gloves. "Who discovered the body?"

Officer Llewellyn, a short stocky guy with a blond mustache, jerked a thumb over his shoulder at the emergency vehicles that had crowded the trailhead. "Two sanitation workers."

Glancing at the ground covered in a thick carpet of leaves, twigs and berries, Jake asked, "Any footprints?"

Llewellyn spoke again. "Not that we noticed, sir. No tire tracks, either, except for the sanitation truck's, but then, a car making its way down here in the middle of the night might be noticed."

"I figured he must've parked farther down and hiked here. Cameras on the parking lot?" He hadn't noticed any and Llewellyn's partner confirmed.

"No cameras, sir."

"Okay, thanks. Just keep the press out. I'm expecting my partner, and then we'll let the forensics team get to work." Jake ducked under the tape the officers had strung up between three trees and a stubby bush, keeping his eyes trained to the ground.

The officers had been correct. The thick carpet of dead plant life yielded no footprints or impressions when you walked on it. When Jake reached the lifeless body of the young brunette, he circled her. The queen of hearts protruded from her mouth and her left hand lay palm up, missing its little finger.

All the other copycats had taken their own trophies, and now the task force knew that the killers must've been sending the severed finger to The Player. He had to be getting some vicarious pleasure from this, but Jake knew the fingers from the other killers couldn't compare to the ones The Player had taken for himself twenty years ago.

He left the card in place for the crime scene photographer and crouched next to the body to verify the cause of death. With a gloved finger, he flicked a lock of hair from the woman's throat to reveal a necklace of deep purple bruising. Strangulation, but did her killer also use drugs to incapacitate her? The first copycat had relied on drugs to get women into his car. The second killer had attacked while his prey slept. The third had used the victims' natural state of intoxication to overpower them.

Footsteps crunched the ground, and Jake jerked his head to the side. Billy, dapper in a navy blue suit and pocket square, shook out a pair of gloves as he approached. His partner had obviously spent the night at his own place, and he'd had time to dress for work. They didn't call him Cool Breeze for nothing.

Stopping a few feet away from the body, Billy surveyed the area, his nostrils flaring, no doubt taking in every fallen leaf and every broken twig. Then he continued toward Jake and crouched beside him. "How's Kyra holding up?"

"She's doing okay. I told her to take the day off, but when she heard about this murder, she said Quinn would've wanted her to continue her work."

"She's probably right." Billy lifted the woman's left wrist to inspect the gaping wound on her hand, and her charm bracelet tinkled. "Bastard. Another woman murdered on The Player's orders on the very day Quinn dies. That's a slap in the face, man."

A muscle at the corner of Jake's eye throbbed. "The Player wouldn't have known about Quinn's death yet. Besides, we don't know if he's giving his minions the precise day for a killing or not."

"But we know he's directing them." Billy's jaw tensed for a second.

Jake rose, brushing his hands against his jeans. "Are there people on the task force still saying that the person orchestrating these murders is not necessarily The Player?"

Billy gave a sharp nod. "Me? I'm gonna go with Detective Roger Quinn's instincts and knowledge of the case. He made it clear that nobody could've known about the yellow diamond wedding ring missing from one of The Player's victims except The Player himself."

"Then we'll proceed accordingly, because I believe it, too." Jake pointed to the ground leading away from the body toward a denser area of the forest. "You see a little disturbance in the pattern of the detritus here?"

"If by detritus, you mean the stuff on the ground? Yeah." Billy joined him and stirred the accumulation of leaves, bark and stems with the gleaming toe of his shoe. "Not a trail, exactly, but a disturbance of some sort."

Jake followed the disruption of the material on the soil surface toward a bush, where it seemed to veer off toward the left. "Could he have walked this way for some reason?"

Billy answered, "Maybe he thought this would be a better place to dump the body and then changed his mind—too secluded."

"Maybe. I'd like to get a couple of uniforms to follow this path, if they can see it. I'm not losing my mind, am I?" Jake fingered a twig, freshly snapped from another bush. "Looks like someone went through this area not too long ago."

"You are not losing your mind. I see it, too, and you know I'm no outdoorsman skilled at tracking."

"Yeah, you're not exactly Daniel Boone." With his gaze pinned to the forest floor, Jake followed a route through the trees and bushes that someone had traversed recently. A few pieces of trash—food wrappers, a trashed sock, even a few old cigarette butts—littered the area, but the stuff had been around forever.

Billy whistled behind him. "I found something."

Jake spun around and charged toward Billy, who was holding up a piece of white paper. "It's not old, is it?"

Waving the paper, Billy said, "It's a receipt—from two days ago."

Jake clapped his partner on the back. "Daniel Boone ain't got nothing on you, brother."

KYRA SMOOTHED A hand down the thighs of her gray slacks and straightened her shoulders as she walked into LAPD's Northeast Division. It seemed weird coming here, knowing she wouldn't get to mull over her workday and the murders with Quinn later. She had a hard time remembering he was gone from her life forever.

No. She pressed a hand against her heart. He'd always be here, with her always. She sniffed and shoved her sunglasses to the top of her head. She waved at the officer manning the front desk and jogged upstairs to the task force war room.

She poked her head inside. Jake and Billy hadn't made it back from the crime scene yet, but by the way everyone buzzed around the room, she knew they had a fourth copycat killer on the loose.

As she scooted a chair up to her desk and pulled out her laptop, her phone rang. She glanced at the unknown number before she answered. "Hello?"

"Is this Kyra Chase?"

"It is. Who's this?"

The person on the other end of the line sighed. "I hoped this was the right number. This is Terrence Hicks. I'm Roger Quinn's attorney."

"Yes, I know. Quinn told me years ago he'd retained you to handle his estate planning. He gave me your card."

"I'm sorry that we finally have to meet this way. Quinn thought very highly of you…no, more than that. He loved you like a daughter."

Kyra's nose tingled again and she snatched a tissue from the box on her desk. "I—I was going to call you."

"I'm sorry to intrude on your grief, but I know Quinn would've wanted me to contact you as soon as possible." Hicks paused. "You know, Quinn left almost everything to you. You're his primary beneficiary."

"I know he wasn't that close to his sister's children, and Charlotte didn't have any nieces and nephews." Kyra chewed her bottom lip. "I suppose that means the Venice house."

"The house in Venice and the cabin in Big Bear. Back in the day, Quinn and Charlotte liked to go up to the mountains for a little skiing in the winter, a little fishing in the summer."

"I remember that cabin."

"Well, it's yours now. When can we meet, Ms. Chase? I can come out to you. There's no will to file. Quinn had a living trust, and you're the beneficiary. Clean and simple."

"Please call me Kyra." She tapped her phone's calendar and perused her appointments. She'd had two patients from her practice cancel on the same afternoon. "I have some availability tomorrow afternoon, if that works."

"I will clear my calendar for you. Quinn was my favorite client."

When she ended the call, Kyra drummed her fingers against her phone. Quinn had always told her he planned to leave her the house in Venice. She'd loved that house, but she didn't know if she'd be able to live there without Quinn or Charlotte.

She entered her appointment with Terrence Hicks into her phone and flipped open her laptop. As she launched her email, Jake and Billy strode into the room. Jake looked fresh in a charcoal suit and dark blue shirt. He and Billy must've stopped off at his place on the way over here.

Jake clapped his hands. "Listen up, everyone. Yes, it's true. We have a fourth copycat killer. Body dumped in the Angeles National Forest, no identification yet, but Cool Breeze here is going to get started on the missing person reports, and he needs a couple of people to help him. In the meantime, we found a receipt from a Walmart in Glendora—time-and date-stamped, so we can pull the video. As long as those cameras are working, we should be able to identify the owner of this receipt quickly."

Someone yelled out, "You think it's the killer?"

"Might be." Jake held up his hand. "Also, as you probably know, retired detective Roger Quinn passed away yesterday, suspected coronary. We'll keep you posted on the funeral. Let's honor Quinn and nail this guy like the others...and The Player who's giving them their marching orders. No briefing today. I gotta get going on this footage."

Kyra said a little prayer that the store's cameras would lead them right to the killer. A receipt at the dump site might not be enough to file charges, but once the detectives had someone in their sights, collecting evidence and tying that someone to the victim and the crime scene made things easier. They'd have his car and his home to search.

Several minutes later, Jake stopped by her desk and perched on the edge. "Are you doing okay? You really shouldn't be here today."

"I'm all right. I'd rather be here where Quinn had his second home than at my apartment by myself." She dabbed her nose with the crumpled tissue on her desk. "I got a call from Terrence Hicks already."

"He's fast. What did he tell you?"

"Nothing I didn't already know. Quinn had a living trust and left me everything."

"You're going to have to go through that Venice house—whether you intend to sell it or keep it. Quinn has a lot of junk in there."

She covered her eyes briefly with her hand. "I'm not looking forward to that task."

"I'll help you." Jake rapped on the top of her desk and stood up. "I'm going out to Glendora to have a look at the footage. I called the store, and they have it. They're going to pull it for me before I get there."

Kyra brought up a map of LA County on her computer and jabbed at the screen. "Glendora's not that far from the Angeles Forest. Maybe he lives in that area."

"We'll find out, and then we'll unearth everything about this guy."

She called after his squared shoulders. "Good luck."

After Jake's announcement and departure from the room, the task force members got to work. They'd gone through this routine with three other killers, and now it had become sad second nature.

Kyra still had follow-up to do with the families of the previous victims. The pain didn't evaporate just because their loved ones' killers had been apprehended and in all three cases had died. As she knew all too well, it remained a terrible wound that eventually scabbed over. Then, when you least expected it, that scab could be ripped off by a memory, a smell, a song.

Her phone buzzed and she jumped. Terrence Hicks had a few more questions for her in anticipation of their meeting. She didn't like talking to him because it brought Quinn's death home. When she worked, she could forget about yesterday, forget she had found Quinn unresponsive on the floor of his house when she and Jake were supposed to be joining him for dinner.

When she ended the call with Hicks, Captain Castillo sidled up to her desk. "Are you doing okay? Another copycat killing on the heels of Quinn's death is almost too much to take—for all of us."

"We'll get him this time, Captain…both of them, the fourth copycat and the man who's directing him."

"With Jake and Billy leading the way, I have no doubt." Castillo's already worried forehead creased further. "Are you going to plan Quinn's funeral? Contact the department if you need any help. We pull out all the stops for one of our own."

"I will, and I'm sure Terrence Hicks can assist with that, too."

Castillo's eyebrows shot up to his curly salt-and-pepper hair. "Hicks? You called Hicks already?"

Her cheeks warmed with the implication. "He called me this morning. He'd heard about Quinn's death and wanted to set up an appointment with me."

"Good." Castillo stroked his chin. "Terrence is a good guy. He'll carry out Quinn's wishes to the T. He'll know how to work with the department for the funeral, too."

Hunching forward, she said, "When is the medical examiner going to do Quinn's autopsy?"

Castillo's dark eyes widened. "I know you mentioned an autopsy before, but is it really necessary? I thought he died of a heart attack. He had a history of heart disease, a couple of stents."

"Jake told me that because of who Quinn was, they'd perform an autopsy."

Castillo asked, "Is that what you want?"

Kyra smacked a hand against her chest. "What I want? Do I have a say?"

"As the next of kin and his sole heir, I think you can request they bypass the autopsy." A muscle at the corner of Castillo's eye twitched. "Do you want the autopsy?"

"Absolutely." She wasn't going to admit to Captain Castillo that she had her suspicions about Quinn's death. Quinn did have heart disease, but he'd been doing so much better lately. The meds thinned his blood and kept his blood pressure down—even in the midst of the copycat killings. He hadn't been complaining about his health...and he'd recently made the discovery that his old nemesis, The Player, was alive and well and orchestrating a new crop of serial killers.

Nodding, Castillo turned to go. "Then you'd better talk to the ME."

Jake had never made it back for lunch, and she'd grabbed a sandwich at her desk. He still hadn't returned by the time she started packing up to leave.

She'd noticed some activity at Billy's desk earlier and sauntered across the room after shoving her laptop in its case. She hung over his shoulder as he clicked through and sorted the photos of women who'd gone missing in LA County recently.

She asked, "Any luck?"

"No and no." His cursor hovered over the face of a dark-haired beauty with innocent eyes. He dragged her photo into a folder.

"Two no's? Is that for emphasis?"

"That's a no luck in ID'ing the victim yet, and no luck with that receipt."

Her fingers curled around the back of his chair. "You heard from Jake?"

"He found the person who made that purchase and had that receipt, but it's a woman—single, no boyfriend lurking in the background."

"That's a disappointment, but it could still lead to something. What was she doing out there, or was she even out there?"

"That's what we're going to find out. Jake ID'd her from the credit card info and called her in for an interview."

"That's progress. Did she wonder what it was all about?"

Billy shrugged, not taking his eyes from the monitor. "I didn't get that far in the convo."

"Okay, I'll leave you to it." Because Billy's own sister had gone missing, he had a passionate need to identify the murder victims as soon as possible. She patted his shoulder before gathering her things.

She trailed down the stairs to the lobby of the station. The shift change had already occurred, so the activity level had tapered off down here. As Kyra waved to the desk sergeant, she eyed a young woman sitting all alone in a chair by the window, the setting sun striking her red hair, creating a little glow around her head.

The woman held a crumpled tissue in her hand and periodically dabbed her nose, which practically matched the color of her hair. She had one thin leg encased in black denim curled around her other leg. She looked like a pretzel—a sad pretzel.

With her own loss painfully fresh, Kyra felt a kindred emotion stir in her breast, and she veered from her path to the door to the bereft woman.

Kyra crouched beside her and said, "Are you all right? Can I get you something?"

The redhead jerked, dropping her sodden tissue. "N-no. I'm all right. I mean, everything's wrong, but I'm okay."

Kyra raised her brows and jerked her thumb toward the front desk. "Have you been helped?"

"Oh, yes. I told him that I was here to see Detective McAllister."

Kyra's heart leaped. This must be the owner of the receipt. She took a quick glance around the room and scooted in closer to the woman. "You're the one who lost the receipt."

The woman's eyes widened, their shade of green almost matching Jake's, and her face blanched, causing the freckles to stand out on her nose. "I—I did. Are you a cop?"

Kyra flushed and tossed back her ponytail. "No, but I'm working on the task force."

"Task force?" The woman's voice squeaked.

Kyra pressed her lips together. She'd said too much. Jake probably hadn't even told her where they'd found the receipt or why he needed to talk to her. She flicked her fingers in the air. "An LAPD task force. I know Detective McAllister. I can take you upstairs to wait for him, make you more comfortable, give you a little privacy."

"Oh, yes, please. I'd like that." She peered over her shoulder out the window, her green eyes wide. "Because I think I witnessed a murder."

Chapter Three

Jake burst through the doors of the LAPD's Northeast Division, his stride long in direct correlation to his tardiness. He tripped to a stop when his gaze stumbled across Kyra sitting on a chair next to a blubbering redhead, Kyra's arm around the other woman's shoulders. He squinted. Was this someone connected to Quinn? Looked about two generations removed from Quinn's.

His step faltered as he approached the two women. "Is everything okay?"

Kyra patted the woman's hunched back. "Piper, this is Detective McAllister. Detective, this is Piper Moss. She's your witness."

Jake's eyes narrowed. He knew damn well who Piper Moss was. He was late to their appointment. But what the hell was Kyra doing with her and...? His heart slammed against his chest. "Wait. Witness?"

"That's right." Kyra dropped her voice, although the desk sergeant was the only one who had a chance of hearing anything over the couple screaming at each other in the corner.

Kyra continued. "Piper was in the Angeles National Forest last night...where she saw someone dump a body."

Jake had to fold his arms to keep himself from rubbing his hands together. Didn't seem the right move for the moment. "Thanks for coming, Ms. Moss. Let's go upstairs."

Piper made a grab for Kyra's hand. "Can she come, too?"

Kyra *did* have a way of insinuating herself into people's lives. She'd done a damn good job infiltrating his mind, body and soul. "Of course. Kyra is a therapist and victims' rights advocate. She works closely with the department."

"I need an advocate…and you can call me Piper."

Jake ushered Kyra and Piper up the stairs ahead of him. Had Kyra been able to extract the information out of Piper that she'd been in the Angeles National Forest last night, or had Piper come here to tell him that herself? She could've claimed that the receipt fell out of her purse somewhere. Why hadn't she come forward before his call?

When they reached an interrogation room, Jake herded them inside. "Can you tell us what happened last night, Piper?"

The young woman shot a quick glance at Kyra, who gave her a barely perceptible nod. "I went to the Angeles National Forest last night to kill myself."

Jake had been scribbling on a notepad, and his pen went off the edge. "You were going to commit suicide out there?"

"Yes." Piper's lower lip trembled, and Kyra grabbed her hand with its stubby red fingernails.

"I'm sorry, Piper." Jake put down his pen. "Why would a young woman like you want to end your life?"

She lifted her narrow shoulders. "My brother died in a motorcycle accident last year, I got fired from my job a few months ago, my girlfriend broke up with me and I'm camping out on the couch of a friend. Life just sucks right now."

Jake had never been happier for Kyra's presence. Piper needed a level of comfort he didn't think he had in him. Kyra had saved him from uttering some stupid, useless homilies by offering Piper her heartfelt solace. Every word out of Kyra's mouth rang with a sincerity that couldn't be faked.

When Piper was able to meet Jake's eyes again, he said, "What were you going to do to yourself up there, Piper?"

"OD on pills." She ran a hand through her thick hair. "I know, so bourgeois."

Jake swallowed. He didn't realize methods of suicide could be categorized by class. "Are you in danger of hurting yourself now?"

"No, what happened last night made me think twice about ending my life." Her thin frame shuddered.

"What did happen last night?" He picked up his pen.

"Can I ask you one question first?"

"Go ahead."

"How did you know I'd been in the forest? I know there aren't any cameras there. I checked." She snapped her fingers. "You asked about my trip to Walmart, didn't you? You must've found my receipt."

"That's exactly what happened. We were investigating a murder this morning and found your receipt. We thought it might be our killer."

"Until you saw me on the footage, right?" She tapped her chest twice with her flattened hand. "You know I didn't kill anyone."

"I didn't think you had, but I thought you might have a husband or a boyfriend who did."

"I don't have anyone." Her lower lip protruded, and Jake held his breath, waiting for another round of sobbing.

Kyra plucked a few tissues and handed them to Piper. "You don't have anyone right now, but you're here doing something incredibly brave."

Jake cleared his throat. "Let's get back to last night. You were there to…kill yourself, and you saw someone with a body."

"That's right."

"Stop." Jake held up his hand. "Where did you park, and did you see any other cars there?"

"I parked in the lot near the trailhead, the Garcia Trail. Mine was the only car there. I wouldn't have parked there otherwise. I hiked down the trail, and was, you know, contemplating my crappy life. Then I heard noises coming from the other end of the trail, and I got scared. Weird, huh? I'm there to kill myself, but I'm afraid that someone else is going to do it first."

"Not weird at all." Jake splayed his hands on the table in front of him. "It was cloudy last night. How much did you see?"

"Not much. When I heard the person coming, I hid behind a bush. A man walked down the trail with something over his shoulder. He made a crinkling noise as he walked."

Jake cocked his head. "Crinkling?"

"I heard it when he chased me, too. Sort of sounded like a garbage bag."

"H-he saw you? He chased you?" Kyra put a hand to her throat.

Jake kept his face impassive and eased a slow breath from his mouth. "How soon after he got there did he notice you?"

"Pretty quickly. He walked up with the body over his

shoulder, looked around for a bit. He stopped in one spot, which, unfortunately for me, was right across from my bush. I must've made a sound because he jerked his head up and stared right at me."

"That's when you ran?"

"Took off like a rabbit." She tapped her fingers on the tabletop. "I got a head start on him, and I think that plastic bag he was wearing slowed him down. I was able to scramble up to my car and take off."

"You were very, very lucky."

"Gave me a new lease on life. All the stuff that happened, except for my brother, it doesn't seem so bad now. I could be that dead girl in the forest." Piper hugged herself, digging her fingers into her upper arms.

"What can you tell me about his appearance? I know it was dark, but height, weight, hair, clothing?"

Piper took a deep breath. "He was tall, or maybe that's because I was crouched down. He seemed big to me— not overweight but not skinny. He had a baseball cap on, dark, but I didn't see any words, pictures or letters on it. I couldn't see his clothes, but that's probably because he had a trash bag over his body."

Jake drilled the point of his pen into the piece of paper. That would explain why they hadn't found any fibers on the victims' clothing. "You're doing great, Piper."

Jake continued his interview with Piper. Her brush with danger had given her a new perspective on her life, so in a weird way, Copycat Four had saved a life just after he'd taken another.

Piper hadn't seen enough of the killer's face to help with a composite, so Jake slipped her a card and said, "If you remember anything else about this guy, anything at all, even if it seems minuscule, let me know."

"He's not going to know—" Piper glanced at Kyra "—I mean, nobody's going to know that I saw him, right?"

Jake shook his head. "I have no intention of telling the press that we have a witness."

"Okay, I feel better." She slumped in her chair. "That's why I didn't call the police to tell them what I saw. I was afraid. When I saw the news later that a body had been found right where I was, I figured I better tell someone. Really. I'm not just saying that because you called me first."

"I understand. It must've been frightening, but you're here now and you've been a big help."

"It's not just because I was scared, either. I didn't want to admit what I was doing there." Piper shoved a thumbnail between her teeth and worried it.

"Call me anytime, day or night, if you have those feelings again." Kyra added her card to Jake's. "What pills were you going to use? Do you still have them?"

"Some antianxiety meds I've been on and off since my brother's death." Piper unzipped the purse slung across her body and resting in her lap. She shoved her hand into the largest compartment. "I do still have them, but I haven't even taken one after my...encounter last night."

"I'm not saying you shouldn't have them if you legitimately need them for anxiety, but maybe you don't need to have so many of them. Are you currently seeing a psychiatrist?"

"No." Piper's eyebrows collided over her nose as she dug deeper into her purse. "My regular doctor prescribes them."

Piper swung her purse onto the table and dumped the contents. She began pawing through loose change, tubes of lipstick, a sticky breath mint and receipts. No wonder she'd lost one from her purse.

"Are you looking for your pills?" Kyra asked.

Her hands still splayed in the hodgepodge of items from her bag, Piper looked up, her eyes glassy and wide. "They should be here. They were in my purse last night, and I hadn't even left my friend's couch today until I came here."

Kyra slid a glance at Jake. "Could they be in your car?"

"My purse was zipped. I just opened that part of it now. I left my sunglasses in the car, and my keys and phone are in the outside pocket." Her chewed fingernails clawed into the table. "I dropped them there. I must've lost them last night. I remember I had them. I'd taken them out of my purse and when I heard that freak coming, I shoved them back into my purse. I bet I missed the opening and then I didn't zip up my purse and that's how the receipt flew out. I left my pill bottle there. Did you find it?"

Jake's mind had been racing along with Piper's narrative. "Just the receipt."

Grabbing the roots of her hair with both hands, Piper moaned and rocked forward. "He has them. He found them. He knows who I am."

"We don't know that for sure." Kyra rubbed a circle on Piper's back. "Jake?"

"We didn't find a pill bottle there. Otherwise, we would've been able to ID you a lot faster than through that receipt." Jake didn't bother to point out that Piper's address wouldn't be on that prescription label, but there would be enough information on it to track her down for someone savvy enough with computers or devious enough—and they knew this guy was both.

"Because he took it. He took it." Piper shoved the items on the table back into her purse, her hands shaking so badly that half the stuff wound up on the floor.

As Kyra bent over to pick up the items, Jake said, "Even if he gets your address, and I'm not saying he can't or won't, you're no longer living there, right? He's not going to track you down to your friend's house."

"My girlfriend still lives at my old place. The condo is in both our names." Piper grabbed her phone and scrolled through the display. "I've been trying to reach Erica all day. I wasn't too worried before because she keeps telling me not to call or text her and I've been trying to let her go, but I wanted to let her know what happened last night—not the suicide part, but the rest of it."

"We'll notify her." Jake kept his own voice calm in the face of Piper's rising hysteria and his own uneasiness.

"Forget that. I need to see her now. I need to warn her to be careful." Piper jumped up from the table, and her chair fell back.

"We're not going to let you go there alone. Right, Detective?" Kyra tipped her head toward the door.

Jake grabbed his notepad and pushed back from the table. Had he expected his day to end any differently? "Where's the condo?"

"I-it's in West Hollywood. Are you coming?"

"We're taking you there."

On the drive over, Kyra tried to talk Piper down, but the young woman's agitation increased the closer they got to the condo until she was practically bouncing around the back seat.

Jake parked in front of the pink stucco building on a street that housed similar condo complexes converted from apartments. He twisted in his seat. "Piper, you stay here with Kyra. I'll check on Erica and let her know what's going on. If she wants to talk with you, I'll call Kyra and you can come up. The way things stand between you two, we don't need to add a domestic dispute to your life."

When he got Piper's assent in the form of a sniffle and a drop of her head, Jake exited his vehicle and walked between the two stately palm trees that guarded the front door of the building. He buzzed the number Piper gave him, but nobody replied. He was about to use Piper's key on the front door when two men walking out held it open for him. So much for security.

He cruised past a bank of brass mailboxes and a few potted palms on his way to the elevator and rode it up to the third floor. A carpet hushed his footsteps as he read the numbers on the doors on his way down the hallway. When he reached Erica's, he knocked and took a step back, standing in full view of the peephole. As he fished his badge from his front pocket, he glanced down and noticed a dark scuff at the bottom of the door. He ran a finger along the doorjamb, looking for a break or splintered wood.

He knocked again, calling out, "Erica? I'm a detective with the LAPD. I need to talk to you."

He pulled Piper's key chain from his pocket. She was still on the title, and she'd given him permission to enter. He rapped his knuckles against the door again as he pushed it open.

His heart pounded when he stepped on some broken glass. As he ventured another few steps into the living room, his eye tracked from the upended coffee table to the lamp on its side to a cracked picture on the floor.

Erica had put up a good fight. His gaze rested on the body splayed across the couch.

She'd lost.

Chapter Four

Kyra scrambled after Piper, her high-heeled boots doing her no favors, as Piper dashed up the stairwell of the condo building.

Jake could be having a civilized conversation with Erica right now and Piper's appearance might upset everything. Kyra's heels clanged on the steps after Piper's sure-footed ascent on a pair of Chucks. She heard the fire door squeal open above her, and she cursed silently. Jake had given her one job to do—keep Piper in the car.

The door slammed shut, the sound ringing down the stairwell. Panting, Kyra scaled the final staircase from the second to the third floor and shoved open the fire door. As she burst into the hallway, she saw Piper stumbling backward from the open door of a unit, her hands clapped over her mouth.

Despite the fear coursing through Kyra's body and weakening her knees, she raced forward, her heart hammering in her chest. As she drew closer to Piper, the woman dropped her hands and screamed through her gaping mouth.

Jake shot out into the hallway and hovered over Piper. "Don't go in there. You don't need to look at her. I've called 911."

Doors up and down the hallway either cracked or flew open, and heads popped out of the condos.

Jake waved his hands. "Police business. Stay inside for now, please."

When Kyra reached Piper, the younger woman threw herself into Kyra's arms and sobbed. "She's dead. She's dead. It's all my fault. I should've told her."

Meeting Jake's flashing eyes over Piper's head, Kyra murmured, "You couldn't have known. Nobody knew."

The phone Jake gripped in his hand rang, and he pivoted back into the condo. After speaking for a few seconds, he shouted over his shoulder. "The first responders are here. I'm going to let them up."

Piper shook her head. "It's no use. She's dead."

Squeezing Piper's arm, Kyra said, "They need to process the scene. They'll find this guy. Let's wait somewhere else while they do their jobs."

"I'm not leaving her." Piper dug her heels into the carpet and flattened her hands against the wall behind her.

The elevator dinged and the doors opened on two sheriff's deputies from West Hollywood and two EMTs.

Kyra waved at them from down the hall. "Over here."

Jake plunged back into the condo ahead of them, and Kyra could see him through the door talking to the deputies. This area belonged to the LA County Sheriff's Department, not the LAPD, but as Copycat Four was most likely Erica's killer, the task force would be involved.

With Jake no longer present, giving orders, a few of the residents wandered into the hallway and peppered Kyra with questions, as they stared at Piper pacing back and forth.

Kyra stopped twisting her fingers into knots and tried to look authoritative. "There's been an accident. The police will talk to you later."

Maybe someone had seen or heard something. Kyra had only gotten a peek into Erica's place, but it looked like there'd been some disruption. The killer had been reckless coming after who he thought was Piper, so he must've been desperate to shut her up.

The police would have to keep quiet about the motivation for this murder and never let the killer know he'd murdered the wrong woman. His witness was still alive and if not exactly well, she'd be out for vengeance.

Piper's mental state worried Kyra. The young woman had already been through so much. Would the death of Erica lead her to another suicide attempt? Piper hadn't seemed too serious about the first attempt, but you could never tell.

More cops poured out of the elevator, and one duo began approaching the neighbors. Kyra tried to tune in, but she couldn't hear their conversation other than a few gasps and a few mentions of Erica's name. She peered into the corner near the elevator and noticed the camera.

As Piper careened past her for the hundredth time, Kyra caught her arm. "Your car's still at the station. Can you call a friend? We can give you a ride home if you want to leave your car there. You shouldn't be alone."

Piper broke away from her and sank to the floor, her head on her knees.

Finally, Jake peeled away from the scene inside the condo. "We can take Piper back to her friend's place."

"That's what I told her." Kyra tipped her head toward the knots of people clustered up and down the hallway. "Did anyone hear anything?"

Jake dipped his head to hers. "Time of death appears to be in the afternoon. A lot of these people were working. The one guy who works at home is a film editor and had headphones on most of the day. One or two people work a night shift and could've been home during the time of the murder. We'll talk to them later."

"Did you notice the cameras?"

"Sheriff's department is on it now. They're going to send the footage to the task force tomorrow." His gaze slid to Piper on the floor, her chin to her chest, arms wrapped about her legs, and he whispered, "She needs to move."

"I'll get her going."

After much coaxing and assurances, Kyra and Jake convinced Piper to leave the building and got her back to the station. Her friend met them there and followed her back to his place after assuring Kyra he'd keep an eye on her.

Kyra slumped in her chair at her desk. "Did you ever think tracking down the owner of that receipt would lead to this?"

"It must've happened just as Piper said." Jake ran a hand through his hair. "She dropped her prescription bottle, the killer found it, tracked down her address and killed the person living there—only he killed the wrong person."

"I didn't want to ask you in front of Piper, but did he commit the murder like a copycat?" She folded her arms and tucked her hands at her sides. "Strangulation, playing card, severed finger?"

"Nope. I'm guessing he didn't want us to connect this murder with his ritualistic ones. Although he did strangle Erica, he used a cord instead of his hands. Looks like he stole some cash from her purse, probably to throw us off. He may not realize we've even spoken to Piper. We certainly haven't announced there was a witness this time."

"Do you intend to keep that out of the press?"

"As much as possible." Jake ambled back to his desk to pack up for the night.

They'd been gone so long with Piper, they had the Copycat Player task force room all to themselves. Now Kyra just wanted to get home and prepare for her meeting with Terrence Hicks tomorrow. "Does it look like Copycat Four might've left some evidence at Erica's place?"

"He left a mess. That's for sure. I'm counting on something to turn up." Jake hitched his bag over his shoulder. "The killer got in deep when he broke one of The Player's rules, one The Player never broke himself...leave no witnesses."

THE FOLLOWING DAY, Kyra didn't go into the station. She had clients to see at her office in Santa Monica. She'd been able to move one afternoon appointment to the morning to clear her schedule for Hicks, and now she checked the clock on her desk to see if she'd have time to pick up something to eat before Hicks's arrival at her apartment. She'd crammed all her work into the first half of the day and had missed lunch completely.

She'd offered to meet Hicks at his office in Century City, but he told her Quinn would be scowling down at him if he didn't make everything as easy as possible on her.

Jake had been able to contact the medical examiner on her behalf this morning to make sure he'd be performing an autopsy on Quinn. He'd assured Jake that was his plan all along. Not that Kyra expected a different cause of death from the heart disease that had plagued Quinn for the past several years, but what kind of detective's daughter would she be if she didn't make sure?

On the short drive from her office to her apartment, Kyra cruised past a deli and picked up a turkey sandwich.

She ordered a second for Hicks, just in case. Quinn would be scowling down on *her* if she didn't treat his attorney right. She still couldn't believe she'd lost the only father she'd ever known, and her eyes blurred with tears on the rest of her way home.

When she got to her apartment, she shooed Spot, the stray cat, away from her door, dumped her purse on the low wall that separated her kitchen from the entryway, and placed a notepad, pen and her laptop on the coffee table.

As she wolfed down her sandwich and a diet soda, she kept her eye on the security footage from her phone. Jake had insisted she install security cameras around her apartment after The Player had gotten too close for comfort.

She didn't know the person taunting her with remnants of her past was The Player until recently, and the knowledge had made the teasing more sinister and frightening. He'd never attempted to physically harm her, but he hadn't put physical violence behind him. He'd killed twice to protect his interests—a homeless woman in Santa Monica who had done his bidding and a true crime blogger who'd gotten too close to one of The Player's copycats. Had he killed Erica, too? Had Jake even thought of that possibility?

When the doorbell rang, she jumped even though Terrence Hicks was right on time and she could see him standing at her door from her phone. She balled up the waxy paper from her sandwich and tossed it in the trash.

She opened the door on the compact attorney, his fit frame outfitted in a navy-blue suit, his bald pate gleaming and a tidy goatee accentuating his chin. He looked exactly like his pictures on the internet.

He thrust out his hand. "Ms. Chase, I'm Terrence

Hicks. It's a pleasure to finally meet you after hearing about you from Quinn these past ten years."

"Kyra, remember?" She invited him inside and offered him the sandwich, which he declined, and a diet soda, which he accepted.

She popped the tab on the can in the kitchen and poured the fizzing liquid over some ice in a glass as Terrence settled on the couch. She carried the drink to him and said, "Is this okay? We can work on the kitchen table if that's easier."

"This is fine." He took the glass from her hand and placed it on a coaster. Then he opened his own laptop next to hers and plopped a thick folder onto his lap. "Quinn did everything right. All his assets are in a living trust, and you are the sole beneficiary, except for a few charitable concerns and small items. His most valuable asset was his home in Venice, which, as you can imagine, is worth over two million dollars—and it's paid off."

Kyra glanced around the small apartment she'd been renting for more than five years. Should she move into Quinn's house? She pinned her hands between her knees. She couldn't imagine being there without him.

The transfer of Quinn's assets went smoothly. She signed where Terrence told her to sign, made a few decisions regarding taxes and even discussed Quinn's funeral arrangements. Terrence had all the right contacts at the LAPD and had already set things in motion.

An hour later, Terrence began to stuff the papers and legal documents back into his briefcase and mentioned Jake's name.

Kyra jerked her head up from shuffling through her own set of documents Terrence was leaving with her. "What about Jake?"

"Quinn altered his trust recently, leaving a few items to J-Mac. I haven't called him yet, but I plan to do that today."

"Quinn left Jake something in his will?" Kyra raised her eyebrows as she collected Terrence's empty glass. "He really *did* have expectations for us."

Terrence cracked a smile, his teeth white against his dark face. "I told you. Quinn had your future all mapped out for you."

"What did Quinn leave him, or am I not allowed to ask that?"

"A few weapons." Terrence reached into his briefcase and pulled out an envelope. "And this. I do have to place this in Jake's hand and I don't know what's in it, but I have some business at the Northeast Division and I can give it to him there."

She eyed the envelope suspiciously. "Ugh, I hope there's not some sort of care and feeding of Kyra Chase in there."

Terrence chuckled as he slipped the envelope in a side pocket of his bag. "It might be. Quinn worried about you."

"I know, and all that time I should've been worrying about him." Kyra pressed a fist against her lips to stop the sob that threatened to escape.

Terrence placed a hand on her shoulder and gave it a gentle squeeze. "You took good care of Quinn. He told me himself."

"Thank you, Terrence. I'll be in touch about the funeral. The ME is doing an autopsy."

"I figured as much."

She walked Terrence to the door, and he stopped suddenly, digging into the pocket of his jacket. "I forgot to give you the keys to the houses."

"I have my own key to the house in Venice."

"I know that, but this makes it official." He dangled a key chain from his fingers and dropped it into her waiting palm. "Let me know what you plan to do with the house—move in or sell it. No hurry."

"Good, because I'll have to think about it."

When the attorney left, Kyra shook out some kibble into a bowl for the missing Spot, who'd left in a huff after she'd shunned him. As she passed through the kitchen, she snatched the extra sandwich from the fridge and curled up in front of the TV with a glass of wine.

Then she put on the next episode of the show she and Quinn had been watching together—a show he'd never finish—and drank deeply.

"WHAT DID HICKS WANT?" Captain Castillo strolled into the nearly empty task force war room and sat on the edge of Billy's desk. "Plans for Quinn's funeral?"

Jake glanced up from the thick envelope Hicks had left him, Quinn's bold writing scrawled across the front, and dropped it on his desk. "Yeah, we talked about that. There's a lot to do, but Hicks has gone through this before for other clients."

He didn't want to read any last words Quinn had for him in front of the captain.

Castillo's gaze flicked to the envelope before meeting Jake's eyes. "West Hollywood Sheriff's Department hasn't come up with much at the scene of Erica Fuentes's murder, have they?"

"They sent the footage over, and the guy knew he was on camera, because he avoided it as much as possible and wore a thick jacket, a hat and a hoodie. Can't tell much from that. He did have a box in his hands, as if he were a delivery guy. Maybe that's how he got her to open the door, and then he kicked it open once she cracked it. We don't see anything again until he leaves with the box under his arm and is able to avoid the cameras on his way out of the building. We checked for parking tickets on the street during that time, canvassed the neighbors, looked at other footage in the area—nothing."

Castillo picked at a cuticle. "You ever think this might be The Player cleaning up for one of his minions, like he did with that crime blogger?"

"Billy and I thought about it. Could be, but that still doesn't give us any more evidence than what we got."

"How's the real witness?"

"Hanging on. Kyra spoke with her over the phone today. She's more upset about the death of her girlfriend now than she is about witnessing that body dump." Jake shrugged into his jacket.

Castillo hopped off the desk. "Kyra doing okay?"

"She's fine. She wants to go to Quinn's house tomorrow, which I think is a little too soon, but once she makes up her mind, there's no stopping her. I guess it's progress. At first, she didn't think she'd ever be able to return to that house."

"That's a prime piece of property."

"It is." Jake raised his brows at the unusually loquacious captain, hoping he'd take the hint to wrap it up.

Castillo said, "I'll let you get going. Long days for everyone. Your daughter doing okay after the kidnapping?"

Jake swept Quinn's envelope from the desk and tucked it in the inside pocket of his jacket. "She's recovered. Maybe even learned a lesson or two—I know her mother and I learned a few things about social media accounts."

"It's a tough age. Not looking forward to going through that stage with my two youngest. When my older kids were teens, social media wasn't as pervasive."

"Gotta keep vigilant." Castillo was on his second marriage and had two young kids with this wife, although his older daughter was married and expecting Castillo's first grandchild. Jake had missed a lot of Fiona's childhood years, but was eager to experience it all with his and Kyra's children—if he could persuade her to go down that path with him.

Finally, Castillo made a move, and Jake walked out of the room with him, waving to a few of the officers staying behind. Everyone on a task force had a job to do, and some of that work was better suited to a quiet office and quiet phones.

Castillo peeled off at his own office, and Jake jogged down the stairs and exited the building. Before getting into his car, he sloughed off his jacket and snatched the envelope from the pocket. He slid behind the steering wheel of his unmarked sedan and slipped his thumb beneath the sealed flap of the envelope.

He pulled out several sheets of paper. One listed a description of some weapons Quinn was leaving to Jake. The second page contained a note from Quinn. In the note, Quinn explained to Jake that he had some files related to The Player locked away in a safe. He'd ended the note with a cryptic statement about how Jake would understand why he kept the file a secret once Jake looked through it.

The crease between Jake's eyebrows deepened when he got to the third sheet. He smoothed the paper over the steering wheel and studied the map Quinn had sketched—a real, live treasure map. Only X didn't mark the spot out in the desert or even in a storage unit like Kyra's foster brother had kept.

Quinn had buried his treasure under the floorboards of his house in Venice. Even more mysterious was Quinn's final directive that Jake not tell Kyra about this file. Jake's mouth got dry. It must be something horrendous about her mother's murder Quinn had never told her.

He'd follow Quinn's instructions to a T, but he'd have to figure out how he was going to lift up some floorboards in a room in a house that Kyra now owned.

THE FOLLOWING EVENING, after a full day of work and a quick bite to eat from a fish market on the Santa Monica Pier, Jake drove Kyra to Quinn's house to start looking around. Kyra wasn't planning to start packing up anything, but she did want to find a nice suit for Quinn's burial and get a feel for whether she could live in the house.

Jake didn't press the issue, but he was hoping she'd start thinking about the idea of moving in with him. She could still hang on to the Venice house and rent it out— but this wasn't the time or the place.

He parked his car as close to the canal walk streets as he could, conscious of Quinn's map tucked in the back pocket of his jeans as they crossed the bridge to the red door of Quinn's house—Kyra's house.

With shaky fingers, she inserted the key and turned the handle. Jake reached around her to push open the door.

Kyra hesitated on the threshold, clutching the key chain at her side, her gaze glued to the spot where they'd discovered Quinn's body.

Jake nudged her back gently. "I'm right behind you."

He followed her into the living room, and his nose twitched at the air, already musty even though the house had been empty just a few days. He didn't detect any odor of death and released a pent-up breath. "I'm going to open some windows and the back door just to get some air in here."

On his way to a window to yank up the sash, he glanced down at the hardwood floor beneath a throw rug in front of the fireplace—Quinn's secret hiding place.

As he grabbed the window, Kyra gasped behind him and he spun around.

Standing in front of a built-in bookcase, Kyra turned to him, her eyes wide and her face pale. "Someone's been here, Jake. Someone broke into Quinn's house."

Chapter Five

Jake's eyebrows jumped to his hairline, but his face didn't reflect the panic she felt clawing at her chest. Didn't he see? If someone broke into Quinn's place, maybe that person was also responsible for Quinn's death.

Surveying the room, Jake said, "What makes you say that? Everything's shut up tight, or it was until I opened this window. The dead bolt on the front door was locked, wasn't it?"

She chewed her bottom lip and grabbed the two pictures from the bookcase. She thrust them in front of her. "These were out of place."

"Two pictures were out of place on a shelf and you jump to break-in?" Jake cocked his head. "That's a big leap. How do you know Quinn didn't rearrange them or move them to get a book?"

"I feel it." Her gaze darted around the room, alighting on cushions tucked into the corners of the couch, a blank pad of paper next to Quinn's landline phone, the corner of the throw rug in front of the mantel turned back—slight differences around the room that made the hair on the back of her neck quiver.

"Let me check the sliding back door." He strode toward Quinn's little dining area and checked the handle and the track of the door where Quinn had an extra lock inserted. "Both in place, just like I left them."

He yanked open the slider, and a cloud of salty sea air wafted into the room. "Remember, I checked all the doors and windows the night Quinn died. There was no sign of any break-in, Kyra."

"I know that. I remember." Clasping her hands in front of her, she did a turn in place. "I can't put my finger on it. The room feels different…ruffled."

Planting his hands on the kitchen table, Jake hunched forward. "Different from usual or different from the last time you were here…when we found Quinn?"

"That's it." She folded her arms and hunched her shoulders. "At first, I thought someone had broken in and killed Quinn."

Jake's mouth dropped open, and she continued to talk over him. "But now that I'm looking around, the differences I'm noticing are since our previous visit when we discovered Quinn's body."

"You think someone broke into Quinn's house and ruffled a few items after he died? Have you checked to see if anything has been stolen? Could be a tweaker or something, knowing the house is empty." Jake walked back into the living room and stood before the fireplace, his arms crossed, his feet planted on the rug.

"He has a safe in his bedroom closet. You wanted to look at that anyway, right? You told me Quinn had left you some weapons. Those would be in that safe."

"Do you have the combination with you?"

Kyra patted her purse. "I brought some of that info with me—including what should be in the safe. I think two of the guns he left to you are in there."

"I know he has a Makarov 9mm in there, a classic, and

a German Luger." Jake peered around the room. "You don't see anything missing? Where's Quinn's computer?"

"He always used a desktop computer because he liked the monitor size, and he kept that in his office. This house has three bedrooms and two bathrooms. Besides his bedroom, one he kept as a guest room, and he turned the other into an office." She crooked her finger at Jake. "This way."

Her breathing had returned to normal once she realized she hadn't felt this disruption in Quinn's house the night he died, but only now. Of course, that night had been a whirlwind of emotions, and maybe she hadn't been attuned to the changes.

Jake followed her down the hallway, and she ducked into the first bedroom on the left. Quinn's computer sat on a desk with some sticky notes fluttering off the edges of the monitor and some bits of paper dotting the surface area of the desk.

Shuffling the mouse to wake up the computer, she said, "I know he didn't have this password-protected."

When the monitor came to life, Jake jabbed a finger at the tabs at the top of the browser. "Looks like Quinn was on Websleuths, the true crime site where The Player met his minions, and Sean Hughes's true crime blog, *LA Confidential*. He was following along with the investigation more than we thought."

"More than *you* thought." She clicked on the *LA Confidential* blog, which displayed the article where Hughes had outed her as the daughter of one of The Player's victims and detailed her troubled past as the killer of one of her foster fathers—in self-defense. Hughes had also functioned as the conduit between Jake and the third copycat, and had been murdered for his trouble.

She closed the browser and all the tabs with a click

of the mouse. "We know his computer wasn't stolen.
Doesn't mean someone didn't look at his files. Like I
said, no password."

"Safe?" Jake jerked his thumb over his shoulder.

Kyra brushed past him and led him to the master bedroom, where Quinn had still slept in the king-size bed
he'd shared with Charlotte. He'd admitted to Kyra once
that he still left room for his wife on the left side, as if
he expected her to be there one morning.

Blinking back tears, Kyra flicked the light switch
on the outside of the walk-in closet and yanked open
the door. Quinn had left one whole side of this closet
empty, too, after Kyra had helped him pack up Charlotte's
clothes. Now she'd have to do the same for his.

"The safe's in the corner, bolted to the floor." She
fished a piece of paper from the purse strapped across
her body. "I have the combination."

Jake held out his hand. "Let me."

"Are you afraid something's going to jump out at me?"
She held on to the paper for a second before slapping it
into his palm. "Go for it."

Jake crouched before the safe with the combination in
one hand. He read out the numbers as he punched them
into the keypad. A little scale of notes trilled, and a small
display flashed green.

"Just like a hotel safe." As Jake paused, she nudged
him in the back with her knee. "You *are* nervous about
opening the safe."

"Just hoping those pieces are still in here." He pulled
open the door of the safe and plunged his hand inside.
"Guns, cash and a few envelopes. Do you want me to
take it all out?"

"Yes, please. I'm guessing one of those envelopes has

info about his living trust and Terrence's phone number." She backed out of the closet. "Bring it out to the bed."

Jake emerged from the closet clutching several items to his chest with one arm, his other arm at his side with an old-fashioned-looking gun dangling from his fingertips. "The man was true to his word."

"Those are the weapons you expected to see in there?"

"They are." He dropped the contents of Quinn's safe on the neatly made-up bed and ran his hand along the barrel of one of the guns. "This piece is worth a lot of money. If you'd rather sell it and take the money, that's okay."

"That is most definitely *not* okay. Quinn cherished those guns, and that's why he wanted you to have them." She pushed three bundles of bills to the side and picked up one of the envelopes. She peeked inside, thumbing through some papers. "As I expected—instructions for his trust and Terrence's business card, which Quinn had given me some time ago."

"And the other envelope?" Jake made a grab for the envelope as she reached for it. He eyed the contents and let out a long breath. "Banking information, which I'm sure Hicks already has."

Kyra consulted a sheet of paper she'd pulled out of her purse. "Guns and cash. That's what he indicated, so it's all here."

"Nothing's been stolen from the house." Jake lifted his shoulders. "I think you're being fanciful about the idea that someone's been here. It's your mind playing tricks on you because Quinn's gone."

She sucked in her lower lip, and Jake dropped the gun he'd been caressing to the bed and took her in his arms. "Are you sure this isn't too soon for you? Let's grab Quinn's suit and get out of here for now. I can pour you a glass of wine and give you a nice massage."

Curling her arms around his neck, she planted a kiss on his mouth. "I'm so glad you're with me. Heart disease or no heart disease, I don't think Quinn could've ever left me unless he felt sure someone could protect me and make me happy—someone like you."

Jake ran a hand through the loose strands of her hair. "Quinn has nothing to worry about. I'm right by your side."

His warmth enveloped her, and she murmured against his solid chest. "So, Quinn didn't leave you instructions for my care and feeding? You're doing it of your own free will?"

Jake's frame stiffened in her arms, and she poked his side. "He *did* leave you instructions."

He backed out of her embrace and pinched her chin. "Don't be ridiculous. I told you. He left me descriptions of the two guns he wanted me to have. He already knew I'd be here to love and protect you."

"How'd I get so lucky?" She plucked at his shirt. "I'm going to dive back into the closet and collect Quinn's good suit. We can come back later to clean house. I—I may need some time before I can get to that."

"Take all the time you need, babe." He hoisted his two new pieces. "I'll put these back in the safe. What do you want to do with the cash? Looks like there's a bundle, couple grand at least."

"You can put that back, too. I'm thinking of giving it to that boxing gym here in Venice. Quinn had mentored a few of those young men who worked out there a couple of years ago." She wiped her nose with the back of her hand. "I think he'd like that."

"I think so, too." Jake flicked on the light to the walk-in closet and carried the guns and the cash to the back.

As he crouched in front of the safe, Kyra bumped him

with her knees. "Sorry. I'm trying to get around you to the blue suit in the plastic. Thank goodness he had that dry-cleaned recently. I believe the last time he wore it was for the funeral of that officer who was ambushed in Crenshaw. He probably never imagined his next time would be for his own funeral."

"Quinn always paid his respects. There will be a huge turnout for his funeral." Still on his haunches, Jake shifted out of her way and then stood up. "This closet's too small for the both of us. You get the suit and I'll lock up the windows and doors I opened."

As Jake slipped out of the closet, the empty hangers on Charlotte's side of the closet clacked and swayed, and the cellophane plastic protecting Quinn's suit whispered between her fingertips. Kyra swallowed and lifted the hanger from the rod. She carried the suit from the closet and laid it across the bed. Then she dipped back into the closet to look for a shirt, tie and shoes.

While she packed up the items on the bed, Jake appeared in the doorway of the bedroom. "The house is locked up. Do you want some help with that?"

"Yes, please." Kyra zipped up the garment bag and hoisted a small overnight suitcase over her shoulder. "I suppose I bring this stuff to the mortuary. I don't even have a mortuary."

Covering her face with her hands, she sank to the edge of the bed. "I don't know what I'm going to do."

The bed dipped as Jake sat beside her and draped an arm over her shoulder. "You do know what to do. You're doing it. You move ahead and think about and grieve for Quinn while you're doing it."

With Jake's help, she made it out of the house in one piece. As she walked past Quinn's neighbors, who had a gathering of friends in their front yard, one of the guys raised his beer and called out. "To Quinn."

The rest followed his lead, and Quinn's name echoed along the canal.

Kyra raised her hand. The night of Quinn's death, she'd resisted the urge to question his neighbors. The scene hadn't looked suspicious to the responding officers, nor to Jake, so they didn't canvass the neighborhood asking questions. The neighbors had known that Quinn passed, so if they'd had anything to report, they would've done so…right?

By the time they reached her apartment just about five miles away from Quinn's house, a lethargy had seeped into Kyra's bones. She could barely brush her teeth and pull the covers back on her bed.

As she drifted off, she could hear Jake putting away Quinn's things in her spare bedroom, taking out the trash and feeding Spot.

Kyra snuggled into her pillow, her eyes heavy.

Jake hovered over her, his breath warm on her cheek, and she felt a stab of guilt that she didn't want to make love. Maybe Jake thought she needed that closeness right now. Maybe she did.

She rolled onto her back and reached for him. "Coming to bed?"

"You looked so peaceful, I was going to let you sleep and then sneak out."

Her lashes fluttered, and she saw that he was still fully dressed. "I didn't mean to shut you out. You can spend the night. I thought you would."

"It's not that late, and I don't have any work clothes here." He brushed the hair from her eyes. "But I'll stay if you want me to."

"You're right." She aimed a blurry-eyed squint at her

digital alarm clock on her nightstand. "It's not late at all—just feels like it. You can leave. Then you can go straight to work in the morning. I'll be okay."

"Are you sure?"

"I'm half asleep anyway." She cupped his strong jaw with her hand. "I'll see you tomorrow. Thanks for everything."

He kissed her hungrily. "Everything's locked up. Security systems are on."

"I'm fine. I'll see you tomorrow."

He kissed her again and then slipped from her room like a thief in the night. The best kind of thief, as he'd completely stolen her heart.

JAKE GOT BEHIND the wheel of his car and tossed Quinn's key chain in the cup holder. Quinn didn't want Kyra to know about the second bequest, and that involved a little subterfuge. Kyra's mood had made things a little easier for him. He'd have a hard time making love to Kyra knowing he planned to sneak to Quinn's behind her back.

He'd plotted ahead—leaving the safe in the closet unlocked to give himself an excuse to go back. But he hadn't needed it. The events of the past few days had drained Kyra. His poor baby couldn't even keep her eyes open.

Jake took the route down Lincoln back to Quinn's house. He parked on the street and launched into Quinn's neighborhood on the Venice canals. He crossed the water lilting against its manmade barrier as the wooden bridge huffed and wheezed. Quinn's rowdy neighbors had called it a night. Kyra had told him the guy next to Quinn was the drummer from an '80s rock band that still did reunion tours. Nice work if you could get it.

Jake reached Quinn's red door and used the key to let himself in. He turned on a lamp and studied the neat room. Had Kyra's sensitivity played tricks with her mind, or had someone really gotten in here after Quinn's death for a search? What could they be searching for? Kyra had already confirmed nothing of value was missing, although a former homicide detective like Quinn could possess many more valuables than cash, jewelry and electronics—and Jake was about to uncover one of those items.

He withdrew Quinn's map from his pocket and shook it out. The old detective must've gotten a little melodramatic in his old age, as he probably could've described the location of the floorboard with words just as well as pictures.

Kneeling by the fireplace, Jake flipped back the throw rug, which looked an awful lot like those pillows Kyra had on her couch. He checked the map in the light from his cell phone and counted the floorboards from the edge of the fireplace.

He pressed on the edges of the wood slats until he felt a rim, and then pulled a knife from his pocket. He slid the blade along the edges and lifted.

About ten minutes later, he had a pile of wood pieces at his elbow and a gaping hole in the floor. His nose twitched as he aimed his light into the crevasse, the odor of brine strong. Something gleamed when the beam of his light hit it. He reached in with one hand and curled his fingers around the hard edge of a metal box.

With cobwebs clinging to his hand, he pulled it out. He balanced the slim container on his palms and blew dust from its surface. He sneezed. If someone *had* gotten into Quinn's house, he or she hadn't gotten this far.

Clutching the metal container, Jake backed up to Quinn's recliner. He sank into the chair and turned on the lamp next to it.

The container looked like something you might use for classified documents. It had an actual locking device on it, but Quinn had provided Jake with the combination, just as he'd left the combination to the safe in the closet for Kyra.

Jake held the piece of paper beneath the yellow glow of the lamp and memorized the numbers. His fingers played across the surface of the lockbox, entering the combination.

When it clicked, he hesitated. Holding his breath, he opened the lid on the box. His gaze alighted on a plain manila envelope with no label on the outside.

He used his fingernails to bend the clasp, still firm, still in place. He lifted the flap and pulled out a sheaf of papers. His eyebrows collided over his nose.

He held in his hands a crime scene report, yellowed at the corners. It resembled the ones the LAPD used today with a few alterations.

His pulse jumped when he read the date and location at the top of the page. Why did Quinn have a copy of the crime scene report of Jennifer Lake's murder holed up in his floor?

He flipped through the pages at the top. He'd read the report of Kyra's mother's murder many times before. So many times, in fact, he practically had it memorized— that's how he spotted some minor differences. Time, body condition and location were all the same, but there were slight changes from the original. Or was this the original?

He continued shuffling through the pages until he got to the end with a description of the child, Kyra, at the scene. Jake skimmed down that page and then sat up, his heart beating erratically in his chest.

He'd just spotted a huge difference from the original report. The child, Marilyn Lake, had not been in the bedroom when the officer, patrolman Carlos Castillo, arrived. She'd been sitting beside the dead body of her mother, the phone from the 911 call still clutched in her hand.

Furthermore, the child hadn't been asleep in her bed when The Player had killed her mother. She'd been peering at him from a crack in her bedroom door.

Kyra Chase had witnessed her mother's murder. She'd seen The Player with her own two eyes.

Chapter Six

A day later Jake stared at the stills from the condo's security cameras with unseeing eyes.

Kyra witnessed her mother's murder. She'd seen The Player. Quinn knew all along. The words kept thrumming through his head on a nonstop loop.

Did Kyra remember? No. That's why Quinn had hidden the file under his floorboards. She didn't remember what she saw as a child, and Quinn never told her she'd been a witness. Quinn never told anyone. The department never knew, the press never knew and The Player himself never knew. Or did he?

Jake ran a hand across his mouth. Was that why The Player had kept tabs on Kyra all these years? He knew he'd left a witness and had been waiting for the other shoe to drop. But it never had. Did he realize why his secret had been safe with Kyra? Did he know Quinn had done everything in his power to protect that eight-year-old girl, even if it meant ignoring an important lead?

Quinn hadn't included a description of the killer in that initial report. Maybe Kyra told him nothing more than that the killer had been a man. She'd been a traumatized child and clearly she'd forgotten whatever it was she saw.

Jake's gaze wandered from his computer screen to the back of Kyra's head as she sat at her desk across the room, her blond ponytail swaying slightly as she typed on her keyboard. Quinn hadn't wanted Kyra to know, hadn't wanted her to remember, but Jake didn't play those games. He was honest, almost to a fault. How could he keep this from Kyra?

He bit the inside of his cheek so hard, he tasted the metallic flavor of blood on his tongue. How would it help her to know? How would it help the case? She didn't remember that she'd seen The Player—Quinn had made sure of that—and she wouldn't remember now.

There had actually been a conspiracy of silence between Quinn and Castillo.

Castillo had been the responding officer the night of Jennifer Lake's murder. He had to have known Jennifer's daughter saw the killer. But Castillo had kept quiet, too. Why?

Falsifying a report like that could mean big trouble, but Quinn and Castillo had kept this pact for twenty years. Why would Castillo jeopardize his career like that? Quinn did it for Kyra, and he could've retired at any time if the brass found out what he did. Quinn didn't care, but Castillo's career was on the upswing.

Jake drummed his thumbs against the keyboard. In fact, Castillo's career took a steep trajectory upward around the time of The Player homicides. Quinn had added the young patrolman to the task force, and Castillo had made a name for himself.

Was that the payoff? Silence for a career boost?

He blinked, and it took him a few second to realize Kyra had twisted around in her chair and was trying to catch his attention. He lifted his eyebrows, and she tapped her phone.

He swiped his personal cell from his desk and read Kyra's text inviting him to lunch. He hadn't talked to her all morning. He'd been true to his word last night and headed home after digging up his final bequest from Quinn. The report now was nestled securely in his own home safe.

He responded in the affirmative to Kyra's lunch invite and returned to the video from Erica's condo, showing her killer skulking down her hallway minutes before he forced his way into her place to murder her—thinking she was the witness in the Angeles National Forest.

A ripple of fear coursed down his spine. Had The Player instructed his minions to kill any witnesses because he had left one himself twenty years ago?

Leaning forward, he studied the hunched-over form, obscuring the killer's real height. The baggy hoodie concealed his body type, and the hat pulled low over his forehead hid his face. This guy could be a hundred men walking the streets of LA right now. Eyewitness accounts provided some of the weakest evidence for a case. Show five different people the same scene and ask them to recount it later, and those five people were very likely to give you five different accounts.

"How long are you going to stare at that, brother?" Billy clapped him on the shoulder. "Nothing to see."

"Did you catch him leaving, by any chance?"

"As we suspected, he left through an unmonitored back door. He could've headed out to a car anywhere along there. No luck."

Jake pushed away from his desk and crossed his hands behind his head. "The sheriff's department doesn't have much evidence from inside the condo, either. He must've been wearing gloves, no prints anywhere. They're looking for hair, fibers, but with no suspect, those could belong to anyone. There is a partial shoe print where he kicked open the door, but it's a common sneaker, and we can't tell the size because we don't have the whole sole of the shoe."

Billy held up a finger. "One piece of good news, if you want to call it that. We got a call today about a young woman missing for a couple of days. Could be our victim. Description matches."

"I have lunch in a minute." Jake shut down the video on his laptop. "Do you want me to stick around for the ID instead?"

"No, I got it covered. The missing woman's brother is coming in. I'll let you know either way." Billy plucked his cell phone from his pocket and paused. "I heard our man Quinn left you a couple of sweet pieces."

"Word gets around, doesn't it?" Jake grabbed his jacket from the back of his chair. "Yeah, Quinn left me some…interesting stuff."

Kyra had left the war room before him. It was a game they played to keep their interactions at the station professional, even though everyone knew they were in a relationship and often had lunch together. As Jake reached the door, he almost bumped into Captain Castillo charging into the room.

Holding up his hands, Jake said, "Whoa, excuse me, Captain. You in a hurry?"

"I was on my way to speak to Billy about the possible ID on the vic."

"He just told me. I hope we can give that poor girl on the slab a name." As he squeezed past Castillo, the captain touched his arm.

"Did you and Kyra have a chance to go out to Quinn's to look for the items he left you?"

Jake's expression froze in place. Without a flick of his eye, he said, "I looked at the weapons he left me and decided to keep them in his safe for now, and Kyra picked out a suit for the burial. We'll be back to clean up."

Castillo skimmed a hand through his salt-and-pepper hair. "You might need some help. Quinn has a lot of stuff in that house."

"Have you been there recently?"

"N-no, not recently, not for several months."

"It's not too bad. I can help Kyra get the house in shape, whether she wants to keep it, sell it or live in it. We'll go through everything."

Jake stayed just long enough to see Castillo's face pale under his brown skin. He wanted to talk over this development with Kyra, but like Castillo, he was keeping a secret. Damn, he hated secrets.

As he exited the station, Kyra caught up with him, nudging him in the back with her purse. "Wait up."

He pretended to stumble and grabbed her arm. "I thought you didn't want to be seen with me at the station."

"We're coworkers having lunch. That's allowed, isn't it?" She tried to shake him off, but he tightened his grip.

"So is this." He leaned over and kissed her on her blushing cheek. "It's not like I'm your boss or you're mine. Hell, you don't even technically work for the LAPD. You're a contractor, and we're paying you for your service. Besides, it's too late for decorum now."

"Because everyone knows we're an item." She squeezed his hand before jerking free. "Doesn't mean we have to feed the rumor mill."

He stabbed at his remote and unlocked the car. Then he beat Kyra to the passenger side and opened her door. "I like the sound of that—feeding the rumor mill. What would we have to do to get that going?"

"Don't—" she flattened her hand against his belly as she slid into the car "—even think about it."

Jake practically jogged to the driver's side. Kyra's mood seemed to be lifting. The visit to Quinn's last night had been tough for her to bear. How much tougher would it have been had she discovered she'd witnessed her mother's murder and Quinn had been hiding it from her all these years?

He couldn't tell her just yet. He'd been thinking about breaking it to her over bowls of steaming pho, but he didn't want to bring her down. Right now, he was more interested in finding out why Castillo had kept Quinn's secret. They'd both colluded in changing a police report for a murder scene.

Fifteen minutes later, they were sitting across from each other at a small table crowded with their drinks and a tray filled with cilantro, jalapeños, bean sprouts and a variety of other condiments to enhance their pho.

Kyra planted her elbows on the table and twirled the straw in her drink. "You seem preoccupied. Did you get anything more out of that video?"

"His hoodie, hat and baggy clothes hid his identity well. He left via an unmonitored back door, so we have no footage at the front of the building." He spread his hands on the table. "Not much to go on, but Billy may be identifying the victim today."

"That should help. Gives you another crime scene if you know where he abducted her." She took a sip of her drink. "Something else?"

He couldn't discuss his suspicions about Castillo with her without telling her the truth about the night her mother died—and he wasn't ready to do that yet.

He shrugged. "Wondering when this is going to end. I want Fiona down here for Christmas, but not if I'm still working this case or, God help us, another copycat killer case."

She covered his hand, curled into a tight ball on the table. "You know when this is going to end. It's going to end when you stop The Player."

"I'm afraid you're right. How can we catch The Player?" He shoved a hand into his hair. "Maybe Quinn and I will be alike in more ways than I want to count. Maybe The Player will outplay both of us."

"He's shown himself." She stopped as the waitress appeared with two bowls of pho, steam curling from the surface. When the server left, Kyra continued. "You have tools at your disposal that Quinn could only dream of twenty years ago. He had faith in you…and so do I. You can do this, Jake, you and Billy and the whole task force."

"Damn, I miss Quinn." He sniffed, and it wasn't because he'd just dumped some jalapeño in his soup. "He was my sounding board. He was my friend."

Kyra smoothed the pad of her thumb along the inside of his wrist. "He felt the same way about you."

Jake blinked and sipped from his spoon, his nose tingling. That was the pho—maybe. "I didn't see you earlier in the morning. Were you able to get Quinn's suit to the funeral home?"

"Not yet, but I did get the name of the mortuary from Terrence." She sprinkled some cilantro on top of her soup and glanced up. "The coroner hasn't released Quinn, umm, Quinn's body yet. Is that normal?"

"Haven't heard from him yet—I mean, her. Dr. Ellis is doing the autopsy. Her husband is a cop, and I know she'll take special care to do a thorough job."

"That's good to hear." She plunged her spoon into her pho. "Hey, I meant to ask you. You did take the keys to Quinn's house, didn't you? Tell me you did."

He gulped the spicy soup too fast and choked. "I discovered this morning that I had them in my pocket. I probably forgot to give them back to you after I locked up last night."

"Okay, that's a relief. I thought I lost them. I mean, I still have my own key to the house, but I wouldn't want to lose Quinn's set."

He asked, "Are you still convinced someone broke into Quinn's place after he was killed to search it?"

"Convinced?" She waved her hand in front of her puckered lips and took a sip of her drink. "As we didn't notice anything missing, I'm not so sure. But I swear, certain items seemed…placed, as if someone wanted to put everything back just as he'd found it."

Jake jerked his head. "Did Castillo have a key to Quinn's place?"

"Captain Castillo?" Kyra narrowed her eyes. "Why would you ask that? What would the captain want from Quinn's house?"

Jake shoved a spoonful of soup, chock-full of veggies and chicken, into his mouth to give himself time to think. Just because the thought came to him in a flash, he didn't have to give voice to it.

"Not that he'd want anything—" besides the police report he and Quinn had eighty-sixed in favor of a revised version "—but maybe he went in there to pay his respects, look around. You said yourself, nothing was missing."

"That's a thought. I'm not sure if Captain Castillo had a key, though. Not sure why he would."

Because they were partners in a cover-up.

"Just thinking outside the box." Jake swiped a napkin across his mouth. "Speaking of thinking outside the box, do you think it would be worth it to hypnotize Piper?"

Kyra dropped her spoon. "Hypnotize her? You mean to see if she remembers anything more about the killer?"

"Do you believe in that sort of thing?"

"I absolutely do, and I think we have one of the best hypnotherapists in the business right here in LA. I'm not sure it would help Piper, though. It's not like she can't remember him. She does, but she saw him in the dark at a distance, and he was wearing a hoodie and a hat—just like when he killed Erica. I don't believe a hypnotherapist could get anything else out of her. She hasn't buried the memory. She just didn't get a good look at him." She gave him a thumbs-up. "I'm impressed. You've come a long way, from a guy who didn't trust therapists several months ago to someone who's suggesting hypnosis for a witness."

"Why wouldn't I? I've been schooled by the best." He dabbed at several cilantro leaves on the table and crushed them between his fingers. "But you do believe hypnosis can uncover blocked memories."

"I do. I've seen it work. Why? Do you have some memories you want unlocked?" She winked at him.

"Me? I have a few I'd rather forget." Pushing his bowl away, he changed the subject. "Fiona wants to know if she can do a video chat with you later. She wants to interview you about your job for a class assignment."

Kyra turned pink. She and his daughter had gotten off to a rocky start, probably because they were too similar, but ever since Kyra risked her life to save Fiona's, his daughter had become Kyra's biggest fan—next to him.

"Have her text me. I'd be more than happy to help out."

"At least she doesn't want to interview me. I couldn't tell her half the stuff I do." He held up his cup and shook it, rattling the ice. "Do you want a refill before we head back? I haven't heard from Cool Breeze, so I don't think they ID'd the victim yet. He probably needs my help."

"I'll tell him you said that." She handed him her cup. "Diet, lots of ice."

When he got back to the table after topping up their drinks, Kyra shoved his phone at him. "Can you call Dr. Ellis before we leave and ask about Quinn's autopsy, please?"

"I'll do it in the car. That way, I can put it on speaker so you can hear."

They grabbed their drinks and headed back to the car. Once inside, Jake pulled out his phone. He scrolled through his contacts and placed a call to the coroner's office.

Someone at the front desk of the ME's office picked up on the second ring, and Jake put his phone on speaker for Kyra. "This is Detective Jake McAllister. I'm calling for Dr. Ellis regarding an autopsy."

"Oh, Detective McAllister, Dr. Ellis has a note to call you. I'm looking at it right here. She had a meeting, but I think they just broke up. I'll let her know you're on the phone."

"Thanks." Jake nodded at Kyra and said, "She's probably done. You can let Terrence know."

A woman's breathless voice came over the line. "Jake? I'm glad you called. Your ears must've been burning, as I was going to call you right after my meeting."

"Perfect, Deirdre. Are you finished with Quinn's autopsy? We have a big funeral to plan."

Deirdre paused. "Uh, not so fast, Jake."

Jake's heart skipped a beat. Licking his lips, he shot a glance at Kyra. Maybe putting the doc on speaker wasn't the best idea.

"Does that mean you're not finished?"

"I have to do some toxicology follow-up, and that could take a few days." He heard some papers shuffling across the line, and then Deirdre cleared her throat. "I found a needle puncture on Quinn's body."

Kyra's hand had been creeping toward his leg, and now she grabbed his thigh.

Jake's nostrils flared with a snort. "Are you suggesting Quinn was using drugs?"

"No evidence of that. One pinprick between his first and second toe on his left foot." Deirdre paused again, this one causing the hair on Quinn's arms to stand on end.

"What are you saying, Deirdre?"

"I'm suggesting Detective Roger Quinn may have been murdered."

Chapter Seven

Kyra dug her fingernails into Jake's leg. The sound of Dr. Ellis's words still echoed in the car. She wanted to scream. She wanted to punch the dashboard. She wanted to know more.

"I can't tell you much other than that right now, Jake."

Kyra tugged on Jake's sleeve. She didn't want to say anything that might get him in trouble for allowing her to listen in, so she kept silent, but Dr. Ellis had to spill more details after making that shocking pronouncement.

Jake dipped his chin to his chest. "You can tell me what led you to that suspicion, Deirdre. You have to give me more than that."

She sighed but delivered. "When I started Quinn's examination, I vowed to do my very best for him. Sure, I had his medical records and knew about the heart disease, saw the stents for myself, but those stents were doing their job. His arteries were clear enough that if he'd had an angiograph the day he died, it wouldn't have shown enough closure for another stent or bypass surgery. He was managing, so I looked elsewhere. I'd noticed two things when we removed his clothing—his right shoe was tied differently from his left and his right sock was on inside-out. Would I have bothered with those details if I'd seen atherosclerosis in his arteries? Nope. But it got me thinking. May have even learned a thing or two from you, J-Mac."

Kyra pressed a hand to her heart, which was in danger of galloping out of her chest. She knew it. Deep down she'd known it all along.

Dr. Ellis took a sip of something and continued. "So, I took a look at that foot, examined the area between the toes where addicts often shoot up—not that I believed for a minute Quinn was using. He didn't have any of the signs of addiction or habitual use. Lo and behold, I discovered a pinprick. Looked a helluva lot to me like a syringe. So I ordered another set of toxicology reports."

Jake asked, "What are you looking for, Deirdre?"

She clicked her tongue. "You know, Jake. I'm looking for a drug that can simulate a heart attack, some kind of stimulant."

Jake talked to the doctor for a few more minutes about timing and schedules, but the roaring in Kyra's ears had blocked their conversation.

As soon as Jake ended the call, Kyra turned to him and grabbed his arm. "I knew it. He killed him."

Jake sat with his head down, the phone cupped between his hands. "The Player? You think The Player killed Quinn?"

"Who else?" She rubbed her arms. "I just don't know how he could've gotten into Quinn's house. How did he manage to shoot him up between his toes?"

Lifting his head, Jake scratched his jaw. "You remember Quinn had the bump on the back of his head."

She froze, pressing her hands against her bouncing knees. "The first responders, and even you, figured he got that when he fell, hitting his head on the coffee table. He was in the right position for that."

"What if that was a setup? What if someone hit Quinn

on the head to knock him out, and then pulled off his shoe and sock to shoot him up, put the shoe and sock back on—incorrectly—and then positioned him to make it look like the heart attack, which was induced, caused him to fall and hit his head?"

Kyra covered her mouth and she rocked forward.

"Death by heart attack instead of a fall because it would be expected, given his condition." Jake gripped the steering wheel, his knuckles white. "It's just speculation."

She shot back in her seat, adrenaline rushing through her body, the wheels in her brain clicking. "Damn good speculation, Detective. Quinn would be proud, but how?"

"How what?"

"Quinn never would've allowed a stranger into his house. Never would've turned his back on one."

"Maybe The Player is no stranger to Quinn."

"I don't even know what that means." Kyra massaged her temples, now throbbing. "You think Quinn knew who The Player was?"

"Listen." Jake squeezed the back her neck. "What if The Player is one of Quinn's acquaintances? This person comes to Quinn's house and Quinn lets him in because he knows him. Quinn turns his back on him, the guy hits him with something and then arranges the heart attack, never imagining a sharp ME like Dr. Ellis would think to look between his toes."

Kyra ground her teeth together, her jaw tight. "If it happened that way, I will never let this rest. I won't be satisfied until the man who murdered my mother *and* my father is brought to justice."

As soon as they got back to the station, Billy swooped in on Jake and carried him away. An hour later, they made public the name of the first victim of the fourth copycat killer.

Ashley Russell had been a young woman struggling to make it in LA. Her brother had told Billy that she'd been attending AA meetings, and had been at one the evening she disappeared. The task force would send someone to question people at the AA meeting, but they probably wouldn't get too far with the people there who wanted to maintain their anonymity and the anonymity of others.

Kyra glanced around the room and shut down her laptop. The team would give her more information on Ashley and her family and friends tomorrow. She had a brother in the picture, so Kyra would most likely start with him if he requested assistance. Nobody would miss her now, and her only patient of the afternoon had canceled.

She had a little of her own detective work to do. Neither Dr. Ellis nor Jake would be releasing any news about Quinn's autopsy until the ME office completed it and the second set of toxicology tests came back. That gave her time to do some amateur sleuthing.

She slipped out of the war room without a second glance and drove straight to Quinn's house in Venice. Quinn didn't have security cameras at his house. Venice contained several dodgy areas, but the neighborhood in the canals wasn't among them. Thieves would have to lug anything they stole out of the neighborhood on foot, which must be a deterrent.

Quinn's car still claimed his parking spot outside of the canals, so Kyra parked along the street. She always kept her key to Quinn's house on her key chain, but now she had Quinn's key chain, as well—the one Jake had forgotten to leave at her place last night.

She pulled it from her purse now, and gripped it in

her hand as she crossed the bridge to his house. She let herself in and stood on the threshold for a minute, surveying the room. It *did* have an air of being tidied. She hadn't imagined that last night, and Dr. Ellis's bombshell today gave her more proof.

Perhaps the killer himself had returned to the scene of his crime to gather evidence or make sure he hadn't left anything behind. If he were a friend of Quinn's, he could explain his presence if caught.

She released the breath she'd been holding and stepped into the room, leaving the door open behind her. If Quinn's toxicology results came back positive for some type of amphetamine in his system and his death was declared a homicide, the CSIs would descend on this house with a fury. But what would they find?

Quinn's prints, hers and Jake's would be all over the place. If Clive Stewart, their fingerprint tech, picked up others, those people would have to provide alibis. There's no way Quinn's friend-turned-killer came in wearing gloves. Of course, he could've wiped his prints after the murder. Even though the end of fall was near, nobody was wearing gloves in LA at this time of the year.

She covered her mouth with one hand. How could The Player have befriended Quinn? Quinn didn't make friends easily, didn't socialize much and was highly suspicious of new acquaintances. That tiny speculation that The Player could be a cop tickled the edges of her mind. Was that what they were looking at?

She took a turn around the room, examining the areas that had caught her attention last night—the bookcase with the two pictures straightened instead of facing the room at an angle, the pillows on the couch neatly tucked into the corners instead of shoved against the back cushion, the throw rug…

She tripped to a stop. Last night, the corner of the rug had been turned back. Now it was straight. She or Jake must've flicked it into position.

She crouched beside the place where they'd discovered Quinn's body and peered at the corner of the coffee table. The EMTs had noted the fresh lump on the back of Quinn's head, and Jake and the other cops on the scene had assumed he'd hit it on his way down, collapsing from the heart attack.

Jake had even spotted a smear of blood on the wood, but that would be easy to arrange. From her position on the floor, Kyra tilted back her head, imagining the scene. Quinn had fallen a few steps from the kitchen. Had he and his guest gone into the kitchen for something to drink?

She and Jake had figured Quinn had been coming out of the kitchen with a glass of water in his hand. The glass hadn't broken when Quinn went down but had rolled onto the area rug in front of the fireplace, spilling its contents along the way.

But what if someone had gone into the kitchen with him? What if Quinn had been bringing that water for someone else? She'd always been after Quinn to drink more water. He didn't like it and preferred soda or iced tea. Maybe that water had been for someone else.

If his fake friend were behind Quinn, though, he might've had his own drink. They hadn't found a second glass, of course, but the killer could've left it on the counter while he went after Quinn to knock him down. Once he had him on the floor, unconscious or disoriented, he pulled off his shoe and sock and shot him up between the toes, never believing someone would be looking for needle marks on retired detective Roger Quinn.

Kyra sprang up from the floor and barreled into the

kitchen. She'd left the glass Quinn dropped in the sink, and it still sat there, undisturbed. She yanked open the dishwasher. When Quinn ate alone, he preferred to wash his dishes by hand, and his dishwasher reflected this. A handful of utensils stuck up from the basket on the side, a few plates nestled neatly in a row and one glass commanded the entire top tray.

She eyed the glass. Could that be the one? She'd ask Jake to collect it as evidence and have Clive run it for prints. Quinn's should be the only prints on the glass. Would the killer be careless enough to leave a glass in the dishwasher?

She sidestepped to the cupboard where Quinn kept his dishes and pulled open the cabinet door. Similar glasses to the one in the sink and the dishwasher stood at attention in a row on the shelf. One stuck out from the others. Had the killer rinsed out his glass, dried it, wiped it clean and put it back in the cupboard? She'd mention this one to Jake, too.

If Quinn's death had been a murder, and she had to keep telling herself that wasn't a forgone conclusion yet, enough people had trudged through the crime scene to render it useless.

A light tap on the open front door had Kyra clutching her throat and spinning around.

"Kyra, is that you? It's Rose." Rose Bernstein, one of Quinn's neighbors and friends, poked her fluffy blond head into the house.

Patting her chest, where her heart thumped back to normal, Kyra called out, "Yes, Rose. I'm in the kitchen."

She closed the cupboard and returned to the living room, where Rose had one tentative foot over the threshold.

"When I saw the open door, I was hoping it was you."

Rose tugged her sweater around her thin frame, slightly stooped with osteoporosis. "May I?"

"Of course." She waved Rose into the room. "Come in."

Rose floated forward, stretching out her hands, the blue veins running crisscross on the backs under thin skin. "My dear girl, I'm so sorry for your loss."

Kyra met her halfway, and the older woman wrapped her in a hug, patting her back, enveloping her in a scent of faded lilacs. When Rose finally released her, Kyra had to grab a tissue from her purse. She'd never met any of her grandparents, but Rose smelled exactly how she'd always imagined a grandma to smell.

"Quinn was your friend, too. I know you're going to miss him."

"Who am I going to cook for now? My son and the grandkids live in New York." She shrugged a set of narrow shoulders. "But now I feel guilty about all those meals I sent to Quinn. He probably shouldn't have been eating lasagna with four different cheeses."

"He loved your cooking." Kyra squeezed her arm, sealing her own lips. It could be the lasagna had nothing to do with Quinn's death. "When was the last time you saw Quinn?"

Rose shook her head. "That's the sad thing. I had been away in Palm Springs, visiting my sister for a few days. I heard about his death from the neighbors when I got back. I wasn't even here. Didn't even see him before he died."

Kyra sucked in her bottom lip. No use asking Rose if she'd seen or heard anything unusual. She wouldn't bother questioning Quinn's nearest neighbor, the drummer next door. She'd leave that up to Jake or Billy once they started investigating Quinn's death as a homicide.

Had Quinn really known The Player all these years and not felt something from him? Some vibe? Some connection?

The Player obviously was very good at appearing human. He'd lived among normal people for years, maybe even had a wife and children. You always had to wonder if the families of serial killers were telling the truth when they proclaimed dear old dad was just like any other father on the block. The BTK killer had walked his daughter down the aisle.

A little shiver crept over Kyra's flesh, and she squared her shoulders, recalibrating. "I'm sorry you missed saying goodbye to Quinn, but none of us knew our last time was a goodbye. Do you want to have a seat? I was just going through Quinn's kitchen to…see what I could throw out."

"I can't stay long, but don't worry about that kitchen. I can clean it up for you. Unless you want any of the food, I can dispose of it and donate the nonperishables to a shelter I work with here in Venice." Rose dangled a single key from a ring. "Quinn and I had keys to each other's places. I can give it to you now, or I can hang on to it and see about that kitchen."

"You're so kind. That would be helpful, but can you hold off on doing anything in the kitchen until I tell you to move ahead?"

"Of course, whatever you need." Rose reached out and patted Kyra's hand. "I'm glad I saw you today. When I noticed the door open, I thought it might be you and I had missed you yesterday, and then you didn't come back with Jake—Detective McAllister."

"Come back?" Kyra tilted her head to the side. Had someone been in the house after she and Jake left last night? "We didn't come back. Did you see someone in the house?"

"I know you didn't come back, but your young man returned later."

Kyra's cheeks warmed at the thought of Jake being her *young man*, but Rose had it wrong and maybe she saw the killer. "Jake and I went back to my place, and then he went home. He didn't go to Quinn's house."

"Oh." Rose fluffed her perm. "Maybe he forgot something and didn't mention it to you, but it was definitely Jake I saw last night. Poco, my Chihuahua, had to take a potty break around midnight, so I walked him outside. I saw Jake coming across the bridge. I almost called out because I thought you might be with him, but he was alone."

"H-he went into the house?" And then Kyra remembered Jake handing over Quinn's key chain at lunch. He claimed he'd forgotten he had it in his pants pocket.

"He let himself into the house with a key and turned on a light in the living room." Rose knitted her eyebrows. "That's all right, isn't it? He was a friend of Quinn's. In fact, Quinn adored that man, and, well, he's a police officer."

Kyra blinked rapidly. "Of course it's okay. He probably stopped here on the way back to his place because he forgot something when we were here earlier."

"Well, I'm glad I got to see you." Rose made a move for the front door. "Let me know when I can get into that kitchen. I want to help you in any way I can. Quinn would want that."

Kyra walked Rose to the door and watched the birdlike woman cross the wooden bridge to her own side of the neighborhood, her house across from Quinn's.

Even after Rose disappeared into her house with a wave, Kyra stayed on the porch, watching the seawater lap against the concrete barrier that formed the canal. Jake might have forgotten something at Quinn's earlier, but he had all that time during lunch to tell her and a perfect opportunity to mention it when he returned Quinn's key chain to her.

She clenched her teeth and stepped back inside her house, slamming the door behind her. Jake didn't tell her because he'd come sneaking back here on his own.

Because Jake had a secret.

Chapter Eight

Captain Carlos Castillo had a secret, had kept it for twenty years.

Jake watched Castillo through narrowed eyes as the captain leaned over Billy's computer to study the stills of Erica's killer. Why had Castillo agreed to change that report? He'd put his career on the line by agreeing to appease Detective Roger Quinn.

Castillo's actions ever since the copycat killers had surfaced several months ago had been suspect. The captain had been jumpy, stressed out, overly curious about Jake's budding relationship with both Kyra and Quinn.

Had he been the one searching Quinn's place after the old detective's death? Had he been searching for that report to squelch it? Castillo had to know that Jake would have the same concerns about that report going public. Kyra's safety had to be Jake's priority, just as it had been Quinn's.

Had Castillo gone even further than breaking and entering? Had he gone to Quinn's that day demanding that he destroy the original report? When Quinn refused, had he hit him over the head? No. If Dr. Ellis was correct about the injection between Quinn's toes, his murder had been deliberate and planned—not a moment of fury.

That didn't mean Castillo and Quinn hadn't argued

about this before. Castillo could've planned to take out Quinn once he realized the detective wouldn't come around to his way of thinking and destroy that report.

Why hadn't Quinn burned the original report? Maybe he knew deep down, as Jake did, that Kyra had a right to know the truth about the night of her mother's murder. She'd want to know.

"Something to add, J-Mac?" Castillo must've felt Jake's stare and now met Jake's eyes with his own, dark and unfathomable.

Jake twitched his head. "Just wondering if you guys had any luck with the zooming, but it doesn't sound like it."

"This guy—" Billy flicked his finger at the screen "—looks like thousands of other white guys in LA. He's too smart to smile at the camera."

"Not too smart to go after a witness and then wind up killing the wrong person." Jake glanced up at the door of the war room for the hundredth time that morning.

Kyra had gone off and done her own thing yesterday afternoon when they'd been scrambling to notify Ashley's family and questioning her brother. She'd sent him a terse text last night and hadn't answered his texts so far today. He hoped Quinn's death wasn't hitting her particularly hard right now, especially as that death might be a murder.

Billy replied, "He didn't want to violate one of The Player's rules—don't leave any witnesses—but he went overboard. Maybe he'll stop at Ashley, seeing how he messed up so much."

"Let's hope so." Castillo rapped his knuckles on the desk and made a quick exit.

Jake drilled the captain's back with his gaze as he left the room. Castillo had gotten that sheen on his forehead when Billy had mentioned witnesses. If Jake wanted the whole story about Jennifer Lake's murder, he had to confront Castillo. But first, he needed some proof or at least some ammunition.

He ducked his head and tapped the keyboard to bring up the personnel database. He didn't have access to go into anyone's individual files, but he could view their progress through the LAPD—time on the job, promotions, accolades, that kind of thing.

He clicked on the link for the Northeast Division, where Castillo had spent his entire career. After looking left and right, Jake pulled the laptop closer to him and scrolled down the alphabet to find Castillo's name. He selected it.

Captain Carlos Castillo's glorious career with the LAPD tumbled down the screen. Jake scanned the very beginning of Castillo's positions, and then zeroed in on the few years The Player was active.

Castillo had been working patrol during that time, and that's why he'd been the first to respond to a child's 911 call that her mother was dead. The year before that, Castillo had supported a drug task force. Jake hunched forward, clicking through the cases that the task force had solved.

He'd read about this before. Armando Sandoval, a drug kingpin from the Sinaloa cartel, had controlled the streets of LA during this period, and the LAPD had formed a task force, LA Impact, to bring him down. The team had been mostly successful, reeling in the small fish first, the pushers on the corners and in the playgrounds. They'd squealed on the bigger fish and so on and so on, until the task force reached Sandoval, the big whale— or shark would be a better term. The DEA had ended up killing Sandoval in a gun battle at the border, but LA Impact had had a hand in the confrontation.

He scrolled through some of the cases, and his hand jerked when Quinn's name popped up. He'd been investigating the murder of a young woman who'd been shot in her car while her son wailed in his car seat in the back. Quinn had discovered that the woman's boyfriend, and the father of her baby, was one of Sandoval's dealers.

Jake drilled down further into the report. Tony Galecki had graduated from selling on the corner to distributing and managing a team of dealers. But something had gone wrong. Tony double-crossed the cartel by cutting the original product, selling more of it and pocketing what he thought the cartel would never notice. He was wrong. The cartel noticed everything. Tony's girlfriend paid the price.

The report didn't end with the girlfriend's death and Tony's arrest, though. The stacks of cash Tony had accumulated had gone missing. Looked like Internal Affairs had been called in for a hot minute, but the issue had been resolved. Tony had recanted his story about the missing money, and the investigation went away.

Jake dug some more, and his fingertips buzzed. Much of IA's suspicions had been directed at Carlos Castillo. He'd done a search of Tony's place, including a storage unit. He found packets of the diluted product but never found Tony's money.

Jake's heart skipped a beat when he saw some of the personal evidence IA had started to investigate about the hotshot patrolman. Castillo had been going through a divorce at the time. Jake had seen the happy family pictures in Castillo's office, which had come after the first marriage. Divorces were expensive—he knew all about that even though he'd gotten off easily. Tess had just wanted their marriage over so she could start again with Brock. His ex had gotten a friend of hers from law school to handle their divorce and it had been as painless and inexpensive as possible. But Jake realized what it could've been—something more like Castillo's.

IA was about to look into some of Castillo's finances at the time, but that ended when Tony admitted he'd lied about the money being missing. Claimed he and his girlfriend had already spent most of it or had given it away.

Steepling his fingers, Jake minimized the screen and leaned back in his chair. Quinn had been involved in a murder case that had found its way onto the LA Impact task force, a task force that Castillo had worked. This had occurred just prior to the formation of The Player task force.

Jake drummed his fingers on the desk. What had happened to Tony Galecki's money? The cartels didn't tolerate lying or stealing, ironically enough, but the sums had to be high for them to take out a woman with her baby. Had Tony and his girlfriend been able to spend that much and that fast? Why had Tony changed his mind at the last minute?

He planned to find out.

He jumped when Billy nudged his arm. "Earth to Jake. Are you down for some lunch?"

"Lunch already?" Jake rubbed his eyes. "That went fast."

"Did you find anything worth reporting?" Billy jabbed his finger at Jake's laptop, the LAPD screensaver innocuously bouncing from one edge to the other.

"Nah. You?"

"Nothing on the videos, nothing at the crime scene in the Angeles National Forest. Copycat Four must've followed The Player's other rules, even though he messed up the witness one."

The Player had messed up that rule himself.

Jake tapped his keyboard to wake up his computer. "You go ahead and get the car started. I'm gonna check one more thing and I'll meet you in the parking lot."

Jake watched Billy leave the room before bringing up the database for prisoners in LA County. Would Galecki still be inside for the drug charge?

He looked him up and discovered he'd served less than ten years on that conviction, his sentence reduced for cooperation. Had he survived in prison after collaborating against the cartel? A few more searches indicated he had survived prison life and currently resided in Boyle Heights. Jake jotted down the address. It was his lucky day. He'd rather see Tony in person than try to question him over the phone.

After his lunch with Billy, he dropped his partner at the station and took the car to East LA. He found Tony's address not too far off the freeway and above an office for a moving company—LA Movers and Shakers. Clever.

He parked his sedan next to a moving truck, open in the back, and checked in at the small office. Obviously just a place to direct traffic and schedule moves, the office sported a desk stacked with invoices and littered with paper cups and soda cans. Several metal filing cabinets hunched behind the desk, a bulletin board with a Laker Girls calendar hanging from it at an angle graced one wall and a few dollies were shoved into the corner.

Jake had taken a few steps into the office and turned his head at the sound of footsteps on the gravel in the parking lot behind him.

A young man with dark brown hair and several tattoos marching up his arms clenched his fists at his sides and said, "What do you want?"

Jake stepped aside to let the man bump past him into the office. "Customer service not a requirement in the moving business?"

A blush rose to the young man's tawny cheeks. "You're not here to schedule a move. You're a cop."

"What gave me away?" Jake's lips twisted up on one side.

"The suit, the car out there." The man tilted his chin in an aggressive manner, his beard practically bristling. "I seen enough of you over the years. He's not here."

"You know I'm looking for Tony Galecki?"

"Aren't you always? He done his time. He built this business when he got out. He hasn't done nothing since."

"I believe you." Jake held up his hands, realizing that this young man was most likely Galecki's son—the one who'd been in the car with his murdered mother. Jake swallowed. This boy had been younger than Kyra when his mother had been murdered, but he must've experienced some of the same trauma as she had.

"I'm not here to harass your father. I just have a few questions to ask him about that time—when your mother was killed."

The son blinked. "He ain't got nothing to say about that anymore."

"AJ, let me be the judge of that."

Jake spun around to find Tony Galecki hovering in the doorway, his arms crossed over his wiry frame, his head cocked to the side. Although Galecki had a receding hairline, he'd gathered what hair he did have in a ponytail that hung down his back.

Jake thrust out his hand. "Mr. Galecki, I'm Detective

McAllister with LAPD Homicide. I'd like to ask you a few questions about your arrest twenty years ago."

Galecki hesitated before grabbing Jake's hand. "This is my son, AJ."

Jake shook Galecki's hand and then extended it to AJ, who'd stuffed his own hands in his pockets.

"Son, show the man respect."

AJ pulled a hand from his pocket and gripped Jake's briefly before hiding it in his pocket again.

"Do you have a minute, Mr. Galecki?"

"Call me Tony." He jerked his thumb over his shoulder. "AJ, prep that moving van. A crew's taking it out tomorrow morning."

"Yes, sir." AJ squeezed between his father and Jake and left them in the small office.

"Who raised him? Seems like a good kid."

Galecki circled the desk and plopped down on the wheeled chair. "My parents. Lucinda's parents couldn't deal. They blamed me for her death. They're not wrong. What do you want after all this time, Detective? It wasn't a cold case. We all know who did it and why."

Jake grabbed a stool, the only other place to sit, and straddled it. "I was looking at your case recently and noticed you'd made a claim that money had been stolen from you."

Galecki narrowed his eyes and ran a thumb down his mustache. "You wired or anything?"

"This isn't official business, Tony. I'm looking into something else. Nobody has to know about our meeting—not even the cops." Jake circled his finger in the air. "Where'd you get the money to start this business?"

Galecki's lips stretched over his teeth in a grim smile. "A little money I had waiting for me on the outside."

"Drug money?" Jake's pulse ticked slow and heavy in anticipation.

"Hey, I'm not proud of it, man. My stupidity caused the death of my woman. I ain't never getting over that." Galecki lifted his shoulders, and Jake noticed the tattoo on his neck that had been refashioned into the word *Baby*.

Jake knew that tattoo had once been AB for the Aryan Brotherhood. Most prisoners had to swear their allegiance to a gang inside if they wanted to survive, but Galecki seemed like he wanted to disavow all that now.

Jake took a deep breath. "But?"

"But they were offering. You know what I mean? Make the theft charges go away for the cops and get a cut of the money. My parents got the cash and they saved it for me, even though I told them to spend it on AJ."

"Who offered you the deal?"

"The old cop. The one who came to tell me first about Lucinda's murder. He didn't know yet that I was working for the cartel and Lucinda's death was a hit. I don't think he's the one who stole my money, though. It was the drug cops who done that."

Jake licked his lips, his throat dry. "Do you remember the name of the old cop who offered you the deal?"

"Oh, yeah. I remember 'cuz he was good to Lucinda's parents and AJ. He was all about AJ, wanted to make sure he didn't go into the system, you know? He kept in touch with Lucinda's parents and mine to check up on the baby. Good guy—except for the corruption. Never could figure out how a cop like that could cover for someone else's theft—but then, you guys stick together, don't you?"

"What was his name, Tony? What was the name of this cop who told you to lie?"

Tony shrugged. "Detective Roger Quinn."

Chapter Nine

Kyra bustled into the task force war room and grabbed the back of her chair, shooting a glance over her shoulder at Jake's desk. She blew out a breath and collapsed in front of her computer.

She'd decided she had to confront Jake. If he were snooping around *her* house, she wanted an explanation. She'd cooled off some after talking to Rose yesterday. Maybe he'd had an inkling that Quinn had been murdered, didn't want to worry her and headed over to the house to check out a clue.

Anytime Jake had lied to her or kept the truth from her, it had usually been in her best interests. She could actually say the same about her lies—most of the lies she'd told Jake had been in her best interests, too.

She'd gotten over that once Jake had proven to her time and again that he wanted to stick by her regardless of her mistakes and deceptions. Now she had to do the same for him. If he'd lied to her about going back to Quinn's, it had probably been for a good reason—at least in his mind.

She'd been ignoring his texts, giving herself a cooling off period.

She'd texted Jake back this afternoon, and now he was ignoring her messages. She glanced at Billy on the phone. He'd probably know the whereabouts of his partner.

When Billy ended his call, Kyra sauntered to his desk. "Hi, Billy. I just wanted to make sure you passed my info along to Ashley's family."

"I did. Her brother's in bad shape." His lips twisted. "I can relate."

She took the chair next to his, which happened to be Jake's, and leaned into his space. "Has your PI had any luck yet?"

Billy's younger sister had gone missing several years ago, and he'd recently hired a PI, Dina Ferrari, to help him find out what happened. The second copycat, Cyrus Fisher, had started his spree by murdering two African American women, which had triggered Billy, big-time.

"Dina got a line on a guy the family didn't even know was in Sabrina's life at the time. His name never came up. Dina's tracking him down now. I feel hopeful, but, man, talking to Ashley's brother ripped me apart."

"I'm here anytime you want to talk."

"I appreciate that." He pointed at Jake's desk. "You know where he is?"

"I was going to ask you. I haven't heard from him since this morning. I was...busy, so I didn't answer him. By the time I got around to responding, he'd gone radio silent."

"We had lunch, and then he took the car to look into something, didn't tell me what." Billy snapped his fingers. "Actually, you might be a bigger help to me than J-Mac in this. Some of Ashley's AA group agreed to talk to me about the night she went missing. They're a cagey bunch. Maybe they'll be more forthcoming with a therapist there. You game?"

"Where are you meeting them?"

"At the AA meeting site—a church in Glendale. That's where her brother found her car."

"I'll come with you. I saw clients this morning and figured I'd do some work at the station this afternoon, but as none of Ashley's friends or family has contacted me yet, I might as well go with you."

As they left the war room together, Captain Castillo grabbed Billy's arm. "Where's J-Mac?"

"He's the man in demand, but I don't have a clue." Billy jerked his thumb at Kyra. "Kyra and I are going to talk to Ashley's AA group. Find out if they saw anything unusual that night or noticed a difference in her behavior."

"Good, good." Castillo waved his hand in the air. He barreled into the war room anyway, as if he intended to stake out Jake's desk.

Billy shook his head as they made for the staircase. "That man needs to chill…or retire."

"He has seemed rattled lately." Kyra knew Jake had his own suspicions about Captain Castillo, but he'd never been anything but helpful and nice to her—probably on Quinn's orders.

On the drive to the church, Billy asked her about the funeral plans for Quinn.

Kyra glanced at Billy's profile, his smooth, dark skin displaying not one crease of worry or consternation. Either Jake hadn't told his partner about Dr. Ellis's findings, or Jake had told him to keep the information on the down-low.

Kyra fiddled with her phone in her lap, keeping her eyes downcast. "As far as I know, the autopsy isn't done yet. At least, I haven't been notified. Quinn's attorney, Terrence Hicks, is going to do most of the arrangements with the department."

"I'm sure Terry will do it up right with the bagpipes

and everything." Billy clasped her hand briefly. "Going to be hard on you."

"Has been and will be." She sniffed. "Everyone has been great, though, and Quinn himself made it easier on me. He'd been planning for this moment for quite a while."

"Most cops do."

They finished the drive on a lighter note with Kyra teasing Billy about his dating life. He was separated from his wife and had been going out with one of Kyra's friends, a TV reporter, but both Billy and her friend had assured her their relationship was casual.

As soon as Billy pulled up outside the church, their sober mood returned. Most likely, Ashley Russell had been snatched from this parking lot. The cops had no evidence indicating how the killer had taken her.

The area around her car showed no signs of a struggle. Her car itself yielded no clues. But someone had lain in wait for a vulnerable woman, recovering, perhaps emotional, and had taken her away and murdered her.

She exited Billy's car and glanced up at the eaves of the church. "No cameras?"

"Not a one." He gestured toward the side of the building. "The meeting room is over here. Has its own entrance."

Kyra pulled on her jacket as she followed Billy around the corner. A door stood open and Billy poked his head inside the room.

He called out, "Marcia?"

Kyra heard a woman's voice answering from the depths of the room. "That's me. Are you Detective Crouch?"

Billy waved to Kyra. "I am, ma'am. I brought a therapist with me. Kyra Chase works on our task force."

Kyra stepped through the door after Billy, catching a whiff of coffee and piety. She'd smelled a lot of piety during her stint with one of her foster families. Church every Sunday and hell to pay after at home if the foster mom didn't think you were paying attention at the service or hadn't sung loudly enough or hadn't put your money in the plate. Those parents had been believers, all right—believers in spare the rod, spoil the child. So they'd been quite liberal with the rod, and Kyra had run away from that home so many times, the foster parents had come to believe even God Himself couldn't save her.

Marcia left off fussing over a table filled with cookies and that coffeepot to greet them. "What a wonderful idea to have a therapist working with the police. I think some of us will feel more comfortable with Kyra here."

"Thank you." Kyra shook hands with Marcia, whose round cheeks bunched into a smile.

"Have a seat." Marcia's blue eyes twinkled as she indicated the chairs already in a circle. "I promise, you don't have to confess anything."

"Good, because we're hoping to get some answers from you about Ashley's last meeting here." Billy folded himself into one of the metal chairs.

Marcia remained standing. "Would you like some coffee?"

Both Kyra and Billy declined, so Marcia took a seat next to Kyra. "I feel guilty about Ashley's murder."

Kyra nodded. "That's not uncommon. What do you think you did or didn't do that put her in harm's way?"

Marcia ran her fingers through her curly dark hair, laced with gray. "She was my co-hospitality person. When I couldn't bring the refreshments, Ashley stepped up. I was running late and asked her to fill in. She picked up some coffee and snacks and then stayed after the meeting ended to clean up—that comes with the duties. That's why she was in the parking lot on her own that night. That's why nobody witnessed her abduction."

As they talked to Marcia, a few other people filtered into the room, nervously sidling up to the refreshment table and grabbing coffee and cookies before joining the circle. They didn't introduce themselves, and she and Billy didn't ask. If one of them had something pertinent, Billy could always get the information later.

Billy ran his finger around the circle. "All women? No guys come to this meeting?"

Marcia answered for all of them. "This is a women's-only AA meeting. Some of us find it easier to share with other women. There are men-only meetings, as well. There are meetings for LGBTQ, some for parents, some for singles. Something for everyone to feel comfortable."

Billy hunched forward, elbows on his knees. "The fact that this is a women's-only meeting is published someplace? Someplace public?"

Marcia answered, her eyes bright with fear, as the other women rustled around her. "Of course. There's a website for AA meetings in Southern California. Anyone can see that."

One of the other women on the far side of the circle, her hands wrapped around a Styrofoam cup of coffee, asked, "You think he targeted our group because of that? Do you think any one of us could've been his victim that night?"

"We just don't know." Billy clasped his hands between his knees. "This guy could've been stalking Ashley, knew she came to this meeting and ambushed her. But I'll tell you what. Let me know what time this meeting gets out, and I'll make sure a Glendale PD officer swings around on patrol at that time."

The rest of their conversation with the women gave them nothing. Ashley hadn't been any different that night. None of the women had seen anyone lurking near the church, and every one of them had left before Ashley—and now blamed themselves for it.

How had the killer known Ashley would be the last to leave? Were the women's fears warranted? Copycat Four would've been satisfied with any one of them?

Billy was right. The task force had nothing on this guy yet—even though he'd committed a second murder within twenty-four hours of the first. The Copycat Player Task Force still hadn't released that information. They wanted to protect Piper, make the killer believe he'd gotten his witness.

By the time they left the meeting, the sun had dipped low in the sky and the temp in the shade made Kyra shiver.

She slid into the passenger seat of Billy's car and took out her phone, which she had silenced. She puffed out a small breath when she saw a text from Jake, and then sucked it back in when she read the message.

He asked her to his place for dinner tonight and indicated he had something important to tell her. Had he gotten confirmation from Dr. Ellis? Had he found something the night before in Quinn's house?

Billy punched the ignition. "Everything okay?"

"Heard from Jake finally."

"Did he say where he'd been?"

"No. Do you want me to ask?"

"He'll tell me if it's important."

Apparently, what he had to tell *her* was important. She texted him back that she was on her way to the station with Billy and would drop by his house for dinner.

They hit some traffic on the freeways. By the time

they got to the Northeast Division, the shift change had already occurred, and most of the detectives had left the station.

Billy pulled right up to the front door. "Okay if I drop you here? I don't need to go in. I took all my stuff with me, and I'll bring the car home tonight."

"This is fine. Thanks for taking me along, even though we didn't get much out of the meeting."

"I wouldn't say that. He may be hitting up late-night meetings where women are likely to be going out to their cars alone in places that probably don't have security cameras. Every bit helps."

Kyra thanked him again before climbing out of the sedan. Entering the building, she waved at the night sergeant at the front desk. She jogged up the stairs. A smattering of people hunched over their computers or phones in the task force room, and she called out a hello here and there.

She'd left her laptop on her desk when she'd gone to the AA meeting with Billy, and she woke it up now and checked her emails. Ashley Russell's brother, Wade, had contacted her, and she replied to let him know her availability for tomorrow.

As she skimmed through the rest of the messages, Captain Castillo appeared at the door of the war room. He didn't usually stay this late, and his disheveled appearance and dark circles under his eyes signaled he should've gone home hours ago.

Kyra smiled. "You're here late, Captain."

"I was waiting for you, Kyra. Do you have a minute?"

"Me?" She glanced behind her to make sure there were no other Kyras in the room.

"When you're free."

"Just let me wrap up, and I'll drop by your office." He

left, and as she logged off her laptop, she mulled over why he'd want to see her. He must want to discuss Quinn's funeral. Soon enough, everyone would know Quinn had been murdered. That would probably double the attendance at his funeral.

She didn't need to return to this room, so she hitched her laptop case over one shoulder and her purse over the other. She trooped down to Castillo's office with both bags banging against her hips.

He'd left the door open in invitation as there were few people left on the floor, but when she stepped inside, he asked her to shut the door. A flutter of trepidation invaded her bones.

She nudged the door closed with her foot and dropped her bags to the floor. When she sat in the chair across from his desk, she gripped the arms.

Captain Castillo spent several seconds straightening items on his orderly desk and then asked, "How are the funeral arrangements for Quinn going?"

Kyra's shoulders slumped, and she uncurled her fingers. He *did* want to talk about Quinn's funeral, not that that discussion didn't pose its own pitfalls. "I'm really not the person to ask. Terrence Hicks is organizing everything right now. I think once he gets certain concessions from the department, he'll present me with choices, and then I'll be more involved in the planning."

He cocked his head. "I haven't heard from Terrence at all yet…or the ME's office. They're not done with the autopsy?"

"The ME hasn't notified me that she's done with the autopsy." She folded her hands in her lap to keep her fingers from fidgeting.

"She?" Castillo's gaze sharpened, and Kyra felt it probing her face.

"Jake mentioned a Dr. Ellis was doing the autopsy, and he called her *she*."

"I know Dr. Ellis. She's thorough and professional."

Would Castillo find Dr. Ellis all that professional if he knew she'd given Jake info on the sly and dropped the word *murder* in his ear?

She cleared her throat. "That's what Jake said. Maybe that's why it's taking a long time."

"You would think with Quinn's history, the autopsy would be a mere formality."

Except for the shoe, the sock and the needle mark between his toes.

"I'm happy to say I'm not familiar with the process of an autopsy." She lifted her shoulders. "When I get the word that the examination is complete, I'll contact Terrence, and he'll move forward with the plans."

Castillo fiddled with a pen on his desk, and Kyra waited, the silence stretching between them so tightly she felt as if she could reach up and pluck it. Was that all he wanted to ask her? Why'd he ask her to his office and close the door?

The knock from outside startled them both. Castillo dropped the pen, which rolled to the floor unheeded, and Kyra jumped in her seat, kicking over her bag. The noise snapped the tension in the room.

Castillo called out, "Come in."

When Jake opened the door, Kyra widened her eyes. She hadn't expected to see him until later for dinner.

But if she was surprised, her emotions were nothing compared to Captain Castillo's. His sharp intake of breath caused Kyra to glance at him behind his desk. His mouth had gone slack, and a sheen of moisture had popped out on his forehead. Castillo ducked down to retrieve the pen, his voice sounding muffled. "What can I do for you, McAllister? Surprised to see you here so late."

"Are you?" Jake stepped into the room, clicking the door behind him. "Were you going to tell Kyra the truth, or should I?"

A choking sound came from the captain, and his eyes bulged from their sockets. "He told you."

Kyra jerked her head back toward Jake, his jaw hard, steely resolve vibrating from his body. What was going on?

"If you mean Tony Galecki, then the answer is yes."

"Who the hell is Tony Galecki?" Kyra leaned back from Jake's looming frame, which was suffocating the space in the office.

Castillo closed his eyes for a second, took a deep breath and clasped his hands beneath his chin as if in prayer. "I actually *was* going to tell her."

"Because you knew I talked to Galecki today. Do you have an alert on his file?"

Kyra still had no idea who Galecki was or what they were talking about, but Jake's question pinged Castillo between the eyes. His brown skin flushed deeply.

"I'm sure Galecki told you everything. Why wouldn't he?" Castillo jabbed a finger at Jake. "Are you willing to destroy Kyra's faith in Quinn, the only father she knew?"

Kyra's heart slammed against her rib cage, rattling it, and her clammy hands gripped the edge of Castillo's desk. "What is he talking about, Jake?"

Crossing his arms, Jake leaned against Castillo's office door. "Quinn left me more than those weapons in his will, Kyra."

"Okay." She smoothed her hands over the thighs of her slacks. "Is that why you went back to his place the other night when you told me you were going home?"

His eyebrows jumped. "How'd you…?"

"Rose saw you. What else did Quinn leave you?"

"A crime report—from the night your mother was murdered."

She glanced at Castillo, who listened with closed eyes, his nostrils flared with his heavy breathing. "We have that crime report. *I* have that report."

"You have the revised report, the official report, the report that was filed by Officer Castillo." Jake spread his hands in front of him. "Quinn left me the original report."

Her adrenaline surged, and prickles of anger danced across the back of her neck. "Are you trying to tell me Quinn lied on a police report? That he deliberately changed a report and let it stand as the truth?"

Castillo snorted, and Jake glared at him as he answered, "He did."

Kyra rocketed to her feet, using the arms of the chair as leverage. "Quinn would never do that. He was a good cop, an honest cop."

Jake reached for her, but she reared back. "He would if it meant he could protect you. He was a good cop, but he was a better man."

"Protect me?" She thrust her finger against her chest. "How would submitting a fraudulent police report protect me?"

Jake lifted one shoulder, his green eyes dark and murky. "Because you witnessed your mother's murder that night. Marilyn Monroe Lake saw The Player."

Chapter Ten

The room spun, and Kyra threw out an arm to brace her hand against the wall. Her lips moved automatically before her brain formed the words. "No, I didn't."

Jake took her free hand in his. "You did, Kyra. It was right there in the report. The attack on your mother woke you up. You stood at your bedroom door and saw the end of your mother's struggle."

"I didn't." She shook her head, and her ponytail whipped back and forth. "Why would Quinn lie about that? I could've described the killer. I could've helped catch him. I was a witness."

Guiding her back to the chair, Quinn said, "Because he saw you, too."

She ended up in the chair with a plop that jarred her teeth. "H-he saw me? That's what I told Quinn?"

"That's what you told *me*." Castillo had slumped in his own chair, his head in his hand. "Then you repeated the story when Detective Quinn came onto the scene. Quinn told me right then and there that the killer could never know you admitted to seeing him. We changed the report to indicate that you'd slept through the whole thing. You were never listed as a witness, and The Player must've believed you'd forgotten, too traumatized to remember locking eyes with him."

"I *don't* remember. I don't remember any of it." Kyra placed a hand at her throat. "I can't believe Quinn lied, actually changed a crime scene report. And you—" she narrowed her eyes at Castillo behind his desk "—why would you agree to something like that?"

Castillo, his face stamped with anxiety in every line, shot Jake a look. "Ask him."

"That's not important now, Kyra. Just know that Quinn did it to protect you. He didn't want to expose you to The Player's scrutiny. He wanted to keep you off his radar."

"It explains why I *have* been on his radar all these years. He knew I saw him, thought I could ID him, and he wanted to keep tabs on me. He's been testing me during the copycat slayings, making sure I wasn't a viable witness." She chewed on her bottom lip. "Why did he leave that report for you, Jake?"

"He was passing along the torch for your protection to me." He gripped the back of his neck with his hand. "I failed. My first instinct was to honor his wish, but I knew you'd want to know."

"Maybe it was no longer his wish, Jake. Maybe that's why he left it to you instead of Captain Castillo." She tipped her head toward Castillo. "Maybe he knew you'd do the right thing."

Castillo's tongue darted out of his mouth. "Wh-what are you going to do with the information, specifically the information from Tony Galecki?"

"Relax. I'm not going to do anything with it…right now." Jake extended his hand to Kyra. "Let's go to my place. We'll have dinner and talk over everything."

She took his hand, and his warmth and strength gave her courage. She stood up on legs she thought were going to fail her minutes before. Whoever Tony Galecki was and whatever happened between him, Quinn and Castillo, she'd deal with it later. She had some important decisions to make tonight…and Jake would be by her side to help.

They left Castillo to his tormented thoughts and re-grets, and Jake walked her to her car.

"Follow me to my house. I have some steaks and red wine and a warm bed."

"And advice? Are you going to have that, too?"

"I don't know about advice, but we can talk it all out." He opened her car door. "I can be your therapist tonight."

She kissed him lightly, and then slid behind the wheel of her car. As she waited for Jake's sedan to pull out of the parking lot, her mind raced in circles. She'd witnessed her mother's murder. She'd seen The Player.

Quinn had been looking out for her the minute he met her. He'd changed a report to protect her. She never would've believed that of him.

When Jake's car appeared, she stepped on the gas and followed him out to the street. When had she forgotten she'd witnessed the murder? She'd been eight years old. She remembered most of that night. She remembered Quinn coming into the room, his suit slightly rumpled, his already graying hair sticking up like he'd just rolled out of bed, his comforting arms around her as she trem-bled in shock and fear. She even remembered the smell of his aftershave, which he continued to use years later.

A tear trembled on her eyelashes, blurring Jake's taillights ahead of her, and she dashed it away. Quinn shouldn't have risked his career for her. Maybe she would've been able to ID The Player and stop his deadly reign of terror. If Quinn had caught him twenty years ago, he wouldn't be active today, encouraging others to follow in his evil footsteps.

She chose to believe that's why Quinn saved the initial

report and left it with Jake. He knew Jake would do the right thing…and protect her. Once the copycat killings began, maybe Quinn realized she had to know the truth.

But what would she do with the truth?

She followed Jake's car up the winding roads of the Hollywood Hills to his house. When they made it inside, she collapsed on the couch that faced the glass wall overlooking the twinkling lights of the city.

He brought her a glass of wine as she toed off her shoes, and then sat beside her, pulling her feet into his lap. "Did the ride over give you time to process?"

"Not really. I still find it hard to believe Quinn would do something like that. It could've ended his career."

"He had a long career already, and I guess he figured your safety was more important than his job." He drove his thumb into the arch of her foot. "Your safety is important to me, too, Kyra. I told you because you had a right to know."

She lightly tickled the inside of his wrist. "Not because I busted you?"

"I didn't know Rose had ratted me out when I charged into Castillo's office tonight. I just wasn't sure what he was telling you." Jake scuffed his knuckles across his jaw. "I don't trust him."

"Are you going to tell me what he did? Why did he agree to go along with Quinn's decision to scrap the original report and lie?"

Jake pulled his bottom lip between his teeth. "It's not a favorable story for Castillo—but it's not a favorable story for Quinn, either. Are you sure you want to hear it?"

"I've already reached the conclusion that Quinn was not as honest as I thought he was. I might as well hear it all. It's not going to change my opinion of him as the best damned father a girl could've had." She cupped her wineglass with both hands and took a swig, the dark, fruity liquid warming her throat.

"It goes back to an LAPD drug task force called LA Impact. Castillo was on that task force and arrested Tony Galecki, a dealer for the Sinaloa cartel. Quinn had been investigating the murder of Galecki's girlfriend, and the murder investigation dovetailed with the drug task force."

"What does this all have to do with me and my mother's murder?"

"Galecki had been skimming—cutting the drugs, selling more than his allotted amount and pocketing the extra cash. That's why the cartel assassinated his girlfriend."

Kyra hunched her shoulders. "Terrible. Go on."

"When Galecki was arrested, he claimed he had fat stacks, and when the cops couldn't find his money, Galecki accused them of stealing it."

Kyra covered her mouth with her hand. "Castillo stole Galecki's money?"

Jake nodded, his lips pressed together. He obviously didn't want to spill the rest—the part that made Quinn look bad.

She took another sip of wine and cupped it on her tongue before swallowing it and continuing Jake's story for him. "Quinn knew about the theft and made it go away for Castillo as long as he lied about the report."

Jake replied, "Quinn made a deal with Galecki, let him keep a cut of the money, let Castillo keep his, and the future captain kept his mouth shut about the night of your mother's murder in exchange."

"Did Quinn take any of the money?" She folded her hands across her stomach to suppress the butterflies.

"No. He wanted nothing out of the deal except for Castillo to keep quiet about your witnessing the murder."

Kyra slumped against the pillow. Quinn hadn't been

the straight arrow she'd always believed him to be, but that didn't matter.

"The worst is over." Jake held up his hands. "That's all I got."

"But that's not all you have." Kyra narrowed her eyes. "You have the original report. Quinn left that, didn't he?"

"Yeah." Jake's Adam's apple bobbed as he swallowed, and he hadn't even taken a sip of wine.

"I'd like to see it, Jake. I need to see it."

"I will hand it over to you on one condition." He waved a finger in the air. "You eat a decent meal tonight. I'm going to grill some steaks, cook potato wedges and toss a salad—and you're going to eat it."

"It's a deal. Gimme." She snapped her fingers, and he lifted her legs from his lap and pushed off the couch.

As he jogged upstairs, probably to retrieve the report from his safe, Kyra took her wineglass to the kitchen and dumped in a little more of the ruby-red liquid, which sloshed up the sides. She had a feeling she'd need something to get through the report—not that she hadn't read its replacement a countless number of times.

Jake returned, a sheaf of papers pinched between his fingers. He placed the report on the coffee table. "I'm leaving it here, and I'm going to make dinner."

"Thanks." She raised her glass in salute and sauntered back to the couch, eying the stack of papers as if it were an explosive device. It just might be.

Jake buzzed around the kitchen, running water, chopping and clanking pans, but the noises couldn't distract her from the words in front of her.

The story unfolded pretty much as she'd read from the dog-eared report she kept in her own safe at home. A female child had called 911, and Officer Carlos Castillo had responded to the duplex in Hollywood. Upon entering the residence, he'd discovered a young girl, sobbing on the phone with the 911 operator still on the line, her hands, legs and feet slick with blood, next to the dead body of a woman she claimed was her mother.

Upon examination of the body, Castillo realized the serial killer The Player had struck again based on the card in the woman's mouth, her missing finger and her death by strangulation. The blood on the child had come from her mother's hand and another cut her mother had suffered from a broken vase, indicating the woman had put up a fight.

Castillo tried to question the child, but she wouldn't or couldn't answer him. He put in a call immediately to Detective Roger Quinn, the lead detective on The Player case. Quinn was in the area and showed up before any other emergency personnel. He was also able to get the girl to talk to him.

Here's where the stories diverged, and Kyra took a gulp of wine before continuing. According to Quinn, the girl reported she was in her bedroom and heard noises. She got up, peeked through a crack in her door—and saw the man who murdered her mother.

She must've made a noise because the man looked up from his gruesome deeds, and his eyes met the girl's. Quinn got a garbled description of the killer from the victim's daughter. The first responders arrived, and the report continued with the familiar sequence of events.

Kyra blew out a wine-scented breath and placed the papers on the polished wood of the coffee table. She sniffed the air and realized Jake was still in the kitchen cooking.

She got to her feet and leaned on the kitchen island to watch him sweep the rest of the chopped veggies into two bowls. "Jake?"

"Yeah?"

"In the report, Quinn mentioned that I gave a garbled description of the killer."

"I know." He stuck the cutting board in the sink and rinsed it off. "Maybe he realized your eyewitness account wouldn't be that useful, and that helped him decide it wasn't worth risking your safety over it."

"Don't make excuses for him. Any eyewitness report would be helpful." She ran a finger around the rim of her glass. "Neither he nor Castillo included any details of my description in the report. What did I claim? A man with red eyes and horns killed my mother? Was Quinn already thinking of chucking my eyewitness account to protect me?"

"You can imagine what he was thinking." Jake circled the island and put the salad bowls on the table. "Scared, shocked little girl locking eyes with a killer. He didn't want to expose you—especially if your account wasn't going to be helpful. Sit."

She picked up her glass and sat down. She waited until Jake had slid the steaks and potatoes onto plates and set them on the table. When he sat to her left, she grabbed her fork and toyed with her salad. She'd promised him she'd eat, but her appetite hadn't returned since they found Quinn on the floor of his house. The punches had kept coming in quick succession.

The savory smell of the steaks made her mouth water, and she dug into her salad first. The wine, the food—and the company—slowly unwound the knots in her belly, and she was able to cut into her steak with gusto.

She waved her fork dripping with steak sauce. "This is so good. I didn't realize how hungry I was."

"Good, keep eating. You need your strength. The

other shoe hasn't even dropped about the cause of Quinn's death."

She dropped her knife, and it clattered against her plate. "Jake, you don't think Captain Castillo had anything to do with Quinn's death, do you?"

He stared into his wineglass as if looking for the answer there. "I admit I suspected it at first, but I don't think he's a killer. He and Quinn must've discussed the report numerous times. I believe Quinn told Castillo that he'd kept the report, and I believe Castillo wanted him to destroy it—for both their sakes. There was no reason for Castillo to believe Quinn was going to come clean about the report."

"Really?" She swirled the mingling fat from the steak and the sauce on her plate with the tines of her fork. "Not even when the copycat killers started operating? We both noticed Castillo's unease when one copycat succeeded the other."

"Castillo may have wanted Quinn to destroy the report, but he knew Quinn wouldn't go public. He wanted to protect you." Jake dug his elbows into the table and balanced his chin on his fists. "I do believe that Castillo is the one who searched Quinn's house, though."

"You're probably right about that." She pushed her plate away. "That was yummy. You're a good cook."

"I have my repertoire. Too bad my daughter's a vegetarian these days, as my repertoire pretty much is this meal."

Patting her stomach, Kyra said, "It hit the spot. I haven't felt this relaxed since…"

She covered her eyes with her hand, and Jake jumped out of his chair and circled behind hers. He placed his hands on her shoulders and said, "It's all right. We'll get justice for Quinn—one way or another. Finish relaxing on the couch. I'll clean up."

"No, you don't. Look at you." She pinched his dress shirt between her fingers, his sleeves rolled up to expose the end of the tiger tattoo on his forearm. "You haven't even changed out of your work clothes. You get comfortable and I'll do the dishes."

He relented and dropped a kiss on the top of her head. "You twisted my arm."

As he went upstairs, she stacked their plates and rinsed them at the sink. She loaded the dishwasher and cocked her head as she heard the shower upstairs. Imagining Jake's body beneath the stream of water, she almost dropped the dishes to scamper upstairs to join him.

They hadn't made love for a while, and she missed the closeness. She'd been on edge and resentful of Jake for keeping his midnight visit to Quinn's house a secret from her, but his revelations tonight had shored up her faith in him and deepened her love. She needed him more than ever.

She finished cleaning up, poured more wine for Jake, and took her glass to the window, where she swirled the dark liquid and stared at the shimmering lights below. Quinn had risked so much to protect her. She wished she could've protected him in the end. If someone had murdered him, who? Not Castillo. She agreed with Jake. The captain was no killer—corrupt, but no killer.

The Player? She shivered despite the warmth of the wine and food in her belly. Had Quinn known The Player all this time? He never would've turned his back on a stranger in his house—never would've let a stranger into his house in the first place. Had The Player been hiding in plain sight?

She heard a step on the stairs and shifted her gaze

from the city lights to Jake's reflection in the glass. He'd changed into a pair of basketball shorts and a white T-shirt. Now she felt overdressed. She should remedy that.

He made a detour to the counter and picked up the glass she'd left for him. Meeting her eyes in the window, he prowled behind her until he stood at her back, one arm wrapped around her waist.

She inhaled his soapy scent, which could never mask the pure masculine essence that emanated from his body. "You smell good."

He dipped his head and kissed the side of her throat. "You taste good."

She undulated her hips against his pelvis, and he gasped and said, "That's quite a greeting."

Holding her wineglass away from her, she started to turn toward him, but he stopped her and took the glass from her hand. "Let me have that. You, stay right here."

She relinquished her wine, and he took a step back and placed both glasses on a side table. Then he snuggled up against her back again, his hands splaying across her stomach, his tongue tickling the lobe of her ear.

She reached down and steadied her hands against his bare thighs, her back arching. "Not fair. I'm still in my work clothes."

"Do you want me to fix that for you?"

She purred, "If you promise always to be my handy-man."

He chuckled in her ear as he undid the first three buttons on her blouse. He loosened the hem of her top from the waistband of her slacks and pulled it over her head, sighing as he plucked at the lacy camisole beneath. "You have to make things complicated for me."

He peeled the camisole from her body and then took care of business with her bra. "Halfway there."

She'd already kicked off her shoes. As Jake fumbled with her slacks, she shooed away his hands and released the button and zipper to help the poor guy out.

He needed no further invitation. He hooked his fingers in her waistband and pulled down her slacks, catching her panties on the way. As her pants pooled at her feet, she stepped out of them and kicked them to the side.

"Now *I'm* overdressed." He made quick work of his T-shirt and shorts and sealed his naked body against hers, his warm skin sending sparks through her veins.

She closed her eyes to slits so she could see Jake's large hands roaming across her naked flesh. He gently eased her shoulders and chest forward, and she braced her forearms against the glass. Then he slipped his hand between her legs.

The coolness of the window contrasting with the hot thumping between her thighs made her gasp. His fingers teased her swollen folds, and she brushed her bottom against his erection prodding her from behind.

He nestled his head in the crook of her neck and nibbled on her collarbone as he continued to stir her to climax. Gritting her teeth, she held her breath, the multicolored lights from the city streets fusing into a rainbow glow. She let out a harsh breath that fogged the window, and then scooped it in again as the tension in her body built to a breaking point.

Shoving two fingers inside her, he stroked her heated flesh on the outside until she exploded. She cried out with her orgasm, bucking against him as she braced her hands against the slick glass.

She still clenched around his fingers, her climax shuddering through her body. He withdrew them and entered her from behind. He thrust into her, and she clawed at the window. He had one arm securely curled around her waist, and she rode him hard, smacking her backside against his pelvis as they rocked together.

His big frame heaved as his climax took him, and he nearly lifted her off her feet. As he slowed his pace and trembled behind her, he hugged her body to his, spooning her from behind, and they slid to the floor together.

Breathing heavily, she reached up behind her and wound one arm around his neck. She turned her head and kissed his salty arm wrapped around her waist. "That was…unexpected."

They'd been mutely enjoying each other's bodies, and her voice cracked with the words.

He pulled out of her and drew her into his lap, his brow furrowed. "Not what you wanted?"

"*Exactly* what I wanted and needed. I just thought we'd head up to your bedroom and slip between the sheets."

"There's still time for that. When I saw you at the window, I had to have you—then, there, now, always."

She snuggled against his chest, her hands resting lightly on his legs straddling her. "Are you sure nobody can see us out there?"

"The only building that reaches this height is that one." He tapped his finger against the glass at a multistory office building across the way and below the Hollywood Hills. Can you see anyone through those little square windows?"

She squinted. "I can barely see the little squares."

"There's your answer—no audience."

She drew a heart in the condensation still fogging the glass. "I love you, Jake."

He made a noise in the back of his throat and pulled her closer, burying his face in her messed-up hair. "I love you, too, and I'll do anything to keep you safe. Maybe I should've never told you about Quinn's deception."

"I know you want to protect me, just like Quinn did, but you were right to tell me. I'm not saying Quinn was wrong to keep the secret, but he was my father. You're my lover, my partner, my equal."

He let out a long breath. "I'm glad you feel that way. Now it's out in the open, and maybe you're safer for it."

"I wouldn't say that." She stroked the hair on his leg.

His body stiffened behind her. "Why do you say that?"

"You know why, Jake."

"I do?"

"Sure you do. You even mentioned it at lunch when you hadn't told me Quinn's secret yet."

His hold on her tightened. "What do you mean, Kyra?"

"I mean, I'm going to undergo hypnosis to bring me back to the night of my mother's murder. I'm going to remember seeing The Player, and I'm going to identify him—and that will put me in danger. Let him try to stop me."

Chapter Eleven

Jake slurped his lukewarm coffee and glanced across the task force war room over the rim of his cup. He and Kyra had spent most of the weekend together, and Kyra had already warned him she'd be in late, as she had a client in Santa Monica and errands. He didn't press her, but was one of those errands contacting that shrink, or rather, the hypnotist?

She'd mentioned to him that a world-renowned hypnotherapist lived right in their backyard, and one of her colleagues had worked with him on a professional level before. He's the one she'd tagged to help her delve into those memories.

Just like Quinn, Jake had known that the fact Kyra had been an eyewitness to her mother's murder could put her at risk, but nobody today had to know she'd discovered that information. Castillo would keep quiet because it was in his best interests to do so. Jake would keep mum about it, too.

One of the cops on the task force broke Jake's line of sight to Kyra's desk, and Jake refocused his gaze on the eager face, eyes glowing behind a pair of glasses. "What is it, Luberger?"

Luberger slid a photo of a woman's wallet onto Jake's desk. "We think we found Copycat Four's trophy."

Jake lifted the piece of paper by the corner and studied the open wallet. "The driver's license is missing."

"That's right." Luberger drilled a finger against the photo. "It should be right there, and Ashley's brother confirmed she kept her license in her wallet behind the plastic shield. He can't find it anywhere."

"Please tell me Clive got to this wallet before you guys had your paws all over it."

Hearing his name, Clive planted himself in front of Jake's desk, a grim twist to his lips. "I did, but he must've been wearing his gloves when he took the license because there were no prints on that wallet save Ashley's."

Pounding his fist on the desk, Jake said, "I thought this guy would be sloppier than the rest. He had a bad start to his career."

When Jake's phone rang, he held up his finger. "Hold on, both of you, for a second."

When he saw the number for the LA County Coroner's Office on his display, his heart slammed against his chest. He answered, "McAllister."

"Jake, it's Deirdre. It's going to come out sooner or later, so I'm giving you a heads-up. Quinn's tox report came back and he had higher than normal levels of amphetamines in his system. None of his meds would've caused that. Given that, the puncture between his toes and the anomalies of the shoe and sock on that foot, we're classifying Quinn's death as a homicide."

Although he'd been expecting this, Jake curled his hand around the edge of his desk. "A homicide made to look like natural causes."

"That's right. My office has already notified Chief Sterling of our report, but I wanted to tell you personally."

"Thanks, Deirdre. When are you sending the report over?"

"It's already been sent to the chief."

He ended the call and was staring blankly at his phone when Clive cleared his throat.

"Something up, Detective?"

"Yep." Jake pushed up from his desk and braced his hands on it as he shouted, "Attention, everyone. Retired detective Roger Quinn was murdered."

The room exploded with outrage and activity. It was the response Jake wanted. He wasn't going to wait for the chief or Castillo. He clapped his hands. "You know what this means, right? This investigation belongs to us, to this task force. There is no way Quinn's murder is not linked to The Player and the copycat killers. The Player must've known Quinn had been offering assistance to our task force, that eventually with our newer technology today Quinn might be able to offer a piece of evidence that we could track back to The Player. It was Quinn who gave us the piece that allowed us to link the copycats directly to The Player. So, let's do this."

At the end of his pep talk, Kyra had sidled into the room, her face white and her eyes round.

Jake strode toward her and grabbed her hand. "You heard."

"I knew it. I always knew it."

"You can't go back to the Venice house today. We're going in and processing it as a crime scene, although I don't want to think about the evidence that might have already been compromised there."

"How did The Player get into Quinn's house? If Quinn didn't know him, maybe The Player sent someone else to do the deed—someone posing as a delivery person."

"We'll figure it out. Everyone is pumped for this one."

Billy sailed into the room, fist in the air. "Hope you all

don't plan to get any sleep in the next several weeks. I just heard from dispatch. We have another copycat slaying."

THE LIGHT SMATTERING of rain hit the windshield, and Billy tapped the wipers to whisk it off the glass. "I hope this rain isn't washing away any evidence."

Jake used his fist to wipe the condensation from the inside of the window. "What evidence? They never seem to leave any."

"Not true, my man. He left a witness. He left Piper."

"And all she was able to give us was a hunched-over man in dark clothes and a hoodie."

"Her presence lured him out to take a chance. We'll get him. I'm confident. We nailed the other three, didn't we? The Player trained them, too, and they all made mistakes. Number Four is careless." Billy shot him a glance from the corner of his eye. "The Player's been careless, too. Did he think he could kill Quinn and get away with it?"

"He thought Quinn's death would come back as natural causes, but he messed up by replacing Quinn's sock and shoe incorrectly. That tipped off the ME."

"And you know this how?" Billy raised his eyebrows as he took the turnoff for the Angeles National Forest.

"A little inside information." Jake shook his head. "Damn, I wish we'd processed that house as a crime scene when we first found Quinn's body. Kyra knew."

"How's she doing? She looked rattled in the war room before we left, but I suppose that's natural. She's had it rough."

"She's coping." Jake sealed his lips after the pronouncement. Billy had no idea how rough it was about to get for Kyra, but nobody, not even his trusted partner, had to know what Kyra planned to do.

It had been a long drive to the dump site, and when

Billy pulled up, emergency vehicles clogged the road. The responding officers from the LA County Sheriff's Department had known immediately what they had on their hands, and had cordoned off the area in anticipation of the arrival of detectives from the Copycat Player Task Force.

Now Jake and Billy moved through the scene, snapping gloves on their hands and trudging toward the soggy crime scene tape.

A sheriff's deputy from the Altadena division intercepted them, raindrops beading on his khaki uniform. "Detectives, I'm Deputy Lawson. I was the first on the scene. Early-morning bird watchers discovered the body—same MO as the others—card between the lips, missing finger, manual strangulation, no sexual assault evident."

They questioned Lawson for a few more minutes, and then dove into the crime scene. Jake hovered over the body, his gut knotted. The rain hadn't dislodged or damaged the stiff, glossy playing card in the victim's mouth. The blood beneath her hand where the killer had removed her finger had soaked into the dirt.

Crouching down, Jake reached out to trace the purple necklace of bruising around her throat. Another necklace of shiny gold winked at him, and he hooked his finger beneath the chain and pulled it away from her flesh. This guy took driver's licenses, not jewelry.

A couple of attachments tinkled as he dropped the necklace. He went in for a closer look, cupping the discs in his hand, and he cocked his head. "Hey, Billy, what does this mean?"

Billy squatted beside him and squinted at the medallions. "They have Roman numerals and some writing. What do the words say?"

"Brother, you need reading glasses." Jake nudged his partner with his shoulder and tipped his head to read the words around the circle of the disc. "It says, 'To thine own self be true.' Then around the triangle in the middle are the words 'Unity, service and recovery.'"

Jake's pulse jumped. "Is this what I think it is?"

Billy dipped his head. "It's a recovery chip or whatever from AA."

"Boom. We have our link."

THE FIRST THING Billy did when he got back to the station was contact Marcia from the AA meeting at the church in Glendale. With Jake listening in, Billy gave Marcia a description of their murder victim.

Still on the phone, Billy shook his head at Jake and said, "Thanks, Marcia. If something comes up, be sure to give me a call."

Billy slumped in his chair. "She's pretty sure that description doesn't match any of the members at the women's-only meeting there."

Shrugging, Jake said, "He'd have to be pretty stupid to take his prey from the exact same meeting and location, but he does have some connection to these meetings. Maybe he's met women there before, was able to play on their vulnerability and figured it was a good place to hunt for victims."

"I told you, the guy's sloppy." Billy coughed. "Hey, man, I'm bringing a team of CSI folks to Quinn's house today. The captain asked me to take a lead on this."

"I know. Don't worry about it." Jake clapped Billy on the back. "Castillo sent me a text with the news. Thought I was too close to the situation."

Billy's eyes widened. "He sent you a text? That's cold, man."

Jake brushed it off. The text hadn't surprised him at all—neither the content nor the delivery. He didn't disagree with Castillo's determination that his relationship with Quinn and Kyra might cloud his judgment and hinder the investigative process into Quinn's homicide, and notification by text suited Castillo's purposes right now. The captain hadn't been alone with Jake since Jake discovered his theft of Tony Galecki's drug money.

It suited Jake's purposes, too. He preferred to keep Castillo off balance.

Billy smacked a piece of paper on Jake's desk. "I made a list for you. These are the most recent missing persons reports. They're all entered, and you can look them up online now."

"I'll do this right away, partner."

Grabbing his jacket, Billy turned toward Jake. "You know I'll keep you posted on everything."

"I know that. Go get our man some justice." Jake held out his fist for a bump and Billy obliged.

When his partner left, taking most of the task force's CSI team with him, Jake pulled out his phone to text Kyra. He'd expected her to be here when he got back, and her empty desk had given him a start.

He breathed a little easier when she responded that she had an appointment with Wade Russell, Ashley's brother. The poor guy had been traumatized by his sister's murder. Hell, Billy was still devastated by his own sister's disappearance after all these years.

Jake had gotten through three reports for women who looked nothing like Copycat Four's victim when a call came through on his work cell from the desk sergeant downstairs. "McAllister. Whatcha got, Lomeli?"

"I have a call on the line from a hysterical woman about her roommate who didn't come home last night.

Today, she found her car parked in the place where the roommate was last headed, some church."

A muscle in Jake's jaw ticked. "She was going to church yesterday on a weekday?"

"AA meeting."

"Put her through. What's her name?"

"Remy Tran."

The first thing Jake heard from Remy was a shaky breath and a sob. "H-hello?"

"Ms. Tran? Remy? This is Detective McAllister. Can you tell me everything you told the sergeant?"

She repeated the story she'd told Lomeli, adding that her roommate was supposed to come home after the AA meeting for a get-together at the roommate's house they shared in Alhambra. "I was kind of setting her up on a blind date with one of my friends, and thought maybe she got cold feet. But when she didn't come home the rest of the night, I freaked. Tina never does that. She's not into partying, you know?"

"What does Tina look like, Remy?"

After Remy had given him an accurate description of the woman they'd just found with a card between her lips, Jake swallowed. "What's Tina's last name, Remy?"

"Valdez. Tina Valdez. I'm by her car right now."

Jake shot up in his seat. "Don't touch the car, Remy. You got that?"

"No, no. I haven't touched the car because I know there's something wrong. The stuff from Tina's purse is all over the seat and floor. I can see her phone. She'd never leave her phone, never leave her purse. Then I just heard another body was found at Angeles." She broke down, and Jake couldn't get her to listen to another word for several seconds.

Where was Kyra when he needed her?

When Remy's sobs had tapered off to hiccups, Jake continued in what he hoped was a soothing voice. "Give me the address of the church, Remy, and I'll be out as soon as I can. I'm going to call the Pasadena PD for you because they can get there before I do. Can you hold on for a few more minutes?"

"Y-yes." She recited the church's name and address.

After reassuring Remy again, Jake called the Pasadena PD and told them to secure the car and the area around it. Then he grabbed his jacket and went in search of a CSI team to send out to Pasadena. Billy had already gathered the A team for Quinn's house, but the LAPD housed a large number of professionals.

He burst into the lab, and a young woman glanced up, her eyebrows disappearing beneath her thick, dark bangs. "Detective McAllister? Clive isn't here. He went out to the Quinn scene."

"I know that. You're...?"

"I'm sorry." She scooted around the table in the center of the room where she'd been hunched over a laptop. "I'm Lori Del Valle. I'm a fingerprint tech, too. I just started last year."

Definitely not the A team.

"I have a possible crime scene in Pasadena. We need to process a car. I need a photographer and a CSI who can vacuum properly and test fluids. Now."

"We have a team." Lori jerked her thumb over her shoulder, her dark eyes shimmering with excitement. "I'll tell them. Address?"

He gave her the address, and she scribbled it down. "The scene is being secured by Pasadena PD. I'll meet you all out there."

Jake strode out of the lab and almost collided with

Kyra. She grabbed his arm. "I heard on the news she was another copycat victim."

"Verified. Are you busy right now?"

"Just have some notes to do. Why?"

"I think we located the victim's car. It's at a church in Pasadena."

Her fingers dug into his arm. "Church? Another AA meeting?"

"That's right. The roommate's there, and she's distraught, to say the least. Might help to have you there."

"I'll be right on your tail."

Five minutes later, Jake pulled out of the parking lot and flicked on his strobe lights to cut through traffic faster. The sooner he reached that car, the better.

With traffic slowing in the rain, the trip northeast to Pasadena took him twenty minutes. Kyra wouldn't be there for another fifteen.

Remy Tran had used the term *parking lot* loosely. A small patch of asphalt with spaces for five cars, tops, bordered one edge of a community room at the back of the church. The little red Honda protected by crime scene tape huddled on a gravel strip not meant for parking but used anyway.

Jake looked up at the building when he exited his car. He didn't expect to see cameras, and his surveillance confirmed his hunch. His gaze shifted to a petite woman, her black hair covering her face as her head dropped between her knees. Yeah, Remy needed Kyra, stat.

Jake introduced himself to the PPD cop and flashed his badge. "I have a CSI team on the way. I appreciate your securing this for us."

The cop gave him a thumbs-up. "The fact that this creep is doing his hunting in our area has us ready to go. Anything you guys need from us."

"Have you talked to the roommate?"

"Can't get much out of her. She's destroyed."

As Jake walked toward Remy, her head popped up, and she jumped to her feet, wringing her hands. "Are you the cop I spoke to on the phone?"

"That's right, Remy. I'm Detective Jake McAllister." He gestured to the curb. "Do you want to sit back down?"

"No." She paced away from him a few feet and wiped a hand across her wet and swollen face. "What next? Are you going to take her car away?"

"We're going to get inside first and search it here."

"The car's unlocked now, but it was locked." Remy's hand plunged into her purse, and the keys jangled in her trembling fingers. "I have an extra key. I told you I didn't touch the car, but I pressed the remote to unlock it and it clicked, so I know it was locked. I left it unlocked."

"That's fine. Thanks for telling me."

"C-can I stay here while you look?"

"Of course, but can you do something for me first? You don't have to right away, but if you're up to it, can I show you a picture of the victim we discovered today?"

"Dead?" She covered her mouth with both hands. "A picture of someone dead?"

He'd blundered. "I'll tell you what. There's someone on the way, Kyra Chase, and she's going to sit with you. If you feel like looking at the picture, so we can ID your friend—if it's her—let Kyra know. That's all. No pressure."

She sank to the curb again, wrapping her arms around her knees and bowing her head.

Jake pulled out some gloves and a few bags for evidence on his way to the roped-off car. Head down, he examined the area around the car. Gravel moved easily, and he spotted shoeprints that looked like the soles of Remy's flip-flops. The rain had created a few puddles in areas where divots formed in the gravel. Signs of a struggle.

He stepped over those spots, hoping to retain any evidence, and opened the driver's side door. Tina hadn't left her keys in the ignition, and the killer probably wouldn't have been able to lock up the car with the key fob inside the vehicle. Copycat Four took her keys, which meant he probably had the key to the house she shared with Remy.

He checked the interior of the car and didn't see any blood or any other disturbances, except the purse. He shook out an evidence bag, plucked up the mostly empty purse with his gloved fingers and dropped it inside. He scanned the contents from the purse that littered the passenger seat and the floor beneath it.

The items represented standard issue for most young women's bags—a tube of lipstick, a small bottle of aspirin, a few pens, random coins—things his own daughter had started carrying in a pocketbook. He squeezed his eyes closed and reached for the wallet.

A few credit cards and a grocery store rewards card occupied the slots, but the plastic enclosure where someone might typically keep a license was empty. He ran his thumb along the plastic, and it slid off. How had he removed the license wearing gloves? Latex gloves like the ones he had on wouldn't have given him enough traction to get that license. He placed the wallet in a separate evidence bag.

He heard a commotion and glanced over his shoulder. The CSI team, including Lori Del Valle, had arrived together in a van, and Kyra had just pulled up in her car. He backed out of Tina's vehicle, clutching the evidence bags.

Back on firm ground, he waved at the CSIs. When they formed a semicircle around him, he pointed at the ground. "We need some photos here. Looks like a scuffle took place outside the car, but I'm not sure the rain and wind left any footprints. The flip-flops belong to the roommate, who discovered the car. You can take her prints, too, to rule them out."

One of the techs he didn't know asked, "Any blood in the car or other bodily fluids?"

"Not that I can see." He held up the evidence bags. "These contain the contents of her purse, and I want particular attention focused on the wallet. He removed her driver's license."

He gave a few more instructions and then cut off Kyra making a beeline to the forlorn roommate hunched over on the curb. "That's Remy Tran. She's really upset. I told her you were on your way. She didn't want to look at a picture of the dead woman."

"I wouldn't think so. She's her roommate, so she probably has pictures of Tina on her phone. I'll have her show you one of those and you can compare it to the deceased."

Jake smacked his forehead. "Of course."

Kyra lowered her voice as they walked toward Remy. "Anything in the car?"

"Not much. Seems like the killer accosted Tina outside the vehicle, and then threw her purse into the front seat before he abducted her. He also snagged her license, or maybe he had her take it out for him."

When they reached Remy, Jake introduced Kyra and left them together. While he waited, he asked the deputy a few more questions, and talked to several of the bystanders who'd gathered in bunches, their eyes narrowed, their whispers hushed.

Kyra waved him over, and he approached her and

Remy, who had at least stopped crying and had gotten to her feet.

"Show him the picture of Tina, Remy." Kyra patted Remy on the arm.

Bracketing her phone with trembling fingers, Remy held out her phone to Jake.

Jake studied the two smiling young women, and his gut rolled. The woman next to Remy had shoulder-length brown hair and expressive brown eyes…and she now lay on a slab at the coroner's office.

His gaze shifted from the photo on the phone to Remy's tear-filled eyes. She knew already, had known from the moment she'd heard about the body and found her roommate's car on the side of this church. "I'm sorry, Remy."

Remy sagged, and Kyra caught her before she sank to the ground. Jake knew Kyra could handle this woman's grief a lot better than he could, so he turned back to Tina's car.

The tech's vacuum whined as it sucked up fibers and fragments from the back seat of the car, to be analyzed later. Lori, the fingerprint tech, hopped out of the van and strode toward him.

"Detective McAllister, I dusted the purse and the wallet."

"Really?" He raised an eyebrow at her. "I thought you'd just take those back to the station to wait for Clive."

"You know, Clive—" She shook her head. "Never mind. You said the wallet was important, so I thought we could take care of it here."

This one was ambitious. He'd have to warn Clive to watch his back.

"Okay, that's great. Thanks." He started to pivot, and she stopped him with a hand on his arm.

"The thing is, Detective McAllister, I found something on the plastic shield of the wallet. Someone left a latent print…and it didn't belong to Tina."

Chapter Twelve

Sitting across from Jake at the Uncommon Grounds coffee house, Kyra listened to him berate himself with a curve to her lips. That's one of the things she loved about him. Most men would've glossed over his interaction with Lori Del Valle without a second thought.

"I just dismissed Lori, didn't expect her to have anything, and she turns up with that print. I'd been thinking of her as second-rate all along when I couldn't get Clive. Even worse, I suspected her of playing office politics when it sounded like she was going to criticize Clive." He ran a hand through his dark hair, which stood up on end. "Do you think I did that because she's a woman?"

"You have a lot of strong females in your life, starting with your daughter. I think you underestimated Lori because you thought of her as part of the B team when Billy took all the CSI first-stringers to Quinn's. Face it. You had low expectations of the entire team, regardless of their gender."

"You're probably right. That just makes me an ass." He swirled the dregs of his coffee and took a sip.

"I mean, when you growled at me for joining the task force, I didn't think it was because I was a woman." She lifted her shoulders and winked. "I knew it was because you hated therapists."

"Definitely an ass." He rubbed his thumb on the back of her hand. "Speaking of therapists, did you reach that Chai Gellman character?"

"His name is *Shai* Gellman and he's a renowned hypnotherapist, not a character." She rapped his knuckles with a plastic spoon. "I left him a message, but he hasn't responded yet."

"You're sure you want to do it?"

"Of course I do." Kyra tapped her head. "Those memories are buried in there somewhere, and I want access to them. Look, Quinn may have been overreacting from the beginning. It doesn't sound like I had much to offer in the way of a description of The Player, and maybe I don't know."

Jake said, "I want to be there with you when you go."

"I'd like that, but you know it's not all going to come to me in one appointment. It could take several sessions, and it might not work at all."

"I'm prepared for that. Are you? Maybe we won't need it. Maybe the CSI A team will gather enough evidence at Quinn's house to find his killer and ID him as The Player."

"Maybe you should've sent the B team to Quinn's instead of the first team." She planted her elbows on the table. "What did you mean when you said Lori Del Valle criticized Clive? I've never heard of anyone criticizing him before."

"Did I say 'criticize'?" Jake popped the lid off his coffee and stared inside the cup as if trying to read tea leaves instead of coffee grounds. "She didn't exactly do that. It was during one of my finer moments when I told her I'd expected her to bring the wallet back to the lab at the station for Clive, rather than dust for prints herself. She started to say something about Clive and then backed off, so it seemed as if she was going to badmouth him. She could've just been thinking he'd be busy with the other crime scene. Anyway, Clive trained her well, and she lifted the latent print off the wallet."

"And it's not Tina's."

"It's not Tina's. We also have the AA connection. I didn't get a chance to tell you." He grabbed his work phone, which he'd been toying with ever since they sat down for coffee to wait for Billy to get back from Quinn's, and tapped it a few times. "Tina was wearing her AA anniversary medallions at the time of her murder."

Kyra leaned over the table to look at the picture on Jake's phone. Her pulse jumped as she noticed the purple bruises around Tina's neck beneath the gold chain of the necklace. Yeah, it's a good thing Jake hadn't shown the picture of Tina's dead body to Remy.

He cupped the phone in his hand again. "That's why the location of the car piqued my interest. I knew we were probably looking at another AA meeting abduction."

"You called that in on the way over here?" She and Jake had headed straight to Uncommon Grounds after the crime scene. It had been too late for lunch and too early for dinner, and Jake needed to decompress after searching Tina's car.

"Called that in and asked one of the task force officers to track down the meeting Tina attended, and to see if he can schedule a group get-together like the one you and Billy had with Ashley's group. I also asked Lori to send the print over to Officer Reppucci so she could enter it into AFIS, the national fingerprint database."

"You're closing in on this fourth copycat." She thudded a fist against her chest. "I feel it here."

When Jake's phone rang in his hand, they both jumped. He answered after the first ring. "How'd it go, Billy?"

As Billy rambled on the other end of the line, Jake's face, tense with anticipation, relaxed.

Kyra sat back in her seat and finished her coffee. It didn't sound promising from Jake's side of the conversation, but they'd just gotten started. Evidence had to be hauled back to the lab and examined and tested. When Jake asked Billy about the misplaced glass in the cupboard, she held her breath, but Jake's face told her nothing.

When he ended the call, he slammed the lid on his cup. "Not much, as you could probably tell."

"Clive got the glass I noticed when we were last there?"

"He bagged it. I don't think he dusted any items there except for windows and doors."

"Unlike the enterprising Lori." She grinned, wrinkling her nose. "Stop beating yourself up over that. Just apologize to her, and that'll go a long way."

Jake lifted his empty cup. "Are you ready? Billy and I have a lot to discuss. I have to fill him in on the identification of Tina Valdez and the evidence from her car."

"I'm ready."

When they got back to the station, Jake and Billy put their heads together, and Kyra sat in front of her computer to follow up on a list of Tina's friends Remy had given to her. Her cell phone buzzed, and she recognized Dr. Gellman's number.

Turning her back to the busy room, she scooted her chair toward the corner. "Hello, this is Kyra Chase."

"Kyra, this is Shai Gellman returning your call."

"Thank you for calling me back, Dr. Gellman."

"Shai, please. How can I help you?"

In a low voice, she explained she had some traumatic

childhood memories she wanted to reclaim. She'd get into the details with him if he accepted her as a patient.

"Are these memories of events you suspect occurred or ones that you know occurred and can't recall?"

"I know they occurred, and I can't remember them—it. It was one memory in particular. I recall the events surrounding the memory but not that one piece."

"Is there someone alive who can verify the memory for you?"

Only if you count a serial killer who'd rather see me dead than remember. "No."

"How old were you, Kyra?"

"I was eight years old."

Shai took a deep breath. "I'm not going to lie to you or pretend I don't know who you are. I followed your story last month from Sean Hughes's blog, so I know about your past. I know your mother was a victim of The Player twenty years ago, and I know you killed a foster father in self-defense. Is this memory from one of those two incidents?"

Kyra bit her lip. "The first. Does that make a difference?"

"It doesn't make a difference to me. I just didn't want you to come in here under false pretenses and then discover later that I knew all about you. We need to have trust between us. You're in the field, so you understand that."

"Thank you for telling me. It doesn't matter to me, either. Is this something you think you can help me with?" Kyra sucked in her bottom lip and stared at a spot on the wall.

"I do. I'd like to help you. I can see you as early as tomorrow, as I just had a cancellation. Will eleven o'clock work for you?"

Her gaze wandered toward Jake's desk, where he and Billy were still yakking. Jake would never be able to make an afternoon appointment, and she'd promised him he could come along. "Something later in the day would work better, the later the better, actually. I have my work on the LAPD task force and my own clients to see. It doesn't have to be tomorrow."

"Hold on." Shai clicked on a keyboard as Kyra held her breath. "I'll tell you what. I can see you at five o'clock tomorrow, if that works."

"That's perfect." Having notoriety helped in the strangest ways, but she'd take it.

When she got back to her email, she paused as she noticed a message from an unknown address. Her breath caught in her throat as she clicked on it, and then her breathing returned to normal when she saw the message from a therapist she'd contacted for a family member of one of Mitchell Reed's victims. The therapist had wanted to let Kyra know that she'd scheduled her first appointment with the client.

Kyra didn't know if she should expect any more communication from The Player. During the first three copycat slayings, The Player had been in contact with her, posing as someone else, of course—teasing, tormenting and torturing her about her past. He'd been quiet so far, but she didn't know if it was because they'd finally identified him as The Player or if he had something else planned for her.

As Kyra responded to the therapist's email, Morgan Reppucci, one of the few female officers on the task force, walked by her desk and squeezed her arm. "Lori Del Valle just finished prepping the fingerprint she took from Tina Valdez's wallet for me to run through the Automated Fingerprint Identification System. Keep your fingers crossed."

"Can I tag along when you pick it up?" Kyra scooted her chair back from her desk and snapped her laptop closed. She didn't know if Jake had gotten the opportunity to apologize to Lori for making assumptions about her. Not that Kyra was Jake's apologist, but she didn't want Lori to have a bad opinion of him. She wanted to see the print, anyway.

"Come on." Morgan crooked her finger at Kyra. "I'm excited that J-Mac gave the task to me. Of course, we haven't had much luck with prints yet. Jake did find that print from Copycat Two, Cyrus Fisher, but we couldn't match it in the system. What's weird about that is Fisher must've submitted false prints for the secret clearance he held at the aerospace company where he worked. That definitely would've come up in AFIS."

Kyra followed Morgan into the lab, where a young woman with glasses and dark hair scooped into a low chignon sat at a table. She flushed when she looked up, which made her look younger. Kyra couldn't blame Jake too much for thinking she might be too green to handle the job.

Scoping out the room, Kyra asked, "Where's Clive?"

Lori pulled her glasses off. "He came back with a ton of prints from Quinn's house, started working on those and then had to leave for a doctor's appointment. I know how to prep a print to run through AFIS."

Ouch. Did Jake's dismissal still sting? Kyra smiled. "Obviously—you're a rock star. Detective McAllister was impressed you took the initiative and dusted that wallet in the field. Who knows? We might still be waiting for Clive to get back from the doctor."

"He told me, *and* he apologized for dismissing me, but

I didn't really take it like that. Clive keeps a tight grip on this department, and I'm sure he's communicated that to Detective McAllister. Anyway, glad I could help." Lori hopped off her stool and thrust out her hand. "By the way, I'm Lori Del Valle. You're Kyra Chase, right? And I know Officer Reppucci."

As Kyra shook Lori's hand, Morgan said, "Call me Morgan. Us ladies have to stick together in this field. Is it ready to go?"

"You're emailing the request to AFIS, correct?"

"I am." Morgan wandered to the table and peered over Lori's shoulder. "Nice. It's pretty clear."

"I think it is." Lori tapped the table next to the prepped print. "I'm going to scan this and email it to you, Morgan. You can use that format for AFIS."

Kyra glanced from one woman to the other. "Is it true a match can come back within an hour now?"

Lori nodded. "If there's a rush on it, and there's always a rush for prints from a murder scene, especially a serial killer case like this. I'm sure Detective McAllister already put in the request for this print."

"He did." Morgan pumped her fist. "Let's do this."

Kyra and Morgan returned to the task force room, where Morgan perched in front of her computer to await Lori's email, and Kyra looked through the family contacts for Tina Valdez that Remy had sent her. Remy needed as much help as Tina's family would. Finding Tina's car and discovering that she'd been murdered had wrecked Remy.

About forty-five minutes later, a vibration rippled through the room, and Kyra jerked her head up. She narrowed her eyes as she watched Morgan talking to Jake and Billy, her face alight, her shoulders pulled back.

She'd done it. They had a match.

Within minutes, Jake and Billy grabbed their jackets. Before he left the war room, Jake winked at her.

A few other officers had left with the detectives, but Morgan remained at her desk, so Kyra scurried across the room and huddled next to her. "The fingerprint matched one in AFIS?"

"It did." Morgan twisted her head around. "It's not a secret…except from the press, of course. Jake and Billy just went out to surveil the guy—check out his home and workplace. They don't want to tip him off yet."

"Who is he?"

"His name is Adam Walker. He lives in Glendale, so he's definitely in the area of the abductions, and he works at an IT help desk."

Kyra blew out a breath. You just never know about anyone these days. "Is that where his prints came from? His job?"

"Not that job. Apparently he used to work in construction and did a job at a school. Most licensed, bonded construction companies fingerprint their workers if they have a project at a school and are around kids. Maybe he forgot his prints were on file for that job."

"Or maybe he never intended to leave his prints when he murdered these women." Kyra held up both of her hands with her fingers crossed. "Let's hope he's the guy and the task force can stop him before he commits a fourth murder."

Jake and Billy hadn't returned by the end of the day. They must still have Walker under surveillance. They wouldn't want to play their hand yet in case Walker led them to more evidence.

As she walked down the hallway to take the stairs, Captain Castillo called out to her from his office. She poked her head inside, and he waved her into a chair.

She shut the door behind her. "Are you sure you don't want to talk to Jake?"

"I just want to ask you what you're doing about that information?"

Did she owe it to Castillo to tell him her plans? He'd kept Quinn's secret all this time, although for personal reasons, so she supposed she owed him something. She took a deep breath. "I don't know what Jake's doing, but I'm going to see a hypnotherapist and try to recover that memory. I don't know if it'll work or not, but I need to give it a try."

"I think that's a good idea. I'm not sure it will help the case, but I think it's something you need to do." The captain rubbed his chin. "If the rest of it gets out, it's going to hurt Quinn's legacy."

Kyra held up her hands. "I have nothing to do with that, Captain Castillo."

Thankfully, his phone rang and he dismissed her from his office.

She had no clients, and Quinn's house was still off limits to her, so she headed to her apartment in Santa Monica when she left the station. Jake's daughter, Fiona, texted her while she was driving regarding her interview. When Kyra got home, she called her.

"Hi, Fiona. Do you want to ask me those questions now?"

"Do you have time?"

"As long as you don't mind some answers between chews. I'm going to eat while we talk, if that's okay."

Fiona paused. "Is my dad there?"

"Your dad is working."

"As usual." Fiona snorted. "I'm going to record our conversation so I can get quotes later. Is that okay?"

"That's fine with me."

Kyra spent the next half hour eating leftover pasta and answering questions about her career. As Fiona started to wrap up the interview, Kyra asked, "Do you think being a therapist or psychologist is something you'd like?"

"Sounds interesting." Fiona paused. "Does listening to people's problems all day make you depressed?"

"No, because by talking about their problems, they're taking the first step toward healing, and that's exciting. Does that make sense?"

"I get it. It's like when my friends are upset over a boy or something and they talk about it, they usually end up laughing about it and plotting their revenge."

Kyra choked on her water. "Yeah, something like that."

The conversation put a smile on Kyra's face that didn't go away as she cleaned the kitchen and fed Spot. Twenty minutes after she ended the conversation with the daughter, the father called her.

She answered the phone. "Busy afternoon?"

"Busy and frustrating. We went to the suspect's work location first and contacted his supervisor, who told us he left early that day for a doctor's appointment. So we left and did a stakeout at his house, a place he rents alone, but no luck there. His car wasn't in the driveway, and it didn't look like anyone was home. The car could be in the garage, but no lights came on in the house, and there was no activity."

"Morgan told me his name. Maybe Walker's sick and went to bed when he got home from the doctor's visit."

"Maybe. Billy and I called it a day, and two other detectives in an unmarked vehicle are taking over the stakeout. We also have an APB on his car, but with instructions to call it in, not to pull it over. Again, we don't want to tip him off or spook him."

"At least if he is holed up in his house and decides

to go on any late-night hunting expeditions, he'll have a tail."

"Exactly. Any activity in the war room after we left?"

"Nope. Seems like everyone got down to business when you and Billy left, doing whatever you instructed them to do." She cleared her throat. "I did have a conversation with Captain Castillo before I left. I told him about my plan to uncover that memory."

"Castillo isn't going to tell anyone."

"He wanted to know what you planned to do."

"I don't even know yet."

Kyra told Jake about the interview with his daughter and about the appointment with Shai the following day. He assured her he'd come with her if he wasn't sitting on Walker.

The rain started pattering against the window, and Spot yowled at the front door. Kyra swung it open for the mangy cat and said, "You're getting wimpy in your old age, Spot. What's a little rain?"

The cat slipped into the apartment and curled up on the edge of the carpet that led into the living room. Spot wasn't into naked affection.

Kyra turned on the TV and settled on the couch with a cup of tea. When a text came through on her phone, she figured it was one of the McAllisters. She swept the phone from the coffee table and read the text from an unknown number, her heart tripping over itself in her chest.

Do you want to find Walker?

She responded.

Who is this?

The sender answered with an address in Hollywood and a warning.

No lights and sirens.

What did that mean? If she called the police, Walker would be gone? Jake had indicated Walker didn't know they were onto him. He and Billy hadn't rushed in with guns blazing. They'd wanted to surveil him first, trip him up, gather more evidence. One print on Tina's wallet wouldn't convict Walker.

Why had this anonymous tipster contacted her? How did he know her, her number, or that she even knew about Walker? Chewing on her bottom lip, she studied the texts.

Only one person had her number and had been contacting her regularly throughout the killing sprees of each copycat. Had The Player surfaced again to give her a heads-up about Walker? Why? Why would he want to reveal one of his minions to her?

She wouldn't call the police, but if The Player thought she'd come alone, he hadn't been paying attention. Of course, if she thought Jake would invite her along, *she* hadn't been paying attention. She'd have to time this just right.

She bounced up from the couch, turned off the TV and put her mug of tea in the sink. Then she shimmied out of her flannel pajama bottoms and stepped into a pair of dark jeans. She pulled a T-shirt over her camisole and slipped her feet into some soft-soled sneakers.

Stepping over Spot, who gave her the evil eye, she grabbed a black jacket with a hood from the hall closet and pocketed her weapon. She nudged Spot with the toe of her shoe. "You, out."

The cat stretched and flicked his tail at her, but he fol-

lowed her and stepped into the drizzle when she opened
the door. She locked up and headed for her car—next
stop, Hollywood.

She'd plugged the address the text had given her, ignoring the 15 at the end of it, into her phone's GPS and
followed the directions. Over thirty minutes later, she
cruised into Hollywood and obeyed the voice from her
phone that took her to a side street off Hollywood Boulevard. Two dilapidated motels occupied one side of the
street, and she identified the second one on the right as
her destination.

The number following the directions now made sense;
15 was the number of the motel room. She rolled past the
entrance to the small parking lot, overgrown with bou-
gainvillea, the petals from the flowers sticking to the
wet pavement. Two palm trees guarded the office, the
fronds littering the walkway to the sagging screen door.

She passed the motel and did a U-turn at the end of
the block, heading back toward the lights of the boulevard. She snatched her phone from the outside pocket of
her purse. Jake couldn't keep her away now because she
was already here.

Her phantom texter hadn't contacted her again. Was
he watching her? She pulled her gun from her pocket and
placed it on the console. Then she called Jake.

"Hey, I was just thinking about you, too."

She hated to crash his good mood. "Jake, I got an
anonymous text about Walker. I'm guessing you didn't."

"I did not. Anonymous? Is La Prey back?"

Glancing in her rearview mirror at the darkness of
the street behind her, she said, "We both know the guy
who's been calling himself La Prey is The Player. Listen,
he gave me an address for Walker in Hollywood. It's a
run-down motel."

Jake drew in a sharp breath. "How do you know that from an address? Did you look it up online?"

"I'm sitting across the street from it." Her muscles tensed.

He didn't explode, but he did mutter a few choice curses under his breath. "Tell me you did not go into that motel."

"I didn't. I'm waiting for you. The texts also warned me not to call the cops, but you don't count because he had to know I'd contact you. You don't want to careen in here with patrol cars on full alert anyway, right?"

"You could've called me and stayed in Santa Monica."

"Naw, I can't do that, Jake, and you know it. I'm in this up to my eyeballs."

"Give me the address and sit tight. Do you have your gun?"

"Of course."

"Keep it handy, and if you're parked in an isolated area, move."

She gazed over the top of her steering wheel at the lights of the busy boulevard. "I'm facing Hollywood Boulevard."

"I'm on my way."

He ended the call, and she expected him in about fifteen minutes. He knew those winding roads in the Hollywood Hills like the back of his hand.

When she saw the motorcycle zip onto the side street fourteen minutes later, she finally relaxed her clenched muscles. He walked the Harley she'd inherited from her foster brother and sold to him up to her window.

She buzzed it down, and Jake flipped up the visor on his rain-spattered helmet. He jerked his thumb over his shoulder. "It's that dump?"

"That's it. Room number 15."

"I suppose it won't do any good to ask you to wait in the car."

"None at all." She grabbed her weapon from the console and flipped up her hood.

She waited while Jake parked his bike in front of her car. He took her arm and they crossed the street, looking like two ninjas all in black.

Jake bypassed the front office and counted the numbers nailed to the doors. Some had fallen off, but they located number 15 around the corner of the parking lot.

Jake's step faltered. "That white car out front is Walker's. Now, I'm going to insist that you stay back so I can get a handle on things here. It looks like I can get a look into the room from the gap in the blinds."

"Okay, it's all yours." She took several steps away from the door and wandered toward the back of the motel. Two more rooms rounded out this side of the building, and then the back of the motel faced an alley and a patch of wild growth that could've been another parking lot.

The wind lifted the ends of her hair and carried the scent of the wet asphalt through the air. She wrinkled her nose at the smell of garbage. A dumpster hunched where the pavement met the overgrown weeds.

The hair on the back of her neck quivered, and she clutched the gun in front of her. She crept forward on silent feet, holding her breath, the stench getting stronger as she approached the dumpster. Standing on her tiptoes, she flipped back the hard plastic lid, and peered inside at the trash and flattened cardboard boxes with the flashlight on her phone.

She went down on her heels and staggered back a few steps, the light from her phone picking out something behind the dumpster in the long grass.

With her gun leading the way, she circled the dumpster and choked. A man, his head sticky with a dark substance, lay on his back, one arm extended to the side, his eyes wide open.

But Adam Walker couldn't see anything anymore.

Chapter Thirteen

The scream came from outside, not inside the neat motel room, and Jake reared back from the window. He spun around, his heart thundering in his chest, but Kyra wasn't where he'd left her.

He rounded the corner of the building, where a door to one of the rooms cracked open, throwing a sliver of light onto the buckled pavement. He hadn't imagined the scream. Others had heard it, too.

Heading for the back of the motel, his gun clutched in his hand, he took the final corner and stumbled into an alley. He spotted Kyra next to a dumpster, her hand raised, her face a pale oval beneath the hood of her jacket.

He rushed toward Kyra, and she pointed behind her, wordlessly. He smelled the body before he saw it. It hadn't been there long, but the rain had ripened the flesh for decomposition. Before approaching it, he yelled over his shoulder, "Call 911."

With Kyra's steady voice in the background, Jake peered at the face, the light from his cell phone illuminating the one side of the man's face not covered in blood. He had an exit wound on the right side of his forehead. He'd most likely been shot in the back of the head, execution style, and he'd spun onto his back maybe in midturn, or the killer had rolled him over.

His fingers itched to dig into the man's pocket for his wallet to confirm his identity, but Jake hadn't brought any gloves with him and he didn't want to muck up this crime scene. He rose to his feet and called Billy. His partner had already heard Kyra's 911 call, so Jake said, "I think we found Adam Walker."

An hour later, Jake waded through officers from LAPD's Hollywood Division and his own task force to reach Kyra standing by the motel's front office, now awash in white light. Once the sirens blared on the scene, several of the motel's guests had ventured from their rooms, some peeking out from behind their doors and others hanging on the fringes of the scene, asking questions.

When he reached Kyra's side, he asked, "Are you doing okay?"

"I'm fine. Nobody told me directly the dead man's identity, but I'm guessing he's Adam Walker." She raised her eyebrows at him hopefully.

"It is Walker. Not only did we find his driver's license in his wallet, we found Ashley Russell's and Tina Valdez's licenses. He's our guy."

Kyra's shoulders slumped a little with the verification, but she continued to twist her fingers in front of her. "Why'd he do it, Jake? Why did The Player rat out one of his own?"

"I've been thinking about that ever since you called me. Remember the other copycat killers, and how they acted? Cannon pretty much chose death by cop. He had to know I was going to shoot once he threatened you with that knife. Fisher actually did kill himself with that cyanide tablet, and do you recall Mitchell Reed's question when we burst in to take him down and rescue you?"

She worried her bottom lip. "He said something like, 'Did he send you?'"

"Yeah, I think he meant The Player. He'd told The Player where he was holding you. He wanted special props for capturing The Player's favorite plaything—you. But in the end, he knew The Player would rather see him dead than arrested." Jake jerked his thumb over his shoulder. "Same thing here. He knew we were closing in on Walker, so he took him out before we could get to him."

"How did he know? The task force never announced Walker as a suspect."

Jake shrugged. "Maybe he was watching Walker's place. Maybe he made me and Billy earlier. Maybe Walker noticed us and told The Player—big mistake." Jake circled his finger in the air. "He just checked in to this dump today. He was on the run, but he couldn't outrun The Player."

Kyra said, "I offered up my phone with the text messages on it, but nobody seemed interested. Are you just assuming he sent those messages from a burner phone? Shouldn't you check? Jordy Cannon stole a phone to make a call about the body he left in Malibu Canyon where the fire was raging, and it led you to a location and eventually his capture—I mean, death."

"We already know where the messages came from, Kyra. The Player sent them to you from Walker's cell phone."

"Oh." She folded her arms over her midsection. "Did any of the other guests see anything? Hear anything?"

"The only thing they heard was your scream when you discovered Walker out back. The gun must've had a silencer." He cocked his head and asked the question that had been bothering him since that scream. "Why'd you go back there? What led you to the body? The stench wasn't strong enough yet to reach the motel."

"I can't tell you. It was as if something was pulling me around the back, to the dumpster and beyond." She placed a hand at her throat. "It's as if The Player and I have this connection."

He curled an arm around her shoulder and pulled her close. "That's going to end. I'm going to make sure of it."

"*I'm* going to make sure of it." She flipped up her hood as the clouds above ushered in another spate of rain. "I forgot to tell you that I have an appointment with Dr. Gellman tomorrow at five. Can you make it? You won't be watching for Walker anymore, but you don't have to go."

"I want to go with you. Five is good. Is he closer to your place or mine?"

"Closer to mine. His office is in Brentwood."

"I'll try to be there for you, but we'll be busy tomorrow trying to tie Walker to the three murders. Thank God this guy was held to three."

"I guess we have The Player to thank for that, but then he was partly responsible for the murders of Ashley, Tina and Erica." She squeezed his arm. "Don't worry if you can't make it to the appointment. You can't come inside during the hypnosis, anyway, and I promise to tell you all about it. Shai warned me that it might take several sessions. It's not like I'm going to remember everything after being under just once."

Jake shook his head. "I would hate that—someone in my brain, having control over me."

"It's not exactly like that." She pulled her jacket close. "Are you done here? I think I am, right? I've given my statement, offered up my phone. I can't say I feel sorry for the guy."

"Nobody's asking you to." He placed his hands on her shoulders. "Can I ask you to wait a minute? I have a few things to wrap up, and then I want to see you home."

"Jake, don't be ridiculous. It's late, it's raining, you're on a motorcycle. I'll be fine. I have security cameras at my place, strong locks and a gun. If The Player wanted me, he could've ambushed me when I got to the motel without you."

"Yeah, about that." He clenched his jaw. He knew it wouldn't do any good to get on her about her risky behavior. She had a stake in this case, a…connection to The Player. She felt entitled to know every part of the investigation and to be involved in it. She *had* been involved until this point, and there was no way she'd back off now.

She tugged at his sleeve. "You can walk me to my car."

He blew out a breath that fogged in the chilly air. "It's the least I can do."

They wended their way through clutches of people, including the press, and crossed the street without anyone following them. Jake turned and surveyed the people on the sidewalk in front of the motel. Was he here? Had The Player stayed to view his handiwork? They'd been taking the videos at every crime scene since the first copycat killer and hadn't been able to identify anyone who'd been at more than one of them—outside of the cops, CSI and media. Why would tonight be any different?

Kyra unlocked her door and turned to face him. "I'll call you when I get home."

He watched her drive toward Hollywood Boulevard and turn left. Why did The Player have to keep pulling her into his sick games? He suspected The Player might be yearning for the notoriety he'd shunned twenty years ago. Maybe The Player thought it was time to get caught—and Jake was ready to oblige the evil bastard.

THE FOLLOWING DAY, Jake stood in the middle of Adam Walker's house in Altadena. Copycat Four had left in a hurry—dishes in the sink, perishable food in the fridge, mail on the floor, and closets and drawers gaping open in the bedroom.

Clive was picking up prints throughout the house, and Geoffrey, another member of the Forensics team, was sifting through Walker's dirty clothes in the hopes of finding some DNA from the victims. They'd towed Walker's car from the motel parking lot, and the techs had already notified Jake that they'd discovered one long strand of brown hair—Tina's?

Brandon Nguyen had already secured Walker's laptop from the motel room and had started a forensic analysis on it. Jake was confident they'd be closing the case on Copycat Four shortly.

But that sense of satisfaction eluded him. He was happy to offer justice to the families, but the main perpetrator was still roaming the streets, still had Kyra in his sights. The Player might be setting up a fifth copycat right now. He'd clearly abandoned Walker, had, in fact, killed Walker, but it didn't mean he'd given up his diabolical school for serial killers.

When he checked the time on his phone, he grimaced. Kyra had that appointment at five o'clock today, and he'd wanted to be there for her, but it wasn't looking good. He knew she'd been busy today with Tina's family and trying to set up a group session for the family members of all the victims. Once they'd learned a few months ago that Kyra herself was a family survivor of The Player, their trust in her had gone through the roof. They shared that bond.

"Look at these," Billy called from across the room and bobbled some tokens in the palm of his hand.

"What are those?" Jake strode across the room and

peered into Billy's hand at the AA sobriety medallions. He shook his head. "He must've gotten the idea that these women in recovery would make good victims while he was actually attending meetings himself. He wouldn't have attended Ashley's meeting, as that was for women only and there's no evidence yet he attended Tina's, but he obviously attended meetings somewhere."

Billy's hand closed around the medallions. "Who even knows if the guy was in recovery? Could've all been a scam."

"I'm just hoping The Player left as much evidence as Walker when he killed him."

"Don't count on it." Billy held up his fingers and ticked off each one. "No prints at the scene, nobody saw a car, a person, heard a voice, a gunshot, no cameras at the no-tell motel. Looks like a ghost murdered Walker."

"A ghost who used the same weapon that killed the true crime blogger, Sean Hughes, a few months ago."

Billy spread his hands. "Where's the weapon? Where are the prints from Quinn's place? Where are the witnesses from Quinn's place? How are we going to trip up this guy?"

Geoffrey interrupted them, holding a large plastic bag in front of him. "I have some clothes here and a pair of shoes we can test. I think we're going to have some overwhelming evidence against Walker."

"Oh, I forgot." Billy dipped into the pocket of his suit jacket. He held out a prescription pill bottle between his thumb and forefinger. "Here's the pill bottle that belongs to Piper Moss."

"Kyra already contacted Piper to let her know Erica's killer was probably dead. That'll put Piper's mind at ease."

"At least someone's happy about this case." Billy

punched Jake's shoulder. "C'mon, man. We've got our guy. He's not going to kill anyone else. He messed up by leaving that witness. It was the beginning of the end for him."

"I'm ecstatic." Jake aimed a finger at his face. "This is my ecstatic look, and you're right. Walker never should've left the witness at the scene and tried to take care of her later."

Knots tightened in Jake's gut. The Player had made the same mistake. Would he fix it twenty years later?

"Don't worry about it. I'm fine." Kyra put her phone on speaker and stuck it in her cup holder. "I'm on my way to the appointment now, and I'm sure Shai will just scratch the surface with me. If I'm too rattled to drive after the session, I'll order a car. You guys killed it today and sealed the deal. I was able to spread good news to all the family members."

"The Player handed him to us. He may have even planted all the evidence so there would be no doubt we had Copycat Four."

"Stop saying that." Kyra squeezed the steering wheel. "Lori lifted Walker's print from Tina's wallet. You would have tracked him down eventually. The Player gave you nothing. He killed Walker out of self-preservation."

"Okay, okay. I'm glad we ended this for the victims— or at least this chapter. It never really ends for them, does it?"

"No. It just becomes a part of you." Kyra blinked. "Hey, I just took the freeway exit for Brentwood. I'll call you when I'm done. Maybe I'll hand you The Player."

"Take it slow and easy... I love you."

Kyra's heart bumped against her chest. Jake usually

reserved those words for postcoital bliss, but she'd take them anytime, anywhere. "I love you, too, J-Mac."

She drove the rest of the way to Shai Gellman's office with a silly smile twitching her lips. She parked on San Vicente along the green strip and jogged across the street to the two-story office building with its red-tiled roof and courtyard ringed with fragrant plumeria and jasmine crawling along the low stucco walls. A fountain gurgled in the center of the courtyard, shimmering water tumbling from a lion's gaping jaws. Shai's office occupied the bottom level, tucked beneath the stairs that led to the upper floor.

Leaves floated in little puddles of water left over from yesterday's rain, encouraged by the shade that shrouded Shai's office door. The gray skies threatened more of the same for this evening, and LA rejoiced at the precipitation that cleared the air and soaked the parched hillsides. Of course, too much saturation could lead to mudslides, and they'd had their share of wildfires at the end of the summer to make that a real possibility. The city always seemed to perch on the cusp of paradise and disaster, sort of mirroring her life.

Shai had a discreet sign by the side of his dark wood door, and Kyra tried the handle. Some therapists locked their front doors to keep all but clients out of their offices. Shai wasn't one of them.

Kyra nudged the door with her hip, and the scent of nag champa engulfed her as she stepped inside the waiting room. A small candle burned in the corner, its flame flickering with the breeze from the open door.

The door to Shai's inner sanctum stood halfway open, and a low voice floated from that room. "Come on in."

Kyra bypassed the button on the wall outside and pushed open the door.

A small-statured man rose from a cushion on the floor and glided forward, a smile wreathing his face. "Welcome. I'm Shai."

Kyra felt his presence like a big, warm hug, and a smile tugged at her own lips as she extended her hand. "Nice to meet you, Shai. I'm Kyra."

He squeezed her hand between his two soft, chubby ones. "I'm glad you're here. Don't worry. You don't have to sit on the floor—unless you want to. My previous client left an hour ago, and I was meditating."

"I'm sorry I kept you late."

"No apologies, please." He flicked his ponytail, laced with gray, over one shoulder. "This is a blame-free, apology-free zone."

Kyra suppressed a smile. Jake was right about one thing. He would've hated this. Tipping her head toward the door, she asked, "Do you always keep the door to your inner office wide open like that?"

"Only for my last appointment of the day—and you're it." Spreading his hands, Shai said, "Have a seat. Something to drink?"

"No, thank you."

She allowed her own clients to sit where they wanted, although not one of them ever sat in her chair. She would've allowed it and incorporated it into their therapy session. She spotted Shai's place in a second, which had his name written all over it: a comfortable chair, not too deep, with a round table next to it containing a cup of tea and a notebook with a jeweled pen beside it.

She settled in the oversized chair across from his, and immediately felt its comforting embrace.

He sank into his own chair. "Tell me what you know about the memory before we start, Kyra."

"Apparently, I witnessed my mother's murder when

I was eight years old. I saw the killer. The detective on the scene wanted to protect me, so he never revealed this to anyone. H-he must've told me when I was a child that I didn't see what I thought I saw. I have no recollection of the event, and I have no recollection of ever thinking I saw the killer. I always believed I'd slept through my mother's murder, and the detective affirmed this over and over throughout my childhood so that it became my truth. It's what I believed until recently when I saw the original police report from that night with the information that I'd seen the killer—and he'd seen me."

Shai steepled his fingers beneath his chin, the expression on his face never flickering. "Did you give a description of the killer in that report?"

"No." She rubbed her hands on her slacks. "Does that sound like an impossible task?"

"The memory exists, whether you can access it or not. It exists. It's never impossible to reach that memory if your mind is open and you truly want it."

"Oh, I want it." She swallowed her last word. Did she? It could mean the identification of The Player, or it might mean nothing at all. Was she hanging all her expectations on this one memory? What if it didn't have the desired results? She'd have nothing. The prospect of recovering the memory gave her hope. The reality might dash all that hope.

When she met Shai's sparkling eyes, slightly turned up at the corners, she knew he'd read every thought that had crossed her mind.

"Do you want it, Kyra?"

She grabbed the overstuffed arms of the chair and straightened her shoulders. "I do."

"I assume you've been hypnotized before, as you're a

therapist yourself." Shai reached over the side of his chair, took a sip of tea and picked up the ornate pen.

"Yes, I've been to a few workshops and underwent hypnosis as part of the sessions." She held up a hand. "Before you ask, yes, I'm susceptible."

"Good." The pen winked in the low light as he waved it at her. "Make yourself comfortable. Release your grip on the chair. I'm going to record our session. Is that all right with you?"

"Fine." Kyra flexed her fingers and then unzipped one of her boots. "Okay to remove my shoes?"

"Whatever works for you." He aimed the pen at a couch. "You can lie down if you like."

"I prefer this chair. I could get lost in this chair. I need one of these in my office."

"Nice, isn't it?" Shai's eyes twinkled. "One of my secret weapons."

Kyra removed her boots and tucked one foot beneath her thigh, relaxing against the cushions. "I'm ready."

Shai held up the gleaming pen. "Another one of my secret weapons. I'd like you to watch it and listen to my voice. Sink into that chair, relax. Unclench every muscle. Clear your mind. Start breathing deeply."

Focusing on the pen that gleamed in the semidarkness, Kyra pulled in a long breath through her nose and blew it out through her mouth. Something Quinn's wife, Charlotte, used to tell her when she'd run to their house away from another foster home flickered across her brain. In with the butterflies, out with the bees. A smile touched her lips. Were Quinn and Charlotte together now?

Shai's voice soothed her nerve endings. "You're so at ease now, so relaxed. You're warm and comfortable. Your mind is open. Your eyes are starting to get heavy. It's all right. You can close them."

The glow of the jeweled pen got blurry, as Kyra's eyelids fluttered. She'd entered a dark, safe space where Shai's voice guided her.

"You're eight years old, Kyra. You're Marilyn now. Your mother calls you Mimi. You're living with your mother. It's the end of the summer. Hot. Do you remember?"

Her chin dropped to her chest. "Hot. Santa Ana winds. I'm going to start third grade in a week. I like school."

"Good. You live alone with your mother, but there's someone else there that night."

Kyra's eyelids flicked. "That night?"

"The night your mother was murdered."

The darkness became a tunnel, and she was rushing toward a pinhole of light that grew larger and larger as she tumbled through the space. The light blinded her and she squeezed her eyes tight. "Someone killed my mom."

"That's right, Mimi. You were there. You saw him. Do you remember?"

A sharp crack had her scrambling from her bed. Sometimes Mom had friends over—sleepy-eyed men who smiled at her over their morning coffee before they left and she never saw them again. Could Mom be seeing one of those friends tonight?

She crept toward her bedroom door and eased it open. It creaked. Through the crack, she saw Mom on the floor, along with a broken vase—a pretty blue vase that Mom bought cheap at the Salvation Army because the color matched their eyes. Mom always said her eyes would make her a famous actress.

Those eyes now bulged from their sockets as Mom clawed at the gloved hands around her throat. The man on top of Mom had something on his head. A white cap? A stocking?

Turn around. Turn around. "Turn around."

The room spun, and Mimi tried to keep her eyes on the man's head. Her vision narrowed, and the tunnel sucked her back into the darkness. "Turn around."

"Kyra?"

Her eyelashes fluttered, and she focused on Shai's face. "I was there. I saw him, but he wouldn't turn around."

"Do you think that's what happened that night? He never did turn around. You never got a look at his face."

She shook her head...hard. "He turned around. I know he did. I expected him to, but I wasn't ready. I wasn't prepared to see him. I noticed he had his head covered with something white or flesh-colored—a cap or maybe a stocking."

"Maybe he pulled a stocking over his face. Maybe that's why your description to the detective was confusing." Shai hunched forward, his forearms on his knees. "How are you feeling? Are you okay?"

"I'm fine." She glanced at Shai's magic pen. "Sh-should we try again?"

He smiled. "Next session."

Kyra stretched her legs in front of her and then pulled on her boots. "Thanks, Shai. I'm confident I can get there."

"So am I. You're a good subject. Most therapists are." He pushed to his feet and tossed his pen onto his desk. "Anything for the road? Water? Coffee?"

"My road's not that long. I'm over in Santa Monica, but thanks." She hitched her purse over her shoulder. "You're staying? I thought I was your last client tonight."

"Just some work to finish up, and I prefer doing it here rather than at home."

Kyra paid for her session, and they scheduled another

in two days. She waved at Shai on her way out of the
office as he stood by the doorway of his therapy room.

Those clouds from earlier had made good on their
promise, and raindrops splattered against the pavers in
the courtyard and pinged against the pool of water in the
fountain. The heels of her boots clicked as she walked
down the sidewalk of the short, empty street that led to
the busier San Vicente, where she'd left her car.

As she passed the corner of one building, a slick
sound, like someone moving in a wet jacket, caught her
attention. The hairs on the back of her neck stood on end,
and she reached into her pocket for her pepper spray. Before she could start to pivot on the toes of her boots, an
arm came around her from behind and crooked around
her throat.

A muted whisper touched her ear. "Now I'm gonna
do you like I did your mother."

Chapter Fourteen

Kyra's muscles coiled and her gaze dropped to the arm in the black jacket that had a stranglehold around her neck. A black glove covered his hand. She tried to twist her head, but the pressure increased. The man's other arm pinned her right arm against her side, and she couldn't get to her purse...or her gun.

But the fingers of her left hand curled around her pepper spray. She wheezed as her attacker squeezed tighter, and she slipped her thumb beneath the release on the canister. In one fluid movement, she pulled her hand from her pocket, aimed the pepper spray over her shoulder and pressed the button.

Immediately, his grip slackened and he hacked. Again, she tried to turn around to get a look at him, but he pushed her hard to the ground. As she hunched on her hands and knees, sucking in air, her assailant stomped on her back and she collapsed.

Still coughing, the muffled sound telling her he had a mask or covering over his face, he kicked her in the side. As she tried to roll over, like a turtle trying to gain purchase, a man's voice rose above the sound of her own harsh breathing.

"Hey, hey. What's going on? Stop!"

Her attacker abandoned his half-hearted efforts to kill

her and ran. She felt the whoosh of his jacket as he took off, and she curled into a fetal position.

She needed help. She needed Jake.

JAKE CAREENED ONTO San Vicente and made a beeline for the emergency lights. Kyra had been calm and coherent on the phone, but her voice sounded like that of a three-pack-a-day, thirty-year smoker.

He didn't bother trying to head down the small street off the boulevard, so he parked his car at the corner and jogged toward the two patrol cars and the ambulance. This street contained small office buildings and businesses, not residences, so the crowd of people rubbernecking was smaller than it might have been.

His pace quickened when he saw Kyra sitting in the back of an ambulance, her legs dangling over the back bumper. A small man with a ponytail held her hand.

Jake started talking before he reached them. "Are you all right? Do you need to go to the hospital?"

She reached out to him with her other hand, a white bandage wrapped around it. "I'm okay."

"You sound…rough. He tried to choke you? What happened to your hand?" He took it gently in his own and traced a finger around the bandage.

"He did choke me. Came at me from behind, and I scraped my hand when I went down." She tried a wink and failed. "But you know me. I never walk alone without a few weapons on me. I got him with my pepper spray."

"Good for you. Did you get a look at him? Did anyone?" He held his breath and glanced at the little man, who smelled like incense.

"I saw his arm as he wrapped it around me—black jacket with a black glove. I could tell from his hold on me that he was about average height, not quite six feet tall.

I know he was wearing some kind of mask because his whisper and his cough sounded muted, and I don't think he could've made a renewed attack on me if the pepper spray had hit him full-on in the face."

"Renewed attack?" Jake's pounding heart picked up speed and he turned to the man with the ponytail. "Did you see him?"

"No, I came out later when I heard the commotion."

"Sorry." Kyra drew back into the ambulance so Jake could get a better look at the man. "Jake, this is Dr. Shai Gellman. Shai, this is Detective Jake McAllister."

Jake gripped Shai's pudgy hand but didn't squeeze too hard. "Thanks for coming to her assistance."

"I'm afraid all I did was offer moral support." Shai pointed to a couple talking to an LAPD officer. "They're the ones who stopped the attack."

Jake squinted at the pair. "Did they see anything?"

"Just a man attacking me, but they scared him off." She nudged him. "Go talk to them and the officers. Shai will stay with me, and the EMT is hovering, waiting to prod me with more instruments."

Jake nodded to the EMT on his way to the couple and the patrol officer. He flipped open his wallet to flash his badge. "LAPD Homicide Detective Jake McAllister."

"Homicide?" The woman's gaze darted to Kyra, and she clutched her throat in just about the same area where Kyra's sported angry, mottled flesh. "Isn't she okay?"

"She's fine, but her attack is related to a series of homicides. I know you answered the officer's questions, but did you see the attacker?"

The tall, gangly man jerked his thumb over his shoulder. "I was picking my wife up from her realty office and walking her to my car that I'd left on San Vicente. There's never enough parking on this street. We saw that woman on the ground by the corner of the building, and a man was standing over her, kicking her."

Hot rage thumped through Jake's veins. "Did you see his face?"

"He was wearing a mask, like a ski mask with slits for his eyes and mouth." The woman covered her face with her hands.

The man continued. "I yelled at him. He didn't even look up. He swung around and took off running. I—I would've followed him, but I didn't know if he had a gun or a knife."

"No, you did the right thing. Did he run toward San Vicente?"

"He ran between those two buildings. That's where I was thinking he was probably hiding. The woman said he surprised her from behind." The guy draped his arm around his wife, who shivered from the rain, or fear. "Did he mug her or something? My wife said I was crazy for picking her up on the nights when she closed out the office by herself because this is a safe area, but you never know, do you?"

"You don't. Keep picking up your wife." Jake clenched his jaw. If he'd been at the appointment with Kyra, this never would've happened.

Jake questioned the couple for several more minutes, and then turned his attention to the officers who arrived on the scene first. They'd canvassed the area and found no other witnesses. Shai only came out when he heard the man yelling at Kyra's assailant. He'd seen nothing.

One of the officers mentioned a camera outside a bank on San Vicente, but as the attacker didn't leave that way, it wouldn't do much good. With a glance at Kyra, still under the ministrations of the EMT, Jake swept aside the fronds of a large sago palm and crept toward the area between the two buildings.

The guy could've easily hidden here, waiting for Kyra, stepped out and secured her around the neck. He could've killed her on the sidewalk, or more likely, could have dragged her back here, out of sight.

He followed the path between the two buildings, which led to a small parking lot. He looked for cameras but found none. The lot abutted the sidewalk of another street. The attacker could've run in several directions.

When he went back to the street where Shai's office was located, the couple had left and the sparse crowd that had gathered had dispersed. The cops had waited for him and promised to send him their report when they had it ready to go.

Jake talked to the EMTs, who were about to release Kyra, and then he and Kyra walked Shai to his car before turning toward San Vicente together.

When they reached the corner, Kyra grabbed his arm. "You know it was The Player, right? He told me he wanted me dead like my mother. If I hadn't maced him first and that couple hadn't been coming down the street, I'd be dead."

The same thought had been circling in his brain ever since she'd called him to tell him about the attack. He couldn't deny it, and the words he whispered to her proved it. "How did he know you were here? Who knew you were going to see Shai?"

"You, me, Shai and—" her eyes grew big and her body stiffened "—Captain Castillo."

"That's right. You did tell Castillo."

"I—I felt he had a right to know." She pressed a hand against her lower back, where The Player had kicked her, and grimaced. "Captain Castillo is not The Player. If I'd seen my mother's killer and then the same guy waltzed in for the 911 call, I'd have known him then."

"I never thought Castillo was The Player, but how did The Player find out about Shai Gellman?" They'd started walking again, and Jake's legs felt like wooden posts beneath him. Could The Player really be a cop? Who else would Castillo tell, and why?

"I don't know. I swear I only told Castillo." Kyra pulled her keys from her purse and stabbed at the key fob. The lights on her car flashed once.

Jake took in the busy street. Cars whizzed past on either side of the green strip down the middle of the boulevard, and people bustled through the crosswalks to get from their cars to restaurants and from their places of work. "Were you followed?"

"What?" Kyra snapped her head around and winced, grabbing the back of her neck.

"Could someone have followed you from the station? You did come here directly from the Northeast Division without going home first, right?" He eyed her work slacks and sweater beneath her jacket, her hair half in and half out of her customary ponytail she wore for work.

"I did, but I didn't notice anyone following me."

"Did you look?"

"No." She pressed a hand to her forehead. "The Player already knows where I live and work. He doesn't have to follow me, even though I *am* careful when I walk to and from my car. That's why I had the pepper spray ready."

"So, someone could've been following you and you wouldn't have known?" He circled her car as she opened the driver's side door.

"I suppose so." She hunched her shoulders. "That means he was watching me on the street and knew where I went."

Jake slipped on a pair of latex gloves from his pocket and crouched on the sidewalk next to her car. He aimed the light from his cell phone at her chassis. On his knees, he crawled to the other side of the car, his hand trailing over the metal that comprised the underside of her vehicle. When his gloved fingers stumbled across a rectangular shape that moved when he nudged it, he ducked his head under the car, the light playing over the area where his fingers picked at the device.

He pulled it off and cupped it in his hand as he rose to his feet. "He didn't have to follow you. He attached this GPS device to your car. He may have been on your tail to see where you went when you got here, or maybe he just watched you walk toward the side street and then took up his position."

Kyra seemed to crumple and grabbed on to the car door before she slid to the ground. "How? Where did he do this?"

Jake took two big steps to catch her in his arms. "It's like you said, Kyra. He knows where you live and work. He could've attached it at any time. He even knew your car was parked on the same street as that motel where he told you to find Walker."

"C-can I see it? I want to know what one looks like—just in case." She held out her cupped hand.

"Don't manhandle it on the off chance he left some prints." He held the device out to her, his fingers on the edges.

She took it from him the same way and examined it. "Should I leave it on the car, so I don't tip him off?"

"No." He wiggled his fingers and she placed the GPS in his hand. Using his fingernail, he opened the rectangle and shook out a flat disc. "With the battery gone, it's not going to function."

He snapped the device back together, peeled off one of his gloves and inserted the GPS into the glove, tying it off at the end.

Kyra placed a hand against her throat. "He means business now, doesn't he? No more fooling around. He wants to kill me."

Jake kissed her gently on the lips. "He's gonna have to go through me first."

THE FOLLOWING MORNING, Jake didn't even glance at Kyra's desk when he walked into the task force room. She'd told him she was taking the morning off.

He'd made sure she got home all right last night, put her to bed and hung out in her living room with Spot to keep watch. She had a top-notch security system at her apartment, but there was no way he wanted to leave her after the night she'd had.

Maybe The Player had gotten the jump on her, literally, because she'd been focused on her session with Shai. She confirmed that under Shai's guidance, she'd gone back to the night of her mother's murder and had seen the killer—or at least the back of his head. She'd had a strong sense that The Player had turned around that night and looked at her, but the hypnosis wouldn't take her there—yet.

She'd also been sure The Player had been wearing something over his head or some kind of white or beige cap, which seemed odd—black ski mask like last night, yes, but light-colored cap? Maybe once he turned around, she couldn't see his face, anyway. He didn't like the idea that The Player might know Kyra was seeing a hypnotherapist.

He'd pay a visit to Captain Castillo to make sure he hadn't let that information slip to anyone. As he turned the corner from the war room, he almost plowed into a woman heading the opposite direction and pulled back.

"Sorry."

She brushed her black hair from her eyes and held up her hands. "Totally on me. Mind on other things."

"Guilty." He assessed her athletic frame, and then snapped his fingers. "You're Dina Ferrari, right? I'm Billy Crouch's partner. I know you're helping him with his sister's disappearance."

She thrust out her hand. "Billy may have mentioned you once or twice. Nice to meet you."

"How long have you been in the PI business?"

"Couple of years." She tilted her head, and her straight hair slipped over one shoulder. "Are you vetting me for Cool Breeze?"

"He seems happy with your work." He patted his pocket for the glove with the GPS device tied up inside, and remembered he'd left it at Kyra's place. "I do have a question for you, though, if you don't mind—professional question."

"My favorite kind."

"I thought I read about a program or something you can put on your phone that detects bugs and GPS devices. Do you have something like that?"

"Absolutely. For yourself? The department?"

"Both. I want it on my phone, but it's for work on the task force."

"Tax deductible." She grinned. "I can text you the link and you can buy and download it right to your phone. It's really easy to use, like a scanner. It'll pick up the waves of a bug and the signal of a GPS. You can get a detector that will have your phone emitting beeps and squeals."

"Sounds perfect." He dipped his hand into his pocket for his personal cell phone and asked for her number. He called her and stored the contact. "Send it to me when you have it. I really appreciate it."

"Anytime, Detective."

Jake continued down the hallway to Castillo's office and listened for voices before tapping on the closed door. At Castillo's invitation, Jake poked his head inside the office.

Castillo's face immediately flushed, and he blinked. Jake was probably the last person Castillo wanted to see.

"Can I have a word?"

"Shut the door." Castillo folded his hands on the desk. "Have you decided what you're going to do yet?"

Jake sat on the arm of the chair. He didn't plan to stay long. "Look, Kyra has the information you and Quinn kept from her all these years, and she's taking steps. I don't see any reason to spread that story around—especially with Quinn's memorial and funeral right around the corner."

Castillo seemed to collapse in his chair. His chin quivered and he wiped a hand across his mouth. "I appreciate that."

Folding his arms, Jake said, "I'm not doing it for you, Castillo. I'm doing it for Quinn and for Kyra. She told you she was seeing a hypnotherapist to recover memories of that night, right?"

"She mentioned it. I told her it was a good idea. She needs to try to remember that night to put it behind her."

"You know The Player attacked her last night."

"Of course I heard. I am still in charge of this task force."

"He attacked her when she was leaving her appointment with the hypnotherapist."

Castillo's sharp intake of breath told Jake he didn't

know that part. "Did you mention Kyra's intention to undergo hypnosis to anyone?"

"No." Castillo smacked his hand on his desk. "Why would I do something like that? That only hurts me. You think I blabbed that information, and that's how The Player tracked her down?"

Jake scratched his chin. "No. He had other methods of tracking her down."

Castillo's phone rang the same time Jake's cell buzzed, but instead of dismissing him, Castillo held up a finger. "Hold on."

As the captain answered his call, Jake checked his phone and saw a text from Dina. She worked fast. Jake tapped the link, downloaded the app and paid for it, all while Castillo talked on the phone.

He opened the app and made a few selections, but Castillo interrupted him. "I wanted to let you know that I'm retiring."

Jake glanced up, raising his eyebrows. "You are? You afraid I'm going to rat you out?"

"I just can't be in command of people who don't respect me. You'll never get that respect back for me, and I know it's only a matter of time before you tell Billy. You two tell each other everything, as it should be. You're good as partners and two of the best detectives in the department—and no, I'm not just blowing smoke."

Jake started to answer, but his phone buzzed in his hand and started making chirps and high-pitched squeals. He stared at the red lines jumping on the display and jerked to his feet.

He held the phone in front of him and shifted his gaze to Castillo's wide eyes and open mouth. Jake put his finger to his lips and scribbled on Castillo's whiteboard.

Your office is bugged.

Chapter Fifteen

Kyra sucked in a sharp breath that rasped against her sore throat. She took a sip of tea laced with honey and said, "How do you know Captain Castillo's office is bugged?"

"I ran into Billy's PI at the station, and she sent me a link to a bug tracker that works from phones. I was in Castillo's office playing around with it, and it went off."

Wrapping her hands around the warm mug, Kyra asked, "Did you find the bug?"

"We found it attached to a lamp on his desk—tiny thing. We left it there."

She choked on her next sip of tea, which didn't do her throat any favors. "You left it?"

"We didn't want to tip off anyone listening that we found it. Castillo's leaving the device there and not having any confidential conversations in his office, but we're thinking of a way we can trip up the person who planted the bug."

"What does this mean, Jake?" Kyra massaged her temples with her fingertips. "Who could possibly get into the captain's office to plant a bug?"

"It could be the cleaning crew." He cleared his throat. "Or a cop."

"You and Quinn always had your suspicions that The Player could be someone on the inside. Nobody wants to think a cop is a killer, working against his coworkers." Kyra picked up the latex glove that contained the GPS tracker from her car and swung it from her fingertips. Was that why The Player always seemed to know where she was? "D-do you think that's how...my attacker knew I'd be at Shai's office last night?"

"Possibly, or it could be the tracker on your car."

"What are you going to do with this information, Jake?"

"Castillo has agreed to keep quiet about it for now. He's going to make a list of people who have been in his office the past few weeks."

"Why two weeks? This could've been going on since the copycat slayings started last summer. He could've been keeping tabs on all the cases."

"Maybe, but bugs have to be replaced at some point."

She swallowed, placing her hand against her bruised neck. "Then what? What are you going to do with Castillo's list?"

He answered abruptly. "Start making discreet inquiries."

"You're going to start investigating members of the task force?"

"I have to, Kyra. Something isn't right when the captain of a task force has his office bugged." Jake paused. "Unless it's Internal Affairs doing the bugging. Maybe they already know Castillo is a dirty cop, and they're trying to catch him in the act. If so, they got an earful the other day when I came to him with what I'd found out about Galecki."

"Can you ask IA without jeopardizing the upper hand you have with this knowledge?"

Jake whistled through his teeth. "I'm not sure. I don't want to play my hand too soon. Let's keep this quiet for now. I'll tell Billy and that's it. We can both do a little investigating on the side—just looking at schedules and possible alibis. We know The Player attacked you last night. We can start looking into the time frame for that, and for the night Walker got whacked."

"I will keep mum."

"How's your throat today? You sound hoarse, like you have a cold."

"It hurts, but it's better than it was this morning. I canceled all my appointments today, and I'm just exchanging emails with the Copycat Killers' victims' families. Tina's and Ashley's friends and families were relieved their killer is dead, and I haven't heard from Erica's family yet." She paused and swirled her tea. "You did find enough evidence in Walker's house and car to tie him to the slayings, right?"

"Oh, yeah. His car was a treasure trove of evidence—hair, fibers, DNA—we got it all. Seems he was only careful when he dumped the body, not when he transported it. He probably figured he'd have time to clean out his car before we got a line on him, but he wasn't counting on his mentor to end his killing spree."

"I'm holding my breath for a fifth. No offense, Detective, but I'm ready for the Copycat Player Task Force to break up."

"I am, too, and I have a feeling we've seen the end of the copycats."

"What makes you say that?" Her muscles tensed. She'd had the same feeling, but the alternative didn't bode well for her.

"The Player ended it himself. He stopped killing after his own reign of terror twenty years ago because he was afraid he'd get caught, or maybe he was locked up during that time, but I think he realizes he's closer than ever to getting nailed today. I think he's done. He can hibernate for another twenty years."

Kyra released a breath. "Except for one loose end."

"He's not going to get to you, Kyra." Jake's phone beeped with a call on the other line. "Stay put today. I'll drop by after work and bring you some chicken soup. Gotta go."

When the call ended, she cupped the phone in her hand and brought up her security cam for the outside of her apartment. Besides her neighbor upstairs and across the way doing his laundry, she didn't see any movement. The Player wouldn't come to her apartment. He must know about the security cameras by now.

He'd never been caught on camera yet—not when he'd run over the homeless woman in Santa Monica after she'd done some dirty work for him, not when he murdered Sean Hughes, the blogger who was in contact with Copycat Three, not when he killed Quinn, not when he shot Copycat Four and not when he attacked her last night. He'd made some bold moves but hadn't shown his hand yet.

Would remembering his face in Shai's office really make a difference? She could help a sketch artist with a composite, but she'd be recalling a man twenty years younger. It could be that her mother knew The Player, and maybe Kyra knew his name, too, as one of her mother's many male *friends*. If that were the case, she could ID him, give him a name, but that's not how The Player operated. He'd killed strangers.

It didn't matter. She'd carry on with the hypnotherapy and hope for the best—even if it were just for her own peace of mind.

She dragged her computer into her lap and rubbed her hands together. More work while she dreamed of chicken soup with Jake.

THE NEXT DAY, Kyra stood in front of the mirror and adjusted a scarf around the bruising on her neck. She didn't need any more attention or sympathy today at the station.

As she gulped down some orange juice standing up in the kitchen, she noticed the glove with the GPS device from her car secured inside on her coffee table. Jake had forgotten to take it with him again. He must be convinced The Player hadn't left prints on it, but Kyra wanted to make sure. She rinsed out her juice glass, stuck it in the dishwasher and swung by the living room to pick up the tracker.

As promised, Jake had delivered the chicken soup last night, along with a box of throat lozenges and probably more tea than had been dumped in Boston Harbor. He'd stayed with her most of the night, but didn't sleep over. He had a busy day today, and she'd shooed him out.

She knew he hated leaving her alone in her own place, but he was also on the feed for her security cams around her apartment. She had a feeling he watched them more obsessively than she did.

An hour later when she got to the station and entered the task force war room, her gaze darted around the desks and studied the faces of the team members. She could usually gauge the point in an investigation by the activity level of the task force. People scurried about today, lots of phone calls and plenty of tapping away on keyboards, but the action lacked the manic, intense feel of when a killer was on the loose. They had their man—or at least one of them.

Her head automatically swung toward Jake's desk,

but she knew he'd be out for most of the day. She pulled her laptop from her bag and grabbed the tied-up latex glove, setting it on her desk beside the computer. Once she logged in, checked her messages and sent Shai a text to confirm their appointment later today, she shoved back her chair and grabbed the glove, her phone and her makeup bag to touch up her bruises in the ladies' room.

She waved to Captain Castillo in the hallway on her way to the forensics lab, but had no intention of stepping inside his office as long as the bug was there. He and Jake could figure out a sting on their own. She didn't want someone listening to her.

She swept into the lab, pinching the glove between her fingers. "Ah, Clive. Just the man I was looking for."

He glanced up, the fluorescent light in the ceiling making his bald pate look yellowish. "Hello, Kyra. Can I help you?"

She twitched the scarf at her neck. Those lights would do a number on her bruises, too. The other cops might know about the attack on her the night before last, but not all the techs would know.

Holding out the glove, she said, "Jake found this GPS tracker on my car. He had gloves on when he handled it and dropped it in here. We thought there might be prints."

Clive cocked his head. "Someone's tracking you?"

"Long story."

"This isn't another one of your off-the-record requests, is it, Kyra?" He clenched his jaw.

"No." She placed the glove on the table in front of him, along with her phone and makeup bag. "Jake is fully aware of this and would've brought it in to you himself, but he left it at…in my car, after disabling it, of course. You can call and check with him if you like."

She'd asked Clive to do a favor for her before, and

when Jake had found out, he wasn't happy. Clive usually did things by the book.

A smile stretched his thin lips. "I trust you. I can't get to it right away, though. Plenty of prints to process from Walker's house and car."

"That's fine. Just like the card you dusted for me, I'm pretty certain the person who planted it didn't leave any prints."

"You never know." He untied the glove and withdrew a plastic bag for appropriate evidence labeling. "I'll let J-Mac know if I find anything. Tied to the copycats?"

"Could be." She didn't feel like going into her whole relationship with The Player.

"Hi, Kyra. What brings you to our sweatshop?"

Kyra turned toward the door and smiled at Lori on the threshold. "Are you accusing Clive of being a hard taskmaster?"

"Never. We're just swamped with work right now—that's a good thing."

"And I just dumped some more on Clive, so I'll leave you guys to your work." She twisted back to sweep up her phone and makeup. "Lunch sometime?"

"Absolutely." Lori winked. "Once the chains come off."

Kyra held up her hand to Clive, who'd already bagged and boxed the GPS device. "Thanks, Clive."

Kyra made a detour to the restroom, and when she placed her phone on the vanity, she saw Shai's text message confirming their appointment—the last of the day again.

A few hours later, rubbing the back of her neck, she'd wished she'd suggested lunch with Lori today. Jake's and Billy's desks were still vacant, and it became apparent she had a sandwich from the deli down the block in her future.

She spent the rest of the afternoon tying up some loose ends with the victims' families and discussing Quinn's memorial and funeral arrangements with Terrence. The ME's office had called her this morning and let her know she could have Quinn transported to the mortuary. Terrence had picked one out and told her he'd handle everything, although she'd insisted on meeting him at the funeral home with Quinn's suit.

Jake had texted her a few times and reminded her that he'd be meeting her when her session with Shai ended to follow her home. If he could put a guard on her 24/7, he'd opt for that.

She packed up for the day and tried to tiptoe past Captain Castillo's open office door, but he called out to her. She backpedaled and hung on to the doorjamb. "I was just on my way out."

"I won't keep you. I spoke to Terrence today, and he told me he talked to you about the plans for Quinn."

She nodded. "He knows so much more about these things than I do, so I'm going to let him take the lead. He's consulting me about a few personal touches, but I sure wish we could catch Quinn's killer before the memorial. It doesn't seem right to hold it when the guy who murdered him is running around."

"Don't lose hope." Castillo winked, and Kyra understood he didn't want to say more.

She didn't, either, and she pulled away from his door with a wave of her hand.

She'd allowed herself an hour and fifteen minutes to get to Shai's office, and turned down San Vicente with ten minutes to spare. Shai's office occupied a street with restricted parking, so that fact relegated her to grabbing a spot along the median strip of San Vicente again. This busy boulevard hadn't given her problems last time, but she balked slightly as she turned the corner onto the street where she'd been attacked.

Her breath flowed a little easier when she saw a few people parking their cars and darting in and out of the office buildings along the tree-lined street. The sun hadn't completely set yet but painted long shadows on the leaf-dappled sidewalk. As Kyra approached the courtyard of Shai's building, she slid her hand into the gun pouch on the outside of her purse—just in case.

She hadn't hit the right mood for a hypnosis today. Taking a deep breath, she approached Shai's office door and shoved it open. Her greeting died on her lips as she noticed the door to Shai's inner office firmly closed.

He'd told her last time he left that door open for his last appointment—her. The hair on her arms stood on end as a chill rippled up her spine. "Shai?"

She glanced over her shoulder at the courtyard, the trees surrounding it blocking out the setting sun. She slammed the door behind her…and locked it. Pulling her weapon from her purse, she crept toward the door to Shai's inner sanctum and called his name again. As long as she didn't accidentally shoot him, he'd understand her caution.

With the gun gripped in one hand, she tried the door handle with the other. She sucked in a breath as it gave beneath her fingers. Raising her weapon, she pushed open the door, the sweet woodsy scent of the candle barely perceptible over another smell, like wet pennies.

She shuffled into the room. As her eyes adjusted to the low light, she picked out open drawers and papers strewn about the floor. With her heart galloping in her chest, she stumbled toward Shai's desk, her purse sliding from her shoulder, and almost tripped over his legs protruding from behind the desk.

Stifling a scream, she dropped to her knees and grabbed Shai's warm hand. *Warm.* His hand was warm, despite the wound on the side of his head, soaking the carpet with his blood.

He moaned, and Kyra yanked the scarf from her neck and wrapped it around his head. "Hold on, Shai. I'm going to call 911. You're going to be okay."

She sprang to her feet to retrieve her purse where she'd dropped it by the door. As she grabbed it, a clicking sound had her whipping her head toward the outer office and the front door.

Her blood ran cold as she saw the door handle twist.

Chapter Sixteen

Jake careened around the corner and screeched to a halt behind the emergency vehicles, abandoning his car in the middle of the street. He vaulted over the crime scene tape and grabbed the first officer he saw. "What happened here?"

The cop shook him off. "Sir, you're going to have to wait behind the line."

Jake flipped out his badge with an unsteady hand. "What's going on?"

"Someone was attacked in one of the offices. It doesn't look good."

The wheels of the gurney the EMTs were rolling into the office building courtyard squealed, grating against his ears. Jake swallowed. "I-is she dead?"

"She?" The officer shook his head. "The victim is a male, an older male, and he's still alive."

Relief making his knees weak, Jake staggered through the courtyard, clutching his badge. When he walked into Shai's office, he rushed to Kyra perched on the edge of a chair, and fell to his knees in front of her. Blood smeared her blouse, and dabs of it dotted her cheek.

His hands circled her waist. "Are you all right? What happened?"

A sob bubbled to her lips, and she swayed forward

grabbing his shoulders. "It's Shai. The Player got in here and attacked him."

"The officer out front said he was still alive."

"Barely." Her fingers dug into his jacket. "I thought at first he'd been shot. There was so much blood around his head, but then I saw the paperweight on the floor later, after the police came. He was here. The Player was here."

"He attacked Shai and then left before you came?" Maybe The Player hadn't known about Kyra's appointment today. He couldn't imagine the killer would give up a chance to harm Kyra.

"He was still here, waiting for me." Her gaze flew to the front door of the office. "When I first walked into the office, I sensed something was off. Shai told me he always left the door to his therapy space open before his last patient. It was open the previous time, but this time it was closed. So when I walked into the office, I closed the door behind me…and locked it."

"You think The Player would've tried to come in behind you?"

Her eyes widened. "I know he did. After I found Shai, I ran back to get my phone to call 911. Someone was trying the door from the outside. He would've come in, maybe surprised me when I was with Shai."

Jake took her hands in his. "What did you do? Where did he go?"

"I had my gun. I aimed it at the door and told him if he stepped into the office, I'd shoot. Told him if he didn't leave, I'd shoot right through the door. He left."

"You didn't see him?"

"No."

"Did Shai see him?"

"I don't know. Shai was moaning and alive when I found him, but he lost consciousness before the paramedics arrived." Kyra popped up from her chair as the EMTs wheeled the gurney from Shai's therapy room. "Is he going to make it?"

One of the EMTs called out to her. "He's still alive. Still unconscious."

Jake stood up and wandered toward the inner office, where papers littered the floor and drawers and cabinets gaped open. "He was looking for something."

Kyra touched his arm. "I'm pretty sure he was looking for notes from my session two days ago. He wants to know what I'm remembering."

"Then stop remembering." Jake squeezed her hand. "You don't have to remember. We'll catch him this time. We'll stop him. He's stepped back into the light, and he's careless, nervous. He's not the precise killer he was twenty years ago. We'll get him, and you don't have to do another thing."

"No video footage of him, no prints, no witnesses. He's still careful, Jake. He still knows how to play the game. Even if I can give you a description of what he looked like twenty years ago, that might help. It's more than you have now."

A muscled ticked at the corner of Jake's mouth. "Shai's hurt. He's not going to be able to help you anymore. In fact, I'm going to request that Castillo remove you from this task force. You're in communication with all of the victims' families. You work with them, and leave the investigation part to us."

Kyra's eyes flashed blue fire, but then she took a deep breath. "Let's pray Shai is going to pull through."

"I'll call the hospital as soon as they get him there." He touched a finger to her cheek. "You have his blood on you."

"You should've seen my hands before the EMTs

cleaned them. I staunched the bleeding on his head wound with my scarf."

"If he lives, it will be because of you."

She dug into her purse for a tissue and dabbed the blood on her face. "I was just going to call you when you came charging in here. You were early."

"As soon as I finished reviewing some evidence with Billy, I took off. Figured I'd park right in front of Shai's office and wait for you in the courtyard. I wasn't going to have you take any chances this time, but I didn't realize he'd come at you another way. I wonder why he didn't just wait for you in Shai's office and ambush you when you came in."

She lifted her shoulders. "He probably didn't know whether or not Shai had any more patients coming. He most likely waited until one left, came into the office, attacked Shai, searched for my session notes and then left before someone else could come. He was probably staking out the courtyard, waiting for me or making sure nobody else was coming."

The hair on the back of Jake's neck stood at attention. "Do you think he knew you had an appointment?"

"I don't know. Maybe he was just here to hurt Shai and search his office. My showing up was the cherry on top."

"Your being alive and unhurt was my cherry." He put his arm around her and pulled her close. "When I saw the emergency vehicles at Shai's office and heard someone had been attacked, everything went dark for me. I thought I'd failed you."

She kissed his jaw. "You never have, and you never will."

BY MIDAFTERNOON the next day, Kyra knew Jake meant business when he told her he wanted her off the task force and shielded from the investigation into Quinn's murder. He'd given her no updates, and everyone seemed to be tiptoeing around her.

He'd only called to tell her about Shai's condition—holding steady but still not conscious. Jake also believed Shai's hospitalization would put an end to her sessions. But while Jake had slept at her place last night, she'd practiced self-hypnosis and had gotten as far as she had with Shai, stopping in exactly the same place—just when The Player was about to turn and show his face. Maybe without Shai's guidance she wouldn't be able to get any further, but she wasn't going to stop trying.

She didn't think Jake would allow her to ever spend one night on her own again until the task force caught The Player. He'd already invited her over tonight for the entire weekend. It's the only thing that still gave her hope that he'd share the progress of the investigation with her. She didn't think he'd be able to resist talking to her about it all weekend—and she'd be there to encourage him. The weekend couldn't come soon enough.

He and Billy had another busy day with briefings, a press conference and meetings with Chief Sterling. Once the chief found out that Jake and Billy believed The Player was responsible for Quinn's death, he wanted them to go full speed ahead on the investigation—without her.

She knew Jake and Billy had also started the unsavory task of delving into the whereabouts of some of the cops at the Northwest Division during the times of some of the murders. The cops would also have to be of a certain age and have been around during The Player investigation twenty years ago. She didn't envy them that task, even if the subjects might not ever find out they were under suspicion.

At the end of the day, with most of the task force clearing out, she stretched and ran her hand along her desk. She'd miss this desk, this room, her spot in the corner.

Clive poked his head in the door, peering across the room. "J-Mac and Billy still gone?"

"They left around lunch and I haven't seen them since, and don't think I will." Until tonight, snug in Jake's arms, where she could start to work on him.

She blinked as she noticed Clive still standing there, his brow right up to his shaved head wrinkled. "Can I help you with something?"

His gaze snapped to her eyes, his face smoothing. "Of course. I should be showing you instead."

Her heart bumped in her chest. "Showing me what?"

"It's regarding the GPS tracker found on your car."

She put a hand to her throat, where the bruises from the attack a few nights ago were yellowing. "You found prints?"

"I found...something." He put a finger to his lips and twisted his head to the side, scanning the war room, depleted of most of its soldiers. He lowered his voice. "I know Jake and Billy suspect someone on the inside. I don't want to raise any suspicions or alarms—especially if I'm wrong."

"But if you're right?" Butterflies swirled in her empty stomach, and she flattened her hand against her waist.

"Then I have a pretty good idea who put that device on your car, and that's going to lead us right to The Player."

She grabbed her phone. "I'll text Jake."

Clive inclined his head. "And if I'm wrong? If *we're* wrong? I heard a rumor that J-Mac is kicking you off the task force. Will he allow us to do this little investigation—if he knows about it?"

She stared at the phone in her hand. If she told Jake

about this, even if she could reach him now, he'd probably tell her to wait, step back.

Clive continued in a soft voice. "I did a favor for you once, Kyra. Dusted that playing card for prints—off the record. I even caught heat for it. You said back then you'd buy me lunch. This would be more appreciated than lunch."

"All right. What do you want me to see? Is it in the lab?"

"I need to lift some prints off-site. I can take you over in my car, and we can be back here within an hour. If it's nothing, no harm, and we'll keep it to ourselves. Nobody's reputation takes a hit."

Kyra hesitated. Did Clive mean that he was going to lift prints from a possible suspect on the sly?

His phone rang, and he held up a finger. "My wife. That's right, sweetheart. I am going to be late, but not too late. Dinner is still on with the Carsons. If I have to meet you at the restaurant, I will."

When he ended the call, he held up his phone. "Monthly dinner plans with friends. When I thought I might be taking J-Mac out to this location, I warned my wife, but she's good. Ready?"

If she could hand this to Jake, if she could do this for Quinn, it would make it all worthwhile. "Yes. I need a few minutes to pack up."

"That's perfect. Meet me at my car. It's a white Prius parked on the street." He patted the black bag hanging off one shoulder. "I have my materials."

When Clive left the room, Kyra logged off her laptop and stuffed it into the case. She grabbed her jacket off the back of the chair and surveyed the room. A few members of the task force talked on the phone or clicked away on their computers. Nobody looked up. If Clive knew Jake planned to boot her off the task force, these team members probably already saw her as persona non grata.

She hitched her bag over her shoulder and strode out of the room to meet Clive. If she and the fingerprint tech could solve this thing, they'd all be singing a different tune—including Jake.

JAKE SAID GOOD-NIGHT to his partner in the parking lot of the station and then made his way to the task force war room. He half expected Kyra to be there, as she hadn't answered his last text, which could mean she was hard at work. He burst through the door and glanced at her empty desk. His gaze shifted to the few task force members still at their desks.

One of the cops called out over his computer. "You just missed her."

Jake smiled to himself. He and Kyra hadn't done a very good job keeping their relationship a secret from the rest of the task force. But he didn't care anymore. She'd be off the task force soon enough. He had to keep her away from the investigation into The Player for her own safety.

She probably hadn't texted him back because she was driving home to pack some clothes for their weekend— but what he had planned for her this rainy weekend didn't require much clothing.

As he sat at his desk and logged in to his computer, he appreciated the quiet of the room. He and Billy had done some discreet inquiries this morning into the locations of the task force members the past few weeks, and they'd started a spreadsheet listing comparisons between those locations and some pivotal dates in The Player's timeline. He wanted to enter some of that data before he left for the weekend.

Fifteen minutes later, he studied the columns, and data for three task force members jumped out at him. Brandon Nguyen had several absences, but the tech guru was a little young to be The Player. He'd have been about Kyra's age at the time of her mother's murder. Still, he had the computer smarts to connect with the copycats. Detective Ned Verona was the right age and had been friends with Quinn. Quinn would've let Verona into his house without a moment's hesitation. Verona had a lot of absences—due to medical. The guy was getting ready to retire. The third person...

"Detective McAllister?"

He glanced up and realized the room had cleared, except for one cop on the phone and Lori Del Valle, the fingerprint tech, standing at the door. "C'mon in and call me Jake. I'm still working for about another fifteen minutes."

"Just wanted to let you know, all the processing from Detective Quinn's house is complete." She held up her hand, her fingers curled into an okay sign, but she said, "Zero. We didn't get anything of substance, nothing to point to a killer."

"I wasn't really expecting anything, Lori." He waved. "Have a good weekend."

He hunched over his laptop again, but he heard tentative clicks across the floor. When he looked up this time, Lori was planted in front of his desk. "Something else?"

Her cheeks flushed. "I just... I wanted to tell you something, but I don't want you to take it the wrong way."

He shoved his laptop away. He hoped this didn't have to do with his boorish assumption earlier that she didn't have the same level of expertise as Clive. He'd hoped they'd put that behind them. "I'm not going to take it any way. What's on your mind?"

"It's Clive." She held up her hands. "I don't want you

to think I'm throwing him under the bus or anything because I want his job. He's supposed to retire anyway."

"Clive?" Jake's pulse ticked up a notch, as he glanced at the third name in the spreadsheet with all the *X*'s in the columns. "What about Clive?"

Lori blew out a breath. "He's been doing some weird things with the evidence on these copycat cases, and even Detective Quinn's crime scene."

A rash of tingles spread across the back of his neck. "What kind of weird things?"

"Well, for one, there was a glass from Quinn's place, and Billy asked us particularly to process it for prints."

"And? From what I understood, there were no prints on the glass."

"That's what Clive put in the report, but that's not altogether true. He never dusted that glass for prints."

Jake's fingertips were buzzing now. "Did you question him about it?"

"I—I didn't." Lori twisted her fingers in front of her. "I wanted to, but that was just after I discovered Walker's prints on Tina's wallet. Clive put me on his blacklist for that."

"For discovering the prints of a killer on a victim's wallet?"

"He told me I shouldn't have done it in the field. I should've brought it back here and let him do it."

"Why would he be upset? It all worked out."

"Did it all work out for him?" She squared her shoulders. "This is what I almost told you at the scene of Tina's car that day. He's been playing fast and loose with these fingerprints. I think he's destroying evidence."

There it was. Lori's words punched him in the gut.

"There's something else. He bagged a GPS device the

other day in the lab, but when I looked for a record of it later, I couldn't find it. He never logged it."

"GPS device?" Jake could barely hear his own voice over the roaring in his ears. He'd left the box at Kyra's. "Where'd he get it?"

"Kyra dropped it off for him."

Jake had pushed back from his desk and was out of his chair before he even knew he was standing. He called to the cop on the phone. "Holt, Holt."

Officer Holt jerked his head up and put the phone down. "Yes, sir?"

"You said I just missed Kyra. Did you see her when she left? Did she leave alone?"

"Yeah, she did. She left by herself—after she talked to someone, all hush-hush."

Jake's tongue felt thick in his mouth. "Who was she talking to?"

"The fingerprint guy—Clive Stewart."

Fifteen minutes later, Jake turned down Clive's street in Studio City. On his way out of the station's parking lot, he noticed Kyra's car, which he hadn't seen when Billy dropped him off. Had she actually gone with Clive in his car? To his home? Why would she do that?

His hands gripped the steering wheel. Why not? She knew Clive. Clive had done a favor for her in the past. Had he lured her with the GPS?

He'd called a patrol car on his way, and one sat across the street from Clive's house now. He'd break down the door himself if he had to get Kyra out of there.

He knew Clive was married. Was his wife out of town? A dark blue compact sat in the driveway of the tidy house. He thought he'd seen Clive get into a white Prius at the station.

The officers got out of their car, and Jake held up his

hand. If Clive had Kyra in this house, he didn't want to spook him.

He stepped onto the porch and rang the doorbell. Maybe Clive hadn't tried anything yet, and Jake could just walk Kyra out of there with the pretense that he had important news for her and knew she had left with Clive. His thoughts stumbled to a stop when a middle-aged woman with blond, chin-length hair opened the door, her eyebrows arched into question marks.

"I'm Detective Jake McAllister. Is your husband at home?"

"My husband?" She drew her sweater around her body in a protective gesture.

Jake showed her his badge. "Clive. I, uh, work with him at the department."

"That bald-headed piece of..." Her hoarse laugh ended in a smoker's cough. "He's not my husband."

Jake stuffed his badge back into his pocket. "You're not Mrs. Stewart? Isn't this Clive's house?"

"Technically, it's still his house, still in his name, but we're divorced. Have been for years. The guy's a creep with mommy issues." She shrugged her shoulders and narrowed her eyes. "This isn't a work call, is it? Did he finally snap?"

Although he was sure the ex-Mrs. Stewart could tell him stories about Clive to curl his hair, he didn't have time to listen. "Where is he? Where does he live now?"

"He lives somewhere in Hollywood. I can't give you the exact address because I don't know it."

Jake slumped. How would he find him? They'd have to ping his phone, Kyra's phone. That could take hours when he probably had minutes. "Do you have anything that might have his address on it? Old mail? Paperwork?"

"No, and he moved recently."

"He moved to Hollywood or he was living in Hollywood and moved?" He'd have to wrap up this conversation that was going nowhere for a chance to ping those phones.

"He moved *to* Hollywood, and no, I didn't ask and he didn't tell me. A friend told me."

"Does this friend have his address?"

"No."

"All right. Thanks, Mrs…" He turned away and waved off the cops.

As he headed toward the sidewalk, his phone already in his hand, Mrs. Stewart called after him. "My friend doesn't have the exact address, but she did see him walking into a fancy high-rise in Hollywood. You know, that one that has a view of the Hollywood Hills, if you're on the right side. I wondered how the hell he afforded that. You know the one I mean?"

Jake knew exactly which one she meant. The plate glass window in his house looked out onto it every night.

Chapter Seventeen

Kyra blinked as Clive pulled into a subterranean garage off of Sunset Boulevard. The darkness was a sharp contrast to the bright lights of the boulevard, where the neon of the flashing signs did battle with the headlights and taillights streaming below them. Those lights had blurred before her eyes, and she swallowed against her dry throat.

She'd thought her throat was improving, but it felt like sandpaper now, and she grabbed the bottle in the cup holder, downing another few sips of the water Clive had offered her when she climbed into his silent electric car. The action of tipping her head back caused the dizziness she'd felt earlier to come crashing down on her in waves. She put her fingers to her temples.

"Are you all right?"

"I feel a little...strange. Is this where we're going? This building?"

"Yes, someone from the station lives here, someone who's been showing too much interest in the fingerprints we've been processing from Quinn's house." He reached into the back seat and patted his black bag. "I'm going to lift some prints, and then we're going to compare them against what I found on the GPS that was attached to your car. If they don't match, no harm, no foul, right?"

"Right." She rubbed her head. "Who lives here?"

"I don't want to say just yet." He parked the car in a slot, and she peered at the number painted on the wall in front of them.

She read the numbers aloud. "2021. Are you parking in someone's space?"

"Don't worry about it. I've scoped out this place already. I know what I'm doing."

Kyra shook her head. What were they doing here? Fingerprints. Fingers. All those missing fingers. Her mother's missing finger.

Clive patted her shoulder. "Are you up for this, Kyra? If you're not feeling well, I can leave you in the car. I just thought you'd want to be a part of this…after all you've been through."

"I do. I do." All those missing fingers.

Clive grabbed his bag and slipped out the driver's side door.

Kyra grabbed the door handle on her side but continued to sit. She wasn't afraid, just…tired.

Clive opened the door for her and helped her out, as if she were ancient, older than Quinn. She stumbled, and he steadied her.

"It's all right. At least we don't have to walk up all those stairs."

He chuckled, and the sound made her feel nauseous for some reason. She'd never heard Clive laugh before. In fact, she'd never heard Clive speak so many words before in all the time she'd known him. And she'd known him…twenty, no, two years. Two years.

He held her arm as he steered her to the back of the parking garage, away from the glass doors.

She pulled against him. "Shouldn't we go that way?"

His grip on her arm tightened, his strong fingers digging into the flesh of her arm beneath her jacket. "I told you. I did reconnaissance first. If we go up the back way and use the freight elevator, nobody will see us. I'm good at reconnaissance."

He marched her silently to a large, dark elevator that smelled like oil. The doors squealed as they opened and shut, and it lumbered up and up. Nineteen, twenty. When it settled, he steered her out of the car, pushed open a fire door and led her to a solid door. When he pulled out a key, she twisted away from him. But when he opened the door, he shoved her inside.

The fog in her brain parted for a few seconds and she grasped at the truth, but it slithered away from her, and she stood in the middle of the sparsely furnished room with her head tilted to one side. "Who lives here? Why are we here?"

Clive clicked his tongue. "I'll tell you later, and we'll gather the prints and run to McAllister with our proof. You'd like that, wouldn't you?"

She nodded, dropping her chin to her chest. She'd tell Jake tonight as he cooked dinner for them—steaks and red wine again.

"But first I want to show you something."

His voice startled her, and she lifted up her head with a Herculean effort, noticing for the first time the telescope positioned at a large window that looked out on the lights of Hollywood—and the hills beyond.

Clive hunched over the telescope, and the recessed lighting in the ceiling glowed on his bald dome, creating a white circle like a cap on his head. *Turn around. Turn around.* The words found their way to her lips. "Turn around."

Clive turned his head, and Kyra was staring into the dark eyes of her mother's killer…again.

"Oh, I see you finally figured it out, little Mimi. Kyra's

a big improvement over Mimi and for sure a big improvement over Marilyn Monroe Lake. Who the hell names their kid Marilyn Monroe? But then, your mother, Jennifer, was a dumb bitch. And a whore. Like my mother. Like my ex-wife. Like you."

She reached for her purse with her gun and realized she'd left it in the car—along with the drugged water.

Instead, Clive pulled out his own weapon and crooked his finger. "Come here. I want to show you something."

Kyra peeled her feet from the carpet and lumbered toward him. Could she push him through the glass? Wrestle the gun away from him? Throw something through the window to attract attention?

Stepping aside, he tapped the telescope. "Have a look. I think you might be interested in what I can see from up here."

She approached the telescope as he adjusted it for her height. When she put her eye to the eyepiece, the view took in the Hollywood Hills across Sunset Boulevard, and as Clive turned a knob on the lens, Jake's house came into focus.

She gasped and staggered back, sinking to the floor, the phone in her jacket pocket digging into her hip.

Clive chuckled, causing her to heave. He'd chuckled the night he turned around and met her eyes after murdering her mother. "Do you know how I know you're a whore, Kyra? I've seen you—all of you. I've watched as *J-Mac* took you against that window, in full view of everyone, your naked body pushed up against the glass. That's how much he cares about you. He knows you're a whore, too."

She couldn't dwell on that right now, couldn't think of Jake, who had no idea where she was. She might be able to watch him from here, pacing his living room floor, calling her, wondering where she'd gone. Wondering if she'd given up on him after he told her he was taking her off the task force. The old Kyra would've done that. But she wasn't the old Kyra. She was the Kyra Quinn always deserved. The Kyra Jake deserved.

She cleared her throat. "You killed Quinn."

"I did." He almost sounded disappointed in himself. "I always liked Quinn, but he was a loose end. His obsession with you is what got him killed. Same with your foster brother, Matt. That's how I was able to keep track of you all those years—first through Quinn and then through Matt."

She had to keep him talking, keep herself active. If she curled up in a corner, she'd die here. The drugs had made her stupid, fuzzy, slow, but she could fight against their effects.

"Why did you stop killing twenty years ago?" Kyra struggled to her feet, stuffing her hand in her pocket and tracing the phone with her fingers. Clive probably thought the phone was still in her purse, along with her gun.

"Technology and new advancements in law enforcement." He flicked his finger against the telescope, where it pinged. "Improvements in DNA testing, mitochondrial DNA testing, genetic databases with idiots sending their DNA in to trace ancestors, cameras everywhere, cell phones, GPS tracking. It's tough being a serial killer today."

"You'll excuse me if I save my pity for the victims."

Clive's lips stretched into a smile. "I admire your... tenacity, Kyra. There were plenty of forces to beat you down, but they never defeated you—until now. I suppose you have Quinn to thank for that. He rescued you, didn't he? He and Charlotte."

"He let you into his house?" She smoothed her thumb across the face of her phone, feeling the imprint of the home button. She had voice activation on her phone and could call or text Jake, but what could she say in the few seconds allotted before Clive stopped her? Maybe just a simple *I love you*.

"Of course. Quinn knew me from the old days. Just like Jake and Billy, Quinn never suspected me. Oh, he may have suspected a cop or two or someone on the inside, but not me." He spread his hands, and for the first time, Kyra noticed their wiry strength. "He let me in, and I avoided witnesses and cameras like I always do. Told him I had something I wanted him to look at regarding The Player case, *my* case. He got us water. I followed him back to the living room and whacked him on the side of the head to make him go down. Then I shot him up with a stimulant. I guess something about how I replaced his shoe and sock tripped me up."

"Something else tripped you up." Kyra placed her thumb on her phone's home button. She had to wander away from him to give herself more time on the phone. "You left your prints on that glass, didn't you?"

His dark eyes narrowed. "How do you know about that? Did that nosy Lori Del Valle tell you something?"

A pulse throbbed in her throat. Did Lori suspect something about Clive? "Lori told me nothing about you. I figured it out myself when I was at Quinn's place. What happened to that glass?"

"I bagged it for processing, but alas—" he threw up his hands "—there were no prints on it."

"I'm sure you saw to that, just like all the other prints in this case. What happened with Fisher's print on the tape? How did that one slip through?"

The nostrils of his long, thin nose flared. "J-Mac found

it at the crime scene. It was a patent print the idiot left. J-Mac saw the print with his bare eyes. I had to process it."

"You killed Yolanda, the homeless lady who helped you send those emails to me and Sean Hughes, the blogger who was communicating with Copycat Three."

"Yes, yes." He waved his hand with the gun in the air. "I took care of all of them, and no, those were not satisfying kills. I did those out of necessity."

"What makes it satisfying for you? What made Clive Stewart a serial killer? Don't you all blame it on your mothers? You called your mother a whore. Is that why other women deserve to die?" She licked her lips. The adrenaline from the knowledge that she finally faced The Player had counteracted the drug in her system, but she still wasn't ready to fight...and he had the gun. She knew he didn't want to shoot her. He wanted to strangle her...just like he did her mother.

"It's a boring tale."

"I doubt that. Why the playing cards? Why the severed fingers? If you're going to kill me, I think I deserve to know. We've been at this game for twenty years, you and I. Before it ends for me, I'd like to know the rules." She meandered toward the window and gazed at the lights below. Too far to jump.

Clive chuckled again and moved toward the door, the gun still clutched in his hand, as if he feared she'd make a run for it now that she'd recovered her faculties. Could she?

"I guess you have a point there, Kyra. I do feel...close to you. You were the only one alive who knew who I was, who I really was, even though you couldn't remember."

"Who was your mother?"

His gaze locked on to her face from across the room,

his own a pale oval against the door. "She was a black-jack dealer in Vegas, part-time hooker. Kind of like your mother."

Kyra nodded in encouragement. She'd always known her mother had traded certain favors for money. Had Clive targeted women like that? Not quite prostitutes but working on the fringes of the sex trade—independent contractors?

"You know what they called her, Mimi?"

"What did they call her, Clive?"

"Pinky." He held up his hand and wiggled his little finger, the one he'd severed from all his victims. "She'd worked in a cannery when she was a teenager and lost her finger. It didn't stop her from dealing, and they all called her Pinky."

The playing cards, the trophy finger—all formed from his messed-up childhood. Her foster brother, Matt, had been abused as a child, shuffled around in foster homes, and had wound up a junkie, in and out of jail. Her own childhood had gone horribly off the rails, and if it hadn't been for Quinn and Charlotte, she could've ended up like Matt. But they hadn't launched a career as a killer.

"Wh-where are all the fingers? You had the copycats take the fingers for you. Did it give you the same thrill?"

"Sadly, it didn't, and now I'm bored with all this. I have one more kill on my list, and then I'm going to retire. I'm retiring from the LAPD, and I'm retiring from killing."

"No, you won't."

His head jerked up. "Excuse me?"

"You won't give it up. You can't. You're driven, and eventually you'll get caught. You don't even seek the fame, do you? You get satisfaction from the perfection of the crime, but you had an unfair advantage. You're not that special, Clive. Once you're no longer *the* fingerprint guy, others will be able to track you down."

"Shut up. I'm tired of hearing you talk. You should be almost comatose by now, but no. You just keep going and going." His face sported red flags and his cheeks puffed out as if he were ready to explode.

She had to make a move. In a loud voice, she said, "I should text Jake."

She shouted the last two words as she pressed her home button and dragged her pocket close to her face. The phone responded in an automated voice, "What do you want to say?"

Clive sputtered and launched forward, shouting something unintelligible.

She brought the phone from her pocket and said the first thing that came to her head. "Twenty, twenty-one, building off…"

Clive tackled her, and they both hit the window hard, the phone flipping out of her hand and spinning across the floor. He smacked her hard across the face, and she kneed him in the groin.

Grunting, he staggered back, but kept the gun pointed in her direction. If he squeezed off a shot, he'd hit her somewhere.

She kicked the telescope, and it topped over on him. She dropped to the ground as he fired the gun. The ear-splitting noise buffeted her eardrums. The window beside him cracked, spider webs rippling along the glass.

She crawled toward his legs beneath a table. If she could wrap her arms around them, she could push him toward the damaged window. They might both go over and fall twenty floors—one for each year of their ac-quaintance—but she'd put an end to The Player.

Clive steadied himself, bracing one hand against

the shattered glass and spotting her under the table. He swung the gun downward.

Kyra coiled her muscles, getting ready to spring, when a loud commotion came through the front door.

Miraculously, Jake's voice bellowed across the room. "Drop it, Clive."

Clive took a step toward Jake, but he wanted her more. He aimed the gun at her between the table legs. She heaved up, lifting the table on her back, ready to rush him.

Another shot rang out, and Clive's eyes widened. He squeezed the trigger of his gun, and the bullet splintered the wood next to her face.

A volley of three, four shots blasted from across the room, and Clive's body danced with the bullets, the window cracking behind him even more. With the gun still in his hand, he staggered back and fell through the window—twenty floors to his certain death.

Epilogue

"I don't get it, Daddy. How'd you know where The Player was holding Kyra? She only gave you the apartment number." Fiona tucked a leg beneath her on the couch and pulled a pillow into her lap.

Jake crossed the room to the plate glass window overlooking the city, the lights even more brilliant in Christmas finery, and crooked his finger at his daughter. "Come here."

She handed the pillow to Kyra seated next to her on the couch and skipped to her father.

Slinging one arm across her shoulders, he pointed out the window, his finger smudging the glass. "You see that building across the way?"

"The tallest one with all the windows?"

"That was the building."

Fiona's mouth dropped open, and she twisted her head to look at Kyra. "For reals? But how'd you know it was that one?"

"I thought Clive was still married and living in Studio City. We all did. But when I got to his house, his ex-wife told me her friend had seen him recently walking into a high-rise on Sunset. I knew right away it had to be that building."

Kyra called from the couch, just to remind Jake. "I

always felt something creepy about that window being exposed to the world."

Fiona turned wide eyes back to the view. "So you went straight to that building from The Player's house?"

"I did, and called backup on the way, but when I got there, I didn't know where to go or where to look. I got the building manager to let me look through the tenants, but Clive didn't live there under his own identity. I was ready to search floor by floor, unit by unit, pull a fire alarm, bring the whole building down if I had to. Then I got Kyra's text. I knew the building had over twenty floors, so I had the manager check the tenant for 2021, and who do you think I found?"

Fiona breathed out with awe of her father. "Clive Stewart? No, wait, The Player?"

Jake tapped on the glass. "Jack Spade."

"Jack Spade, like in the jack of spades card?"

"That's right. When I saw that, I knew. The manager gave me the key. I came up with a SWAT team and listened at the door for a few seconds. When I heard the gunshot, I barreled into the room and uh…stopped him."

Fiona nodded and flicked back her ombré-tinted hair. "You shot him and he fell through the window."

"He had a gun in his hand. He was threatening Kyra."

"Oh, I know you wouldn't have shot him unless you had to, but it's still badass."

Jake cleared his throat. "It's late. If you're going to spend the weekend at Lyric's, you'd better get to bed."

"Mrs. Becker promised to keep an eye on us all weekend, so I won't get kidnapped again."

Jake pulled his daughter close and kissed the side of her head. "I have it all worked out with Mrs. Becker."

"Thanks, Dad." Fiona kissed her father on the cheek and sauntered back to the couch, where she leaned over and hugged Kyra from behind. "I'm so glad you're okay, Kyra. Were you scared when you figured out Clive was The Player?"

Kyra brushed the girl's smooth skin with her fingers. "Remember how scared you were when your cute internet boyfriend turned out to be Copycat Three and kidnapped you?"

"Don't remind me."

"I was that scared."

Fiona dropped a kiss on top of Kyra's head, which made Kyra's heart melt. "I'm glad you're safe, and I'm glad you're gonna marry Dad and be my stepmom."

"Me, too." Kyra squeezed Fiona's hands.

Fiona stepped back and ran up the stairs. She stopped midway, clutching the banister, looking down at them shyly through her lowered lashes. "Are you guys gonna give me some siblings? Mom and Brock refuse. Brock has his two kids from his first marriage, and Mom has me, and that's it for them."

Laughing at Jake's stuttering, Kyra stood up and stretched. "I think we can manage that. Now, go to bed before you give your father a heart attack."

When Fiona traipsed up the stairs with a flourish, Kyra joined Jake at the window. "You really should get some drapes."

"That would ruin the whole dramatic effect." He curled an arm around her waist. "Are you going to start making changes when you move in here?"

"You still have time for your bachelor life before the wedding, and I still need to do some work on the Venice house before I rent it out."

"Quinn's memorial was fitting, wasn't it? Was it everything you wanted?"

"And more. Terrence did a spectacular job."

"And you. Your touches made it special."

"In the end, Quinn did help catch The Player. If Clive hadn't left his prints on that glass at his house and Lori hadn't noticed the irregularities in Clive's behavior, you never would've suspected Clive."

"And if Quinn hadn't raised you to be the…badass you are, I never would've found you." He rubbed a circle on her back. "Do you really want to finish your sessions with Shai?"

"As soon as he's a hundred percent. I owe it to my mom to remember, really remember those last moments of her life. I'm not afraid."

"I know you're not. That's one of the many things love about you. You're fearless in everything you do."

"Not so fearless in love." She cupped his strong jaw in her hand. "Not until I met you."

He bent his head to press his lips against hers, and his kiss scorched her, took possession of her very soul. He murmured against her mouth. "I suppose making love against this window is out now."

"Um, yeah, especially with your daughter upstairs." She flattened her hands against his chest. "Besides, you have a perfectly good bed with just about the same view minus the potential for peepers. I think that will work just as well to get going on Fiona's request."

"Let me put a ring on it first." He swept her up in his arms and carried her to the staircase. "But I'm not opposed to giving you a preview of things to come."

As he held her in his arms going up the stairs, she dropped her head to his shoulder and took in the view of the city lights. From here, the beauty outweighed the evil. Somewhere out there were young women just like her mother, with hopes and dreams. People cared. They helped each other heal and recover. They struggled. They trusted each other. They fell in love.

LA *was* the city of angels, and she'd finally found hers.

* * * * *

COMING SOON!

We really hope you enjoyed reading this book. If you're looking for more romance, be sure to head to the shops when new books are available on

Thursday 8th July

To see which titles are coming soon, please visit
millsandboon.co.uk/nextmonth

MILLS & BOON

LET'S TALK
Romance

For exclusive extracts, competitions
and special offers, find us online:

f facebook.com/millsandboon

𝕏 @MillsandBoon

◎ @MillsandBoonUK

Get in touch on 01413 063232

For all the latest titles coming soon, visit

millsandboon.co.uk/nextmonth

MILLS & BOON

THE HEART OF ROMANCE

A ROMANCE FOR EVERY READER

MODERN

Prepare to be swept off your feet by sophisticated, sexy and seductive heroes, in some of the world's most glamourous and roma... locations, where power and passion collide.

HISTORICAL

Escape with historical heroes from time gone by. Whether your passio... for wicked Regency Rakes, muscled Vikings or rugged Highlanders, a... the romance of the past.

MEDICAL

Set your pulse racing with dedicated, delectable doctors in the high-p... sure world of medicine, where emotions run high and passion, comfo... love are the best medicine.

True Love

Celebrate true love with tender stories of heartfelt romance, from the... rush of falling in love to the joy a new baby can bring, and a focus o... emotional heart of a relationship.

Desire

Indulge in secrets and scandal, intense drama and plenty of sizzling h... action with powerful and passionate heroes who have it all: wealth, st... good looks…everything but the right woman.

HEROES

Experience all the excitement of a gripping thriller, with an intense r... mance at its heart. Resourceful, true-to-life women and strong, fearle... face danger and desire - a killer combination!

To see which titles are coming soon, please visit

millsandboon.co.uk/nextmonth

JOIN US ON SOCIAL MEDIA!

Stay up to date with our latest releases, author news and gossip, special offers and discounts, and all the behind-the-scenes action from Mills & Boon...

 millsandboon

 millsandboonuk

 millsandboon

MILLS & BOON
Desire

Indulge in secrets and scandal, intense drama and plenty of sizzling hot action with powerful and passionate heroes who have it all: wealth, status, good looks…everything but the right woman.